A PORTRAIT OF THE ARTIST
AS A YOUNG MAN

The first, shortest, and most approachable of James Joyce's novels, *A Portrait of the Artist as a Young Man* portrays the Dublin upbringing of Stephen Dedalus, from his youthful days at Clongowes Wood College to his radical questioning of all convention. In doing so, it provides an oblique self-portrait of the young Joyce himself. At its center lie questions of origin and source, authority and authorship, and the relationship of an artist to his family, culture, and race. Exuberantly inventive in style, the novel subtly and beautifully orchestrates the patterns of quotation and repetition instrumental in its hero's quest to create his own character, his own language, life, and art: "to forge in the smithy of my soul the uncreated conscience of my race."

This edition, published for the novel's centennial, is the definitive text, authorized by the Joyce estate and collated from all known proofs, manuscripts, and impressions to reflect the author's original wishes.

* * *

"Magical . . . A coming-of-age story, perhaps the prime example of that genre in English literature . . . Even now, twenty-seven years after reading it for the first time, its moods come back to me."
—Karl Ove Knausgaard, from the Foreword

"One believes in Stephen Dedalus as one believes in few characters in fiction." —H. G. Wells

"[Mr. Joyce is] concerned at all costs to reveal the flickerings of that innermost flame which flashes its myriad message through the brain, he disregards with complete courage whatever seems to him adventitious, though it be probability or coherence or any other of the handrails to which we cling for support when we set our imaginations free." —Virginia Woolf

"[*A Portrait of the Artist as a Young Man* will] remain a permanent part of English literature." —Ezra Pound

PENGUIN CLASSICS (🐧) DELUXE EDITION

A PORTRAIT OF THE ARTIST
AS A YOUNG MAN

JAMES JOYCE was born in Dublin on February 2, 1882. He was the oldest of ten children in a family that, after brief prosperity, collapsed into poverty. In 1902, following his graduation from University College, Dublin, he went to Paris, where he devoted himself to writing poems and prose sketches, and to formulating an "aesthetic system." Recalled to Dublin in April 1903 because of the fatal illness of his mother, he met a young woman from Galway, Nora Barnacle, and persuaded her to go with him to the Continent, where they finally settled, in Trieste, in 1905. They had two children, a son, Giorgio, and a daughter, Lucia. Joyce's first book, the poems of *Chamber Music*, was published in London in 1907, followed by *Dubliners* (1914), *A Portrait of the Artist as a Young Man* (1916), and *Exiles, a play* (1918). In 1920, Joyce moved to Paris, publishing *Ulysses,* the book that brought him international fame, in 1922. His final book, *Finnegans Wake*, was published in 1939. After the outbreak of World War II, Joyce moved back to Zurich, where he had lived during World War I. He died there on January 13, 1941.

KARL OVE KNAUSGAARD is the author of the *New York Times* bestselling six-volume autobiographical novel *My Struggle*, a global literary phenomenon that has won numerous international literary awards and has been translated into more than twenty-five languages. He was born in 1968 in Oslo, Norway, and now lives in Sweden.

SEAMUS DEANE, professor of English and the Donald and Marilyn Keough Professor of Irish Studies at the University of Notre Dame, is a member of the Royal Irish Academy and the general editor of the works of James Joyce for Penguin Classics.

JAMES JOYCE

A Portrait of the Artist as a Young Man

Foreword by
KARL OVE KNAUSGAARD

Edited with an Introduction and Notes by
SEAMUS DEANE

PENGUIN BOOKS

PENGUIN BOOKS

An imprint of Penguin Random House LLC
375 Hudson Street
New York, New York 10014
penguin.com

First published in the United States of America by B. W. Huebsch Inc., 1916
The definitive text, corrected from the Dublin holograph by Chester G. Anderson and edited by
Richard Ellman, first published by The Viking Press, Inc., 1964
Published with an introduction and notes by Seamus Deane in Penguin Books (U.K.) 1992
Published in Penguin Books (U.S.A.) 1993
This edition with a new foreword by Karl Ove Knausgaard published 2016

ISBN 9780143108245

Printed in the United States of America
12th Printing

Set in Sabon Lt Std

Contents

Foreword

The Long Way Home

This year marks the hundredth anniversary of the publication of *A Portrait of the Artist as a Young Man*. Its genesis was long and tortuous—Joyce began writing his novel in 1904—and the road to its canonization as one of the seminal works of Western literature was not short either: the reviews spoke of the author's "cloacal obsession" and "the slime of foul sewers," comments that seem strange today, insofar as it is the subjective aspect of the book, the struggle that goes on inside the mind of its young protagonist, that perhaps stands out to us now as its most striking feature. What appeared at the time to be unprecedented about the novel seems more mundane to us today, whereas what then came across as mundane now seems unprecedented. That Joyce's novel should remain so vital, in contrast to almost all others published in 1916, is down to the fact that the author so forcefully strived toward an idiosyncratic form of expression, a language intrinsic to the story he wanted to tell, about the young man, Stephen Dedalus, and his formative years in Dublin, in which uniqueness was the very point, and the question of what constitutes the individual was the issue posed.

The first time I heard about James Joyce I was eighteen years old, working as a substitute teacher in a small community in northern Norway and wanting to be a writer. That ambition had prompted me to subscribe to a literary journal, and in one of the issues that came in the mail there was a series of articles on the masterpieces of modernism, one of which was Joyce's novel *Ulysses*. The word *modernism* evoked in me a vague notion of machines, futuristic and shiny, and when I read about the tower that Stephen Dedalus—a protagonist of both novels—inhabits at the beginning of the book, I imagined some sort of medieval world of turreted castles, though with cars of the 1920s and airplanes, a place populated by young men reciting works in Latin and Greek—in other words, something very remote from the world in which I resided, with its quaysides and fishing boats, its steeply rising fells and icy ocean, its fishermen and factory workers, TV programs and pounding car audio systems. I longed to get away. What I wanted was to write, and I resolved to read this marvelous work and be illuminated by all its radiance. For me, at that time, literature represented *somewhere else*, and my conception of *Ulysses* was tinged by the books I had read, the boyhood excesses lived out in the French fantasies of Jules Verne, for instance, or swashbuckling classics like *The Count of Monte Cristo, The Three Musketeers, Ivanhoe*, or *Treasure Island*—imaginary worlds in which I had lived half my life, and which for me were the very essence of literature. Literature was somewhere other than me, so I thought, and related to that was another idea I had, that everything of meaning was to be found at the center, that only there did important things happen, while all that occurred on the periphery—where I felt I was—was without significance and unworthy of being written about. History belonged to others, literature belonged to others, truth belonged to others.

Three years later I sat in the library at the University of Bergen reading *Ulysses,* in English. By that time, the literary adventures of my boyhood and youth had been cast aside and my naïve notion of literature's essence adjusted, but the idea of it belonging to others, those with talent and knowledge, who inhabited the center, lingered on. I never related *Ulysses* to my own world, to the young people at the desks around me—even though one of the scenes in the book takes place in a library, among students—not to mention the cobbled streets outside, the gateways and alleys, the shop windows and hoardings, the umbrellas, strollers, raincoats, and overcoats. No, *Ulysses* took place in the language, and the reality the novel described occurred in the land of modernism, in the depths of literature's continent. I read it in the way an archaeologist might excavate an ancient monument, layer by layer, piece by piece, endeavoring thereby to make some mean-

ingful totality of it all, always with my own inferiority and limita-
tions in relation to it clear in mind. It was like an idiot stumbling
over the remains of Troy and trying to make sense of what he had
found.

Since I had an assignment to write about *Ulysses*, I read Joyce's
other books too, among them his first novel, *A Portrait of the
Artist as a Young Man*. And how different it was! Where *Ulysses*
scatters, *Portrait* holds together. Where *Ulysses* describes one day
in a single town, *Portrait* depicts twenty years in a life. And where
Ulysses swells with linguistic inventiveness and gleeful experi-
mentation, *Portrait* swells with . . . well, what? Mood. Even now,
twenty-seven years after reading it for the first time, its moods
come back to me. The rain-drenched school buildings in the
dusk, the circumambient sound of children's voices, the dull thud
of a foot striking a ball, the heavy arc of the ball in the dismal air.
The smell of cold night in the chapel, and the hum of prayer. The
family gathered together on Christmas Day, waiting for the dinner to be served, the fire burning in the fireplace, candles lighting
up the table, the bonds and conflicts that exist between the people seated around it. The father, who talks with strangers in bars
and tells the same stories every time. The narrow, filthy lanes in
which the prostitutes huddle, the yellow gaslights, the smell of
perfume, Stephen's trembling heart. And the birds at evening, circling above the library, dark against the blue-gray sky, their cry
"shrill and clear and fine and falling like threads of silken light
unwound from whirring spools."

A Portrait of the Artist as a Young Man is a so-called *Bil-
dungsroman*, a coming-of-age story, perhaps the prime example
of that genre in English literature. It deals with identity, or more
precisely the way in which identity arises, the events that shape
us and make us who we are. These circumstances are more or
less the same for everyone. We are born into a family, and by virtue of how it receives and relates to us, we become manifest to
ourselves and to others. We learn a language, and though it does
not belong to us alone, but is shared by all members of the community, it is by means of our language that we understand and
express ourselves and that which is all around us. With the language comes a culture, of which, whether we like it or not, we

become a part. Our circles widen, we start school, and the process of our socialization becomes more formal. We learn about the language, our culture and society, and to that first identity within the family a new layer of national identity is added. Within this screen the protagonist, Stephen Dedalus, emerges as an Irish Catholic son of a petty bourgeois family, only to turn against all these categories in the latter half of the novel, rejecting Irish nationalism, rejecting his Catholic religion, rejecting the middle class, insistent on being nobody's son.

The key scene in the book occurs when Stephen is out walking with his friend Cranly and confides to him that he has quarrelled with his mother that morning about religion—because he had refused to receive the Eucharist. Cranly fails to see the problem: Surely he could do it for his mother's sake, regardless of his absent faith? But Stephen is resolute. "I will not serve," he says. But why not? This is the novel's most important question, and the work itself, in its artistic entirety, is the answer. We are not merely the age in which we live, not merely our language, or the family to which we belong, our religion, our country, our culture. We are this and more, insofar as each of us is an individual encountering and relating to all of these categories. But what exactly does this individual comprise? What is its nature, and how do we go about capturing and describing it? How do we even see it, when the tools and instruments at our disposal are precisely of our age, our language, our religion, our culture? In order to reach into the essence of the individual, we must break away from that which is common to us all, and this is what Joyce does in *A Portrait of the Artist as a Young Man*. He ventures inside that part of our identity for which no language yet exists, probing into the space between what belongs to the individual alone and what is ours together, exploring the shifts of mind, the currents of the soul as they flow blindly this way and that, and that we know to be moods and feelings, the unarticulated, more or less salient presence of the soul, that part of our inner being that rises when we are enthused and falls when we are afraid or despairing. *A Portrait of the Artist as a Young Man* is about this, a young man's soul, and what makes Joyce's novel so magical, and what moreover is the true essence of literature, is that the conquest of what belongs to the individual alone, what is special and characteristic, and to Joyce's mind unique, is also what belongs, and is unique, to us. Literature is never the preserve of others, and it knows no center—which is to say that its center is any place at which it exists. Only by refusing to serve, as Stephen does, may the artist do just that: serve. Only by means of a *no* may a book such as *A Portrait of the Artist as a Young Man* emerge into being. And only by means of a *no* may a book like *Ulysses* reach its famous conclusion: "and yes I said yes I will Yes."

KARL OVE KNAUSGAARD
Translated by Martin Aitken

Introduction

A Portrait of the Artist as a Young Man (1916) ends with a beginning. Stephen Dedalus emerges in the last pages of the last chapter as the 'I' who will 'forge . . . the uncreated conscience of my race' (p. 235). The switch from the neuter third-person narrator, commanding a discourse that is dominated by quotation, repetition and carefully construed rhythmical effects, to a first-person whose discourse is by comparison disjointed, careening from petty local detail to the declaration of his solemn ambition, is dislocating for the reader. Yet, for all his lonely self-assertion, Stephen recognizes himself to be a member of a community; it is in relation to the collective, the race, that he formulates his individual aspiration. Similarly, it is in relation to his community that he learns the techniques of individuation, although it is by a process of inversion that he achieves his ambition to be self-born.

Stephen, as child, as boy and as young man, is seduced time and again by siren voices – parental, political, religious, sexual, literary – but concedes ultimately only to his own voice, or to the ventriloquial version of his own voice that he assigns to his 'soul'. That spiritual voicing, although it is the product of a closely exercised discipline of isolation, is not the voicing of a private or personal condition only. It is the voicing of the hitherto unrealized and unexamined condition of a race, the Irish. *Portrait* is among the most important of Irish novels because it is the first to examine the distorted relationship between the Irish community and oppression and to focus upon oppression's ultimate resource – the cooperation of the oppressed. It is a sweet irony that the novel should have appeared in the year of the Easter Rising in

Dublin. The political rebellion and even the cultural resurgence led by Yeats seemed to Joyce insufficient (although notable) attempts on the part of the Irish to break from the psychological dependency that they manifested towards the British and the Roman Catholic imperiums that had between them transformed the Irish into 'A race of clodhoppers!' (p. 231).

It is customary to say that in this, as in other works by Joyce, we witness a reaction to the squalor, paralysis and servility of Irish life. This is true, but the point loses its force unless it is refined further. It is well known that many of the most important modernist writers display a strong dislike of the 'modern world' of late nineteenth- and early twentieth-century mass civilization. A new and profound degeneracy had, it seemed, emerged. To overcome it, authority had to be renovated and reaffirmed; to explain it, the social and political system had to be analysed; to describe it, new modes of representation had to be developed. From Nietzsche to D. H. Lawrence, there is generated in European writing an obsessional, combative, threnodic discourse that is both of and against the white European world's loss of culture and confidence, a patriarchal collapse into disorder and confusion. While it is proper to see Joyce's work in that relation, it is ill-advised to think of him as only one more voice in the general chorus of lamentation. That role is more dramatically and successfully filled by his great compatriot and contemporary, Yeats. Joyce was unforgiving in his analysis of the Irish version of degeneration, but he came to understand that the morbidity of his community's condition was not the consequence of a lost wholeness or of a traditional culture. Instead, it was the adherence to deforming systems of belief and modes of behaviour that kept the Irish in bondage. It was fear of freedom, fear of the body, fear of the complexity of experience that would always be in excess of the conventions which attempted to organize it into stereotyped patterns that wounded the Irish spirit. This fear was all the more pronounced because the conventional systems by which the Irish lived were borrowed, from both London and Rome; even their revival was, in his view, a fake, both because it found its ratification in a misty and suspect past rather than in the present and because it reproduced – in its valorization of manliness, sexual purity, the glory of defeat, the imaginative destiny of the Celt or Gael, the spiritual and religious character of the race – the very features of its colonial–Catholic oppression that it was trying to erase. Degeneracy, insofar as that mobile term could be taken to identify a condition, was the product of tradition not the consequence of its loss.

In his 1904 essay, 'A Portrait of the Artist', Joyce provided an early sketch of himself ('His judgment was exquisite, deliberate, sharp; his sentence sculptural') and of his view of his contemporaries:

> These young men saw in the death of a dull French novelist (Emile Zola) the hand of Emmanuel God with us; they admired Gladstone, physical science and the tragedies of Shakespeare; and they believed in the adjustment of Catholic teaching to every day needs, in the Church diplomatic. In their relations among themselves and towards their superiors they displayed a nervous and (wherever there was a question of authority) a very English liberalism.

He goes on to point up contradictions in the attitudes of his fellow students. Pledged to self-denial, they admired those who were 'wild'; meek in themselves, they greeted rebellion when they met it in the writings and stories of Irish rebels. They preserved 'the union of faith and fatherland' despite its inner tensions and, above all, accepted authority.

> The exercise of authority might be sometimes (rarely) questionable, its intention, never.

In what now reads like an anticipation of *Stephen Hero*, the abandoned novel out of which *Portrait* grew, Joyce goes on to speak of the false antinomies with which, in such a world, he was faced – on the one hand 'sensitiveness', on the other hand 'dullness'. This too is an early indication of one of the ironically presented motifs in *Portrait*, the distinction between the sensitive artist and his dull, sports-playing, subservient friends. As in *Stephen Hero*, he announced his 'Nego', the denial (*'non*

serviam: I will not serve', as it became in *Portrait*) that faced
both ways and caused a furore. He played 'the mocking devil
in an isle twice removed from the mainland, under joint government of their Intensities and their Bullockships' wrote his
'Nego' 'amid a chorus of peddling Jews' gibberish and Gentile
clamour' and was condemned to hell. But 'that outburst over, it
was urbanity in warfare'. That final phrase catches the quality
that distinguishes *Portrait* from *Stephen Hero*. In the latter,
Stephen's war is conducted by frontal assault; in *Portrait* it is
conducted obliquely, by deconstruction rather than by destruction, by an insider who only becomes himself when he becomes
an outsider. But the negativity, the denial, is not barren. It too
has its utopian moment. In the famous closing passage of this
essay, Joyce, deploying the vocabulary of degeneration and
infection, nevertheless writes a prelude to the great finales that
give his most famous works their communal, utopian dimension – as in the short story 'The Dead', as in Molly's soliloquy
in *Ulysses* and Anna Livia Plurabelle's meditation in *Finnegans
Wake*:

> Man and woman, out of you comes the nation that is to come,
> the lighting of your masses in travail; the competitive order is
> employed against itself, the aristocracies are supplanted; and
> amid the general paralysis of an insane society, the confederate
> will issues in action.

This 1904 essay owes much to Ibsen. Like Nietzsche and Freud,
he exposed the pharisaic face (or faces) of bourgeois society. Joyce
is engaged on a similar enterprise, but he is famously different
because, more than anyone else before or since, he situates his
analysis in a specific place and, because he exploits that place's
reputation for wit and eloquence, makes language itself both the
instrument and the object of his analysis.

Dublin in Joyce's writing is not a place in the sense that London is in, say, Dickens or Gissing. Its streets, shops, pubs,
churches and civic buildings are named and located in relation
to one another as though, out of these particularities, a generic
map of The City as such could be drawn. Indeed, the condition

of becoming generic is that of being specific. The problem is that a bridge over a canal, a Findlater's church, a Bank of Ireland, a restaurant that is known by a Dedalus family nickname ('Underdone's', p. 88) may be too miscellaneous to conform to any generic pattern, or their function in relation to such a pattern may be too recondite or obscure, or it may be that what is generic in them is precisely their random, lividly particular nature. This last possibility is the most worrying and challenging, because it raises the possibility that all generic patterns are impositions upon a reality that is always in excess of their embrace and that the very idea of order and meaning is itself a delusion from which we must escape or to which we have to give a reluctant and disillusioned consent. It may be a delusion, but it is all we have got. Equally, it may be a delusion because it is constituted by the very language that we speak and write. Language, we may come to feel, may regulate reality but is not constitutive of it. Yet we can only know this, or say it, in language. It is, therefore, important to recognize from the outset that Joyce's Dublin is a place, a site of linguistic self-consciousness and a point on a map of the modern world that may be only a projection of our desire to give our knowledge a shape that is foreign to or other than it. Above all, it is a place that is named.

NAMING OF PLACE

In Chapter V, Stephen leaves his house in Fairview to go to University College in Stephen's Green. It is, of course, a journey that he regularly undertakes, and he has patterned it for himself as though his walk were a mnemonic device for his reading:

> The rainladen trees of the avenue evoked in him, as always, memories of the girls and women in the plays of Gerhart Hauptmann; and the memory of their pale sorrows and the fragrance falling from the wet branches mingled in a mood of quiet joy. His morning walk across the city had begun, and he foreknew that as he passed the sloblands of Fairview he would think of

the cloistral silverveined prose of Newman, that as he walked
along the North Strand Road, glancing idly at the windows of
the provision shops, he would recall the dark humour of Guido
Cavalcanti and smile, that as he went by Baird's stonecutting
works in Talbot Place the spirit of Ibsen would blow through
him like a keen wind, a spirit of wayward boyish beauty, and
that passing a grimy marine-dealer's shop beyond the Liffey he
would repeat the song by Ben Jonson which begins:

> *I was not wearier where I lay.*   (p. 163)

It is certainly possible (see notes) to identify the places and the
writers mentioned here; it is almost certainly futile to do so in the
hope of gaining access to the meaning(s) of the passage by observ-
ing that there is some correlation between, say, Cavalcanti's 'dark
humour' and the 'provision shops'. The passage is a display of
Stephen's habitual way of going about Dublin, making associations, imposing significances that are private and peculiar to himself. We are only expected, one would guess, to glimpse the basis
of the association, if any hint is given; but we cannot be sure we
have done so. More reasonably, we can assure ourselves that we
can see from such a passage the kind of intellectual dandy Stephen is; the very obscurity of the associations is itself the sign of
his preciousness. Furthermore, the literary associations seem
exotic in relation to the locales that precipitate them. Stephen has
just left a miserable home, picked his way down a waterlogged
lane strewn with mounds of rubbish, heard the screeching of a
mad nun from a madhouse. This programmed walk is a soothing
of his spirit, a way of dealing with a life that has become physically and socially repellent to him. The reader who thinks this
too bland a conclusion still has to confront an even more random
event when, a little later, 'Near the hoardings on the canal' Stephen meets 'the consumptive man with the doll's face and the
brimless hat' (p. 164) and thinks that it must be eleven o'clock –
since this is obviously a regular meeting (note the force of the
definite article in these phrases in affirming the habitual character of this randomness) – looks into a dairy to see a clock that
tells the wrong time and then hears a public clock strike eleven.
This makes him think of his acquaintance, MacCann, of whom

we then get a thumbnail sketch. Between that meeting and the next point in Stephen's journey, Trinity College and the neighbouring statue of Thomas Moore, there is an immense qualitative difference. For the college and the statue are quickly identified as important representations of the young man's cultural heritage and each is repudiated – Trinity's dull, Protestant centrality, Moore's ersatz Catholic–Celtic nationalism. And so on. The journey continues up Grafton Street to where Stephen once witnessed the laying of a slab in memory of the Irish republican patriot Wolfe Tone. To him it was a tawdry occasion. He goes on to the University College buildings in Stephen's Green, where Buck Egan and Burnchapel Whaley were reputed to have said black masses in the days of the Anglo-Irish gentry; and finally he enters to meet the dean of studies, the English convert, with whom he has a famous confrontation over language, religion and aesthetics.

All of Stephen's walks are like this. The walk is itself one of the novel's most effective rhetorical devices, allowing for conversation, flashbacks, meditations, and aligning these in a variety of ways to the geography of the city. The geography implies a history. Insofar as it is public, referring to public buildings and monuments, the history that accompanies it is 'official', national history. Insofar as it is private – hoardings, provision shops, a dairy with a clock – it is 'personal', the history of Stephen, his friendships, his reading and his thoughts. The distinction between the two is not secure, since Stephen is constantly reading the history of his city's monuments in the light of his own preoccupations, making it, so to say, 'personal'; and the personal history is being offered to us in a text and in a context that makes it historical too. Ireland has a story and Stephen has a story, and where they intersect is history. History is, in this sense, Stephen's interpretation of aspects of Ireland's past and of his own present upon which is mounted the reader's interpretation of what Stephen–Joyce writes. For 'Stephen' is, obviously, the name that occurs most often in the novel, and our sense of Dublin as a place is to a large degree formed by the variety of the journeys he undertakes from the ever-shifting abodes of the downward-spiralling

Dedalus family, from Bray to Blackrock, to Mountjoy Square, to Fairview and Drumcondra.

The intensive naming of place, most of it centred on Dublin but stretching also to Kildare and Cork (and to towns like Buttevant, Kilmallock and Moycullen, which make brief appearances), both confirms and disturbs the possibility of seeing the local in larger metropolitan and world-historical terms. Although it is in *Ulysses* and *Finnegans Wake* that we come to realize the full implications of the notion that a reading of history also involves a history of reading, the peregrinations of Stephen in *Portrait* also have this chiasmic function. Reading a city, as Stephen does, involves two different kinds of experience, as we have seen. What we may call the personal brings all that is otherwise anonymous – places like bridges, corners, shops, towpaths, shorelines, tramways – into view as surrounds for all that is officially historical. Important public buildings and monuments stand in relation to these other places like italicized passages in a body of roman type. They are quotations of and from history and they are increasingly incorporated into the geography of Stephen's world, so that, by the close, it is the places of crucial importance to Stephen's development that become, as it were, italicized in the reader's mind – the steps of the National Library, the chapel at Clongowes, Dollymount Strand, and, in an obvious example, Stephen's Green ('Crossing Stephen's, that is, my green', p. 231). The importance of a place depends finally on the importance of being Stephen. It is he who confers value on the city he reads. It is, after all, his city and his reading.

QUOTATION

Portrait begins and ends with quotation. In the interval, quotations are so numerous that they entirely take over the text, as in Chapter III with the hell-fire sermon (quoted as by Fr Arnall, who is himself quoting a seventeenth-century treatise) and the close of Chapter V, which is taken up by quotations from Stephen's diary. It is important that the novel ends by citing the words of the young man who has been its subject; the narrated

Stephen becomes the narrator Stephen. Just as he gradually took over the Dublin that cited and recited itself to him on his wanderings, he also takes over the telling of his own story, finally replacing the words of others with his own words, ultimately achieving elquoence after beginning in baby lispings and mispronunciations. The first quotation is the epigraph to the novel. The 'he' referred to there is Daedalus, to whom Stephen turns in the last sentence of the novel. In the first dozen pages there are quotations from a children's story, a nursery rhyme, a tralala accompaniment to a dance, a version of a hymn, mnemonic sentences from a school text, Stephen's own name and (cosmic) address from the flyleaf of his school-book and, opposite, Fleming's joke verse and three different prayers. The ratio of ten quotations to a dozen pages is at least sustained and often exceeded thereafter.

Quotation assumes a variety of forms in this novel. The villanelle by Stephen in Chapter V (pp. 201–2) is a quotation, but is it in the same category as the sentence we meet a couple of pages earlier?

> Bah! he had done well to leave the room in disdain. He had done well not to salute her on the steps of the library. (p. 204)

Further, a change of tense can indicate more sharply the presence of a narrator who is citing Stephen's words:

> He had told himself bitterly as he walked through the streets that she was a figure of the womanhood of her country . . . (p. 204)

The inflections of the narrative voice that Joyce made more supple and subtle with his 'indirect free style' (or stream-of-consciousness), his interior monologue and, in *Portrait*, with his shading of the third-person narrative towards a first-person account, can bring the whole question of 'reported speech' under scrutiny. Even apart from the passages in the novel that are indented and italicized to indicate that they are quotations and the other passages that are ascribed to formally acknowledged authorities – for example, Cardinal Newman, St Thomas Aquinas – or fictive sources – Fr Arnall, Simon Dedalus, etc. – there are numerous occasions when the alterations of the tense and mood of the verbs indicate the increasing proximity of the third- to the first-person narrative, when the whole narrative reads like a quotation. In the first chapter, as Stephen agonizes about whether he should or should not go to the rector to report his wrongful punishment at the hands of Fr Dolan, the tenses of the verbs shift between perfect, pluperfect and future, and their moods between indicative and conditional, as he hesitates and looks for support to what he had read in his school history texts and to the imagined comments of his schoolfellows (pp. 45–9). It is the exertion of such pressure on the narrative boundaries of the text that robs it of security. The story is constantly being ascribed to Stephen, and by Stephen to someone else, so that the reader is compelled to ask, but never able to answer, the question of the 'identity' of the narrator. Is the narrator the same as the author? Or is the narrator's voice as borrowed, as ventriloquial, as the voices of those in the text that are indisputably quoted?

This is not a technical issue that can be resolved by reference to the history of narrative technique in the novel from Flaubert to Dorothy Richardson, the woman who 'invented' the stream-of-consciousness technique. Joyce may have learned a great deal from his predecessors, but none of them had brought the question of the authority of the author to light as he did. For him, it was a question fundamental to his culture. Time and again, as the systematic exploitation of the rhetorical device of quotation makes clear, this novel returns to the question of origin and source. The Irish speak a borrowed language, having given up their own. Despite his contempt for the dean of studies, Stephen recognizes that

> His language, so familiar and so foreign, will always be for me an acquired speech . . . My soul frets in the shadow of his language. (p. 175)

When he has a 'wrangle' with the Italian lecturer, 'little round-head rogue'seye Ghezzi', about Giordano Bruno, his brief victory is tempered by the memory that Ghezzi's

countrymen and not mine had invented what Cranly the other
night called our religion. (p. 231)

Stephen's aesthetic theory is borrowed from a variety of
sources, most of them theological. His idea of the soul and its
relation to the body is at first a borrowed one too, culled from
the teaching of his religious superiors and later confirmed by his
reading of literature, especially Dante. But, worst of all, Stephen
feels the threat of his borrowed culture when it seeks to co-opt
him, when it tries to recruit him into its system of institutional-
ized borrowing, either through the vocation of the priesthood
(p. 149) or through a commitment to Irish nationalism. He tells
Davin:

—This race and this country and this life produced me . . . I
shall express myself as I am. (p. 188)

When Davin repeats his plea to Stephen to 'be one of us', Stephen replies:

—My ancestors threw off their language and took another . . .
They allowed a handful of foreigners to subject them. Do you
fancy I am going to pay in my own life and person debts they
made? What for? (p. 188)

He will not be borrowed. To be borrowed is, in a sense, to be
used to pay debts others have contracted. Stephen sees no reason
why he should suffer the hangover from the drinking of others.
It is one thing to quote others; it is another to be a quotation in
someone else's anthology of names, whether those be the names
of the members of the Jesuit order, cited several times, or of the
saints, or of the heroes of Irish nationalism or of the uncertain
listings of the names of great English writers, from Marryat to
Newman, Tennyson and Byron (see p. 25).
    The other literary and cultural constituency into which Ste-
phen refused co-option is that of the Irish Literary Revival, led
by Yeats. He quotes Yeats twice (pp. 209, 233) and refers to the
fuss that attended the first night of the poet's *The Countess*

Cathleen, marking the beginning of the Irish National Theatre. The refusal to join with the Revival is important. Joyce avoided all the established versions of cultural nationalism. But there was a kinship between his own project and that of Yeats. Both sought to find for Ireland a language and a literary form or forms that would consort with Irish experience, including the traumatic experience of having lost a language. Although their ways of doing so were very different, their work bears the impress of the same recognition – that Ireland must find its own language or be doomed to quote itself as a stereotype in a language that belonged to others. In the end, Stephen pays a back-handed compliment to the Revival by quoting a mock-version of the kind of new speech to be found in the Revival plays of Lady Gregory and John Millington Synge. It is with this peasant (always a term of contempt in the *Portrait*), John Alphonsus Mulrennan, that Stephen 'must struggle' (p. 234). One of the most effective ways of triumphing over inherited or current cultural languages is to quote them, for in quotation they undergo a torsion that wrenches them from their own context and replaces them in the context of the writer who quotes. It is, finally, a typographical irony on Joyce's part that *Portrait*, like his other works, should be without quotation marks. Their absence is a symptom of the pervasive presence of what they would deny.

FATHERS AND MOTHERS

However, there is, it would seem, an ultimate sense in which Stephen is himself a quote from an original. He is the son of his parents. Although he finds it impossible to experience the expected filial sentiments, his emotional repudiation is not enough to give him the release from parental origin that he craves. In Chapter II, on the trip to Cork with his father, he takes refuge from the paternal grasp by repeating names:

—I am Stephen Dedalus. I am walking beside my father whose name is Simon Dedalus. We are in Cork, in Ireland. Cork is a city. Our room is in the Victoria Hotel. Victoria and Stephen and Simon. Simon and Stephen and Victoria. Names. (p. 83)

But this chanting of names blurs rather than sharpens his sense of self. He suddenly loses contact with his felt memory of the child he had been:

The memory of his childhood suddenly grew dim. He tried to call forth some of its vivid moments but could not. He recalled only names: Dante, Parnell, Clane, Clongowes. A little boy had been taught geography by an old woman who kept two brushes in her wardrobe. (pp. 83–4)

Later, in the pub conversation between his father and one of his former cronies, Stephen is told that he looks like his grandfather, that he has a trace of Cork accent in his speech, and then, when the conversation turns to girls, he hears that, if he is not a 'flirt',

—Then he's not his father's son, said the little old man.
—I don't know, I'm sure, said Mr Dedalus, smiling complacently. (p. 85)

The conversation casts shadows for Stephen. 'Leave him to his Maker', 'I hope he'll be as good as man as his father' – the phrases have a retrospective irony once we have seen Stephen reproduce his father's sexual delinquency when he goes to the prostitute soon after (pp. 91–2), when the name Simon becomes associated with the sin of Simon Magus, simony, the exchange of spiritual for temporal goods (pp. 87–8, 147), and when Stephen exchanges his biological for his spiritual father, Daedalus, at the close. The struggle to create his own father, and thereby to become father to himself, to become, in effect, his own origin, is enabled by his adaptation of the Catholic doctrine of the Trinity, in which this miracle of self-begetting is given an elaborate and detailed formulation (pp. 137–8). The father–son relationship of Daedalus and Icarus is another figure for his ambition, as is the relationship between the priests and Stephen – although the only occasion on which he addresses a priest by the name 'Father' and in return is addressed as 'my child' is in the confessional in Chapter III (pp. 132–3). Although it was conventional, both at school and at university, to address the priests as 'sir', Stephen is alert to the significance of the practice. He thinks of the dean of studies as 'one whom he would never call his ghostly father' (p. 176) and remarks on Davin's solecism in addressing 'the jesuits as father' (p. 187). The fact that they are celibate and 'fathers' brings up the question of the woman, the mother and her role.

Although no one in the novel has a function independent of his or her effect upon Stephen, Mrs Dedalus and Stephen's beloved (E——— C——— on p. 62, 'Emma' on p. 106, a 'certain young lady' in Davin's phrase on p. 187, otherwise 'she') are the most ghostly presences in the book. Both women are associated with celibacy. Emma angers Stephen by consorting with Fr Moran, the 'priested peasant' (p. 205) to whom 'she would unveil her soul's shy nakedness' rather than to Stephen, 'a priest of eternal imagination' (p. 205). Some of Stephen's most rancorous class insults are reserved for priests like Fr Moran or Fr Dolan, although women are often included to give the insult more point. Mrs Dedalus has no first name, Emma has no surname, the priests have no first names, but, even as a child, Stephen is defensive about his own name:

> The great men in the history had names like that and nobody made fun of them. It was his own name that he should have made fun of if he wanted to make fun. Dolan: it was like the name of a woman that washed clothes. (p. 48)

In his anger at her, her image is distorted into memories of young women who had embarrassed or angered him by their coarseness – the flowergirl, the kitchengirl, the girl who had laughed to see him stumble, a girl who had called coarsely after him (p. 204). The support given by women to the Church and to the language movement ('The best helpers the language has', p. 204) is a further proof of their underdevelopment, their almost nameless existence. But their love for the celibate is figured, not as a love for the Holy Ghost, but as a love for a St Joseph figure. This association is threatening because of the implicit betrayal of the cuckold father of Jesus. The link between virginity and harlotry, embodied in the villanelle that he writes but does not send to Emma, is a threat that both confuses and frightens Stephen throughout. From the early schooldays when he is made fun of because he said he kissed his mother before he went to bed (p. 10) to the references to St Aloysius Gonzaga and Pascal, both of whom refused to touch their mothers, as Stephen tells Cranly (p. 224), women are consigned to this dual role. This duality is famously confirmed by Stephen's use of the same phrase on two occasions to characterize two different women as typical of their race. When he hears Davin's story about the peasant woman who invited him to stay with her in the lonely mountain cottage while her husband was away (pp. 168–9), Stephen imagines her as

> a type of her race and his own, a batlike soul waking to the consciousness of itself in darkness and secrecy and loneliness and, through the eyes and voice and gesture of a woman without guile, calling the stranger to her bed. (p. 169)

Later, in his bitterness against Emma's association with Fr Moran, he tells himself

> that she was a figure of the womanhood of her country, a batlike soul waking to the consciousness of itself in darkness and secrecy and loneliness, tarrying awhile, loveless and sinless, with her mild lover and leaving him to whisper of innocent transgressions in the latticed ear of a priest. (pp. 204–5)

Either way, the figure of Irish womanhood, to whatever state of spiritual consciousness she may be coming, is effecting her improvement by betrayal – of the husband in one case, of Stephen in the other. One incident indicates a sexual awakening, the other a stifling of sexuality. But it matters little. Both women are still prefigured as harlot and virgin and neither role is liberating. Each conforms to a stereotype while the passage conflictually speaks of the beginning of an escape from it.

Mother Ireland, Mother Church, Our Blessed Mother, Eve,

Virgin, prostitute, temptress – all of these roles and their accompanying imageries (cold ivory, hot swooning) lead to the erasure of women from Stephen's project of self-origination. They are threats to it because his realization of it demands that he repudiate his feeling both for Emma and for his mother, even though Mrs Dedalus prays that in his exile he

> may learn in my own life and away from home and friends what the heart is and what it feels. (p. 234)

Thus, the grammatical idea of the male person, first, second and third, is closely allied with the theological doctrine of the three Persons of the Trinity; they in turn are incorporated into Stephen's male-gendered aesthetic system, with the Holy Ghost, the Third Person, representing the inspiration that makes the Father speak through the Son and the Son through the Father. The Holy Ghost is the voice of the Father who is speaking the narrative of the Son. In another act of enfolding and unfolding, the Trinity also comes to represent Stephen's alternative vision of the actual familial world from which he too 'proceeds'. The world of his father, Simon Dedalus, and of his mother, who is never named, has its religious analogue in the Holy Family, an icon that Stephen finds to be entirely characteristic of the Ireland and the brand of Catholicism he came to know, bereft of the mystery and severity of the Trinity and also dangerously and seductively carnal, especially in virtue of the central role it assigned to woman, in her role as Virgin and Mother, as betrayer and temptress. It is in *Ulysses* that these specific preoccupations become governing agencies in the narrative. *Portrait*, although it is something quite other than a preparation for *Ulysses*, is a novel shadowed by archetypal disputes that are more emphatically present in its successor.

BODY AND SOUL

A call is bodily, a calling is spiritual. Stephen, whose ears are filled throughout with voices and voicings, has some trouble in distinguishing between these. We hear of 'the cold silence of intellectual revolt' (p. 168) that possesses Stephen, but we hear directly the voices that promote that silence within him. Words have sounds and Stephen is early puzzled by the Saussurean problem of the linkage between these sounds and the meanings they bear. The word 'suck' is 'queer'; the words 'hot' and 'cold' on the taps in the lavatory make him feel hot and cold. That too is 'queer', as is the chill air in the corridor. If he listens, he can hear the gas flame singing when the fellows stopped talking (p. 7). When he thinks of the word 'God', he pursues his laboured thought about it through fourteen repetitions in one paragraph (as well as two occurrences of the French word 'Dieu', p. 12). Stephen's wondering manipulation of his small but growing vocabulary in the first chapter involves a great deal of such repetition. But as his mastery grows, the labyrinthine pursuit of the same word or words through a series of cadences remains with him:

He would fall. He had not yet fallen but he would fall silently, in an instant. Not to fall was too hard, too hard: and he felt the silent lapse of his soul, as it would be at some instant to come, falling, falling but not yet fallen, still unfallen but about to fall. (p. 150)

Many of his quotations are heard – 'Newman had heard this note also' (p. 151); 'remembered only a proud cadence from Newman' (p. 153); beginning to cite the villanelle, his thoughts become 'cries arising unbroken in a hymn' (p. 205) – many are sung, in many instances he repeats them to himself (see pp. 87, 154). We hear of 'A soft liquid joy like the noise of many waters', and in the next paragraph 'A soft liquid joy flowed through the words where the soft long vowels hurtled noiselessly' (p. 209). The speech of others is listened to intensely. Cranly's speech is distinguished at some length from Davin's by virtue of the linguistic echoes that resonate within it (p. 181); the dwarfish man at the National Library has 'a genteel accent, low and moist, marred by errors' (p. 211); 'The voice, the accent, the mind' of MacAlister offends him in the physics theatre (p. 179). In every sense of the phrase, Stephen hears voices, and he is steadfast to his early habit of considering the intimacy between the cadence of the voice, the sounds of the words it speaks and the meanings that he assigns to them. The aural dimension in *Portrait* is crucial because sound is physical and yet disembodied. It is through the channels of the ear that the talkative world of Dublin reaches Stephen's soul.

Taste, touch and sight are also important. Physical sensations are salient in the first three chapters in particular, culminating in the account of the torments of hell-fire in Chapter III. But the aural sense is finally more important, since it is through it that words achieve their various effects. As we have noted, *Portrait* is full of repetitive patterns, pleated phrasings, reiterated cadences of the kind that can be found in the controlled impressionistic prose of writers of the 'decadent' school of the nineteenth century, particularly Walter Pater. But in this novel, the repetitions have a curious and specific function. Stephen is fond of reminding us of his cold and steely resolve, his indifference, his repudiation of the personal for the impersonal – so much so that this becomes a culminating moment in his aesthetic:

> The personality of the artist, at first a cry or a cadence or a mood
> and then a fluid and lambent narrative, finally refines itself out of
> existence, impersonalises itself, so to speak. (p. 199)

The relationship between this 'impersonal' resolve and the myriad subtle sensations that Stephen registers seems contradictory. His iron determination is sheathed in the velvet glove of his sensibility. But this contradiction is bound up with Stephen's attempt to rewrite the conventional distinction between soul and body.

The torments of hell, as described in Chapter III, are of two kinds – physical and spiritual. They are boundless in their extension, incredible in their intensity, unceasing in their variety (pp. 120–1) and, worst of all, they are eternal. Fr Arnall attempts, with a fair degree of success, to make hell a place that can be physically realized rather than an unimaginable condition. But for all the stress of his rhetoric, he cannot overcome the doctrinal difficulty that lies at the heart of the sermon. There are ways of explaining how an infinitely good God could create such a place. But there is no way of explaining how disembodied spirits can feel physical pain, even though various attempts were made to do so (see note 47, p. 256). The categories of the physical and the spiritual are incompatible. Throughout *Portrait*, the intensity with which the physical world is recorded and registered is discrepant with spiritual growth. Body and soul are not born simultaneously, as Stephen explains to Davin. The soul

> has a slow and dark birth, more mysterious than the birth of the body. When the soul of a man is born in this country there are nets flung at it to hold it back from flight. You talk to me of nationality, language, religion. I shall try to fly by those nets. (p. 188)

When physical sensation reaches a sufficient pitch of intensity, the physical world and its words fade. Stephen swoons as often as a heroine in a sentimental novel of the eighteenth century, and the swoon often carries its earlier meaning of sexual intercourse. The lips of the prostitute press on his brain and lips 'as though they were the vehicle of a vague speech'; and as she opens her lips he feels the pressure of her tongue 'darker than the swoon of sin, softer than sound or odour' (p. 92). At Dollymount Strand, the image of the young girl 'had passed into his soul for ever and no word had broken the holy silence of his ecstasy'. He experiences a cosmic sense, as though he were looking down upon the earth. 'His soul was swooning into some new world' (p. 159). In bleaker vein, as he prepares to go to confession, the 'black cold void waste' is apprehended so powerfully that he loses a sense of where he is:

> Consciousness of place came ebbing back to him slowly over a vast tract of time unlit, unfelt, unlived. (p. 129)

From an early stage, he wants 'to meet in the real world the unsubstantial image which his soul so constantly beheld'. When he encountered it, he 'would fade into something impalpable' (p. 58). There are other instances of this spiritual cosmic experience in which world and word fade and the physically vivid

Dublin and Ireland that he knows is left behind. This is Stephen's version of eternity, the realm of art in which 'consciousness of place' ebbs away. It is when the physically real world is most vividly there that it undergoes a change and becomes faint, vague, transmuting itself into a spiritual experience. Because it frees itself from the specific and the actual, it ceases to be personal. Soul is cosmic, the body is political.

Here we can look again at the practice of repetition in this novel. Repetition has its monotonous aspect. It emphasizes for us the asphyxiation of Stephen's surroundings, their limited and limiting character. Repetition also has (like the fires of hell) the quality of variety, endless difference in sameness. It is also a mnemonic device, reminding him (and us) of the ways in which variety can be organized around a number of governing obsessions or tropes. In addition, repetition is a mode of intensification, accumulating power as it progresses, a repeated probing for an exit from its own reiterations. Finally, the practice of repetition is not, of course, confined to words, phrases or sentences. It extends to the organization of incident and episode, allowing us to see the pattern of rise and fall, near-escape and then further imprisonment that gives the work its convoluted form. Out of all these repetitions we see the slow emergence of a Stephen who will no longer be victim to them, just as, on another level, we see the emergence of Stephen into the first and out of the third person, the gradual liberation of his language from that of others. In fact, repetition is, in its monotony, variety and intensity, the rhetoric of hell, and, as in hell, its worst aspect is that it goes on forever. It is from this that Stephen must escape. It is from the very carefully construed, aurally dominant prose, in which one phrase lapses into another, that he must break free into the more staccato, declarative prose of his diary. The animating principle in Stephen's otherwise energy-sapping world is flight. To 'fly by those nets', to watch the flight of birds from the steps of the National Library as auguries of the future (pp. 207–9), to invoke Daedalus and Icarus, 'a hawklike man flying sunward above the sea' (p. 156), is his ambition. But he does not escape *from* his Ireland: he escapes *with* it. He brings it into another world. He wants to absolve it from the fate of sameness, the monotony of a repetition that becomes merely farcical.

IRELAND: TERRITORY AND HISTORY

Writing is extraterritorial even for someone like Stephen (or Joyce), who makes a fetish in his writing about the country and, more especially, the city that he left. In a slightly cryptic moment, just before his interview with the dean of studies, Stephen enters the corridor that leads to the physics theatre. The house once belonged to an Anglo-Irish anti-Catholic, Buck Whaley; now it belongs to the Jesuits:

> The corridor was dark and silent but not unwatchful. Why did he feel that it was not unwatchful? Was it because he had heard that in Buck Whaley's time there was a secret staircase there? Or was the jesuit house extraterritorial and was he walking among aliens? The Ireland of Tone and of Parnell seemed to have receded in space. (p. 170)

The house is, in a sense, haunted by history, but the main point is that it is in Ireland but not of it. Once owned by the gentry, who held it for Britain, and now owned by the Jesuits, who hold it for Rome, it is literally as well as technically 'extraterritorial'. It is an emblem of the British–Roman imperium, anti-Catholic and militantly Catholic, a perfect site for the subsequent conversation with the English Catholic convert dean who is going to make Stephen feel both contemptuous and foreign, an 'alien' in his own country. Yet Stephen's chief complaint is not lodged against either the British or the Roman Catholic imperial systems. It is directed against the Irish themselves who cooperate with these systems and who habitually betray the leaders who attempt to bring them freedom. Stephen too is a bringer of freedom, more spiritual indeed, but, in his view, more basic. Like the political leaders, he too feels the fear of betrayal, although in his case the treachery might take the subtler form of self-betrayal, a concession to the conventional life, whether of the Church or of the new revivalism, of his unconsciously enslaved compatriots.

The famous Christmas-dinner scene is an obvious and early instance of Stephen's introduction to the battle between spiritual leadership and the established British–Roman governance of the country. Dante Riordan defends the role of the Catholic Church in destroying Parnell. Stephen's father and Mr Casey attack it and, by extension, attack the Church's long-standing opposition to Irish republican and Fenian insurrection since 1798. The role of Britain in the Parnell episode is almost entirely ignored and it is only implied in relation to the other episodes mentioned (p. 26). Nevertheless, the political question of freedom and kingship is secondary to what Mrs Riordan calls 'a question of public morality' (p. 26), over which the Church has control. Mrs Riordan was once a supporter of Parnell, as the child Stephen remembers. She hit a man on the head with her umbrella because he took off his hat when the band played the British national anthem (p. 31). In this respect she is like many others – anti-British but not anti-Catholic, even when the Church's position supports the British position. Terrified as he is by the savagery of the row, Stephen recognizes the power of the Church in Mrs Riordan's about-turn.

Parnell is a product of Parnellism. Parnellism is a set of rhetorical procedures for the reading of the Irish past that Joyce and Yeats, with many others, perfected in the period between 1890 and 1940. The first and most important of these procedures was to formulate the Parnell crisis as a confrontation between two forces, one embodied in Parnell himself, the other in the Irish people. This is so obvious that it deserves repetition. Parnell is one agent; the Irish people are another. Each of these agents is then constituted as having a radical bias of personality. Parnell is austere, remote, self-contained, disdainful; the Irish people are, under his influence, an organized community that has, nevertheless, an irresistible longing towards the delinquency and volatility of the mob. This 'mob' impulse is precipitated by the divorce proceedings. The fear of the mob had been one of the bequests of the counter-revolutionary reaction to France since 1789; in Ireland, it took on a local colouring in the opposition to

O'Connellite politics and the mobilization of the Catholic masses. Indeed, both Yeats and Joyce rehearse the standard attacks on O'Connell's demagoguery, on his populism and garrulity, unfavourably contrasting these with Parnell's solitariness and his lack of eloquence. All the stereotypes of Irishness are contradicted by Parnell, confirmed in the Irish people. The conflict between these two agents is one between a highly individuated selfhood and the uniform obedience of the crowd. Parnell almost made the Irish into individuals; that was the real version of Home Rule that he offered. Once they refused it, the battle for individuality was resumed by the artist, availing of the long romantic tradition of radical selfhood to support his position. Parnell is, in that respect, the leader who almost redeemed the Irish from their oppression; but what he revealed was that the oppression was not inflicted by the English alone; the Irish had introjected the oppression; they had become experts in oppressing themselves. That was why they hated individuality, why they hated the artist and why they turned upon Parnell. They could not take on the responsibility of becoming themselves; they turned instead into the infernal mob condition to which earlier in their history they had been reduced.

'Ivy Day in the Committee Room' is, of course, the story in which Joyce's Parnell figures most prominently, although it is through his absence that his presence is most felt. All the stories in *Dubliners* move from repression to epiphany, from a condition of moral inarticulacy to a moment of revelation, even if the revelation is nothing more than an exposure of the initial condition. The *ethos* of Dublin and the *pathos* of the individual Dubliners are interfused. In 'Ivy Day', the gloom and the dilapidation of the committee room, the banked fire, the cheap futilities of the conversations and, above all, the shadowiness of the scene all conspire to remind us that this is Ireland in the despondent years after Parnell's fall. Parnell is a shade, Ireland is in his shadow; Ireland is an underworld populated by shades; the Parnell crisis is shadowed forth again by the dispute about the kind of reception to be accorded to the adulterous English King Edward VII. Dublin is apparently going to welcome the King of England who is adulterous, having destroyed the uncrowned king of Ireland for the same fault. This is a wake for Parnell, haunted by the mysterious figure of the spoilt priest, celebrated by drink – payment for political services – and by bad poetry, sentimentally received. Funeral, wake, underworld, shade, shadow, depression, repetition – these are the indications of the famous Dublin paralysis that has been brought on, in this case, by the shock of Parnell's downfall. The stupefaction of this world is complete. The Irish, having destroyed their leader, have lapsed back into that sodden state of lachrymose concussion from which he had threatened to liberate them.

In 'Ivy Day', it is the crime of Parnell's destruction that is finally admitted so that a reason for the condition of Dublin could be found. But Parnell's death does not explain the pathological state of the inmates of the room. It is their pathological state that explains why Parnell was destroyed. The source of that is in the national character of the Irish people. It is their destiny to be slaves and, in their revolt against this destiny, to be confined to a bogus and eloquent lamentation about it. Their dreadful blarney is the index of their servitude. Parnell's aristocratic hauteur defines him as a person who has selfhood, far removed in his silence and impassiveness from the blether and kitsch sentiment of the democratic rabble. Joyce's valorization of 'silence' (along with 'exile' and 'cunning') as the mark of the artist, the extraordinary personage, gives a historical context to Stephen's version of his own personal and spiritual integrity.

Joyce consistently associates Parnell with the Fenians – not just through the 'phoenix flame' of Hynes's recitation in the *Dubliners* story, but much more specifically in the famous Christmas-dinner scene in *Portrait* and in his essay 'Fenianism'. Mr Casey, Simon Dedalus's guest and friend at the dinner table, is a Fenian who served time for his beliefs. Parnell himself appealed to the Fenians when *in extremis*, in his last campaign, over the heads of his Irish Parliamentary Party supporters. The complicated relationship between Parnell and the Fenians is reduced by Joyce's representation to a close liaison in which both parties seem to share a common insurrectionist aim. Perhaps the main attraction of Fenianism was that it had never been defeated. Despite 1867,

Fenianism survived, in various guises, as a freemasonry of those who were against the British presence. Fenianism was the sea in which the IRB fish swam. Brutal jail sentences, clerical condemnations, the rise of the Home Rule movement and the Land League, reprints of patriotic song books, aided its survival. In Joyce's own words:

> the Fenianism of '67 was not one of the usual flashes of Celtic temperament that lighten the shadows for a moment and leave behind a darkness blacker than before.

Fenianism was as different from Emmet's rebellion, or Young Ireland's 1848 fiasco, as was Parnell from O'Connell. In terms of military incompetence and clownishness, there is not much to choose between 1848 and 1867; nevertheless, the choice was made because, it would seem, '67 was regarded as an origin for Fenianism while '48 was a finale for Young Ireland. More importantly, Fenianism had the reputation, assiduously fostered by its leader, James Stephens, of being an *organized* movement. It was not a mere impulse, not a twitch of the Celtic nervous system. It was, in Joyce's view, a movement that would change the character of the Irish people. This is close to the heart of the Fenian appeal for Joyce and his association of Parnell with the movement. It would change the national character of the Irish people; it might finally relieve them of their junior status as molten Celts and make them into truly individuated Parnellites. Joyce appreciated that, between them, the Fenians and Parnell were achieving the beginnings of a psychological revolution in Ireland. Parnell's destruction – for which the Fenians could not be blamed, as they had, in his view, remained steadfast – was an act of self-mutilation, a turning back into the underworld of servitude even as the Home Rule sun arose above the divorce court and committee room 15.

In short, Joyce's version of Parnell was part of his analysis of the aborted progress of the Irish people from colonial slavery to near-freedom. The double empire of London and Rome weighed so heavily on the Irish because they had grown to love their enslavement and to fear freedom and its responsibilities. What

Parnell had tried to do politically, with the help of the Fenians, Joyce envisaged himself as doing in art, with the very minor help of shadowy forerunners like James Clarence Mangan and in despite of the fake Celticism of W. B. Yeats, Synge and company. He would win Home Rule for art; with him, modern Ireland would truly begin and so too would Irish literature. He would be the uncrowned king of Irish letters and the first writer to give to the Irish people a representation of spiritual freedom.

Ulysses and *Finnegans Wake* extend the issue. This is not the place for an inventory of their varied formal experiments and effects, but the Babel of these works grows out of the more formal, univocal language of their predecessors. For our immediate purpose, it seems remarkable that the heterogeneity of Joyce's later texts coincides with a diminution of the Parnellism that had been so evident in the early books and in the Italian essays and lectures. The later works are stylistically different from the earlier, in part because the whole basis of Joyce's critique of the Irish situation has altered. In them, the Irish people have found their voices. The plural is important. All the pastiche and parody, all the colloquial conversations and ruminations, the songs, the puns, witticisms and so forth are signs of a diversity that contrasts strongly with the fixity of character and the univocal performances previously displayed. Joyce is no longer stereotyping the aristocratic leader and his plebeian followers, just as he is no longer positing the ideal of the remote artist against the philistine mob. He is still preoccupied with the effects of internalized guilt, with the victim's tendency to self-blame for the triumph of his victimizer. Bloom and HCE are both victims of some original fault – Bloom's father's conversion, the condition of being a Jew or a cuckold, or, in Earwicker's case, the anxiety about that original and unspecified thing that happened in the Phoenix Park, the Dublinized version of the Garden of Eden. But he sees this issue in a more various light. The racial propensities of the Irish were no longer for him a legitimate basis for a reading of the Irish situation, as they had been in relation to the Parnell crisis. This is true even though the conventional anthropological distinctions between the Irish and the English had become part of the political discourse of the period. The Fenians provoked Matthew Arnold in *Culture and Anarchy* to make a memorable discrimination:

> And then the difference between an Irish Fenian and an English rough is so immense . . . [The Fenian] is so evidently desperate and dangerous, a man of a conquered race, a Papist, with centuries of ill-usage to inflame him against us . . . But with the Hyde Park rioter how different! He is our own flesh and blood; he is a Protestant . . .

This is the preacher of the new hellenism Joyce mocks in the opening chapter of *Ulysses*. It is this species of racial characterization that Joyce abandons; in abandoning it, he also abandons his Parnellism.

But in *Portrait*, Parnell's death leaves a traumatic impression on the young Stephen. He dreams of the arrival of the catafalque bearing the leader's remains at Kingstown and the mourning crowd patrolled by the vengeful green and maroon figure of Dante Riordan (p. 22). The incident is deeply embedded, both here and in the literature of the subsequent period. Yeats, in his commentary of 1935 on the poem 'Parnell's Funeral', spoke of the four bells that struck, at equally divided intervals, to mark the ending of major historical phases of Irish experience. The first came with the Flight of the Earls; the second with the battle of the Boyne; the third with the arrival of French revolutionary influence 'among our peasants'; and the fourth with the death of Parnell. He then describes how he went to Kingstown to meet Maud Gonne off the mailboat one October morning in 1891 and found an immense crowd there to meet the body of Parnell and escort it to his grave. At Glasnevin – and he cites Maud Gonne and Standish O'Grady as witnesses – a star fell as Parnell's body was lowered into the grave. The bitterness of the Parnell dispute was such, according to Yeats, that it changed Dublin from 'a well-mannered, smooth-spoken city' into the 'foul mouth' he mentioned in 1913 in his first Parnell poem 'To a Shade'. But it also brought with it 'free discussion', the 'passion for reality' and the 'satiric genius that informs *Ulysses, The Playboy of the Western World* . . .' Yeats goes on to mention the Christmas-dinner scene in Joyce's *Portrait*, and then adds:

> We had passed through an initiation like that of the Tibetan ascetic, who staggers half dead from a trance, where he has seen himself eaten alive and has not yet learned that the eater was himself.
>
> As we discussed and argued, the national character changed, O'Connell, the great comedian, left the scene and the tragedian Parnell took his place. When we talked of his pride; of his apparent impassivity when his hands were full of blood because he had torn them with his nails, the preceding epoch with its democratic bonhomie, seemed to grin through a horse collar. He was the symbol that made apparent, or made possible that epoch's contrary . . .

In Chapter V of *Portrait*, Stephen tells Davin:

> —No honourable and sincere man . . . has given up to you his life and his youth and his affections from the days of Tone to those of Parnell but you sold him to the enemy or failed him in need or reviled him and left him for another. And you invite me to be one of you. I'd see you damned first. (p. 188)

He speaks of Irish political leaders here in terms more appropriate to those of a spurned lover ('left him for another'). This allows for a merging of the sexual and political themes. Emma leaves Stephen for 'another', the priest Fr Moran. Not only that, but she is involved with Moran in the language revival movement. That movement and the Gaelic Athletic Association movement, with its revival of the games of Gaelic football and hurling, elicits Stephen's scorn too. In his conversation with Davin he conjoins political betrayal with the Gaelic sports revival:

> —When you make the next rebellion with hurleysticks, said Stephen, and want the indispensable informer, tell me. I can find you a few in this college. (p. 187)

The literary revival too was bogus. Like the others, it was a 'peasant' movement; but like them it was also a repeat perfor- mance, an attempt to make the present a rehearsal of the past. This endless repetition – informers, rebellions, peasant reviv- als, betrayals – is the history from which that other Stephen, in *Ulysses*, is trying to recover:

> —History, Stephen said, is a nightmare from which I am trying to awake. (U. 34)

This remark is an echo of Marx's comment in *The Eighteenth Brumaire of Louis Bonaparte*:

> The tradition of all the generations of the dead weighs like a night- mare on the brain of the living. And just when they seem involved in revolutionizing themselves and things, in creating something that has never before existed, it is precisely in such periods of revo- lutionary crisis that they anxiously conjure up the spirits of the past to their service and borrow names, battle cries and costumes from them in order to act out the new scene of world history in this time-honoured disguise and this borrowed language.

It is just this fancy-dress version of tradition that Joyce flees from, most particularly because it is so loyal to an idea of Ire- land and the Irish as an essentialist place and people, given over to a destiny that is inscribed in the past and will be rein- scribed in the future. What is missing is not only the present but a Joycean present without a peasant in sight – the present of the city which in all its miscellany and plurality cannot be recruited to any single-minded notion of essence or identity. It is important to recognize that the Dublin of Joyce's work is not merely different from Ireland. It is a cancellation of what Ireland had been made into by the various sponsors of the dif- ferent revival movements.

The downward mobility of Stephen's family is a symptom of the fluctuations of city life. The novel is full of the chance meet- ings of life in a small city; yet every meeting is narratively engi- neered into a fixed scheme. Stephen's experience is both monotonous and various, characterized by bouts of apathy and of energy. But its contrasting features are not locked into an endless interchange for him as they are for others. His father replays his adolescent life in Cork and becomes little more than 'a praiser of his own past' (p. 224). Emma too, according to Lynch, 'remembers the past' (p. 233). She remembers her own and Stephen's childhood as well. Stephen will have none of this; remembering the past is an activity that he crudely associates with women:

> The past is consumed in the present and the present is living only because it brings forth the future. Statues of women, if Lynch be right, should always be fully draped, one hand of the woman feeling regretfully her own hinder parts. (p. 233)

In the next entry in his diary, this fascination with the past is linked to Yeats and the Irish Revival. Unlike Yeats's Robartes, Stephen does not want to embrace a long-faded loveliness.

> Not this. Not at all. I desire to press in my arms the loveliness which has not yet come into the world. (p. 233)

It is the imagined future, not the re-imagined past of Ireland, that Stephen seeks. He is a post-modernist beside the modernist Yeats. For him, the past cannot be assimilated to the present; this would only make the difference between them invisible. Stephen is ready to make his 'great mistake' (p. 229). He is going to make Ireland part of History by making it open to the future. Endlessly repeated experience, a reality encountered for the 'millionth time', is going to be made into something that has so far remained 'uncreated'. As in the moments of intense physical realization referred to earlier, the 'spiritual' supervenes and world and word fade. Stephen leaves, flies from repetition and assimilation to his forging, to producing the 'uncreated conscience' which has in fact been produced in a novel that defers the statement of his ambition until after its achievement. Yeats locates Parnell within a survey of Irish history and understands his downfall in relation to a series of stereotyped characterizations that derived from a powerful racial discourse then current. In *Portrait*, Parnell's downfall becomes a crucial family event, a personally traumatic experience and, finally, a model of what Stephen will not become. He is named after the first Christian martyr but he will not be recruited into the ranks of Irish martyrdom. Stephen literally leaves, or prepares to leave, the territory of Ireland for his extraterritorial project – the production of a writing that is not embedded in or reducible to the categories of earlier Irish experience. His art is new and free. It has undergone the process of decolonizing itself from the history by which the Irish have been made. It is, instead, a making, an act of freedom that lifts the historical aloft into a new region. The Dublin of 1904, when the writing began, is translated into the Trieste of 1914, when it ended. Thereafter, the novel appeared in serial form in London in *The Egoist* (1914–15) and in book form in New York in 1916. In those years, the long process of decolonization in Ireland continued, but it was to remain haunted by the mutilated history that Joyce was to reproduce as a shadowy, fragmented nightmare in the pages of *Finnegans Wake*.

IRONY IN *PORTRAIT*

Finally, it is such a cliché of commentary on this novel that Stephen's position is ironized by Joyce that it must be considered. After all, it is the case that the Stephen we finally see is, in many respects, an outrageous prig who has indeed made a 'great mistake'. He forsakes everyone, he goes off armed with a half-baked aesthetic theory that, after mountainous labour, has only produced a little mouse of a poem; he dedicates himself solemnly and humourlessly to an absurdly overstated ambition. He is remarkable only in the pride he takes in his almost preternatural capacity not to feel as others do, and he is ruthless in the execution of a project that can never, by its nature, get off the ground. As further evidence, we need only look at the figure Stephen cuts in the subsequent novel *Ulysses* to recognize that Joyce is here providing us with a part-loving, part-ironic portrait of himself as a (very) young man. This is a view that assumes the existence of a 'character' for Stephen as readily as Stephen himself assumes the existence of a kind of national character for the Irish race, of which he is in some sense an embodiment and to which he is also a highly Parnellite rebuke. It is, of course, a safe assumption, but it needs a qualification.

Stephen is, as he set out to be, self-begotten. He makes himself into a character and he contrasts that act of will on his part with the obedience of his contemporaries, men and women, who have allowed themselves to be constructed by the social, economic and political circumstances of their lives. The Latin tag his father's friends question him on in Cork means either 'Times change and we change with them' or 'Times change and we are changed by them' (p. 85). Either way, Stephen would refuse the sentiment for himself, though not for others. He is his own creation. It may be that there is an irony involved. We may feel that this is one of Stephen's fictions, that he has obviously been created by the circumstances and times into which he was born and lived. We can see what he cannot. But the irony has another extension. If identity is socially constructed, then 'character' as such has no independent status as a category. It is merely the product of a complex of forces. To assign it some prior status, independent of those forces, is to lose the point in relation to Stephen. For it is at the close of the novel, when the ironies are apparently most pronounced, that Stephen clarifies his desire to escape from what is socially constructed and to find freedom for himself and for his race beyond the inherited repertoire the past has made available. Stephen is remarkable precisely because he refuses to become a 'character'; Ireland has to be left because it is full of them. When Stephen takes flight, he is leaving behind not only Ireland but also the nineteenth-century novel and its elaborate apparatus for the siting and description of character. By referring at the close to his 'race' he (or rather Joyce) is recognizing that it is not individual but national character that has become the cynosure of attention in the age of the decline of the European imperial powers. The most effective irony in *Portrait* is in its title. It establishes the difference between what Joycean representation involves and the earlier works, both in painting and in literature, that would have had no difficulty with the idea of portraiture itself. Perhaps, then, it is better to suggest that Joyce's irony is not ultimately directed at Stephen's youth, but at the first word in his title and, thereby, at the underlying assumptions about representation in literature (and in art) which he so potently undermined.

Suggestions for Further Reading

This is a short list of some of the more notable discussions of *A Portrait of the Artist as a Young Man.*

Beja, Morris (ed.), *James Joyce:* Dubliners *and* A Portrait: *A Casebook* (London: Macmillan, 1973)

Blades, John, *A Portrait of the Artist as a Young Man*, Penguin Critical Studies (London: Penguin, 1991)

Burgess, Anthony, *Here Comes Everybody: An Introduction to James Joyce for the Ordinary Reader* (London: Faber and Faber, 1965)

Connolly, James, *Joyce's* Portrait: *Criticisms and Critiques* (London: Peter Owen, 1964)

Gifford, Don, *Joyce Annotated: Notes for* Dubliners *and* A Portrait of the Artist as a Young Man, 2nd edn (Berkeley: University of California Press, 1982)

Kenner, Hugh, *Dublin's Joyce* (London: Chatto and Windus, 1955)

Parrinder, Patrick, *James Joyce* (Cambridge: Cambridge University Press, 1984)

Scholes, Robert, and Kain, Richard M. (eds.), *The Workshop of Daedalus: James Joyce and the Raw Materials for* A Portrait (Evanston: Northwestern University Press, 1965)

Staley, Thomas F., and Benstock, Bernard (eds.), *Approaches to Joyce's* Portrait: *Ten Essays* (Pittsburgh: University of Pittsburgh Press, 1976)

A Note on the Text

A Portrait of the Artist as a Young Man first appeared serially in *The Egoist*, a journal founded by Harriet Shaw Weaver and Dora Marsden, 1914–15. It was first published in book form by Huebsch, New York, 1916. The text used here is that of *A Portrait of the Artist as a Young Man* edited by Chester G. Anderson (New York: Viking; London: Cape, 1964). This was reprinted in the Viking Critical Library edition, edited by Chester G. Anderson. Some obvious errors have been silently corrected.

A Portrait of the Artist as a Young Man

Et ignotas animum dimittit in artes.
– Ovid, Metamorphoses, VIII, 188

I

Once upon a time and a very good time it was there was a moo-cow coming down along the road and this moocow that was coming down along the road met a nicens little boy named baby tuckoo. . . .

His father told him that story: his father looked at him through a glass: he had a hairy face.

He was baby tuckoo. The moocow came down the road where Betty Byrne lived: she sold lemon platt.[1]

> O, the wild rose blossoms
> On the little green place.

He sang that song. That was his song.

> O, the green wothe botheth.

When you wet the bed first it is warm then it gets cold. His mother put on the oilsheet. That had the queer smell.

His mother had a nicer smell than his father. She played on the piano the sailor's hornpipe for him to dance. He danced:

> Tralala lala
> Tralala tralaladdy
> Tralala lala
> Tralala lala.

Uncle Charles and Dante clapped. They were older than his father and mother but uncle Charles was older than Dante.

Dante had two brushes in her press. The brush with the maroon velvet back was for Michael Davitt and the brush with the green velvet back was for Parnell.[2] Dante gave him a cachou[3] every time he brought her a piece of tissue paper.

The Vances lived in number seven. They had a different father and mother. They were Eileen's father and mother. When they were grown up he was going to marry Eileen. He hid under the table. His mother said:

—O, Stephen will apologise.

Dante said:

—O, if not, the eagles will come and pull out his eyes.

> *Pull out his eyes,*
> *Apologise,*
> *Apologise,*
> *Pull out his eyes.*

> *Apologise,*
> *Pull out his eyes,*
> *Pull out his eyes,*
> *Apologise.*[4]

The wide playgrounds were swarming with boys. All were shouting and the prefects urged them on with strong cries. The evening air was pale and chilly and after every charge and thud of the footballers the greasy leather orb flew like a heavy bird through the grey light. He kept on the fringe of his line, out of sight of his prefect, out of the reach of the rude feet, feigning to run now and then. He felt his body small and weak amid the throng of players and his eyes were weak and watery. Rody Kickham was not like that: he would be captain of the third line[5] all the fellows said.

Rody Kickham was a decent fellow but Nasty Roche was a stink. Rody Kickham had greaves in his number and a hamper in the refectory.[6] Nasty Roche had big hands. He called the Friday pudding dog-in-the-blanket. And one day he had asked:

—What is your name?

Stephen had answered:

—Stephen Dedalus.[7]

Then Nasty Roche had said:

—What kind of a name is that?

And when Stephen had not been able to answer Nasty Roche had asked:

—What is your father?

Stephen had answered:

—A gentleman.

Then Nasty Roche had asked:

—Is he a magistrate?[8]

He crept about from point to point on the fringe of his line, making little runs now and then. But his hands were bluish with cold. He kept his hands in the sidepockets of his belted grey suit. That was a belt round his pocket. And belt was also to give a fellow a belt. One day a fellow had said to Cantwell:

—I'd give you such a belt in a second.

Cantwell had answered:

—Go and fight your match. Give Cecil Thunder a belt. I'd like to see you. He'd give you a toe in the rump for yourself.

That was not a nice expression. His mother had told him not to speak with the rough boys in the college. Nice mother! The first day in the hall of the castle when she had said goodbye she had put up her veil double to her nose to kiss him: and her nose and eyes were red. But he had pretended not to see that she was going to cry. She was a nice mother but she was not so nice when she cried. And his father had given him two fiveshilling pieces for pocket money. And his father had told him if he wanted anything to write home to him and, whatever he did, never to peach[9] on a fellow. Then at the door of the castle the rector[10] had shaken hands with his father and mother, his soutane fluttering in the breeze, and the car had driven off with his father and mother on it. They had cried to him from the car, waving their hands:

—Goodbye, Stephen, goodbye!

—Goodbye, Stephen, goodbye!

He was caught in the whirl of a scrimmage[11] and, fearful of the flashing eyes and muddy boots, bent down to look through the legs. The fellows were struggling and groaning and their legs were rubbing and kicking and stamping. Then Jack Lawton's yellow boots dodged out the ball and all the other boots and legs ran after. He ran after them a little way and then stopped. It was useless to run on. Soon they would be going home for the holidays. After supper in the studyhall he would change the number pasted up inside his desk from seventyseven to seventysix.[12]

It would be better to be in the studyhall than out there in the cold. The sky was pale and cold but there were lights in the castle. He wondered from which window Hamilton Rowan had thrown his hat on the haha and had there been flowerbeds at that time under the windows.[13] One day when he had been called to the castle the butler had shown him the marks of the soldiers' slugs in the wood of the door and had given him a piece of shortbread that the community ate. It was nice and warm to see the lights in the castle. It was like something in a book. Perhaps Leicester Abbey was like that. And there were nice sentences in Doctor Cornwell's Spelling Book. They were like poetry but they were only sentences to learn the spelling from.

> Wolsey died in Leicester Abbey
> Where the abbots buried him.
> Canker is a disease of plants,
> Cancer one of animals.[14]

It would be nice to lie on the hearthrug before the fire, leaning his head upon his hands, and think on those sentences. He shivered as if he had cold slimy water next his skin. That was mean of Wells to shoulder him into the square ditch[15] because he would not swop his little snuffbox for Wells's seasoned hacking chestnut,[16] the conqueror of forty. How cold and slimy the water had been! A fellow had once seen a big rat jump into the scum. Mother was sitting at the fire with Dante waiting for Brigid to bring in the tea. She had her feet on the fender and her jewelly slippers were so hot and they had such a lovely warm smell! Dante knew a lot of things. She had taught him where the Mozambique Channel was and what was the longest river in America and what was the name of the highest mountain in the moon. Father Arnall knew more than Dante because he was a priest but both his father and uncle Charles said that Dante was a clever woman and a wellread woman. And when Dante made that noise after dinner and then put up her hand to her mouth: that was heartburn.

A voice cried far out on the playground:

—All in!

Then other voices cried from the lower and third lines:

—All in! All in!

The players closed around, flushed and muddy, and he went among them, glad to go in. Rody Kickham held the ball by its greasy lace. A fellow asked him to give it one last: but he walked on without even answering the fellow. Simon Moonan told him not to because the prefect was looking. The fellow turned to Simon Moonan and said:

—We all know why you speak. You are McGlade's suck.[17]

Suck was a queer word. The fellow called Simon Moonan that name because Simon Moonan used to tie the prefect's false sleeves behind his back and the prefect used to let on to be angry. But the sound was ugly. Once he had washed his hands in the lavatory of the Wicklow Hotel[18] and his father pulled the stopper up by the chain after and the dirty water went down through the hole in the basin. And when it had all gone down slowly the hole in the basin had made a sound like that: suck. Only louder.

To remember that and the white look of the lavatory made him feel cold and then hot. There were two cocks that you turned and water came out: cold and hot. He felt cold and then a little hot: and he could see the names printed on the cocks. That was a very queer thing.

And the air in the corridor chilled him too. It was queer and wettish. But soon the gas would be lit and in burning it made a light noise like a little song. Always the same: and when the fellows stopped talking in the playroom you could hear it.

It was the hour for sums. Father Arnall wrote a hard sum on the board and then said:

—Now then, who will win? Go ahead, York! Go ahead, Lancaster![19]

Stephen tried his best but the sum was too hard and he felt confused. The little silk badge with the white rose on it that was pinned on the breast of his jacket began to flutter. He was no good at sums but he tried his best so that York might not lose. Father Arnall's face looked very black but he was not in a wax:[20] he was laughing. Then Jack Lawton cracked his fingers and Father Arnall looked at his copybook and said:

—Right. Bravo Lancaster! The red rose wins. Come on now, York! Forge ahead!

Jack Lawton looked over from his side. The little silk badge with the red rose on it looked very rich because he had a blue sailor top on. Stephen felt his own face red too, thinking of all the bets about who would get first place in elements,[21] Jack Lawton or he. Some weeks Jack Lawton got the card for first and some weeks he got the card for first. His white silk badge fluttered and fluttered as he worked at the next sum and heard Father Arnall's voice. Then all his eagerness passed away and he felt his face quite cool. He thought his face must be white because it felt so cool. He could not get out the answer for the sum but it did not matter. White roses and red roses: those were beautiful colours to think of. And the cards for first place and second place and third place were beautiful colours too: pink and cream and lavender. Lavender and cream and pink roses were beautiful to think of. Perhaps a wild rose might be like those colours and he remembered the song about the wild rose blossoms on the little green place. But you could not have a green rose.[22] But perhaps somewhere in the world you could.

The bell rang and then the classes began to file out of the rooms and along the corridors towards the refectory. He sat looking at the two prints of butter on his plate but could not eat the damp bread. The tablecloth was damp and limp. But he drank off the hot weak tea which the clumsy scullion, girt with a white apron, poured into his cup. He wondered whether the scullion's apron was damp too or whether all white things were cold and damp. Nasty Roche and Saurin drank cocoa that their people sent them in tins. They said they could not drink the tea; that it was hogwash. Their fathers were magistrates, the fellows said.

All the boys seemed to him very strange. They had all fathers and mothers and different clothes and voices. He longed to be at home and lay his head on his mother's lap. But he could not: and so he longed for the play and study and prayers to be over and to be in bed.

He drank another cup of hot tea and Fleming said:

—What's up? Have you a pain or what's up with you?

—I don't know, Stephen said.

—Sick in your breadbasket, Fleming said, because your face looks white. It will go away.

—O yes, Stephen said.

But he was not sick there. He thought that he was sick in his heart if you could be sick in that place. Fleming was very decent to ask him. He wanted to cry. He leaned his elbows on the table and shut and opened the flaps of his ears. Then he heard the noise of the refectory every time he opened the flaps of his ears. It made a roar like a train at night. And when he closed the flaps the roar was shut off like a train going into a tunnel. That night at Dalkey[23] the train had roared like that and then, when it went into the tunnel, the roar stopped. He closed his eyes and the train went on, roaring and then stopping; roaring again, stopping. It was nice to hear it roar and stop and then roar out of the tunnel again and then stop.

Then the higher line fellows began to come down along the matting in the middle of the refectory, Paddy Rath and Jimmy Magee and the Spaniard who was allowed to smoke cigars and the little Portuguese who wore the woolly cap. And then the lower line tables and the tables of the third line. And every single fellow had a different way of walking.

He sat in a corner of the playroom pretending to watch a game of dominos and once or twice he was able to hear for an instant the little song of the gas. The prefect was at the door with some boys and Simon Moonan was knotting his false sleeves. He was telling them something about Tullabeg.[24]

Then he went away from the door and Wells came over to Stephen and said:

—Tell us, Dedalus, do you kiss your mother[25] before you go to bed?

Stephen answered:

—I do.

Wells turned to the other fellows and said:

—O, I say, here's a fellow says he kisses his mother every night before he goes to bed.

The other fellows stopped their game and turned round, laughing. Stephen blushed under their eyes and said:

—I do not.

Wells said:

—O, I say, here's a fellow says he doesn't kiss his mother before he goes to bed.

They all laughed again. Stephen tried to laugh with them. He felt his whole body hot and confused in a moment. What was the right answer to the question? He had given two and still Wells laughed. But Wells must know the right answer for he was in third of grammar. He tried to think of Wells's mother but he did not dare to raise his eyes to Wells's face. He did not like Wells's face. It was Wells who had shouldered him into the square ditch the day before because he would not swop his little snuffbox for Wells's seasoned hacking chestnut, the conqueror of forty. It was a mean thing to do; all the fellows said it was. And how cold and slimy the water had been! And a fellow had once seen a big rat jump plop into the scum.

The cold slime of the ditch covered his whole body; and, when the bell rang for study and the lines filed out of the playrooms, he felt the cold air of the corridor and staircase inside his clothes. He still tried to think what was the right answer. Was it right to kiss his mother or wrong to kiss his mother? What did that mean, to kiss? You put your face up like that to say goodnight and then his mother put her face down. That was to kiss. His mother put her lips on his cheek; her lips were soft and they wetted his cheek; and they made a tiny little noise: kiss. Why did people do that with their two faces?

Sitting in the studyhall he opened the lid of his desk and changed the number pasted up inside from seventyseven to seventysix. But the Christmas vacation was very far away: but one time it would come because the earth moved round always.

There was a picture of the earth on the first page of his geography: a big ball in the middle of clouds. Fleming had a box of crayons and one night during free study he had coloured the earth green and the clouds maroon. That was like the two brushes in Dante's press, the brush with the green velvet back for Parnell and the brush with the maroon velvet back for Michael Davitt. But he had not told Fleming to colour them those colours. Fleming had done it himself.

He opened the geography to study the lesson; but he could not learn the names of places in America. Still they were all different places that had those different names. They were all in different countries and the countries were in continents and the continents were in the world and the world was in the universe.

He turned to the flyleaf of the geography and read what he had written there: himself, his name and where he was.

Stephen Dedalus
Class of Elements
Clongowes Wood College
Sallins
County Kildare
Ireland
Europe
The World
The Universe

That was in his writing: and Fleming one night for a cod[26] had written on the opposite page:

Stephen Dedalus is my name,
Ireland is my nation.
Clongowes is my dwellingplace
And heaven my expectation.

He read the verses backwards but then they were not poetry. Then he read the flyleaf from the bottom to the top till he came to his own name. That was he: and he read down the page again. What was after the universe? Nothing. But was there anything round the universe to show where it stopped before the nothing place began? It could not be a wall but there could be a thin thin line there all round everything. It was very big to think about everything and everywhere. Only God could do that. He tried to think what a big thought that must be but he could think only of God. God was God's name just as his name was Stephen. *Dieu* was the French for God and that was God's name too; and when anyone prayed to God and said *Dieu* then God knew at once that it was a French person that was praying. But though there were different names for God in all the different languages in the world and God understood what all the people who prayed said in their different languages still God remained always the same God and God's real name was God.

It made him very tired to think that way. It made him feel his head very big. He turned over the flyleaf and looked wearily at the green round earth in the middle of the maroon clouds. He wondered which was right, to be for the green or for the maroon, because Dante had ripped the green velvet back off the brush that was for Parnell one day with her scissors and had told him that Parnell was a bad man. He wondered if they were arguing at home about that. That was called politics. There were two sides in it: Dante was on one side and his father and Mr Casey were on the other side but his mother and uncle Charles were on no side. Every day there was something in the paper about it.[27]

It pained him that he did not know well what politics meant and that he did not know where the universe ended. He felt small and weak. When would he be like the fellows in poetry and rhetoric? They had big voices and big boots and they studied trigonometry. That was very far away. First came the vacation and then the next term and then vacation again and then again another term and then again the vacation. It was like a train going in and out of tunnels and that was like the noise of the boys eating in the refectory when you opened and closed the flaps of the ears. Term, vacation; tunnel, out; noise, stop. How far away it was! It was better to go to bed to sleep. Only prayers in the chapel and then bed. He shivered and yawned. It would be lovely in bed after the sheets got a bit hot. First they were so cold to get into. He shivered to think how cold they were first. But then they got hot and then he could sleep. It was lovely to be tired. He yawned again. Night prayers and then bed: he shivered and wanted to yawn. It would be lovely in a few minutes. He felt a warm glow creeping up from the cold shivering sheets, warmer and warmer till he felt warm all over, ever so warm; ever so warm and yet he shivered a little and still wanted to yawn.

The bell rang for night prayers and he filed out of the study-hall after the others and down the staircase and along the corridors to the chapel. The corridors were darkly lit and the chapel was darkly lit. Soon all would be dark and sleeping. There was cold night air in the chapel and the marbles were the colour the sea was at night. The sea was cold day and night: but it was colder at night. It was cold and dark under the seawall beside his father's house. But the kettle would be on the hob to make punch.

The prefect of the chapel prayed above his head and his memory knew the responses:

> O Lord, open our lips
> And our mouth shall announce Thy praise.
> Incline unto our aid, O God!
> O Lord, make haste to help us![28]

There was a cold night smell in the chapel. But it was a holy smell. It was not like the smell of the old peasants who knelt at the back of the chapel at Sunday mass. That was a smell of air and rain and turf and corduroy. But they were very holy peasants. They breathed behind him on his neck and sighed as they prayed. They lived in Clane, a fellow said: there were little cottages there and he had seen a woman standing at the halfdoor of a cottage with a child in her arms, as the cars had come past from Sallins.[29] It would be lovely to sleep for one night in that cottage before the fire of smoking turf, in the dark lit by the fire, in the warm dark, breathing the smell of the peasants, air and rain and turf and corduroy. But, O, the road there between the trees was dark! You would be lost in the dark. It made him afraid to think of how it was.

He heard the voice of the prefect of the chapel saying the last prayer. He prayed it too against the dark outside under the trees.

*Visit, we beseech Thee, O Lord, this habitation and drive away
from it all the snares of the enemy. May Thy holy angels dwell
herein to preserve us in peace and may Thy blessing be always
upon us through Christ, Our Lord. Amen.*[30]

His fingers trembled as he undressed himself in the dormitory. He told his fingers to hurry up. He had to undress and
then kneel and say his own prayers and be in bed before the gas
was lowered so that he might not go to hell when he died. He
rolled his stockings off and put on his nightshirt quickly and
knelt trembling at his bedside and repeated his prayers quickly
quickly, fearing that the gas would go down. He felt his shoulders shaking as he murmured:

*God bless my father and my mother and spare them to me!
God bless my little brothers and sisters and spare them to me!
God bless Dante and uncle Charles and spare them to me!*

He blessed himself and climbed quickly into bed and, tucking
the end of the nightshirt under his feet, curled himself together
under the cold white sheets, shaking and trembling. But he
would not go to hell when he died; and the shaking would stop.
A voice bade the boys in the dormitory goodnight. He peered
out for an instant over the coverlet and saw the yellow curtains
round and before his bed that shut him off on all sides. The light
was lowered quietly.

The prefect's shoes went away. Where? Down the staircase
and along the corridors or to his room at the end? He saw the
dark. Was it true about the black dog that walked there at night
with eyes as big as carriagelamps? They said it was the ghost of
a murderer. A long shiver of fear flowed over his body. He saw
the dark entrance hall of the castle. Old servants in old dress
were in the ironingroom above the staircase. It was long ago.
The old servants were quiet. There was a fire there but the hall
was still dark. A figure came up the staircase from the hall. He
wore the white cloak of a marshal; his face was pale and
strange; he held his hand pressed to his side. He looked out of
strange eyes at the old servants. They looked at him and saw

their master's face and cloak and knew that he had received his deathwound. But only the dark was where they looked: only dark silent air. Their master had received his deathwound on the battlefield of Prague far away over the sea. He was standing on the field; his hand was pressed to his side; his face was pale and strange and he wore the white cloak of a marshal.[31]

O how cold and strange it was to think of that! All the dark was cold and strange. There were pale strange faces there, great eyes like carriagelamps. They were the ghosts of murderers, the figures of marshals who had received their deathwound on battlefields far away over the sea. What did they wish to say that their faces were so strange?

Visit, we beseech Thee, O Lord, this habitation and drive away from it all . . .

Going home for the holidays! That would be lovely: the fellows had told him. Getting up on the cars in the early wintry morning outside the door of the castle. The cars were rolling on the gravel. Cheers for the rector!

Hurray! Hurray! Hurray!

The cars drove past the chapel and all caps were raised. They drove merrily along the country roads. The drivers pointed with their whips to Bodenstown.[32] The fellows cheered. They passed the farmhouse of the Jolly Farmer. Cheer after cheer after cheer. Through Clane they drove, cheering and cheered. The peasant women stood at the halfdoors, the men stood here and there. The lovely smell there was in the wintry air: the smell of Clane: rain and wintry air and turf smouldering and corduroy.

The train was full of fellows: a long long chocolate train with cream facings. The guards went to and fro opening, closing, locking, unlocking the doors. They were men in dark blue and silver; they had silvery whistles and their keys made a quick music: click, click: click, click.

And the train raced on over the flat lands and past the Hill of Allen. The telegraphpoles were passing, passing. The train went on and on. It knew. There were coloured lanterns in the hall of his father's house and ropes of green branches. There were holly and ivy round the pier-glass and holly and ivy, green and red, twined round the chandeliers. There were red holly and green ivy round the old portraits on the walls. Holly and ivy for him and for Christmas.

Lovely . . .

All the people. Welcome home, Stephen! Noises of welcome. His mother kissed him. Was that right?[33] His father was a marshal now:[34] higher than a magistrate. Welcome home, Stephen!

Noises . . .

There was a noise of curtainrings running back along the rods, of water being splashed in the basins. There was a noise of rising and dressing and washing in the dormitory: a noise of clapping of hands as the prefect went up and down telling the fellows to look sharp. A pale sunlight showed the yellow curtains drawn back, the tossed beds. His bed was very hot and his face and body were very hot.

He got up and sat on the side of his bed. He was weak. He tried to pull on his stocking. It had a horrid rough feel. The sunlight was queer and cold.

Fleming said:

—Are you not well?

He did not know; and Fleming said:

—Get back into bed. I'll tell McGlade you're not well.

—He's sick.

—Who is?

—Tell McGlade.

—Get back into bed.

—Is he sick?

A fellow held his arms while he loosened the stocking clinging to his foot and climbed back into the hot bed.

He crouched down between the sheets, glad of their tepid glow. He heard the fellows talk among themselves about him as they dressed for mass. It was a mean thing to do, to shoulder him into the square ditch, they were saying.

Then their voices ceased; they had gone. A voice at his bed said:

—Dedalus, don't spy on us, sure you won't?[35]

Wells's face was there. He looked at it and saw that Wells was afraid.

—I didn't mean to. Sure you won't?

His father had told him, whatever he did, never to peach on a fellow. He shook his head and answered no and felt glad. Wells said:

—I didn't mean to, honour bright. It was only for cod. I'm sorry.

The face and the voice went away. Sorry because he was afraid. Afraid that it was some disease. Canker was a disease of plants and cancer one of animals: or another different. That was a long time ago then out on the playgrounds in the evening light, creeping from point to point on the fringe of his line, a heavy bird flying low through the grey light. Leicester Abbey lit up. Wolsey died there. The abbots buried him themselves.

It was not Wells's face, it was the prefect's. He was not foxing. No, no: he was sick really. He was not foxing. And he felt the prefect's hand on his forehead; and he felt his forehead warm and damp against the prefect's cold damp hand. That was the way a rat felt, slimy and damp and cold. Every rat had two eyes to look out of. Sleek slimy coats, little little feet tucked up to jump, black shiny eyes to look out of. They could understand how to jump. But the minds of rats could not understand trigonometry. When they were dead they lay on their sides. Their coats dried then. They were only dead things.

The prefect was there again and it was his voice that was saying that he was to get up, that Father Minister[36] had said he was to get up and dress and go to the infirmary. And while he was dressing himself as quickly as he could the prefect said:

—We must pack off to Brother Michael because we have the collywobbles! Terrible thing to have the collywobbles! How we wobble when we have the collywobbles!

He was very decent to say that. That was all to make him laugh. But he could not laugh because his cheeks and lips were all shivery: and then the prefect had to laugh by himself.

The prefect cried:

—Quick march! Hayfoot! Strawfoot![37]

They went together down the staircase and along the corridor and past the bath. As he passed the door he remembered with a vague fear the warm turfcoloured bogwater, the warm moist air, the noise of plunges, the smell of the towels, like medicine.

Brother Michael[38] was standing at the door of the infirmary and from the door of the dark cabinet on his right came a smell like medicine. That came from the bottles on the shelves. The prefect spoke to Brother Michael and Brother Michael answered and called the prefect sir. He had reddish hair mixed with grey and a queer look. It was queer that he would always be a brother. It was queer too that you could not call him sir because he was a brother and had a different kind of look. Was he not holy enough or why could he not catch up on the others?

There were two beds in the room and in one bed there was a fellow: and when they went in he called out:

—Hello! It's young Dedalus! What's up?

—The sky is up, Brother Michael said.

He was a fellow out of the third of grammar and, while Stephen was undressing, he asked Brother Michael to bring him a round of buttered toast.

—Ah, do! he said.

—Butter you up! said Brother Michael. You'll get your walking papers in the morning when the doctor comes.

—Will I? the fellow said. I'm not well yet.

Brother Michael repeated:

—You'll get your walking papers, I tell you.

He bent down to rake the fire. He had a long back like the long back of a tramhorse. He shook the poker gravely and nodded his head at the fellow out of third of grammar.

Then Brother Michael went away and after a while the fellow out of third of grammar turned in towards the wall and fell asleep.

That was the infirmary. He was sick then. Had they written home to tell his mother and father? But it would be quicker for one of the priests to go himself to tell them. Or he would write a letter for the priest to bring.

Dear Mother

    I am sick. I want to go home. Please come and take me home. I am in the infirmary.

Your fond son,
Stephen

How far away they were! There was cold sunlight outside the window. He wondered if he would die. You could die just the same on a sunny day. He might die before his mother came. Then he would have a dead mass[39] in the chapel like the way the fellows had told him it was when Little had died. All the fellows would be at the mass, dressed in black, all with sad faces. Wells too would be there but no fellow would look at him. The rector would be there in a cope of black and gold and there would be tall yellow candles on the altar and round the catafalque. And they would carry the coffin out of the chapel slowly and he would be buried in the little graveyard of the community off the main avenue of limes. And Wells would be sorry then for what he had done. And the bell would toll slowly.

He could hear the tolling. He said over to himself the song that Brigid had taught him.

> *Dingdong! The castle bell!*
> *Farewell, my mother!*
> *Bury me in the old churchyard*
> *Beside my eldest brother.*
> *My coffin shall be black,*
> *Six angels at my back,*
> *Two to sing and two to pray*
> *And two to carry my soul away.*[40]

How beautiful and sad that was! How beautiful the words were where they said *Bury me in the old churchyard!* A tremor passed over his body. How sad and how beautiful! He wanted to cry quietly but not for himself: for the words, so beautiful and sad, like music. The bell! The bell! Farewell! O farewell!

The cold sunlight was weaker and Brother Michael was

standing at his bedside with a bowl of beeftea. He was glad for
his mouth was hot and dry. He could hear them playing on the
playgrounds. And the day was going on in the college just as if
he were there.

Then Brother Michael was going away and the fellow out of
third of grammar told him to be sure and come back and tell
him all the news in the paper. He told Stephen that his name
was Athy and that his father kept a lot of racehorses that were
spiffing jumpers and that his father would give a good tip to
Brother Michael any time he wanted it because Brother Michael
was very decent and always told him the news out of the paper
they got every day up in the castle. There was every kind of
news in the paper: accidents, shipwrecks, sports and politics.

—Now it is all about politics in the paper, he said. Do your
people talk about that too?

—Yes, Stephen said.

—Mine too, he said.

Then he thought for a moment and said:

—You have a queer name, Dedalus, and I have a queer name
too, Athy.⁴¹ My name is the name of a town. Your name is like
Latin.

Then he asked:

—Are you good at riddles?

Stephen answered:

—Not very good.

Then he said:

—Can you answer me this one? Why is the county Kildare
like the leg of a fellow's breeches?

Stephen thought what could be the answer and then said:

—I give it up.

—Because there is a thigh in it, he said. Do you see the joke?
Athy is the town in the county Kildare and a thigh is the other
thigh.

—O, I see, Stephen said.

—That's an old riddle, he said.

After a moment he said:

—I say!

—What? asked Stephen.

—You know, he said, you can ask that riddle another way?

—Can you? said Stephen.

—The same riddle, he said. Do you know the other way to ask it?

—No, said Stephen.

—Can you not think of the other way? he said.

He looked at Stephen over the bedclothes as he spoke. Then he lay back on the pillow and said:

—There is another way but I won't tell you what it is.

Why did he not tell it? His father, who kept the racehorses, must be a magistrate too like Saurin's father and Nasty Roche's father. He thought of his own father, of how he sang songs while his mother played and of how he always gave him a shilling when he asked for sixpence and he felt sorry for him that he was not a magistrate like the other boys' fathers. Then why was he sent to that place with them? But his father had told him that he would be no stranger there because his granduncle had presented an address to the liberator[42] there fifty years before. You could know the people of that time by their old dress. It seemed to him a solemn time: and he wondered if that was the time when the fellows in Clon-gowes wore blue coats with brass buttons and yellow waistcoats and caps of rabbitskin and drank beer like grownup people and kept greyhounds of their own to course the hares with.

He looked at the window and saw that the daylight had grown weaker. There would be cloudy grey light over the playgrounds. There was no noise on the playgrounds. The class must be doing the themes or perhaps Father Arnall was reading a legend out of the book.

It was queer that they had not given him any medicine. Perhaps Brother Michael would bring it back when he came. They said you got stinking stuff to drink when you were in the infirmary. But he felt better now than before. It would be nice getting better slowly. You could get a book then. There was a book in the library about Holland. There were lovely foreign names in it and pictures of strangelooking cities and ships. It made you feel so happy.

How pale the light was at the window! But that was nice. The fire rose and fell on the wall. It was like waves. Someone had put coal on and he heard voices. They were talking. It was the noise of the waves. Or the waves were talking among themselves as they rose and fell.

He saw the sea of waves, long dark waves rising and falling, dark under the moonless night. A tiny light twinkled at the pierhead where the ship was entering: and he saw a multitude of people gathered by the waters' edge to see the ship that was entering their harbour. A tall man stood on the deck, looking out towards the flat dark land: and by the light at the pierhead he saw his face, the sorrowful face of Brother Michael.

He saw him lift his hand towards the people and heard him say in a loud voice of sorrow over the waters:

—He is dead. We saw him lying upon the catafalque.

A wail of sorrow went up from the people.

—Parnell! Parnell! He is dead!⁴³

They fell upon their knees, moaning in sorrow.

And he saw Dante in a maroon velvet dress and with a green velvet mantle hanging from her shoulders walking proudly and silently past the people who knelt by the waters' edge.

A great fire, banked high and red, flamed in the grate and under the ivytwined branches of the chandelier the Christmas table was spread. They had come home a little late and still dinner was not ready: but it would be ready in a jiffy, his mother had said. They were waiting for the door to open and for the servants to come in, holding the big dishes covered with their heavy metal covers.

All were waiting: uncle Charles, who sat far away in the shadow of the window, Dante and Mr Casey, who sat in the easychairs at either side of the hearth, Stephen, seated on a chair between them, his feet resting on the toasted boss.⁴⁴ Mr Dedalus looked at himself in the pierglass above the mantelpiece, waxed out his moustache-ends and then, parting his coattails, stood with his back to the glowing fire: and still, from time to time, he withdrew a hand from his coattail to wax out one of his moustache-ends. Mr Casey leaned his head to one side and, smiling, tapped the gland of his neck with his fingers. And Stephen smiled too for he knew now that it was not true that Mr

Casey had a purse of silver in his throat. He smiled to think how the silvery noise which Mr Casey used to make had deceived him. And when he had tried to open Mr Casey's hand to see if the purse of silver was hidden there he had seen that the fingers could not be straightened out: and Mr Casey had told him that he had got those three cramped fingers making a birthday present for Queen Victoria.[45]

Mr Casey tapped the gland of his neck and smiled at Stephen with sleepy eyes: and Mr Dedalus said to him:

—Yes. Well now, that's all right. O, we had a good walk, hadn't we, John? Yes . . . I wonder if there's any likelihood of dinner this evening. Yes. . . . O, well now, we got a good breath of ozone round the Head[46] today. Ay, bedad.

He turned to Dante and said:

—You didn't stir out at all, Mrs Riordan?

Dante frowned and said shortly:

—No.

Mr Dedalus dropped his coattails and went over to the sideboard. He brought forth a great stone jar of whisky from the locker and filled the decanter slowly, bending now and then to see how much he had poured in. Then replacing the jar in the locker he poured a little of the whisky into two glasses, added a little water and came back with them to the fireplace.

—A thimbleful, John, he said, just to whet your appetite.

Mr Casey took the glass, drank, and placed it near him on the mantelpiece. Then he said:

—Well, I can't help thinking of our friend Christopher manufacturing . . .

He broke into a fit of laughter and coughing and added:

—. . . manufacturing that champagne[47] for those fellows.

Mr Dedalus laughed loudly.

—Is it Christy? he said. There's more cunning in one of those warts on his bald head than in a pack of jack foxes.

He inclined his head, closed his eyes, and, licking his lips profusely, began to speak with the voice of the hotelkeeper.

—And he has such a soft mouth when he's speaking to you, don't you know. He's very moist and watery about the dewlaps, God bless him.

Mr Casey was still struggling through his fit of coughing and laughter. Stephen, seeing and hearing the hotelkeeper through his father's face and voice, laughed.

Mr Dedalus put up his eyeglass and, staring down at him, said quietly and kindly:

—What are you laughing at, you little puppy, you?

The servants entered and placed the dishes on the table. Mrs Dedalus followed and the places were arranged.

—Sit over, she said.

Mr Dedalus went to the end of the table and said:

—Now, Mrs Riordan, sit over. John, sit you down, my hearty.

He looked round to where uncle Charles sat and said:

—Now then, sir, there's a bird here waiting for you.

When all had taken their seats he laid his hand on the cover and then said quickly, withdrawing it:

—Now, Stephen.

Stephen stood up in his place to say the grace before meals:

Bless us, O Lord, and these Thy gifts which through Thy bounty we are about to receive through Christ Our Lord. Amen.[48]

All blessed themselves and Mr Dedalus with a sigh of pleasure lifted from the dish the heavy cover pearled around the edge with glistening drops.

Stephen looked at the plump turkey which had lain, trussed and skewered, on the kitchen table. He knew that his father had paid a guinea for it in Dunn's of D'Olier Street[49] and that the man had prodded it often at the breastbone to show how good it was: and he remembered the man's voice when he had said:

—Take that one, sir. That's the real Ally Daly.[50]

Why did Mr Barrett in Clongowes call his pandybat a turkey?[51] But Clongowes was far away: and the warm heavy smell of turkey and ham and celery rose from the plates and dishes and the great fire was banked high and red in the grate and the green ivy and red holly made you feel so happy and when dinner was ended the big plum-pudding would be carried in, studded with peeled almonds and sprigs of holly, with bluish fire running around it and a little green flag flying from the top.

It was his first Christmas dinner and he thought of his little brothers and sisters who were waiting in the nursery, as he had often waited, till the pudding came. The deep low collar and the Eton jacket made him feel queer and oldish: and that morning when his mother had brought him down to the parlour, dressed for mass, his father had cried. That was because he was thinking of his own father. And uncle Charles had said so too.

Mr Dedalus covered the dish and began to eat hungrily. Then he said:

—Poor old Christy, he's nearly lopsided now with roguery.

—Simon, said Mrs Dedalus, you haven't given Mrs Riordan any sauce.

Mr Dedalus seized the sauceboat.

—Haven't I? he cried. Mrs Riordan, pity the poor blind.

Dante covered her plate with her hands and said:

—No, thanks.

Mr Dedalus turned to uncle Charles.

—How are you off, sir?

—Right as the mail, Simon.

—You, John?

—I'm all right. Go on yourself.

—Mary? Here, Stephen, here's something to make your hair curl.

He poured sauce freely over Stephen's plate and set the boat again on the table. Then he asked uncle Charles was it tender. Uncle Charles could not speak because his mouth was full but he nodded that it was.

—That was a good answer our friend made to the canon. What? said Mr Dedalus.

—I didn't think he had that much in him, said Mr Casey.

—*I'll pay you your dues, father, when you cease turning the house of God into a pollingbooth.*

—A nice answer, said Dante, for any man calling himself a catholic to give to his priest.

—They have only themselves to blame, said Mr Dedalus suavely. If they took a fool's advice they would confine their attention to religion.

—It is religion, Dante said. They are doing their duty in warning the people.

—We go to the house of God, Mr Casey said, in all humility to pray to our Maker and not to hear election addresses.

—It is religion, Dante said again. They are right. They must direct their flocks.

—And preach politics from the altar, is it? asked Mr Dedalus.

—Certainly, said Dante. It is a question of public morality. A priest would not be a priest if he did not tell his flock what is right and what is wrong.

Mrs Dedalus laid down her knife and fork, saying:

—For pity's sake and for pity sake let us have no political discussion on this day of all days in the year.

—Quite right, ma'am, said uncle Charles. Now, Simon, that's quite enough now. Not another word now.

—Yes, yes, said Mr Dedalus quickly.

He uncovered the dish boldly and said:

—Now then, who's for more turkey?

Nobody answered. Dante said:

—Nice language for any catholic to use!

—Mrs Riordan, I appeal to you, said Mrs Dedalus, to let the matter drop now.

Dante turned on her and said:

—And am I to sit here and listen to the pastors of my church being flouted?

—Nobody is saying a word against them, said Mr Dedalus, so long as they don't meddle in politics.

—The bishops and priests of Ireland have spoken, said Dante, and they must be obeyed.

—Let them leave politics alone, said Mr Casey, or the people may leave their church alone.

—You hear? said Dante turning to Mrs Dedalus.

—Mr Casey! Simon! said Mrs Dedalus. Let it end now.

—Too bad! Too bad! said uncle Charles.

—What? cried Mr Dedalus. Were we to desert him at the bidding of the English people?[52]

—He was no longer worthy to lead, said Dante. He was a public sinner.

—We are all sinners and black sinners, said Mr Casey coldly.

—*Woe be to the man by whom the scandal cometh!* said Mrs Riordan. *It would be better for him that a millstone were tied about his neck and that he were cast into the depth of the sea rather than that he should scandalise one of these, my least little ones.*[53] That is the language of the Holy Ghost.

—And very bad language if you ask me, said Mr Dedalus coolly.

—Simon! Simon! said uncle Charles. The boy.

—Yes, yes, said Mr Dedalus. I meant about the . . . I was thinking about the bad language of that railway porter. Well now, that's all right. Here, Stephen, show me your plate, old chap. Eat away now. Here.

He heaped up the food on Stephen's plate and served uncle Charles and Mr Casey to large pieces of turkey and splashes of sauce. Mrs Dedalus was eating little and Dante sat with her hands in her lap. She was red in the face. Mr Dedalus rooted with the carvers at the end of the dish and said:

—There's a tasty bit here we call the pope's nose. If any lady or gentleman . . .

He held a piece of fowl up on the prong of the carvingfork. Nobody spoke. He put it on his own plate, saying:

—Well, you can't say but you were asked. I think I had better eat it myself because I'm not well in my health lately.

He winked at Stephen and, replacing the dishcover, began to eat again.

There was a silence while he ate. Then he said:

—Well now, the day kept up fine after all. There were plenty of strangers down too.

Nobody spoke. He said again:

—I think there were more strangers down than last Christmas.

He looked round at the others whose faces were bent towards their plates and, receiving no reply, waited for a moment and said bitterly:

—Well, my Christmas dinner has been spoiled anyhow.

—There could be neither luck nor grace, Dante said, in a house where there is no respect for the pastors of the church.

Mr Dedalus threw his knife and fork noisily on his plate.

—Respect! he said. Is it for Billy with the lip or for the tub of guts up in Armagh?[54] Respect!

—Princes of the church, said Mr Casey with slow scorn.

—Lord Leitrim's coachman,[55] yes, said Mr Dedalus.

—They are the Lord's anointed, Dante said. They are an honour to their country.

—Tub of guts, said Mr Dedalus coarsely. He has a handsome face, mind you, in repose. You should see that fellow lapping up his bacon and cabbage of a cold winter's day. O Johnny!

He twisted his features into a grimace of heavy bestiality and made a lapping noise with his lips.

—Really, Simon, said Mrs Dedalus, you should not speak that way before Stephen. It's not right.

—O, he'll remember all this when he grows up, said Dante hotly—the language he heard against God and religion and priests in his own home.

—Let him remember too, cried Mr Casey to her from across the table, the language with which the priests and the priests' pawns broke Parnell's heart and hounded him into his grave. Let him remember that too when he grows up.

—Sons of bitches! cried Mr Dedalus. When he was down they turned on him to betray him and rend him like rats in a sewer. Lowlived dogs! And they look it! By Christ, they look it!

—They behaved rightly, cried Dante. They obeyed their bishops and their priests. Honour to them!

—Well, it is perfectly dreadful to say that not even for one day in the year, said Mrs Dedalus, can we be free from these dreadful disputes!

Uncle Charles raised his hands mildly and said:

—Come now, come now, come now! Can we not have our opinions whatever they are without this bad temper and this bad language? It is too bad surely.

Mrs Dedalus spoke to Dante in a low voice but Dante said loudly:

—I will not say nothing. I will defend my church and my religion when it is insulted and spit on by renegade catholics.[56]

Mr Casey pushed his plate rudely into the middle of the

table and, resting his elbows before him, said in a hoarse voice
to his host:

—Tell me, did I tell you that story about a very famous spit?

—You did not, John, said Mr Dedalus.

—Why then, said Mr Casey, it is a most instructive story. It
happened not long ago in the county Wicklow where we are now.

He broke off and, turning towards Dante, said with quiet
indignation:

—And I may tell you, ma'am, that I, if you mean me, am no
renegade catholic. I am a catholic as my father was and his father
before him and his father before him again when we gave up our
lives rather than sell our faith.

—The more shame to you now, Dante said, to speak as you do.

—The story, John, said Mr Dedalus smiling. Let us have the
story anyhow.

—Catholic indeed! repeated Dante ironically. The blackest
protestant[57] in the land would not speak the language I have
heard this evening.

Mr Dedalus began to sway his head to and fro, crooning
like a country singer.

—I am no protestant, I tell you again, said Mr Casey flushing.

Mr Dedalus, still crooning and swaying his head, began to
sing in a grunting nasal tone:

> O, come all you Roman catholics
> That never went to mass.[58]

He took up his knife and fork again in good humour and set
to eating, saying to Mr Casey:

—Let us have the story, John. It will help us to digest.

Stephen looked with affection at Mr Casey's face which
stared across the table over his joined hands. He liked to sit
near him at the fire, looking up at his dark fierce face. But his
dark eyes were never fierce and his slow voice was good to listen to. But why was he then against the priests? Because Dante
must be right then. But he had heard his father say that she was
a spoiled nun and that she had come out of the convent in the

Alleghanies when her brother had got the money from the savages for the trinkets and the chainies.[59] Perhaps that made her severe against Parnell. And she did not like him to play with Eileen because Eileen was a protestant and when she was young she knew children that used to play with protestants and the protestants used to make fun of the litany of the Blessed Virgin. *Tower of Ivory*, they used to say, *House of Gold!*[60] How could a woman be a tower of ivory or a house of gold? Who was right then? And he remembered the evening in the infirmary in Clongowes, the dark waters, the light at the pierhead and the moan of sorrow from the people when they had heard.

Eileen had long white hands. One evening when playing tig she had put her hands over his eyes: long and white and thin and cold and soft. That was ivory: a cold white thing. That was the meaning of *Tower of Ivory*.

—The story is very short and sweet, Mr Casey said. It was one day down in Arklow, a cold bitter day, not long before the chief died. May God have mercy on him!

He closed his eyes wearily and paused. Mr Dedalus took a bone from his plate and tore some meat from it with his teeth, saying:

—Before he was killed, you mean.

Mr Casey opened his eyes, sighed and went on:

—It was down in Arklow one day. We were down there at a meeting and after the meeting was over we had to make our way to the railway station through the crowd. Such booing and baaing, man, you never heard. They called us all the names in the world. Well there was one old lady, and a drunken old harridan she was surely, that paid all her attention to me. She kept dancing along beside me in the mud bawling and screaming into my face: *Priesthunter!*[61] *The Paris Funds! Mr Fox! Kitty O'Shea!*[62]

—And what did you do, John? asked Mr Dedalus.

—I let her bawl away, said Mr Casey. It was a cold day and to keep up my heart I had (saving your presence, ma'am) a quid of Tullamore[63] in my mouth and sure I couldn't say a word in any case because my mouth was full of tobacco juice.

—Well, John?

—Well. I let her bawl away, to her heart's content, *Kitty O'Shea* and the rest of it till at last she called that lady a name that I won't sully this Christmas board nor your ears, ma'am, nor my own lips by repeating.

He paused. Mr Dedalus, lifting his head from the bone, asked:

—And what did you do, John?

—Do! said Mr Casey. She stuck her ugly old face up at me when she said it and I had my mouth full of tobacco juice. I bent down to her and *Phth!* says I to her like that.

He turned aside and made the act of spitting.

—*Phth!* says I to her like that, right into her eye.

He clapped a hand to his eye and gave a hoarse scream of pain.

—*O Jesus, Mary and Joseph!* says she. *I'm blinded! I'm blinded and drownded!*

He stopped in a fit of coughing and laughter, repeating:

—*I'm blinded entirely.*

Mr Dedalus laughed loudly and lay back in his chair while uncle Charles swayed his head to and fro.

Dante looked terribly angry and repeated while they laughed:

—Very nice! Ha! Very nice!

It was not nice about the spit in the woman's eye. But what was the name the woman had called Kitty O'Shea that Mr Casey would not repeat? He thought of Mr Casey walking through the crowds of people and making speeches from a wagonette. That was what he had been in prison for and he remembered that one night Sergeant O'Neill had come to the house and had stood in the hall, talking in a low voice with his father and chewing nervously at the chinstrap of his cap. And that night Mr Casey had not gone to Dublin by train but a car had come to the door and he had heard his father say something about the Cabinteely road.[64]

He was for Ireland and Parnell and so was his father: and so was Dante too for one night at the band on the esplanade she had hit a gentleman on the head with her umbrella because he had taken off his hat when the band played *God save the Queen* at the end.

Mr Dedalus gave a snort of contempt.

—Ah, John, he said. It is true for them.[65] We are an unfortunate

priestridden[66] race and always were and always will be till the end
of the chapter.

Uncle Charles shook his head, saying:

—A bad business! A bad business!

Mr Dedalus repeated:

—A priestridden Godforsaken race!

He pointed to the portrait of his grandfather on the wall to
his right.

—Do you see that old chap up there, John? he said. He was
a good Irishman when there was no money in the job. He was
condemned to death as a whiteboy.[67] But he had a saying about
our clerical friends, that he would never let one of them put his
two feet under his mahogany.[68]

Dante broke in angrily:

—If we are a priestridden race we ought to be proud of it!
They are the apple of God's eye. *Touch them not*, says Christ,
for they are the apple of My eye.[69]

—And can we not love our country then? asked Mr Casey.
Are we not to follow the man that was born to lead us?

—A traitor to his country! replied Dante. A traitor, an adul-
terer! The priests were right to abandon him. The priests were
always the true friends of Ireland.

—Were they, faith? said Mr Casey.

He threw his fist on the table and, frowning angrily, pro-
truded one finger after another.

—Didn't the bishops of Ireland betray us in the time of the
union when bishop Lanigan presented an address of loyalty to
the Marquess Cornwallis?[70] Didn't the bishops and priests sell the
aspirations of their country in 1829 in return for catholic emancipation?[71] Didn't they denounce the fenian movement from the
pulpit and in the confessionbox?[72] And didn't they dishonour the
ashes of Terence Bellew MacManus?[73]

His face was glowing with anger and Stephen felt the glow
rise to his own cheek as the spoken words thrilled him. Mr
Dedalus uttered a guffaw of coarse scorn.

—O, by God, he cried, I forgot little old Paul Cullen![74] Another
apple of God's eye!

Dante bent across the table and cried to Mr Casey:

—Right! Right! They were always right! God and morality and religion come first.

Mrs Dedalus, seeing her excitement, said to her:

—Mrs Riordan, don't excite yourself answering them.

—God and religion before everything! Dante cried. God and religion before the world!

Mr Casey raised his clenched fist and brought it down on the table with a crash.

—Very well, then, he shouted hoarsely, if it comes to that, no God for Ireland!

—John! John! cried Mr Dedalus, seizing his guest by the coatsleeve.

Dante stared across the table, her cheeks shaking. Mr Casey struggled up from his chair and bent across the table towards her, scraping the air from before his eyes with one hand as though he were tearing aside a cobweb.

—No God for Ireland! he cried. We have had too much God in Ireland. Away with God!

—Blasphemer! Devil! screamed Dante, starting to her feet and almost spitting in his face.

Uncle Charles and Mr Dedalus pulled Mr Casey back into his chair again, talking to him from both sides reasonably. He stared before him out of his dark flaming eyes, repeating:

—Away with God, I say!

Dante shoved her chair violently aside and left the table, upsetting her napkinring which rolled slowly along the carpet and came to rest against the foot of an easy-chair. Mrs Dedalus rose quickly and followed her towards the door. At the door Dante turned round violently and shouted down the room, her cheeks flushed and quivering with rage:

—Devil out of hell! We won! We crushed him to death! Fiend!

The door slammed behind her.

Mr Casey, freeing his arms from his holders, suddenly bowed his head on his hands with a sob of pain.

—Poor Parnell! he cried loudly. My dead king![75]

He sobbed loudly and bitterly.

Stephen, raising his terrorstricken face, saw that his father's eyes were full of tears.

The fellows talked together in little groups.
   One fellow said:
   —They were caught near the Hill of Lyons.[76]
   —Who caught them?
   —Mr Gleeson and the minister.[77] They were on a car.[78]
The same fellow added:
   —A fellow in the higher line told me.
   Fleming asked:
   —But why did they run away, tell us?
   —I know why, Cecil Thunder said. Because they had fecked[79] cash out of the rector's room.
   —Who fecked it?
   —Kickham's brother. And they all went shares in it.
   But that was stealing. How could they have done that?
   —A fat lot you know about it, Thunder! Wells said. I know why they scut.[80]
   —Tell us why.
   —I was told not to, Wells said.
   —O, go on, Wells, all said. You might tell us. We won't let it out.
   Stephen bent forward his head to hear. Wells looked round to see if anyone was coming. Then he said secretly:
   —You know the altar wine they keep in the press in the sacristy?
   —Yes.
   —Well, they drank that and it was found out who did it by the smell. And that's why they ran away, if you want to know.
   And the fellow who had spoken first said:
   —Yes, that's what I heard too from the fellow in the higher line.
   The fellows were all silent. Stephen stood among them, afraid to speak, listening. A faint sickness of awe made him feel weak. How could they have done that? He thought of the dark silent sacristy. There were dark wooden presses there where the crimped surplices lay quietly folded. It was not the chapel but still you had

to speak under your breath. It was a holy place. He remembered the summer evening he had been there to be dressed as boat-bearer,[81] the evening of the procession to the little altar in the wood.[82] A strange and holy place. The boy that held the censer had swung it gently to and fro near the door with the silvery cap lifted by the middle chain to keep the coals lighting. That was called charcoal: and it had burned quietly as the fellow had swung it gently and had given off a weak sour smell. And then when all were vested he had stood holding out the boat to the rector and the rector had put a spoonful of incense in it and it had hissed on the red coals.

The fellows were talking together in little groups here and there on the playground. The fellows seemed to him to have grown smaller: that was because a sprinter[83] had knocked him down the day before, a fellow out of second of grammar. He had been thrown by the fellow's machine lightly on the cinder-path and his spectacles had been broken in three pieces and some of the grit of the cinders had gone into his mouth.

That was why the fellows seemed to him smaller and farther away and the goalposts so thin and far and the soft grey sky so high up. But there was no play on the football grounds for cricket was coming:[84] and some said that Barnes would be the prof[85] and some said it would be Flowers. And all over the playgrounds they were playing rounders[86] and bowling twisters and lobs.[87] And from here and from there came the sounds of the cricketbats through the soft grey air. They said: pick, pack, pock, puck: like drops of water in a fountain slowly falling in the brimming bowl.

Athy, who had been silent, said quietly:

—You are all wrong.

All turned towards him eagerly.

—Why?

—Do you know?

—Who told you?

—Tell us, Athy.

Athy pointed across the playground to where Simon Moonan was walking by himself kicking a stone before him.

—Ask him, he said.

The fellows looked there and then said:

—Why him?

—Is he in it?

—Tell us, Athy. Go on. You might if you know.

Athy lowered his voice and said:

—Do you know why those fellows scut? I will tell you but you must not let on you know.

He paused for a moment and then said mysteriously:

—They were caught with Simon Moonan and Tusker Boyle in the square one night.

The fellows looked at him and asked:

—Caught?

—What doing?

Athy said:

—Smugging.[88]

All the fellows were silent: and Athy said:

—And that's why.

Stephen looked at the faces of the fellows but they were all looking across the playground. He wanted to ask somebody about it. What did that mean about the smugging in the square? Why did the five fellows out of the higher line run away for that? It was a joke, he thought. Simon Moonan had nice clothes and one night he had shown him a ball of creamy sweets that the fellows of the football fifteen had rolled down to him along the carpet in the middle of the refectory when he was at the door. It was the night of the match against the Bective Rangers and the ball was made just like a red and green apple only it opened and it was full of the creamy sweets. And one day Boyle had said that an elephant had two tuskers instead of two tusks and that was why he was called Tusker Boyle but some fellows called him Lady Boyle because he was always at his nails, paring them.

Eileen had long thin cool white hands too because she was a girl. They were like ivory; only soft. That was the meaning of *Tower of Ivory* but protestants could not understand it and made fun of it. One day he had stood beside her looking into the hotel grounds. A waiter was running up a trail of bunting on the flagstaff and a fox terrier was scampering to and fro on the sunny lawn. She had put her hand into his pocket where his hand was and he had felt how cool and thin and soft her hand was. She had said that pockets were funny things to have: and then all of a sudden she had broken away and had run laughing down the sloping curve of the path. Her fair hair had streamed out behind her like gold in the sun. *Tower of Ivory. House of Gold.* By thinking of things you could understand them.

But why in the square? You went there when you wanted to do something. It was all thick slabs of slate and water trickled all day out of tiny pinholes and there was a queer smell of stale water there. And behind the door of one of the closets there was a drawing in red pencil of a bearded man in a Roman dress with a brick in each hand and underneath was the name of the drawing:

Balbus was building a wall.[89]

Some fellows had drawn it there for a cod. It had a funny face but it was very like a man with a beard. And on the wall of another closet there was written in backhand in beautiful writing:

Julius Cæsar wrote The Calico Belly.[90]

Perhaps that was why they were there because it was a place where some fellows wrote things for cod. But all the same it was queer what Athy said and the way he said it. It was not a cod because they had run away. He looked with the others in silence across the playground and began to feel afraid.

At last Fleming said:

—And we are all to be punished for what other fellows did?

—I won't come back, see if I do, Cecil Thunder said. Three days' silence in the refectory and sending us up for six and eight[91] every minute.

—Yes, said Wells. And old Barrett has a new way of twisting the note so that you can't open it and fold it again to see how many ferulæ[92] you are to get. I won't come back too.

—Yes, said Cecil Thunder, and the prefect of studies was in second of grammar this morning.

—Let us get up a rebellion, Fleming said. Will we?

All the fellows were silent. The air was very silent and you could hear the cricketbats but more slowly than before: pick, pock.

Wells asked:

—What is going to be done to them?

—Simon Moonan and Tusker are going to be flogged, Athy said, and the fellows in the higher line got their choice of flogging or being expelled.

—And which are they taking? asked the fellow who had spoken first.

—All are taking expulsion except Corrigan, Athy answered. He's going to be flogged by Mr Gleeson.

—Is it Corrigan that big fellow? said Fleming. Why, he'd be able for two of Gleeson!

—I know why, Cecil Thunder said. He is right and the other fellows are wrong because a flogging wears off after a bit but a fellow that has been expelled from college is known all his life on account of it. Besides Gleeson won't flog him hard.

—It's best of his play not to, Fleming said.

—I wouldn't like to be Simon Moonan and Tusker, Cecil Thunder said. But I don't believe they will be flogged. Perhaps they will be sent up for twice nine.[93]

—No, no, said Athy. They'll both get it on the vital spot.[94]

Wells rubbed himself and said in a crying voice:

—Please, sir, let me off!

Athy grinned and turned up the sleeves of his jacket, saying:

> It can't be helped;
> It must be done
> So down with your breeches
> And out with your bum.

The fellows laughed; but he felt that they were a little afraid. In the silence of the soft grey air he heard the cricketbats from here and from there: pock. That was a sound to hear but if you were hit then you would feel a pain. The pandybat made a sound too but not like that. The fellows said it was made of whalebone and leather with lead inside: and he wondered what was the pain like. There were different kinds of pains for all the different kinds of sounds. A long thin cane would have a high whistling sound and he wondered what was that pain like. It made him shivery to think of it and cold: and what Athy said too. But what was there to laugh at in it? It made him shivery: but that was because you always felt like a shiver when you let down your trousers. It was the same in the bath when you undressed yourself. He wondered who had to let them down, the master or the boy himself. O how could they laugh about it that way?

He looked at Athy's rolledup sleeves and knuckly inky hands. He had rolled up his sleeves to show how Mr Gleeson would roll up his sleeves. But Mr Gleeson had round shiny cuffs and clean white wrists and fattish white hands and the nails of them were long and pointed. Perhaps he pared them too like Lady Boyle. But they were terribly long and pointed nails. So long and cruel they were though the white fattish hands were not cruel but gentle. And though he trembled with cold and fright to think of the cruel long nails and of the high whistling sound of the cane and of the chill you felt at the end of your shirt when you undressed yourself yet he felt a feeling of queer quiet pleasure inside him to think of the white fattish hands, clean and strong and gentle. And he thought of what Cecil Thunder had said; that Mr Gleeson would not flog Corrigan hard. And Fleming had said he would not because it was best of his play not to. But that was not why.

A voice from far out on the playground cried:

—All in!

And other voices cried:

—All in! All in!

During the writing lesson he sat with his arms folded, listening to the slow scraping of the pens. Mr Harford went to and fro making little signs in red pencil and sometimes sitting beside the boy to show him how to hold the pen. He had tried to spell out the headline for himself though he knew already what it was for it was the last of the book. *Zeal without prudence is like a ship adrift.* But the lines of the letters were like fine invisible threads and it was only by closing his right eye tight tight and staring out of the left eye that he could make out the full curves of the capital.

But Mr Harford was very decent and never got into a wax.[95]

All the other masters got into dreadful waxes. But why were they to suffer for what fellows in the higher line did? Wells had said that they had drunk some of the altar wine out of the press in the sacristy and that it had been found out who had done it by the smell. Perhaps they had stolen a monstrance[96] to run away with it and sell it somewhere. That must have been a terrible sin, to go in there quietly at night, to open the dark press and steal the flashing gold thing into which God was put on the altar in the middle of flowers and candles at benediction while the incense went up in clouds at both sides as the fellow swung the censer and Dominic Kelly sang the first part by himself in the choir. But God was not in it of course when they stole it. But still it was a strange and a great sin even to touch it. He thought of it with deep awe; a terrible and strange sin: it thrilled him to think of it in the silence when the pens scraped lightly. But to drink the altar wine out of the press and to be found out by the smell was a sin too: but it was not terrible and strange. It only made you feel a little sickish on account of the smell of the wine. Because on the day when he had made his first holy communion in the chapel he had shut his eyes and opened his mouth and put out his tongue a little: and when the rector had stooped down to give him the holy communion he had smelt a faint winy smell off the rector's breath after the wine of the mass. The word was beautiful: wine. It made you think of dark purple because the grapes were dark purple that grew in Greece outside houses like white temples. But the faint smell off the rector's breath had made him feel a sick feeling on the morning of his first communion. The day of your first communion was the happiest day of your life. And once a lot of generals had asked Napoleon what was the happiest day of his life. They thought he would say the day he won some great battle or the day he was made an emperor. But he said:

—Gentlemen, the happiest day of my life was the day on which I made my first holy communion.[97]

Father Arnall came in and the Latin lesson began and he remained still, leaning on the desk with his arms folded. Father Arnall gave out the themebooks and he said that they were scandalous and that they were all to be written out again with the corrections at once. But the worst of all was Fleming's theme because the pages were stuck together by a blot: and Father Arnall held it up by a corner and said it was an insult to any master to send him up such a theme. Then he asked Jack Lawton to decline the noun *mare* and Jack Lawton stopped at the ablative singular and could not go on with the plural.[98]

—You should be ashamed of yourself, said Father Arnall sternly. You, the leader of the class!

Then he asked the next boy and the next and the next. Nobody knew. Father Arnall became very quiet, more and more quiet as each boy tried to answer and could not. But his face was black-looking and his eyes were staring though his voice was so quiet. Then he asked Fleming and Fleming said that that word had no plural. Father Arnall suddenly shut the book and shouted at him:

—Kneel out there in the middle of the class. You are one of the idlest boys I ever met. Copy out your themes again the rest of you.

Fleming moved heavily out of his place and knelt between the two last benches. The others boys bent over their theme-books and began to write. A silence filled the classroom and Stephen, glancing timidly at Father Arnall's dark face, saw that it was a little red from the wax he was in.

Was that a sin for Father Arnall to be in a wax or was he allowed to get into a wax when the boys were idle because that made them study better or was he only letting on to be in a wax? It was because he was allowed because a priest would know what a sin was and would not do it. But if he did it one time by mistake what would he do to go to confession? Perhaps he would go to confession to the minister. And if the minister did it he would go to the rector: and the rector to the provincial: and the provincial to the general[99] of the jesuits. That was called the order: and he had heard his father say that they were all clever men. They could all have become highup people in the world if they had not become jesuits. And he wondered what Father Arnall and Paddy Barrett would have become and what Mr McGlade and Mr Gleeson would have become if they had not become jesuits. It was hard to think what because you would have to think of them in a different way with different coloured coats and trousers and with beards and moustaches and different kinds of hats.

The door opened quietly and closed. A quick whisper ran through the class: the prefect of studies. There was an instant of dead silence and then the loud crack of a pandybat on the last desk. Stephen's heart leapt up in fear.

—Any boys want flogging here, Father Arnall? cried the prefect of studies. Any lazy idle loafers that want flogging in this class?

He came to the middle of the class and saw Fleming on his knees.

—Hoho! he cried. Who is this boy? Why is he on his knees? What is your name, boy?

—Fleming, sir.

—Hoho, Fleming! An idler of course. I can see it in your eye. Why is he on his knees, Farther Arnall?

—He wrote a bad Latin theme, Father Arnall said, and he missed all the questions in grammar.

—Of course he did! cried the prefect of studies. Of course he did! A born idler! I can see it in the corner of his eye.

He banged his pandybat down on the desk and cried:

—Up, Fleming! Up, my boy!

Fleming stood up slowly.

—Hold out! cried the prefect of studies.

Fleming held out his hand. The pandybat came down on it with a loud smacking sound: one, two, three, four, five, six.

—Other hand!

The pandybat came down again in six loud quick smacks.

—Kneel down! cried the prefect of studies.

Fleming knelt down squeezing his hands under his armpits, his face contorted with pain, but Stephen knew how hard his hands were because Fleming was always rubbing rosin into them. But perhaps he was in great pain for the noise of the pandies was terrible. Stephen's heart was beating and fluttering.

—At your work, all of you! shouted the prefect of studies. We want no lazy idle loafers here, lazy idle little schemers. At your work, I tell you. Father Dolan will be in to see you every day. Father Dolan will be in tomorrow.

He poked one of the boys in the side with the pandybat, saying:

—You, boy! When will Father Dolan be in again?

—Tomorrow, sir, said Tom Furlong's voice.

—Tomorrow and tomorrow and tomorrow,[100] said the prefect of studies. Make up your minds for that. Every day Father Dolan. Write away. You, boy, who are you?

Stephen's heart jumped suddenly.

—Dedalus, sir.

—Why are you not writing like the others?

—I . . . my . . .

He could not speak with fright.

—Why is he not writing, Father Arnall?

—He broke his glasses, said Father Arnall, and I exempted him from work.

—Broke? What is this I hear? What is this your name is? said the prefect of studies.

—Dedalus, sir.

—Out here, Dedalus. Lazy little schemer. I see schemer in your face. Where did you break your glasses?

Stephen stumbled into the middle of the class, blinded by fear and haste.

—Where did you break your glasses? repeated the prefect of studies.

—The cinderpath, sir.

—Hoho! The cinderpath! cried the prefect of studies. I know that trick.

Stephen lifted his eyes in wonder and saw for a moment Father Dolan's whitegrey not young face, his baldy whitegrey head with fluff at the sides of it, the steel rims of his spectacles and his nocoloured eyes looking through the glasses. Why did he say he knew that trick?

—Lazy idle little loafer! cried the prefect of studies. Broke my glasses! An old schoolboy trick! Out with your hand this moment!

Stephen closed his eyes and held out in the air his trembling hand with the palm upwards. He felt the prefect of studies touch it for a moment at the fingers to straighten it and then the swish of the sleeve of the soutane as the pandybat was lifted to strike.

A hot burning stinging tingling blow like the loud crack of a broken stick made his trembling hand crumple together like a leaf in the fire: and at the sound and the pain scalding tears were driven into his eyes. His whole body was shaking with fright, his arm was shaking and his crumpled burning livid hand shook like a loose leaf in the air. A cry sprang to his lips, a prayer to be let off. But though the tears scalded his eyes and his limbs quivered with pain and fright he held back the hot tears and the cry that scalded his throat.

—Other hand! shouted the prefect of studies.

Stephen drew back his maimed and quivering right arm and held out his left hand. The soutane sleeve swished again as the pandybat was lifted and a loud crashing sound and a fierce maddening tingling burning pain made his hand shrink together with the palms and fingers in a livid quivering mass. The scalding water burst forth from his eyes and, burning with shame and agony and fear, he drew back his shaking arm in terror and burst out into a whine of pain. His body shook with a palsy of fright and in shame and rage he felt the scalding cry come from his throat and the scalding tears falling out of his eyes and down his flaming cheeks.

—Kneel down! cried the prefect of studies.

Stephen knelt down quickly pressing his beaten hands to his sides. To think of them beaten and swollen with pain all in a moment made him feel so sorry for them as if they were not his own but someone else's that he felt sorry for. And as he knelt, calming the last sobs in his throat and feeling the burning tingling pain pressed in to his sides, he thought of the hands which he had held out in the air with the palms up and of the firm touch of the prefect of studies when he had steadied the shaking fingers and of the beaten swollen reddened mass of palm and fingers that shook helplessly in the air.

—Get at your work, all of you, cried the prefect of studies from the door. Father Dolan will be in every day to see if any boy, any lazy idle little loafer wants flogging. Every day. Every day.

The door closed behind him.

The hushed class continued to copy out the themes. Father Arnall rose from his seat and went among them, helping the boys with gentle words and telling them the mistakes they had made. His voice was very gentle and soft. Then he returned to his seat and said to Fleming and Stephen:

—You may return to your places, you two.

Fleming and Stephen rose and, walking to their seats, sat down. Stephen, scarlet with shame, opened a book quickly with one weak hand and bent down upon it, his face close to the page.

It was unfair and cruel because the doctor had told him not to read without glasses and he had written home to his father that morning to send him a new pair. And Father Arnall had said that he need not study till the new glasses came. Then to be called a schemer before the class and to be pandied when he always got the card for first or second and was the leader of the Yorkists! How could the prefect of studies know that it was a trick? He felt the touch of the prefect's fingers as they had steadied his hand and at first he had thought he was going to shake hands with him because the fingers were soft and firm: but then in an instant he had heard the swish of the soutane sleeve and the crash. It was cruel and unfair to make him kneel in the middle of the class then: and Father Arnall had told them both that they might return to their places without making any difference between them. He listened to Father Arnall's low and gentle voice as he corrected the themes. Perhaps he was sorry now and wanted to be decent. But it was unfair and cruel. The prefect of studies was a priest but that was cruel and unfair. And his whitegrey face and the nocoloured eyes behind the steelrimmed spectacles were cruel looking because he had steadied the hand first with his firm soft fingers and that was to hit it better and louder.

—It's a stinking mean thing, that's what it is, said Fleming in the corridor as the classes were passing out in file to the refectory, to pandy a fellow for what is not his fault.

—You really broke your glasses by accident, didn't you? Nasty Roche asked.

Stephen felt his heart filled by Fleming's words and did not answer.

—Of course he did! said Fleming. I wouldn't stand it. I'd go up and tell the rector on him.

—Yes, said Cecil Thunder eagerly, and I saw him lift the pandybat over his shoulder and he's not allowed to do that.

—Did they hurt much? Nasty Roche asked.

—Very much, Stephen said.

—I wouldn't stand it, Fleming repeated, from Baldy-head or any other Baldyhead. It's a stinking mean low trick, that's what it is. I'd go straight up to the rector and tell him about it after dinner.

—Yes, do. Yes, do, said Cecil Thunder.

—Yes, do. Yes, go up and tell the rector on him, Dedalus, said Nasty Roche, because he said that he'd come in tomorrow again to pandy you.

—Yes, yes. Tell the rector, all said.

And there were some fellows out of second of grammar listening and one of them said:

—The senate and the Roman people[101] declared that Dedalus had been wrongly punished.

It was wrong: it was unfair and cruel: and, as he sat in the refectory, he suffered time after time in memory the same humiliation until he began to wonder whether it might not really be that there was something in his face which made him look like a schemer and he wished he had a little mirror to see. But there could not be; and it was unjust and cruel and unfair.

He could not eat the blackish fish fritters they got on Wednesdays in Lent[102] and one of his potatoes had the mark of the spade in it. Yes, he would do what the fellows had told him. He would go up and tell the rector that he had been wrongly punished. A thing like that had been done before by somebody in history, by some great person whose head was in the books of history. And the rector would declare that he had been wrongly punished because the senate and the Roman people always declared that the men who did that had been wrongly punished. Those were the great men whose names were in Richmal Magnall's Questions.[103] History was all about those men and what they did and that was what Peter Parley's Tales[104] about Greece and Rome were all about. Peter Parley himself was on the first page in a picture. There was a road over a heath with grass at the side and little bushes: and Peter Parley had a broad hat like a protestant minister and a big stick and he was walking fast along the road to Greece and Rome.

It was easy what he had to do. All he had to do was when the dinner was over and he came out in his turn to go on walking but not out to the corridor but up the staircase on the right that led to the castle. He had nothing to do but that: to turn to the right and walk fast up the staircase and in half a minute he would be in the low dark narrow corridor that led through the castle to the rector's room. And every fellow had said it was unfair, even the fellow out of second of grammar who had said that about the senate and the Roman people.

What would happen? He heard the fellows of the higher line stand up at the top of the refectory and heard their steps as they came down the matting: Paddy Rath and Jimmy Magee and the Spaniard and the Portuguese and the fifth was big Corrigan who was going to be flogged by Mr Gleeson. That was why the prefect of studies had called him a schemer and pandied him for nothing: and, straining his weak eyes, tired with the tears, he watched big Corrigan's broad shoulders and big hanging black head passing in the file. But he had done something and besides Mr Gleeson would not flog him hard: and he remembered how big Corrigan looked in the bath. He had skin the same colour as the turfcoloured bogwater in the shallow end of the bath and when he walked along the side his feet slapped loudly on the wet tiles and at every step his thighs shook a little because he was fat.

The refectory was half empty and the fellows were still passing out in file. He could go up the staircase because there was never a priest or a prefect outside the refectory door. But he could not go. The rector would side with the prefect of studies and think it was a schoolboy trick and then the prefect of studies would come in every day the same only it would be worse because he would be dreadfully waxy at any fellow going up to the rector about him. The fellows had told him to go but they would not go themselves. They had forgotten all about it. No, it was best to forget all about it and perhaps the prefect of studies had only said he would come in. No, it was best to hide out of the way because when you were small and young you could often escape that way.

The fellows at his table stood up. He stood up and passed out among them in the file. He had to decide. He was coming near the door. If he went on with the fellows he could never go up to the rector because he could not leave the playground for that. And if he went and was pandied all the same all the fellows would make fun and talk about young Dedalus going up to the rector to tell on the prefect of studies.

He was walking down along the matting and he saw the door before him. It was impossible: he could not. He thought of the baldy head of the prefect of studies with the cruel nocoloured eyes looking at him and he heard the voice of the prefect of studies asking him twice what his name was. Why could he not remember the name when he was told the first time? Was he not listening the first time or was it to make fun out of the name? The great men in the history had names like that and nobody made fun of them. It was his own name that he should have made fun of if he wanted to make fun. Dolan: it was like the name of a woman that washed clothes.

He had reached the door and, turning quickly up to the right, walked up the stairs and, before he could make up his mind to come back, he had entered the low dark narrow corridor that led to the castle. And as he crossed the threshold of the door of the corridor he saw, without turning his head to look, that all the fellows were looking after him as they went filing by.

He passed along the narrow dark corridor, passing little doors that were the doors of the rooms of the community. He peered in front of him and right and left through the gloom and thought that those must be portraits. It was dark and silent and his eyes were weak and tired with tears so that he could not see. But he thought they were the portraits of the saints and great men of the order who were looking down on him silently as he passed: saint Ignatius Loyola holding an open book and pointing to the words *Ad Majorem Dei Gloriam*[105] in it, saint Francis Xavier pointing to his chest, Lorenzo Ricci with his berretta on his head like one of the prefects of the lines, the three patrons of holy youth, saint Stanislaus Kostka, saint Aloysius Gonzaga and blessed John Berchmans,[106] all with young faces because they died when they were young, and Father Peter Kenny sitting in a chair wrapped in a big cloak.

He came out on the landing above the entrance hall and looked about him. That was where Hamilton Rowan had passed and the marks of the soldiers' slugs were there. And it was there that the old servants had seen the ghost in the white cloak of a marshal.

An old servant was sweeping at the end of the landing. He asked him where was the rector's room and the old servant pointed to the door at the far end and looked after him as he went on to it and knocked.

There was no answer. He knocked again more loudly and his heart jumped when he heard a muffled voice say:

—Come in!

He turned the handle and opened the door and fumbled for the handle of the green baize door inside. He found it and pushed it open and went in.

He saw the rector sitting at a desk writing. There was a skull on the desk and a strange solemn smell in the room like the old leather of chairs.

His heart was beating fast on account of the solemn place he was in and the silence of the room: and he looked at the skull and at the rector's kindlooking face.

—Well, my little man, said the rector, what is it?

Stephen swallowed down the thing in his throat and said:

—I broke my glasses, sir.

The rector opened his mouth and said:

—O!

Then he smiled and said:

—Well, if we broke our glasses we must write home for a new pair.

—I wrote home, sir, said Stephen, and Father Arnall said I am not to study till they come.

—Quite right! said the rector.

Stephen swallowed down the thing again and tried to keep his legs and his voice from shaking.

—But, sir . . .

—Yes?

—Father Dolan came in today and pandied me because I was not writing my them.

The rector looked at him in silence and he could feel the blood rising to his face and the tears about to rise to his eyes.

The rector said:

—Your name is Dedalus, isn't it?

—Yes, sir.

—And where did you break your glasses?

—On the cinderpath, sir. A fellow was coming out of the bicycle house and I fell and they got broken. I don't know the fellow's name.

The rector looked at him again in silence. Then he smiled and said:

—O, well, it was a mistake; I am sure Father Dolan did not know.

—But I told him I broke them, sir, and he pandied me.

—Did you tell him that you had written home for a new pair? the rector asked.

—No, sir.

—O well then, said the rector, Father Dolan did not understand. You can say that I excuse you from your lessons for a few days.

Stephen said quickly for fear his trembling would prevent him:

—Yes, sir, but Father Dolan said he will come in tomorrow to pandy me again for it.

—Very well, the rector said, it is a mistake and I shall speak to Father Dolan myself. Will that do now?

Stephen felt the tears wetting his eyes and murmured:

—O yes sir, thanks.

The rector held his hand across the side of the desk where the skull was and Stephen, placing his hand in it for a moment, felt a cool moist palm.

—Good day now, said the rector, withdrawing his hand and bowing.

—Good day, sir, said Stephen.

He bowed and walked quietly out of the room, closing the doors carefully and slowly.

But when he had passed the old servant on the landing and

was again in the low narrow dark corridor he began to walk faster and faster. Faster and faster he hurried on through the gloom excitedly. He bumped his elbow against the door at the end and, hurrying down the staircase, walked quickly through the two corridors and out into the air.

He could hear the cries of the fellows on the playgrounds. He broke into a run and, running quicker and quicker, ran across the cinderpath and reached the third line playground, panting.

The fellows had seen him running. They closed round him in a ring, pushing one against another to hear.

—Tell us! Tell us!

—What did he say?

—Did you go in?

—What did he say?

—Tell us! Tell us!

He told them what he had said and what the rector had said and, when he had told them, all the fellows flung their caps spinning up into the air and cried:

—Hurroo!

They caught their caps and sent them up again spinning sky-high and cried again:

—Hurroo! Hurroo!

They made a cradle of their locked hands and hoisted him up among them and carried him along till he struggled to get free. And when he had escaped from them they broke away in all directions, flinging their caps again into the air and whistling as they went spinning up and crying:

—Hurroo!

And they gave three groans for Baldyhead Dolan and three cheers for Conmee and they said he was the decentest rector that was ever in Clongowes.

The cheers died away in the soft grey air. He was alone. He was happy and free: but he would not be anyway proud with Father Dolan. He would be very quiet and obedient: and he wished that he could do something kind for him to show him that he was not proud.

The air was soft and grey and mild and evening was coming. There was the smell of evening in the air, the smell of the fields in the country where they digged up turnips to peel them and eat them when they went out for a walk to Major Barton's,[107] the smell there was in the little wood beyond the pavilion where the gallnuts[108] were.

The fellows were practising long shies[109] and bowling lobs and slow twisters. In the soft grey silence he could hear the bump of the balls: and from here and from there through the quiet air the sound of the cricket bats: pick, pack, pock, puck: like drops of water in a fountain falling softly in the brimming bowl.

Uncle Charles smoked such black twist[1] that at last his nephew suggested to him to enjoy his morning smoke in a little outhouse at the end of the garden.

—Very good, Simon. All serene,[2] Simon, said the old man tranquilly. Anywhere you like. The outhouse will do me nicely: it will be more salubrious.

—Damn me, said Mr Dedalus frankly, if I know how you can smoke such villainous awful tobacco. It's like gunpowder, by God.

—It's very nice, Simon, replied the old man. Very cool and mollifying.

Every morning, therefore, uncle Charles repaired to his outhouse but not before he had creased[3] and brushed scrupulously his back hair and brushed and put on his tall hat. While he smoked the brim of his tall hat and the bowl of his pipe were just visible beyond the jambs of the outhouse door. His arbour, as he called the reeking outhouse which he shared with the cat and the garden tools, served him also as a soundingbox: and every morning he hummed contentedly one of his favourite songs: *O, twine me a bower* or *Blue eyes and golden hair* or *The Groves of Blarney*[4] while the grey and blue coils of smoke rose slowly from his pipe and vanished in the pure air.

During the first part of the summer in Blackrock[5] uncle Charles was Stephen's constant companion. Uncle Charles was a hale old man with a welltanned skin, rugged features and white side whiskers. On week days he did messages between the house in Carysfort Avenue and those shops in the main street of the town with which the family dealt. Stephen was glad to go with him on these errands for uncle Charles helped him very liberally to handfuls of whatever was exposed in open boxes and barrels outside the counter. He would seize a handful of grapes and sawdust or three or four American apples and thrust them generously into his grandnephew's hand while the shopman smiled uneasily; and, on Stephen's feigning reluctance to take them, he would frown and say:

—Take them, sir. Do you hear me, sir? They're good for your bowels.

When the order list had been booked[6] the two would go on to the park where an old friend of Stephen's father, Mike Flynn, would be found seated on a bench, waiting for them. Then would begin Stephen's run round the park. Mike Flynn would stand at the gate near the railway station, watch in hand, while Stephen ran round the track in the style Mike Flynn favoured, his head high lifted, his knees well lifted and his hands held straight down by his sides. When the morning practice was over the trainer would make his comments and sometimes illustrate them by shuffling along for a yard or so comically in an old pair of blue canvas shoes. A small ring of wonderstruck children and nursemaids would gather to watch him and linger even when he and uncle Charles had sat down again and were talking athletics and politics. Though he had heard his father say that Mike Flynn had put some of the best runners of modern times through his hands Stephen often glanced with mistrust at his trainer's flabby stubblecovered face, as it bent over the long stained fingers through which he rolled his cigarette, and with pity at the mild lustreless blue eyes which would look up suddenly from the task and gaze vaguely into the blue distance while the long swollen fingers ceased their rolling and grains and fibres of tobacco fell back into the pouch.

On the way home uncle Charles would often pay a visit to the chapel and, as the font was above Stephen's reach, the old man would dip his hand and then sprinkle the water briskly about Stephen's clothes and on the floor of the porch.[7] While he prayed he knelt on his red handkerchief and read above his breath from a thumbblackened prayerbook wherein catchwords were printed at the foot of every page. Stephen knelt at his side respecting, though he did not share, his piety. He often wondered what his granduncle prayed for so seriously. Perhaps he prayed for the souls in purgatory or for the grace of a happy death or perhaps he prayed that God might send him back a part of the big fortune he had squandered in Cork.

On Sundays Stephen with his father and his granduncle took their constitutional. The old man was a nimble walker in spite of his corns and often ten or twelve miles of the road were covered. The little village of Stillorgan was the parting of the ways. Either they went to the left towards the Dublin mountains or along the Goatstown road and thence into Dundrum, coming home by Sandyford.[8] Trudging along the road or standing in some grimy wayside publichouse his elders spoke constantly of the subjects nearer their hearts, of Irish politics, of Munster[9] and of the legends of their own family, to all of which Stephen lent an avid ear. Words which he did not understand he said over and over to himself till he had learned them by heart: and through them he had glimpses of the real world about him. The hour when he too would take part in the life of that world seemed drawing near and in secret he began to make ready for the great part which he felt awaited him, the nature of which he only dimly apprehended.

His evenings were his own: and he pored over a ragged translation of *The Count of Monte Cristo*.[10] The figure of that dark avenger stood forth in his mind for whatever he had heard or divined in childhood of the strange and terrible. At night he built up on the parlour table an image of the wonderful island cave[11] out of transfers and paper flowers and coloured tissue paper and strips of the silver and golden paper in which chocolate is wrapped. When he had broken up this scenery, weary of its tinsel, there would come to his mind the bright picture of Marseilles, of sunny trellises and of Mercedes.[12] Outside Blackrock, on the road that led to the mountains, stood a small whitewashed house in the garden of which grew many rosebushes: and in this house, he told himself, another Mercedes lived. Both on the outward and on the homeward journey he measured distance by this landmark: and in his imagination he lived through a long train of adventures, marvellous as those in the book itself, towards the close of which there appeared an image of himself, grown older and sadder, standing in a moonlit garden with Mercedes who had so many years before slighted his love, and with a sadly proud gesture of refusal, saying:

—Madam, I never eat muscatel grapes.[13]

He became the ally of a boy named Aubrey Mills and founded with him a gang of adventurers in the avenue. Aubrey carried a whistle dangling from his buttonhole and a bicycle lamp attached to his belt while the others had short sticks thrust daggerwise through theirs. Stephen, who had read of Napoleon's plain style of dress, chose to remain unadorned and thereby heightened for himself the pleasure of taking counsel with his lieutenant before giving orders. The gang made forays into the gardens of old maids or went down to the castle[14] and fought a battle on the shaggy weedgrown rocks, coming home after it weary stragglers with the stale odours of the foreshore in their nostrils and the rank oils of the seawrack upon their hands and in their hair.

Aubrey and Stephen had a common milkman and often they drove out in the milkcar to Carrickmines where the cows were at grass. While the men were milking the boys would take turns in riding the tractable mare round the field. But when autumn came the cows were driven home from the grass: and the first sight of the filthy cowyard at Stradbrook[15] with its foul green puddles and clots of liquid dung and steaming brantroughs sickened Stephen's heart. The cattle which had seemed so beautiful in the country on sunny days revolted him and he could not even look at the milk they yielded.

The coming of September did not trouble him this year for he was not to be sent back to Clongowes. The practice in the park came to an end when Mike Flynn went into hospital. Aubrey was at school and had only an hour or two free in the evening. The gang fell asunder and there were no more nightly forays or battles on the rocks. Stephen sometimes went round with the car which delivered the evening milk: and these chilly drives blew away his memory of the filth of the cowyard and he felt no repugnance at seeing the cowhairs and hayseeds on the milkman's coat. Whenever the car drew up before a house he waited to catch a glimpse of a wellscrubbed kitchen or of a softlylighted hall and to see how the servant would hold the jug and how she would close the door. He thought it should be a pleasant life enough, driving along the roads every evening to deliver milk, if he had warm gloves and a fat bag of gingernuts in his pocket to eat from. But the same foreknowledge which had sickened his heart and made his legs sag suddenly as he raced round the park, the same intuition which had made him glance with mistrust at his trainer's flabby stubblecovered face as it bent heavily over his long stained fingers, dissipated any vision of the future. In a vague way he understood that his father was in trouble and that this was the reason why he himself had not been sent back to Clongowes. For some time he had felt the slight changes in his house; and these changes in what he had deemed unchangeable were so many slight shocks to his boyish conception of the world. The ambition which he felt astir at times in the darkness of his soul sought no outlet. A dusk like that of the outer world obscured his mind as he heard the mare's hoofs clattering along the tramtrack on the Rock Road and the great can swaying and rattling behind him.[16]

He returned to Mercedes and, as he brooded upon her image, a strange unrest crept into his blood. Sometimes a fever gathered within him and led him to rove alone in the evening along the quiet avenue. The peace of the gardens and the kindly lights in the windows poured a tender influence into his restless heart. The noise of children at play annoyed him and their silly voices made him feel, even more keenly than he had felt at Clongowes, that he was different from others. He did not want to play. He wanted to meet in the real world the unsubstantial image which his soul so constantly beheld. He did not know where to seek it or how: but a premonition which led him on told him that this image would, without any overt act of his, encounter him. They would meet quietly as if they had known each other and had made their tryst, perhaps at one of the gates or in some more secret place. They would be alone, surrounded by darkness and silence: and in that moment of supreme tenderness he would be transfigured. He would fade into something impalpable under her eyes and then in a moment, he would be transfigured. Weakness and timidity and inexperience would fall from him in that magic moment.

Two great yellow caravans had halted one morning before the door and men had come tramping into the house to dismantle it. The furniture had been hustled out through the front garden which was strewn with wisps of straw and rope ends and into the huge vans at the gate. When all had been safely stowed the vans had set off noisily down the avenue: and from the window of the railway carriage, in which he had sat with his redeyed mother, Stephen had seen them lumbering heavily along the Merrion Road.[17]

The parlour fire would not draw that evening and Mr Dedalus rested the poker against the bars of the grate to attract the flame. Uncle Charles dozed in a corner of the half furnished uncarpeted room and near him the family portraits leaned against the wall. The lamp on the table shed a weak light over the boarded floor, muddied by the feet of the vanmen. Stephen sat on a footstool beside his father listening to a long and incoherent monologue. He understood little or nothing of it at first but he became slowly aware that his father had enemies and that some fight was going to take place. He felt too that he was being enlisted for the fight, that some duty was being laid upon his shoulders. The sudden flight from the comfort and revery of Blackrock, the passage through the gloomy foggy city, the thought of the bare cheerless house in which they were now to live made his heart heavy: and again an intuition or foreknowledge of the future came to him. He understood also why the servants had often whispered together in the hall and why his father had often stood on the hearthrug, with his back to the fire, talking loudly to uncle Charles who urged him to sit down and eat his dinner.

—There's a crack of the whip left in me yet, Stephen, old chap, said Mr Dedalus, poking at the dull fire with fierce energy. We're not dead yet, sonny. No, by the Lord Jesus (God forgive me) nor half dead.

Dublin was a new and complex sensation. Uncle Charles had

grown so witless that he could no longer be sent out on errands and the disorder in settling in the new house left Stephen freer than he had been in Blackrock. In the beginning he contented himself with circling timidly round the neighbouring square or, at most, going half way down one of the side streets: but when he had made a skeleton map of the city in his mind he followed boldly one of its central lines until he reached the customhouse.[18] He passed unchallenged among the docks and along the quays wondering at the multitude of corks that lay bobbing on the surface of the water in a thick yellow scum, at the crowds of quay porters and the rumbling carts and the illdressed bearded policeman. The vastness and strangeness of the life suggested to him by the bales of merchandise stocked along the walls or swung aloft out of the holds of steamers wakened again in him the unrest which had sent him wandering in the evening from garden to garden in search of Mercedes. And amid this new bustling life he might have fancied himself in another Marseilles but that he missed the bright sky and the sunwarmed trellises of the wineshops. A vague dissatisfaction grew up within him as he looked on the quays and on the river and on the lowering skies and yet he continued to wander up and down day after day as if he really sought someone that eluded him.

He went once or twice with his mother to visit their relatives: and, though they passed a jovial array of shops lit up and adorned for Christmas, his mood of embittered silence did not leave him. The causes of his embitterment were many, remote and near. He was angry with himself for being young and the prey of restless foolish impulses, angry also with the change of fortune which was reshaping the world about him into a vision of squalor and insincerity. Yet his anger lent nothing to the vision. He chronicled with patience what he saw, detaching himself from it and tasting its mortifying flavour in secret.

He was sitting on the backless chair in his aunt's kitchen. A lamp with a reflector hung on the japanned wall of the fireplace and by its light his aunt was reading the evening paper that lay on her knees. She looked a long time at a smiling picture that was set in it and said musingly:

—The beautiful Mabel Hunter!

A ringletted girl stood on tiptoe to peer at the picture and said softly:

—What is she in, mud?

—In the pantomime, love.

The child leaned her ringletted head against her mother's sleeve, gazing on the picture, and murmured as if fascinated:

—The beautiful Mabel Hunter!

As if fascinated, her eyes rested long upon those demurely taunting eyes and she murmured again devotedly:

—Isn't she an exquisite creature?

And the boy who came in from the street, stamping crookedly under his stone of coal,[19] heard her words. He dropped his load promptly on the floor and hurried to her side to see. But she did not raise her easeful head to let him see. He mauled the edges of the paper with his reddened and blackened hands, shouldering her aside and complaining that he could not see.

He was sitting in the narrow breakfast room high up in the old darkwindowed house. The firelight flickered on the wall and beyond the window a spectral dusk was gathering upon the river. Before the fire an old woman was busy making tea and, as she bustled at her task, she told in a low voice of what the priest and the doctor had said. She told too of certain changes she had seen in her of late and of her odd ways and sayings. He sat listening to the words and following the ways of adventure that lay open in the coals, arches and vaults and winding galleries and jagged caverns.

Suddenly he became aware of something in the doorway. A skull appeared suspended in the gloom of the doorway. A feeble creature like a monkey was there, drawn thither by the sound of voices at the fire. A whining voice came from the door, asking:

—Is that Josephine?

The old bustling woman answered cheerily from the fireplace:

—No, Ellen. It's Stephen.

—O . . . O, good evening, Stephen.

He answered the greeting and saw a silly smile break over the face in the doorway.

—Do you want anything, Ellen? asked the old woman at the fire.

But she did not answer the question and said:

—I thought it was Josephine. I thought you were Josephine, Stephen.

And, repeating this several times, she fell to laughing feebly.

He was sitting in the midst of a children's party at Harold's Cross.[20] His silent watchful manner had grown upon him and he took little part in the games. The children, wearing the spoils of their crackers, danced and romped noisily and, though he tried to share their merriment, he felt himself a gloomy figure amid the gay cocked hats and sunbonnets.

But when he had sung his song and withdrawn into a snug corner of the room he began to taste the joy of his loneliness. The mirth, which in the beginning of the evening had seemed to him false and trivial, was like a soothing air to him, passing gaily by his senses, hiding from other eyes the feverish agitation of his blood while through the circling of the dancers and amid the music and laughter her glance travelled to his corner, flattering, taunting, searching, exciting his heart.

In the hall the children who had stayed latest were putting on their things: the party was over. She had thrown a shawl about her and, as they went together towards the tram, sprays of her fresh warm breath flew gaily above her cowled head and her shoes tapped blithely on the glassy road.

It was the last tram. The lank brown horses knew it and shook their bells to the clear night in admonition. The conductor talked with the driver, both nodding often in the green light of the lamp. On the empty seats of the tram were scattered a few coloured tickets. No sound of footsteps came up or down the road. No sound broke the peace of the night save when the lank brown horses rubbed their noses together and shook their bells.

They seemed to listen, he on the upper step and she on the lower. She came up to his step many times and went down to hers again between their phrases and once or twice stood close beside him for some moments on the upper step, forgetting to go down, and then went down. His heart danced upon her movements like a cork upon a tide. He heard what her eyes said to him from beneath their cowl and knew that in some dim past, whether in life or in revery, he had heard their tale before. He saw her urge her vanities, her fine dress and sash and long black stockings, and knew that he had yielded to them a thousand times. Yet a voice within him spoke above the noise of his dancing heart, asking him would he take her gift to which he had only to stretch out his hand. And he remembered the day when he and Eileen had stood looking into the hotel grounds watching the waiters running up a trail of bunting on the flagstaff and the fox terrier scampering to and fro on the sunny lawn, and how, all of a sudden, she had broken out into a peal of laughter and had run down the sloping curve of the path. Now, as then, he stood listlessly in his place, seemingly a tranquil watcher of the scene before him.

—She too wants me to catch hold of her, he thought. That's why she came with me to the tram. I could easily catch hold of her when she comes up to my step: nobody is looking. I could hold her and kiss her.

But he did neither: and, when he was sitting alone in the deserted tram, he tore his ticket into shreds and stared gloomily at the corrugated footboard.

The next day he sat at his table in the bare upper room for many hours. Before him lay a new pen, a new bottle of ink and a new emerald exercise. From force of habit he had written at the top of the first page the initial letters of the jesuit motto: A.M.D.G.[21] On the first line of the page appeared the title of the verses he was trying to write: To E—— C——.[22] He knew it was right to begin so for he had seen similar titles in the collected poems of Lord Byron.[23] When he had written this title and drawn an ornamental line underneath he fell into a daydream and began to draw diagrams on the cover of the book. He saw himself sitting at his table in Bray the morning after the discussion at the Christmas dinnertable, trying to write a poem about Parnell on the back of one of his father's second moiety notices.[24] But his brain had then refused to grapple with the theme and, desisting, he had covered the page with the names and addresses of certain of his classmates:

Roderick Kickham
John Lawton
Anthony MacSwiney
Simon Moonan

Now it seemed as if he would fail again but, by dint of brooding on the incident, he thought himself into confidence. During this process all these elements which he deemed common and insignificant fell out of the scene. There remained no trace of the tram itself nor of the trammen nor of the horses: nor did he and she appear vividly. The verses told only of the night and the balmy breeze and the maiden lustre of the moon. Some undefined sorrow was hidden in the hearts of the protagonists as they stood in silence beneath the leafless trees and when the moment of farewell had come the kiss, which had been withheld by one, was given by both. After this the letters L.D.S.[25] were written at the foot of the page and, having hidden the book, he went into his mother's bedroom and gazed at his face for a long time in the mirror of her dressingtable.

But his long spell of leisure and liberty was drawing to its end. One evening his father came home full of news which kept his tongue busy all through dinner. Stephen had been awaiting his father's return for there had been mutton hash that day and he knew that his father would make him dip his bread in the gravy. But he did not relish the hash for the mention of Clongowes had coated his palate with a scum of disgust.

—I walked bang into him, said Mr Dedalus for the fourth time, just at the corner of the square.

—Then, I suppose, said Mrs Dedalus, he will be able to arrange it. I mean about Belvedere.

—Of course he will, said Mr Dedalus. Don't I tell you he's provincial of the order[26] now?

—I never liked the idea of sending him to the christian brothers[27] myself, said Mrs Dedalus.

—Christian brothers be damned! said Mr Dedalus. Is it with Paddy Stink and Mickey Mud? No, let him stick to the jesuits in God's name since he began with them. They'll be of service to him in after years. Those are the fellows that can get you a position.

—And they're a very rich order, aren't they, Simon?

—Rather. They live well, I tell you. You saw their table at Clongowes. Fed up, by God, like gamecocks.

Mr Dedalus pushed his plate over to Stephen and bade him finish what was on it.

—Now then, Stephen, he said, you must put your shoulder to the wheel, old chap. You've had a fine long holiday.

—O, I'm sure he'll work very hard now, said Mrs Dedalus, especially when he has Maurice[28] with him.

—O, Holy Paul, I forgot about Maurice, said Mr Dedalus. Here, Maurice! Come here, you thickheaded ruffian! Do you know I'm going to send you to a college where they'll teach you to spell c.a.t. cat. And I'll buy you a nice little penny handkerchief to keep your nose dry. Won't that be grand fun?

Maurice grinned at his father and then at his brother. Mr Dedalus screwed his glass into his eye and stared hard at both his sons. Stephen mumbled his bread without answering his father's gaze.

—By the bye, said Mr Dedalus at length, the rector, or provincial, rather, was telling me that story about you and Father Dolan. You're an impudent thief, he said.

—O, he didn't, Simon!

—Not he! said Mr Dedalus. But he gave me a great account of the whole affair. We were chatting, you know, and one word borrowed another. And, by the way, who do you think he told me will get that job in the corporation? But I'll tell you that after. Well, as I was saying, we were chatting away quite friendly and he asked me did our friend here wear glasses still and then he told me the whole story.

—And was he annoyed, Simon?

—Annoyed! Not he! *Manly little chap!* he said.

Mr Dedalus imitated the mincing nasal tone of the provincial.

—Father Dolan and I, when I told them all at dinner about it,

Father Dolan and I had a great laugh over it. *You better mind yourself, Father Dolan*, said I, *or young Dedalus will send you up for twice nine.*[29] We had a famous laugh together over it. Ha! Ha! Ha!

Mr Dedalus turned to his wife and interjected in his natural voice:

—Shows you the spirit in which they take the boys there. O, a jesuit for your life, for diplomacy!

He reassumed the provincial's voice and repeated:

—*I told them all at dinner about it and Father Dolan and I and all of us we had a hearty laugh together over it. Ha! Ha! Ha!*

The night of the Whitsuntide[30] play had come and Stephen from the window of the dressingroom looked out on the small grassplot across which lines of Chinese lanterns were stretched. He watched the visitors come down the steps from the house and pass into the theatre. Stewards in evening dress, old Belvedereans, loitered in groups about the entrance to the theatre and ushered in the visitors with ceremony. Under the sudden glow of a lantern he could recognise the smiling face of a priest.

The Blessed Sacrament had been removed from the tabernacle and the first benches had been driven back so as to leave the dais of the altar and the space before it free. Against the walls stood companies of barbells and Indian clubs; the dumbbells were piled in one corner: and in the midst of countless hillocks of gymnasium shoes and sweaters and singlets in untidy brown parcels there stood the stout leatherjacketed vaulting horse waiting its turn to be carried up on the stage. A large bronze shield, tipped with silver, leaned against the panel of the altar also waiting its turn to be carried up on the stage and set in the middle of the winning team at the end of the gymnastic display.

Stephen, though in deference to his reputation for essaywriting he had been elected secretary to the gymnasium, had had no part in the first section of the programme but in the play which formed the second section he had the chief part, that of the farcical pedagogue. He had been cast for it on account of his stature and grave manners for he was now at the end of a second year at Belvedere and in number two.

A score of the younger boys in white knickers and singlets came pattering down from the stage, through the vestry and into the chapel. The vestry and chapel were peopled with eager masters and boys. The plump bald sergeantmajor was testing with his foot the springboard of the vaulting horse. The lean young man in a long overcoat, who was to give a special display of intricate club swinging, stood near watching with interest, his silvercoated clubs peeping out of his deep sidepockets. The hollow rattle of the wooden dumbbells was heard as another team made ready to go up on the stage: and in another moment the excited prefect was hustling the boys through the vestry like a flock of geese, flapping the wings of his soutane nervously and crying to the laggards to make haste. A little troop of Neapolitan peasants were practising their steps at the end of the chapel, some circling their arms above their heads, some swaying their baskets of paper violets and curtseying. In a dark corner of the chapel at the gospel side of the altar a stout old lady knelt amid her copious black skirts. When she stood up a pinkdressed figure, wearing a curly golden wig and an oldfashioned straw sunbonnet, with black pencilled eyebrows and cheeks delicately rouged and powdered, was discovered. A low murmur of curiosity ran round the chapel at the discovery of this girlish figure. One of the prefects, smiling and nodding his head, approached the dark corner and, having bowed to the stout old lady, said pleasantly:

—Is this a beautiful young lady or a doll that you have here, Mrs Tallon?

Then, bending down to peer at the smiling painted face under the leaf of the bonnet, he exclaimed:

—No! Upon my word I believe it's little Bertie Tallon after all!

Stephen at his post by the window heard the old lady and the priest laugh together and heard the boys' murmur of admiration behind him as they passed forward to see the little boy who had to dance the sunbonnet dance by himself. A movement of impatience escaped him. He let the edge of the blind fall and, stepping down from the bench on which he had been standing, walked out of the chapel.

He passed out of the schoolhouse and halted under the shed that flanked the garden. From the theatre opposite came the muffled noise of the audience and sudden brazen clashes of the soldiers' band. The light spread upwards from the glass roof making the theatre seem a festive ark, anchored among the hulks of houses, her frail cables of lanterns looping her to her moorings. A sidedoor of the theatre opened suddenly and a shaft of light flew across the grassplots. A sudden burst of music issued from the ark, the prelude of a waltz: and when the side-door closed again the listener could hear the faint rhythm of the music. The sentiment of the opening bars, their languor and supple movement, evoked the incommunicable emotion which had been the cause of all his day's unrest and of his impatient movement of a moment before. His unrest issued from him like a wave of sound: and on the tide of flowing music the ark was journeying, trailing her cables of lanterns in her wake. Then a noise like dwarf artillery broke the movement. It was the clapping that greeted the entry of the dumbbell team on the stage.

At the far end of the shed near the street a speck of pink light showed in the darkness and as he walked towards it he became aware of a faint aromatic odour. Two boys were standing in the shelter of a doorway, smoking, and before he reached them he had recognised Heron by his voice.

—Here comes the noble Dedalus! cried a high throaty voice. Welcome to our trusty friend!

This welcome ended in a soft peal of mirthless laughter as Heron salaamed and then began to poke the ground with his cane.

—Here I am, said Stephen, halting and glancing from Heron to his friend.

The latter was a stranger to him but in the darkness, by the aid of the glowing cigarettetips, he could make out a pale dandyish face, over which a smile was travelling slowly, a tall overcoated figure and a hard hat. Heron did not trouble himself about an introduction but said instead:

—I was just telling my friend Wallis what a lark it would be tonight if you took off the rector in the part of the schoolmaster. It would be a ripping good joke.

Heron made a poor attempt to imitate for his friend Wallis the rector's pedantic bass and then, laughing at his failure, asked Stephen to do it.

—Go on, Dedalus, he urged, you can take him off rippingly. *He that will not hear the churcha let him be to theea as the heathena and the publicana.*[31]

The imitation was prevented by a mild expression of anger from Wallis in whose mouthpiece the cigarette had become too tightly wedged.

—Damn this blankety blank[32] holder, he said, taking it from his mouth and smiling and frowning upon it tolerantly. It's always getting stuck like that. Do you use a holder?

—I don't smoke, answered Stephen.

—No, said Heron, Dedalus is a model youth. He doesn't smoke and he doesn't go to bazaars and he doesn't flirt and he doesn't damn anything or damn all.

Stephen shook his head and smiled in his rival's flushed and mobile face, beaked like a bird's. He had often thought it strange that Vincent Heron had a bird's face as well as a bird's name. A shock of pale hair lay on the forehead like a ruffled crest: the forehead was narrow and bony and a thin hooked nose stood out between the closeset prominent eyes which were light and inexpressive. The rivals were school friends. They sat together in class, knelt together in the chapel, talked together after beads over their lunches. As the fellows in number one were undistinguished dullards Stephen and Heron had been during the year the virtual heads of the school. It was they who went up to the rector together to ask for a free day or to get a fellow off.

—O by the way, said Heron suddenly, I saw your governor going in.

The smile waned on Stephen's face. Any allusion made to his father by a fellow or by a master put his calm to rout in a moment. He waited in timorous silence to hear what Heron might say next. Heron, however, nudged him expressively with his elbow and said:

—You're a sly dog, Dedalus!

—Why so? said Stephen.

—You'd think butter wouldn't melt in your mouth, said Heron. But I'm afraid you're a sly dog.

—Might I ask you what are talking about? said Stephen urbanely.

—Indeed you might, answered Heron. We saw her, Wallis, didn't we? And deucedly pretty she is too. And so inquisitive! *And what part does Stephen take, Mr Dedalus? And will Stephen not sing, Mr Dedalus?* Your governor was staring at her through that eyeglass of his for all he was worth so that I think the old man has found you out too. I wouldn't care a bit, by Jove. She's ripping, isn't she, Wallis?

—Not half bad, answered Wallis quietly as he placed his holder once more in the corner of his mouth.

A shaft of momentary anger flew through Stephen's mind at these indelicate allusions in the hearing of a stranger. For him there was nothing amusing in a girl's interest and regard. All day he had thought of nothing but their leavetaking on the steps of the tram at Harold's Cross, the stream of moody emotions it had made to course through him, and the poem he had written about it. All day he had imagined a new meeting with her for he knew that she was to come to the play. The old restless moodiness had again filled his breast as it had done on the night of the party but had not found an outlet in verse. The growth and knowledge of two years of boyhood stood between then and now, forbidding such an outlet: and all day the stream of gloomy tenderness within him had started forth and returned upon itself in dark courses and eddies, wearying him in the end until the pleasantry of the prefect and the painted little boy had drawn from him a movement of impatience.

—So you may as well admit, Heron went on, that we've fairly found you out this time. You can't play the saint on me any more, that's one sure five.[33]

A soft peal of mirthless laughter escaped from his lips and, bending down as before, he struck Stephen lightly across the calf of the leg with his cane, as if in jesting reproof.

Stephen's movement of anger had already passed. He was neither flattered nor confused but simply wished the banter to end. He scarcely resented what had seemed to him at first a silly indelicateness for he knew that the adventure in his mind stood in no danger from their words: and his face mirrored his rival's false smile.

—Admit! repeated Heron, striking him again with his cane across the calf of the leg.

The stroke was playful but not so lightly given as the first one had been. Stephen felt the skin tingle and glow slightly and almost painlessly; and bowing submissively, as if to meet his companion's jesting mood, began to recite the *Confiteor*.[34] The episode ended well for both Heron and Wallis laughed indulgently at the irreverence.

The confession came only from Stephen's lips and, while they spoke the words, a sudden memory had carried him to another scene called up, as if by magic, at the moment when he had noted the faint cruel dimples at the corners of Heron's smiling lips and had felt the familiar stroke of the cane against his calf and had heard the familiar word of admonition:

—Admit.

It was towards the close of his first term in the college when he was in number six. His sensitive nature was still smarting under the lashes of an undivined and squalid way of life. His soul was still disquieted and cast down by the dull phenomenon of Dublin. He had emerged from a two years' spell of revery to find himself in the midst of a new scene, every event and figure of which affected him intimately, disheartened him or allured and, whether alluring or disheartening, filled him always with unrest and bitter thoughts. All the leisure which his school life left him was passed in the company of subversive writers whose gibes and violence of speech set up a ferment in his brain before they passed out of it into his crude writings.

The essay was for him the chief labour of his week and every Tuesday, as he marched from home to the school, he read his fate in the incidents of the way, pitting himself against some figure ahead of him and quickening his pace to outstrip it before a certain goal was reached or planting his steps scrupulously in the spaces of the patchwork of the footpath and telling himself that he would be first and not first in the weekly essay.

On a certain Tuesday the course of his triumphs was rudely broken. Mr Tate, the English master, pointed his finger at him and said bluntly:

—This fellow has heresy in his essay.

A hush fell on the class. Mr Tate did not break it but dug with his hand between his crossed thighs while his heavily starched linen creaked about his neck and wrists. Stephen did not look up. It was a raw spring morning and his eyes were still smarting and weak. He was conscious of failure and of detection, of the squalor of his own mind and home, and felt against his neck the raw edge of his turned and jagged collar.

A short loud laugh from Mr Tate set the class more at ease.

—Perhaps you didn't know that, he said.

—Where? asked Stephen.

Mr Tate withdrew his delving hand and spread out the essay.

—Here. It's about the Creator and the soul. Rrm . . . rrm . . . rrm . . . Ah! *without a possibility of ever approaching nearer.* That's heresy.

Stephen murmured:

—I meant *without a possibility of ever reaching.*[35]

It was a submission and Mr Tate, appeased, folded up the essay and passed it across to him, saying:

—O . . . Ah! *ever reaching.* That's another story.

But the class was not so soon appeased. Though nobody spoke to him of the affair after class he could feel about him a vague general malignant joy.

A few nights after this public chiding he was walking with a letter along the Drumcondra Road[36] when he heard a voice cry:

—Halt!

He turned and saw three boys of his own class coming towards him in the dusk. It was Heron who had called out and, as he marched forward between his two attendants, he cleft the air before him with a thin cane, in time to their steps. Boland, his friend, marched beside him, a large grin on his face, while Nash came on a few steps behind, blowing from the pace and wagging his great red head.

As soon as the boys had turned into Clonliffe Road[37] together they began to speak about books and writers, saying what books they were reading and how many books there were in their fathers' bookcases at home. Stephen listened to them in some wonderment for Boland was the dunce and Nash the idler of the class. In fact after some talk about their favourite writers Nash declared for Captain Marryat[38] who, he said, was the greatest writer.

—Fudge! said Heron. Ask Dedalus. Who is the greatest writer, Dedalus?

Stephen noted the mockery in the question and said:

—Of prose do you mean?

—Yes.

—Newman,[39] I think.

—Is it Cardinal Newman? asked Boland.

—Yes, answered Stephen.

The grin broadened on Nash's freckled face as he turned to Stephen and said:

—And do you like Cardinal Newman, Dedalus?

—O, many say that Newman has the best prose style, Heron said to the other two in explanation. Of course he's not a poet.

—And who is the best poet, Heron? asked Boland.

—Lord Tennyson,[40] of course, answered Heron.

—O, yes, Lord Tennyson, said Nash. We have all his poetry at home in a book.

At this Stephen forgot the silent vows he had been making and burst out:

—Tennyson a poet! Why, he's only a rhymester!

—O, get out! said Heron. Everyone knows that Tennyson is the greatest poet.

—And who do you think is the greatest poet? asked Boland, nudging his neighbour.

—Byron, of course, answered Stephen.

Heron gave the lead and all three joined in a scornful laugh.

—What are you laughing at? asked Stephen.

—You, said Heron. Byron the greatest poet! He's only a poet for uneducated people.

—He must be a fine poet! said Boland.

—You may keep your mouth shut, said Stephen, turning on him boldly. All you know about poetry is what you wrote up on the slates in the yard and were going to be sent to the loft for.

Boland, in fact, was said to have written on the slates in the yard a couplet about a classmate of his who often rode home from the college on a pony:

> *As Tyson was riding into Jerusalem*
> *He fell and hurt his Alec Kafoozelum.*[41]

This thrust put the two lieutenants to silence but Heron went on:

—In any case Byron was a heretic and immoral too.

—I don't care what he was, cried Stephen hotly.

—You don't care whether he was a heretic or not? said Nash.

—What do you know about it? shouted Stephen. You never read a line of anything in your life except a trans[42] or Boland either.

—I know that Byron was a bad man, said Boland.

—Here, catch hold of this heretic, Heron called out.

In a moment Stephen was a prisoner.

—Tate made you buck up the other day, Heron went on, about the heresy in your essay.

—I'll tell him tomorrow, said Boland.

—Will you? said Stephen. You'd be afraid to open your lips.

—Afraid?

—Ay. Afraid of your life.

—Behave yourself! cried Heron, cutting at Stephen's legs with his cane.

It was the signal for their onset. Nash pinioned his arms behind while Boland seized a long cabbage stump which was lying in the gutter. Struggling and kicking under the cuts of the cane and the blows of the knotty stump Stephen was borne back against a barbed wire fence.

—Admit that Byron was no good.

—No.

—Admit.

—No.

—Admit.

—No. No.

At last after a fury of plunges he wrenched himself free. His tormentors set off towards Jones's Road,[43] laughing and jeering at him, while he, torn and flushed and panting, stumbled after them half blinded with tears, clenching his fists madly and sobbing.

While he was still repeating the *Confiteor* amid the indulgent laughter of his hearers and while the scenes of that malignant episode were still passing sharply and swiftly before his mind he wondered why he bore no malice now to those who had tormented him. He had not forgotten a whit of their cowardice and cruelty but the memory of it called forth no anger from him. All the descriptions of fierce love and hatred which he had met in books had seemed to him therefore unreal. Even that night as he stumbled homewards along Jones's Road he had felt that some power was divesting him of that suddenwoven anger as easily as a fruit is divested of its soft ripe peel.

He remained standing with his two companions at the end of the shed, listening idly to their talk or to the bursts of applause in the theatre. She was sitting there among the others perhaps waiting for him to appear. He tried to recall her appearance but could not. He could remember only that she had worn a shawl about her head like a cowl and that her dark eyes had invited and unnerved him. He wondered had he been in her thoughts as she had been in his. Then in the dark and unseen by the other two he rested the tips of the fingers of one hand upon the palm of the other hand, scarcely touching it and yet pressing upon it lightly. But the pressure of her fingers had been lighter and steadier: and suddenly the memory of their touch traversed his brain and body like an invisible warm wave.

A boy came towards them, running along under the shed. He was excited and breathless.

—O, Dedalus, he cried, Doyle is in a great bake[44] about you.

You're to go in at once and get dressed for the play. Hurry up, you better.

—He's coming now, said Heron to the messenger with a haughty drawl, when he wants to.

The boy turned to Heron and repeated:

—But Doyle is in an awful bake.

—Will you tell Doyle with my best compliments that I damned his eyes? answered Heron.

—Well, I must go now, said Stephen, who cared little for such points of honour.

—I wouldn't, said Heron, damn me if I would. That's no way to send for one of the senior boys. In a bake, indeed! I think it's quite enough that you're taking a part in his bally old play.

This spirit of quarrelsome comradeship which he had observed lately in his rival had not seduced Stephen from his habits of quiet obedience. He mistrusted the turbulence and doubted the sincerity of such comradeship which seemed to him a sorry anticipation of manhood. The question of honour here raised was, like all such questions, trivial to him. While his mind had been pursuing its intangible phantoms and turning in irresolution from such pursuit he had heard about him the constant voices of his father and of his masters, urging him to be a gentleman above all things and urging him to be a good catholic above all things. These voices had now come to be hollow-sounding in his ears. When the gymnasium had been opened he had heard another voice urging him to be strong and manly and healthy and when the movement towards national revival had begun to be felt in the college yet another voice had bidden him to be true to his country and help to raise up her fallen language and tradition.[45] In the profane world, as he foresaw, a worldly voice would bid him raise up his father's fallen state by his labours and, meanwhile, the voice of his school comrades urged him to be a decent fellow, to shield others from blame or to beg them off and to do his best to get free days for the school. And it was the din of all these hollow-sounding voices that made him halt irresolutely in the pursuit of phantoms. He gave them ear only for a time but he was happy only when he was far from them, beyond their call, alone or in the company of phantasmal comrades.

In the vestry a plump freshfaced jesuit and an elderly man, in shabby blue clothes, were dabbling in a case of paints and chalks. The boys who had been painted walked about or stood still awkwardly, touching their faces in a gingerly fashion with their furtive fingertips. In the middle of the vestry a young jesuit, who was then on a visit to the college, stood rocking himself rhythmically from the tips of his toes to his heels and back again, his hands thrust well forward into his sidepockets. His small head set off with glossy red curls and his newly shaven face agreed well with the spotless decency of his soutane and with his spotless shoes.

As he watched this swaying form and tried to read for himself the legend of the priest's mocking smile there came into Stephen's memory a saying which he had heard from his father before he had been sent to Clongowes, that you could always tell a jesuit by the style of his clothes. At the same moment he thought he saw a likeness between his father's mind and that of this smiling well-dressed priest: and he was aware of some descration of the priest's office or of the vestry itself, whose silence was now routed by loud talk and joking and its air pungent with the smells of the gasjets and the grease.

While his forehead was being wrinkled and his jaws painted black and blue by the elderly man he listened distractedly to the voice of the plump young jesuit which bade him speak up and make his points clearly. He could hear the band playing *The Lily of Killarney*[46] and knew that in a few moments the curtain would go up. He felt no stage fright but the thought of the part he had to play humiliated him. A remembrance of some of his lines made a sudden flush rise to his painted cheeks. He saw her serious alluring eyes watching him from among the audience and their image at once swept away his scruples, leaving his will compact. Another nature seemed to have been lent him: the infection of the excitement and youth about him entered into and transformed his moody mistrustfulness. For one rare moment he seemed to be clothed in the real apparel of boyhood: and, as he stood in the wings among the other players, he shared the common mirth amid which the drop scene was hauled upwards by two ablebodied priests with violent jerks and all awry.

A few moments after he found himself on the stage amid the garish gas and the dim scenery, acting before the innumerable faces of the void. It surprised him to see that the play which he had known at rehearsals for a disjointed lifeless thing had suddenly assumed a life of its own. It seemed now to play itself, he and his fellow actors aiding it with their parts. When the curtain fell on the last scene he heard the void filled with applause and, through a rift in the side scene, saw the simple body before which he had acted magically deformed, the void of faces breaking at all points and falling asunder into busy groups.

He left the stage quickly and rid himself of his mummery and passed out through the chapel into the college garden. Now that the play was over his nerves cried for some further adventure. He hurried onwards as if to overtake it. The doors of the theatre were all open and the audience had emptied out. On the lines which he had fancied the moorings of an ark a few lanterns swung in the night breeze, flickering cheerlessly. He mounted the steps from the garden in haste, eager that some prey should not elude him, and forced his way through the crowd in the hall and past the two jesuits who stood watching the exodus and bowing and shaking hands with the visitors. He pushed onward nervously, feigning a still greater haste and faintly conscious of the smiles and stares and nudges which his powdered head left in its wake.

When he came out on the steps he saw his family waiting for him at the first lamp. In a glance he noted that every figure of the group was familiar and ran down the steps angrily.

—I have to leave a message down in George's Street,[47] he said to his father quickly. I'll be home after you.

Without waiting for his father's questions he ran across the road and began to walk at breakneck speed down the hill. He hardly knew where he was walking. Pride and hope and desire like crushed herbs in his heart sent up vapours of maddening incense before the eyes of his mind. He strode down the hill amid the tumult of suddenrisen vapours of wounded pride and fallen hope and baffled desire. They streamed upwards before his anguished eyes in dense and maddening fumes and passed away above him till at last the air was clear and cold again.

A film still veiled his eyes but they burned no longer. A power, akin to that which had often made anger or resentment fall from him, brought his steps to rest. He stood still and gazed up at the sombre porch of the morgue and from that to the dark cobbled laneway at its side. He saw the word *Lotts*[48] on the wall of the lane and breathed slowly the rank heavy air.

—That is horse piss and rotted straw, he thought. It is a good odour to breathe. It will calm my heart. My heart is quite calm now. I will go back.

Stephen was once again seated beside his father in the corner of a railway carriage at Kingsbridge.[49] He was travelling with his father by the night mail to Cork. As the train steamed out of the station he recalled his childish wonder of years before and every event of his first day at Clongowes. But he felt no wonder now. He saw the darkening lands slipping past him, the silent telegraphpoles passing his window swiftly every four seconds, the little glimmering stations, manned by a few silent sentries, flung by the mail behind her and twinkling for a moment in the darkness like fiery grains flung backwards by a runner.

He listened without sympathy to his father's evocation of Cork and of scenes of his youth, a tale broken by sighs or draughts from his pocketflask whenever the image of some dead friend appeared in it or whenever the evoker remembered suddenly the purpose of his actual visit. Stephen heard but could feel no pity. The images of the dead were all strange to him save that of uncle Charles, an image which had lately been fading out of memory. He knew, however, that his father's property was going to be sold by auction and in the manner of his own dispossession he felt the world give the lie rudely to his phantasy.

At Maryborough[50] he fell asleep. When he awoke the train had passed out of Mallow[51] and his father was stretched asleep on the other seat. The cold light of the dawn lay over the country, over the unpeopled fields and the closed cottages. The terror of sleep fascinated his mind as he watched the silent country or heard from time to time his father's deep breath or sudden sleepy movement. The neighbourhood of unseen sleepers filled him with strange dread as though they could harm him: and he prayed that the day might come quickly. His prayer, addressed neither to God nor saint, began with a shiver, as the chilly morning breeze crept through the chink of the carriage door to his feet, and ended in a trail of foolish words which he made to fit the insistent rhythm of the train; and silently, at intervals of four seconds, the telegraph-poles held the galloping notes of the music between punctual bars. This furious music allayed his dread and, leaning against the windowledge, he let his eyelids close again.

They drove in a jingle across Cork while it was still early morning and Stephen finished his sleep in a bedroom of the Victoria Hotel.[52] The bright warm sunlight was streaming through the window and he could hear the din of traffic. His father was standing before the dressing-table, examining his hair and face and moustache with great care, craning his neck across the waterjug and drawing it back sideways to see the better. While he did so he sang softly to himself with quaint accent and phrasing:

> *'Tis youth and folly*
> *Makes young men marry,*
> *So here, my love, I'll*
>   *No longer stay.*
> *What can't be cured, sure,*
> *Must be endured, sure,*
>   *So I'll go to*
>   *Amerikay.*

> *My love she's handsome,*
> *My love she's bonny:*
> *She's like good whisky*
>   *When it is new;*
> *But when 'tis old*
> *And growing cold*
> *It fades and dies like*
>   *The mountain dew.*[53]

The consciousness of the warm sunny city outside his window and the tender tremors with which his father's voice festooned the strange sad happy air, drove off all the mists of the night's ill humour from Stephen's brain. He got up quickly to dress and, when the song had ended, said:

—That's much prettier than any of your other *come-all-yous*.[54]

—Do you think so? asked Mr Dedalus.

—I like it, said Stephen.

—It's a pretty old air, said Mr Dedalus, twirling the points of his moustache. Ah, but you should have heard Mick Lacy sing it! Poor Mick Lacy! He had little turns for it, grace notes he used to put in that I haven't got. That was the boy who could sing a *come-all-you*, if you like.

Mr Dedalus had ordered drisheens[55] for breakfast and during the meal he crossexamined the waiter for local news. For the most part they spoke at crosspurposes when a name was mentioned, the waiter having in mind the present holder and Mr Dedalus his father or perhaps his grandfather.

—Well, I hope they haven't moved the Queen's College[56] anyhow, said Mr Dedalus, for I want to show it to this young-ster of mine.

Along the Mardyke[57] the trees were in bloom. They entered the grounds of the college and were led by the garrulous porter across the quadrangle. But their progress across the gravel was brought to a halt after every dozen or so paces by some reply of the porter's.

—Ah, do you tell me so? And is poor Pottlebelly dead?

—Yes, sir. Dead, sir.

During these halts Stephen stood awkwardly behind the two men, weary of the subject and waiting restlessly for the slow march to begin again. By the time they had crossed the quad-rangle his restlessness had risen to fever. He wondered how his father, whom he knew for a shrewd suspicious man, could be duped by the servile manners of the porter; and the lively south-ern speech which had entertained him all the morning now irri-tated his ears.

They passed into the anatomy theatre where Mr Dedalus,

the porter aiding him, searched the desks for his initials. Stephen remained in the background, depressed more than ever by the darkness and silence of the theatre and by the air it wore of jaded and formal study. On the desk before him he read the word *Fœtus* cut several times in the dark stained wood. The sudden legend startled his blood: he seemed to feel the absent students of the college about him and to shrink from their company. A vision of their life, which his father's words had been powerless to evoke, sprang up before him out of the word cut in the desk. A broadshouldered student with a moustache was cutting in the letters with a jackknife, seriously. Other students stood or sat near him laughing at his handiwork. One jogged his elbow. The big student turned on him, frowning. He was dressed in loose grey clothes and had tan boots.

Stephen's name was called. He hurried down the steps of the theatre so as to be as far away from the vision as he could be and, peering closely at his father's initials, hid his flushed face.

But the word and the vision capered before his eyes as he walked back across the quadrangle and towards the college gate. It shocked him to find in the outer world a trace of what he had deemed till then a brutish and individual malady of his own mind. His recent monstrous reveries came thronging into his memory. They too had sprung up before him, suddenly and furiously, out of mere words. He had soon given in to them and allowed them to sweep across and abase his intellect, wondering always where they came from, from what den of monstrous images, and always weak and humble towards others, restless and sickened of himself when they had swept over him.

—Ay, bedad! And there's the Groceries[58] sure enough! cried Mr Dedalus. You often heard me speak of the Groceries, didn't you, Stephen. Many's the time we went down there when our names had been marked,[59] a crowd of us, Harry Peard and little Jack Mountain and Bob Dyas and Maurice Moriarty, the Frenchman, and Tom O'Grady and Mick Lacy that I told you of this morning and Joey Corbet and poor little good hearted Johnny Keevers of the Tantiles.[60]

The leaves of the trees along the Mardyke were astir and whispering in the sunlight. A team of cricketers passed, agile young
men in flannels and blazers, one of them carrying the long green
wicketbag. In a quiet by-street a German band of five players in
faded uniforms and with battered brass instruments was playing
to an audience of street arabs⁶¹ and leisurely messenger boys. A
maid in a white cap and apron was watering a box of plants on a
sill which shone like a slab of limestone in the warm glare. From
another window open to the air came the sound of a piano, scale
after scale rising into the treble.

Stephen walked on at his father's side, listening to stories he
had heard before, hearing again the names of the scattered
and dead revellers who had been the companions of his father's
youth. And a faint sickness sighed in his heart. He recalled his
own equivocal position in Belvedere, a free boy, a leader afraid
of his own authority, proud and sensitive and suspicious, bat-
tling against the squalor of his life and against the riot of his
mind. The letters cut in the stained wood of the desk stared
upon him, mocking his bodily weakness and futile enthusi-
asms and making him loathe himself for his own mad and
filthy orgies. The spittle in his throat grew bitter and foul to
swallow and the faint sickness climbed to his brain so that for
a moment he closed his eyes and walked on in darkness.

He could still hear his father's voice.

—When you kick out for yourself, Stephen—as I daresay you
will one of these days—remember, whatever you do, to mix
with gentlemen. When I was a young fellow I tell you I enjoyed
myself. I mixed with fine decent fellows. Everyone of us could
do something. One fellow had a good voice, another fellow was
a good actor, another could sing a good comic song, another
was a good oarsman or a good racketplayer, another could tell
a good story and so on. We kept the ball rolling anyhow and
enjoyed ourselves and saw a bit of life and we were none the
worse of it either. But we were all gentlemen, Stephen—at least
I hope we were—and bloody good honest Irishmen too. That's
the kind of fellows I want you to associate with, fellows of the
right kidney. I'm talking to you as a friend, Stephen. I don't
believe in playing the stern father. I don't believe a son should be

afraid of his father. No, I treat you as your grandfather treated me when I was a young chap. We were more like brothers than father and son. I'll never forget the first day he caught me smoking. I was standing at the end of the South Terrace one day with some maneens[62] like myself and sure we thought we were grand fellows because we had pipes stuck in the corners of our mouths. Suddenly the governor passed. He didn't say a word, or stop even. But the next day, Sunday, we were out for a walk together and when we were coming home he took out his cigar case and said: *By the bye, Simon, I didn't know you smoked:* or something like that. Of course I tried to carry it off as best I could. *If you want a good smoke,* he said, *try one of these cigars. An American captain made me a present of them last night in Queenstown.*[63]

Stephen heard his father's voice break into a laugh which was almost a sob.

—He was the handsomest man in Cork at that time, by God he was! The women used to stand to look after him in the street.

He heard the sob passing loudly down his father's throat and opened his eyes with a nervous impulse. The sunlight breaking suddenly on his sight turned the sky and clouds into a fantastic world of sombre masses with lakelike spaces of dark rosy light. His very brain was sick and powerless. He could scarcely interpret the letters of the signboards of the shops. By his monstrous way of life he seemed to have put himself beyond the limits of reality. Nothing moved him or spoke to him from the real world unless he heard in it an echo of the infuriated cries within him. He could respond to no earthly or human appeal, dumb and insensible to the call of summer and gladness and companionship, wearied and dejected by his father's voice. He could scarcely recognise as his his own thoughts, and repeated slowly to himself:

—I am Stephen Dedalus. I am walking beside my father whose name is Simon Dedalus. We are in Cork, in Ireland. Cork is a city. Our room is in the Victoria Hotel. Victoria and Stephen and Simon. Simon and Stephen and Victoria. Names.

The memory of his childhood suddenly grew dim. He tried to

call forth some of its vivid moments but could not. He recalled
only names: Dante, Parnell, Clane, Clongowes. A little boy had
been taught geography by an old woman who kept two brushes
in her wardrobe. Then he had been sent away from home to a
college. In the college he had made his first communion[64] and
eaten slim jim[65] out of his cricketcap and watched the firelight
leaping and dancing on the wall of a little bedroom in the infirmary and dreamed of being dead, of mass being said for him by
the rector in a black and gold cope, of being buried then in the
little graveyard of the community off the main avenue of limes.
But he had not died then. Parnell had died. There had been no
mass for the dead in the chapel and no procession. He had not
died but he had faded out like a film in the sun. He had been
lost or had wandered out of existence for he no longer existed.
How strange to think of him passing out of existence in such a
way, not by death but by fading out in the sun or by being lost
and forgotten somewhere in the universe! It was strange to see
his small body appear again for a moment: a little boy in a grey
belted suit. His hands were in his sidepockets and his trousers
were tucked in at the knees by elastic bands.

On the evening of the day on which the property was sold
Stephen followed his father meekly about the city from bar to
bar. To the sellers in the market, to the barmen and barmaids,
to the beggars who importuned him for a lob[66] Mr Dedalus
told the same tale, that he was an old Corkonian, that he had
been trying for thirty years to get rid of his Cork accent up in
Dublin and that Peter Pickackafax beside him was his eldest
son but that he was only a Dublin jackeen.[67]

They had set out early in the morning from Newcombe's cof-
feehouse where Mr Dedalus' cup had rattled noisily against its
saucer, and Stephen had tried to cover that shameful sign of his
father's drinking bout of the night before by moving his chair
and coughing. One humiliation had succeeded another: the
false smiles of the market sellers, the curvettings and oglings of
the barmaids with whom his father flirted, the compliments and
encouraging words of his father's friends. They had told him
that he had a great look of his grandfather and Mr Dedalus had

agreed that he was an ugly likeness. They had unearthed traces of a Cork accent in his speech and made him admit that the Lee[68] was a much finer river than the Liffey. One of them in order to put his Latin to the proof had made him translate short passages from Dilectus[69] and asked him whether it was correct to say: *Tempora mutantur nos et mutamur in illis* or *Tempora mutantur et nos mutamur in illis.*[70] Another, a brisk old man, whom Mr Dedalus called Johnny Cashman, had covered him with confusion by asking him to say which were prettier, the Dublin girls or the Cork girls.

—He's not that way built, said Mr Dedalus. Leave him alone. He's a levelheaded thinking boy who doesn't bother his head about that kind of nonsense.

—Then he's not his father's son, said the little old man.

—I don't know, I'm sure, said Mr Dedalus, smiling complacently.

—Your father, said the little old man to Stephen, was the boldest flirt in the city of Cork in his day. Do you know that?

Stephen looked down and studied the tiled floor of the bar into which they had drifted.

—Now don't be putting ideas into his head, said Mr Dedalus. Leave him to his Maker.

—Yerra,[71] sure I wouldn't put any ideas into his head. I'm old enough to be his grandfather. And I am a grandfather, said the little old man to Stephen. Do you know that?

—Are you? asked Stephen.

—Bedad I am, said the little old man. I have two bouncing grandchildren out at Sunday's Well.[72] Now then! What age do you think I am? And I remember seeing your grandfather in his red coat riding out to hounds. That was before you were born.

—Ay, or thought of, said Mr Dedalus.

—Bedad I did, repeated the little old man. And, more than that, I can remember even your greatgrandfather, old John Stephen Dedalus, and a fierce old fireeater he was. Now then! There's a memory for you!

—That's three generations – four generations, said another

of the company. Why, Johnny Cashman, you must be nearing the century.

—Well, I'll tell you the truth, said the little old man. I'm just twentyseven years of age.

—We're as old as we feel, Johnny, said Mr Dedalus. And just finish what you have there, and we'll have another. Here, Tim or Tom or whatever your name is, give us the same again here. By God, I don't feel more than eighteen myself. There's that son of mine there not half my age and I'm a better man than he is any day of the week.

—Draw it mild now, Dedalus. I think it's time for you to take a back seat, said the gentleman who had spoken before.

—No, by God! asserted Mr Dedalus. I'll sing a tenor song against him or I'll vault a fivebarred gate against him or I'll run with him after the hounds across the country as I did thirty years ago along with the Kerry Boy and the best man for it.

—But he'll beat you here, said the little old man, tapping his forehead and raising his glass to drain it.

—Well, I hope he'll be as good a man as his father. That's all I can say, said Mr Dedalus.

—If he is, he'll do, said the little old man.

—And thanks be to God, Johnny, said Mr Dedalus, that we lived so long and did so little harm.

—But did so much good, Simon, said the little old man gravely. Thanks be to God we lived so long and did so much good.

Stephen watched the three glasses being raised from the counter as his father and his two cronies drank to the memory of their past. An abyss of fortune or of temperament sundered him from them. His mind seemed older than theirs: it shone coldly on their strifes and happiness and regrets like a moon upon a younger earth. No life or youth stirred in him as it had stirred in them. He had known neither the pleasure of companionship with others nor the vigour of rude male health nor filial piety. Nothing stirred within his soul but a cold and cruel and loveless lust. His childhood was dead or lost and with it his soul capable of simple joys, and he was drifting amid life like the barren shell of the moon.

Art thou pale for weariness
Of climbing heaven and gazing on the earth,
Wandering companionless . . . ?[73]

He repeated to himself the lines of Shelley's fragment. Its alternation of sad human ineffectualness with vast inhuman cycles of activity chilled him, and he forgot his own human and ineffectual grieving.

Stephen's mother and his brother and one of his cousins waited at the corner of quiet Foster Place[74] while he and his father went up the steps and along the colonnade where the highland sentry was parading. When they had passed into the great hall and stood at the counter Stephen drew forth his orders on the governor of the bank of Ireland for thirty and three pounds; and these sums, the moneys of his exhibition and essay prize, were paid over to him rapidly by the teller in notes and in coin respectively. He bestowed them in his pockets with feigned composure and suffered the friendly teller, to whom his father chatted, to take his hand across the broad counter and wish him a brilliant career in after life. He was impatient of their voices and could not keep his feet at rest. But the teller still deferred the serving of others to say he was living in changed times and that there was nothing like giving a boy the best education that money could buy. Mr Dedalus lingered in the hall gazing about him and up at the roof and telling Stephen, who urged him to come out, that they were standing in the house of commons of the old Irish parliament.[75]

—God help us! he said piously, to think of the men of those times, Stephen, Hely Hutchinson and Flood and Henry Grattan and Charles Kendal Bushe,[76] and the noblemen we have now, leaders of the Irish people at home and abroad. Why, by God, they wouldn't be seen dead in a tenacre field with them. No, Stephen, old chap, I'm sorry to say that they are only as I roved out one fine May morning in the merry month of sweet July.[77]

A keen October wind was blowing round the bank. The three figures standing at the edge of the muddy path had pinched

cheeks and watery eyes. Stephen looked at his thinly clad mother
and remembered that a few days before he had seen a mantle
priced at twenty guineas in the windows of Barnardo's.[78]

—Well that's done, said Mr Dedalus.

—We had better go to dinner, said Stephen. Where?

—Dinner? said Mr Dedalus. Well, I suppose we had better,
what?

—Some place that's not too dear, said Mrs Dedalus.

—Underdone's?[79]

—Yes. Some quiet place.

—Come along, said Stephen quickly. It doesn't matter about
the dearness.

He walked on before them with short nervous steps, smiling. They tried to keep up with him, smiling also at his eagerness.

—Take it easy like a good young fellow, said his father.
We're not out for the half mile, are we?

For a swift season of merrymaking the money of his prizes
ran through Stephen's fingers. Great parcels of groceries and
delicacies and dried fruits arrived from the city. Every day he
drew up a bill of fare for the family and every night led a party
of three or four to the theatre to see *Ingomar* or *The Lady of
Lyons*.[80] In his coat pockets he carried squares of Vienna chocolate for his guests while his trousers' pockets bulged with masses
of silver and copper coins. He bought presents for everyone,
overhauled his room, wrote out resolutions, marshalled his
books up and down their shelves, pored upon all kinds of price
lists, drew up a form of commonwealth for the household by
which every member of it held some office, opened a loan bank
for his family and pressed loans on willing borrowers so that he
might have the pleasure of making out receipts and reckoning
the interests on the sums lent. When he could do no more he
drove up and down the city in trams. Then the season of pleasure came to an end. The pot of pink enamel paint gave out and
the wainscot of his bedroom remained with its unfinished and
illplastered coat.

His household returned to its usual way of life. His mother
had no further occasion to upbraid him for squandering his

money. He too returned to his old life at school and all his novel enterprises fell to pieces. The commonwealth fell, the loan bank closed its coffers and its books on a sensible loss, the rules of life which he had drawn about himself fell into desuetude.

How foolish his aim had been! He had tried to build a breakwater of order and elegance against the sordid tide of life without him and to dam up, by rules of conduct and active interests and new filial relations, the powerful recurrence of the tides within him. Useless. From without as from within the water had flowed over his barriers: their tides began once more to jostle fiercely above the crumbled mole.

He saw clearly too his own futile isolation. He had not gone one step nearer the lives he had sought to approach nor bridged the restless shame and rancour that divided him from mother and brother and sister. He felt that he was hardly of the one blood with them but stood to them rather in the mystical kinship of fosterage, fosterchild and fosterbrother.

He burned to appease the fierce longings of his heart before which everything else was idle and alien. He cared little that he was in mortal sin,[81] that his life had grown to be a tissue of subterfuge and falsehood. Beside the savage desire within him to realise the enormities which he brooded on nothing was sacred. He bore cynically with the shameful details of his secret riots in which he exulted to defile with patience whatever image had attracted his eyes. By day and by night he moved among distorted images of the outer world. A figure that had seemed to him by day demure and innocent came towards him by night through the winding darkness of sleep, her face transfigured by a lecherous cunning, her eyes bright with brutish joy. Only the morning pained him with its dim memory of dark orgiastic riot, its keen and humiliating sense of transgression.

He returned to his wanderings. The veiled autumnal evenings led him from street to street as they had led him years before along the quiet avenues of Blackrock. But no vision of trim front gardens or of kindly lights in the windows poured a tender influence upon him now. Only at times, in the pauses of his desire, when the luxury that was wasting him gave room to a softer languor, the image of Mercedes traversed the background of his memory. He saw again the small white house and the garden of rosebushes on the road that led to the mountains and he remembered the sadly proud gesture of refusal which he was to make there, standing with her in the moonlit garden after years of estrangement and adventure. At those moments the soft speeches of Claude Melnotte[82] rose to his lips and eased his unrest. A tender premonition touched him of the tryst he had then looked forward to and, in spite of the horrible reality which lay between his hope of then and now, of the holy encounter he had then imagined at which weakness and timidity and inexperience were to fall from him.

Such moments passed and the wasting fires of lust sprang up again. The verses passed from his lips and the inarticulate cries and the unspoken brutal words rushed forth from his brain to force a passage. His blood was in revolt. He wandered up and down the dark slimy street peering into the gloom of lanes and doorways, listening eagerly for any sound. He moaned to himself like some baffled prowling beast. He wanted to sin with another of his kind, to force another being to sin with him and to exult with her in sin. He felt some dark presence moving irresistibly upon him from the darkness, a presence subtle and murmurous as a flood filling him wholly with itself. Its murmur besieged his ears like the murmur of some multitude in sleep; its subtle streams penetrated his being. His hands clenched convulsively and his teeth set together as he suffered the agony of its penetration. He stretched out his arms in the street to hold fast the frail swooning form that eluded him and incited him: and the cry that he had strangled for so long in his throat issued from his lips. It broke from him like a wail of despair from a hell of sufferers and died in a wail of furious entreaty, a cry for an iniquitous abandonment, a cry which was but the echo of an obscene scrawl which he had read on the oozing wall of a urinal.

He had wandered into a maze of narrow and dirty streets. From the foul laneways he heard bursts of hoarse riot and wrangling and the drawling of drunken singers. He walked onward, undismayed, wondering whether he had strayed into the quarter of the jews. Women and girls dressed in long vivid gowns traversed the street from house to house. They were leisurely and perfumed. A trembling seized him and his eyes grew dim. The yellow gasflames arose before his troubled vision against the vapoury sky, burning as if before an altar. Before the doors and in the lighted halls groups were gathered arrayed as for some rite. He was in another world: he had awakened from a slumber of centuries.

He stood still in the middle of the roadway, his heart clamouring against his bosom in a tumult. A young woman dressed in a long pink gown laid her hand on his arm to detain him and gazed into his face. She said gaily:

—Good night, Willie dear!

Her room was warm and lightsome. A huge doll sat with her legs apart in the copious easychair beside the bed. He tried to bid his tongue speak that he might seem at ease, watching her as she undid her gown, noting the proud conscious movement of her perfumed head.

As he stood silent in the middle of the room she came over to him and embraced him gaily and gravely. Her round arms held him firmly to her and he, seeing her face lifted to him in serious calm and feeling the warm calm rise and fall of her breast, all but burst into hysterical weeping. Tears of joy and relief shone in his delighted eyes and his lips parted though they would not speak.

She passed her tinkling hand through his hair, calling him a little rascal.

—Give me a kiss, she said.

His lips would not bend to kiss her. He wanted to be held firmly in her arms, to be caressed slowly, slowly, slowly. In her arms he felt that he had suddenly become strong and fearless and sure of himself. But his lips would not bend to kiss her.

With a sudden movement she bowed his head and joined her lips to his and he read the meaning of her movements in her frank uplifted eyes. It was too much for him. He closed his eyes, surrendering himself to her, body and mind, conscious of nothing in the world but the dark pressure of her softly parting lips. They pressed upon his brain as upon his lips as though they were the vehicle of a vague speech; and between them he felt an unknown and timid pressure, darker than the swoon of sin, softer than sound or odour.

III

The swift December dusk had come tumbling clownishly after its dull day and, as he stared through the dull square of the window of the schoolroom, he felt his belly crave for its food. He hoped there would be stew for dinner, turnips and carrots and bruised potatoes and fat mutton pieces to be ladled out in thick peppered flourfattened sauce. Stuff it into you, his belly counselled him.

It would be a gloomy secret night. After early nightfall the yellow lamps would light up, here and there, the squalid quarter of the brothels. He would follow a devious course up and down the streets, circling always nearer and nearer in a tremor of fear and joy, until his feet led him suddenly round a dark corner. The whores would be just coming out of their houses making ready for the night, yawning lazily after their sleep and settling the hairpins in their clusters of hair. He would pass by them calmly waiting for a sudden movement of his own will or a sudden call to his sinloving soul from their soft perfumed flesh. Yet as he prowled in quest of that call, his senses, stultified only by his desire, would note keenly all that wounded or shamed them; his eyes, a ring of porter froth on a clothless table or a photograph of two soldiers standing to attention or a gaudy playbill; his ears, the drawling jargon of greeting:

—Hello, Bertie, any good in your mind?

—Is that you, pigeon?

—Number ten. Fresh Nelly is waiting on you.

—Goodnight, husband! Coming in to have a short time?

The equation on the page of his scribbler began to spread out a widening tail, eyed and starred like a peacock's; and, when the

eyes and stars of its indices had been eliminated, began slowly to
fold itself together again. The indices appearing and disappear-
ing were eyes opening and closing; the eyes opening and closing
were stars being born and being quenched. The vast cycle of
starry life bore his weary mind outward to its verge and inward
to its centre, a distant music accompanying him outward and
inward. What music? The music came nearer and he recalled the
words, the words of Shelley's fragment upon the moon wandering companionless, pale for weariness.[1] The stars began to crumble and a cloud of fine stardust fell through space.

The dull light fell more faintly upon the page whereon another
equation began to unfold itself slowly and to spread abroad its
widening tail. It was his own soul going forth to experience,
unfolding itself sin by sin, spreading abroad the balefire of its
burning stars and folding back upon itself, fading slowly, quench-
ing its own lights and fires. They were quenched: and the cold
darkness filled chaos.

A cold lucid indifference reigned in his soul. At his first violent sin he had felt a wave of vitality pass out of him and had
feared to find his body or his soul maimed by the excess. Instead
the vital wave had carried him on its bosom out of himself
and back again when it receded: and no part of body or soul had
been maimed but a dark peace had been established between
them. The chaos in which his ardour extinguished itself was a
cold indifferent knowledge of himself. He had sinned mortally
not once but many times and he knew that, while he stood in
danger of eternal damnation for the first sin alone, by every suc-
ceeding sin he multiplied his guilt and his punishment. His days
and works and thoughts could make no atonement for him, the
fountains of sanctifying grace having ceased to refresh his soul.
At most, by an alms given to a beggar whose blessing he fled
from, he might hope wearily to win for himself some measure
of actual grace.[2] Devotion had gone by the board. What did it
avail to pray when he knew that his soul lusted after its own
destruction? A certain pride, a certain awe, withheld him from
offering to God even one prayer at night though he knew it was
in God's power to take away his life while he slept and hurl his
soul hellward ere he could beg for mercy. His pride in his own

sin, his loveless awe of God, told him that his offence was too grievous to be atoned for in whole or in part by a false homage to the Allseeing and Allknowing.

—Well now, Ennis, I declare you have a head and so has my stick! Do you mean to say that you are not able to tell me what a surd is?

The blundering answer stirred the embers of his contempt of his fellows. Towards others he felt neither shame nor fear. On Sunday mornings as he passed the churchdoor he glanced coldly at the worshippers who stood bareheaded, four deep, outside the church, morally present at the mass which they could neither see nor hear.[3] Their dull piety and the sickly smell of the cheap hairoil with which they had anointed their heads repelled him from the altar they prayed at. He stooped to the evil of hypocrisy with others, sceptical of their innocence which he could cajole so easily.

On the wall of his bedroom hung an illuminated scroll, the certificate of his prefecture in the college of the sodality of the Blessed Virgin Mary.[4] On Saturday mornings when the sodality met in the chapel to recite the little office[5] his place was a cushioned kneelingdesk at the right of the altar from which he led his wing of boys through the responses. The falsehood of his position did not pain him. If at moments he felt an impulse to rise from his post of honour and, confessing before them all his unworthiness, to leave the chapel, a glance at their faces restrained him. The imagery of the psalms of prophecy soothed his barren pride. The glories of Mary held his soul captive: spikenard and myrrh and frankincense, symbolising the preciousness of God's gifts to her soul, rich garments, symbolising her royal lineage, her emblems, the lateflowering plant and lateblossoming tree, symbolising the agelong gradual growth of her cultus among men.[6] When it fell to him to read the lesson towards the close of the office he read it in a veiled voice, lulling his conscience to its music.

Quasi cedrus exaltata sum in Libanon et quasi cupressus in monte Sion. Quasi palma exaltata sum in Gades et quasi plantatio rosae in Jericho. Quasi uliva speciosa in campis et quasi

*platanus exaltata sum juxta aquam in plateis. Sicut cinnamo-
mum et balsamum aromatizans odorem dedi et quasi myrrha
electa dedi suavitatem odoris.*[7]

His sin, which had covered him from the sight of God, had
led him nearer to the refuge of sinners. Her eyes seemed to
regard him with mild pity; her holiness, a strange light glowing
faintly upon her frail flesh, did not humiliate the sinner who
approached her. If ever he was impelled to cast sin from him
and to repent the impulse that moved him was the wish to be
her knight. If ever his soul, reentering her dwelling shyly after
the frenzy of his body's lust had spent itself, was turned towards
her whose emblem is the morning star,[8] *bright and musical, telling of heaven and infusing peace,*[9] it was when her names were
murmured softly by lips whereon there still lingered foul and
shameful words, the savour itself of a lewd kiss.

That was strange. He tried to think how it could be but the
dusk, deepening in the schoolroom, covered over his thoughts.
The bell rang. The master marked the sums and cuts[10] to be
done for the next lesson and went out. Heron, beside Stephen,
began to hum tunelessly.

My excellent friend Bombados.

Ennis, who had gone to the yard, came back, saying:
—The boy from the house is coming up for the rector. A tall
boy behind Stephen rubbed his hands and said:
—That's game ball. We can scut the whole hour.[11] He won't
be in till after half two. Then you can ask him questions on the
catechism, Dedalus.

Stephen, leaning back and drawing idly on his scribbler, listened to the talk about him which Heron checked from time to
time by saying:
—Shut up, will you. Don't make such a bally racket!

It was strange too that he found an arid pleasure in following
up to the end the rigid lines of the doctrines of the church and
penetrating into obscure silences only to hear and feel the more

deeply his own condemnation. The sentence of saint James which says that he who offends against one commandment becomes guilty of all[12] had seemed to him first a swollen phrase until he had begun to grope in the darkness of his own state. From the evil seed of lust all other deadly sins had sprung forth: pride in himself and contempt of others, covetousness in using money for the purchase of unlawful pleasure, envy of those whose vices he could not reach to and calumnious murmuring against the pious, gluttonous enjoyment of food, the dull glowering anger amid which he brooded upon his longing, the swamp of spiritual and bodily sloth in which his whole being had sunk.[13]

As he sat in his bench gazing calmly at the rector's shrewd harsh face his mind wound itself in and out of the curious questions proposed to it. If a man had stolen a pound in his youth and had used that pound to amass a huge fortune how much was he obliged to give back, the pound he had stolen only or the pound together with the compound interest accruing upon it or all his huge fortune?[14] If a layman in giving baptism pour the water before saying the words is the child baptised? Is baptism with a mineral water valid?[15] How comes it that while the first beatitude promises the kingdom of heaven to the poor of heart the second beatitude promises also to the meek that they shall possess the land?[16] Why was the sacrament of the eucharist instituted under the two species of bread and wine if Jesus Christ be present body and blood, soul and divinity, in the bread alone and in the wine alone? Does a tiny particle of the consecrated bread contain all the body and blood of Jesus Christ or a part only of the body and blood? If the wine change into vinegar and the host crumble into corruption after they have been consecrated is Jesus Christ still present under their species as God and as man?[17]

—Here he is! Here he is!

A boy from his post at the window had seen the rector come from the house. All the catechisms were opened and all heads bent upon them silently. The rector entered and took his seat on the dais. A gentle kick from the tall boy in the bench behind urged Stephen to ask a difficult question.

The rector did not ask for a catechism to hear the lesson from. He clasped his hands on the desk and said:

—The retreat will begin on Wednesday afternoon in honour of saint Francis Xavier whose feast day is Saturday. The retreat will go on from Wednesday to Friday. On Friday confession will be heard all the afternoon after beads. If any boys have special confessors perhaps it will be better for them not to change. Mass will be on Saturday morning at nine o'clock and general communion for the whole college. Saturday will be a free day. Sunday of course. But Saturday and Sunday being free days some boys might be inclined to think that Monday is a free day also. Beware of making that mistake. I think you, Lawless, are likely to make that mistake.

—I, sir? Why, sir?

A little wave of quiet mirth broke forth over the class of boys from the rector's grim smile. Stephen's heart began slowly to fold and fade with fear like a withering flower.

The rector went on gravely:

—You are all familiar with the story of the life of saint Francis Xavier, I suppose, the patron of your college. He came of an old and illustrious Spanish family and you remember that he was one of the first followers of saint Ignatius. They met in Paris where Francis Xavier was professor of philosophy at the university. This young and brilliant nobleman and man of letters entered heart and soul into the ideas of our glorious founder, and you know that he, at his own desire, was sent by saint Ignatius to preach to the Indians. He is called, as you know, the apostle of the Indies. He went from country to country in the east, from Africa to India, from India to Japan, baptising the people. He is said to have baptised as many as ten thousand idolaters in one month. It is said that his right arm had grown powerless from having been raised so often over the heads of those whom he baptised. He wished then to go to China to win still more souls for God but he died of fever on the island of Sancian. A great saint, saint Francis Xavier! A great soldier of God!

The rector paused and then, shaking his clasped hands before him, went on:

—He had the faith in him that moves mountains. Ten thousand souls won for God in a single month! That is a true conqueror, true to the motto of our order: *ad majorem Dei gloriam!* A saint who has great power in heaven, remember: power to intercede for us in our grief, power to obtain whatever we pray for if it be for the good of our souls, power above all to obtain for us the grace to repent if we be in sin. A great saint, saint Francis Xavier! A great fisher of souls![18]

He ceased to shake his clasped hands and, resting them against his forehead, looked right and left of them keenly at his listeners out of his dark stern eyes.

In the silence their dark fire kindled the dusk into a tawny glow. Stephen's heart had withered up like a flower of the desert that feels the simoom coming from afar.

—*Remember only thy last things and thou shalt not sin for ever*— words taken, my dear little brothers in Christ, from the book of Ecclesiastes, seventh chapter, fortieth verse.[19] In the name of the Father and of the Son and of the Holy Ghost. Amen.

Stephen sat in the front bench of the chapel. Father Arnall sat at a table to the left of the altar. He wore about his shoulders a heavy cloak; his pale face was drawn and his voice broken with rheum. The figure of his old master, so strangely rearisen, brought back to Stephen's mind his life at Clongowes: the wide playgrounds, swarming with boys, the square ditch, the little cemetery off the main avenue of limes where he had dreamed of being buried, the firelight on the wall of the infirmary where he lay sick, the sorrowful face of Brother Michael. His soul, as these memories came back to him, became again a child's soul.

—We are assembled here today, my dear little brothers in Christ, for one brief moment far away from the busy bustle of the outer world to celebrate and to honour one of the greatest of saints, the apostle of the Indies, the patron saint also of your college, saint Francis Xavier. Year after year for much longer than any of you, my dear little boys, can remember or than I can remember the boys of this college have met in this very chapel to make their annual retreat before the feast day of their patron saint. Time has gone on and brought with it its changes. Even in the last few years what changes can most of you not remember? Many of the boys who sat in those front benches a few years ago are perhaps now in distant lands, in the burning tropics or immersed in professional duties or in seminaries or voyaging over the vast expanse of the deep or, it may be, already called by the great God to another life and to the rendering up of their stewardship. And still as the years roll by, bringing with them changes for good and bad, the memory of the great saint is honoured by the boys of his college who make every year their annual retreat on the days preceding the feast day set apart by our holy mother the church to transmit to all the ages the name and fame of one of the greatest sons of catholic Spain.

—Now what is the meaning of this word *retreat* and why is it allowed on all hands to be a most salutary practice for all who desire to lead before God and in the eyes of men a truly christian life? A retreat, my dear boys, signifies a withdrawal for a while from the cares of our life, the cares of this workaday world, in order to examine the state of our conscience, to reflect on the mysteries of holy religion and to understand better why we are here in this world. During these few days I intend to put before you some thoughts concerning the four last things. They are, as you know from your catechism, death, judgment, hell and heaven. We shall try to understand them fully during these few days so that we may derive from the understanding of them a lasting benefit to our souls. And remember, my dear boys, that we have been sent into this world for one thing and for one thing alone: to do God's holy will and to save our immortal souls. All else is worthless. One thing alone is needful, the salvation of one's soul. What doth it profit a man to gain the whole world if he suffer the loss of his immortal soul?[20] Ah, my dear boys, believe me there is nothing in this wretched world that can make up for such a loss.

—I will ask you therefore, my dear boys, to put away from your minds during these few days all worldly thoughts, whether of study or pleasure or ambition, and to give all your attention to the state of your souls. I need hardly remind you that during the days of the retreat all boys are expected to preserve a quiet and pious demeanour and to shun all loud unseemly pleasure. The elder boys, of course, will see that this custom is not infringed and I look especially to the prefects and officers of the sodality of Our Blessed Lady and of the sodality of the holy angels to set a good example to their fellow-students.

—Let us try therefore to make this retreat in honour of saint Francis with our whole heart and our whole mind. God's blessing will then be upon all your year's studies. But, above and beyond all, let this retreat be one to which you can look back in after years when maybe you are far from this college and among very different surroundings, to which you can look back with joy and thankfulness and give thanks to God for having granted you this occasion of laying the first foundation of a pious honourable zealous christian life. And if, as may so happen, there be at this moment in these benches any poor soul who has had the unutterable misfortune to lose God's holy grace and to fall into grievous sin I fervently trust and pray that this retreat may be the turningpoint in the life of that soul. I pray to God through the merits of his zealous servant Francis Xavier that such a soul may be led to sincere repentance and that the holy communion on saint Francis' day of this year may be a lasting covenant between God and that soul. For just and unjust, for saint and sinner alike, may this retreat be a memorable one.

—Help me, my dear little brothers in Christ. Help me by your pious attention, by your own devotion, by your outward demeanour. Banish from your minds all worldly thoughts and think only of the last things, death, judgment, hell and heaven. He who remembers these things, says Ecclesiastes, shall not sin for ever. He who remembers the last things will act and think with them always before his eyes. He will live a good life and die a good death, believing and knowing that, if he has sacrificed much in this earthly life, it will be given to him a hundredfold and a thousandfold more in the life to come, in the kingdom without end—a blessing, my dear boys, which I wish you from my heart, one and all, in the name of the Father and of the Son and of the Holy Ghost. Amen.

As he walked home with silent companions a thick fog seemed to compass his mind. He waited in stupor of mind till it should lift and reveal what it had hidden. He ate his dinner with surly appetite and, when the meal was over and the greas-estrewn plates lay abandoned on the table, he rose and went to the window, clearing the thick scum from his mouth with his tongue and licking it from his lips. So he had sunk to the state of a beast that licks his chaps after meat. This was the end; and a faint glimmer of fear began to pierce the fog of his mind. He pressed his face against the pane of the window and gazed out into the darkening street. Forms passed this way and that through the dull light. And that was life. The letters of the name of Dublin lay heavily upon his mind, pushing one another surlily hither and thither with slow boorish insistence. His soul was fattening and congealing into a gross grease, plunging ever deeper in its dull fear into a sombre threatening dusk, while the body that was his stood, listless and dishonoured, gazing out of darkened eyes, helpless, perturbed and human for a bovine god to stare upon.

The next day brought death and judgment, stirring his soul slowly from its listless despair. The faint glimmer of fear became a terror of spirit as the hoarse voice of the preacher blew death into his soul. He suffered its agony. He felt the deathchill touch the extremities and creep onward towards the heart, the film of death veiling the eyes, the bright centres of the brain extinguished one by one like lamps, the last sweat oozing upon the skin, the powerlessness of the dying limbs, the speech thickening and wandering and failing, the heart throbbing faintly and more faintly, all but vanquished, the breath, the poor breath, the poor helpless human spirit, sobbing and sighing, gurgling and rattling in the throat. No help! No help! He, he himself, his body to which he had yielded was dying. Into the grave with it! Nail it down into a wooden box, the corpse. Carry it out of the house on the shoulders of hirelings. Thrust it out of men's sight into a long hole in the ground, into

A PORTRAIT OF THE ARTIST AS A YOUNG MAN

the grave, to rot, to feed the mass of its creeping worms and to be devoured by scuttling plump-bellied rats.

And while the friends were still standing in tears by the bedside the soul of the sinner was judged. At the last moment of consciousness the whole earthly life passed before the vision of the soul and, ere it had time to reflect, the body had died and the soul stood terrified before the judgmentseat. God, who had long been merciful, would then be just. He had long been patient, pleading with the sinful soul, giving it time to repent, sparing it yet awhile. But that time had gone. Time was to sin and to enjoy, time was to scoff at God and at the warnings of His holy church, time was to defy His majesty, to disobey His commands, to hoodwink one's fellow men, to commit sin after sin and sin after sin and to hide one's corruption from the sight of men. But that time was over. Now it was God's turn: and He was not be hoodwinked or deceived. Every sin would then come forth from its lurkingplace, the most rebellious against the divine will and the most degrading to our poor corrupt nature, the tiniest imperfection and the most heinous atrocity. What did it avail then to have been a great emperor, a great general, a marvellous inventor, the most learned of the learned? All were as one before the judgmentseat of God. He would reward the good and punish the wicked. One single instant was enough for the trial of a man's soul. One single instant after the body's death, the soul had been weighed in the balance. The particular judgment[21] was over and the soul had passed to the abode of bliss or to the prison of purgatory or had been hurled howling into hell.

Nor was that all. God's justice had still to be vindicated before men: after the particular there still remained the general judgment. The last day had come. Doomsday was at hand. The stars of heaven were falling upon the earth like the figs cast by the figtree which the wind has shaken. The sun, the great luminary of the universe, had become as sackcloth of hair. The moon was bloodred. The firmament was as a scroll rolled away. The archangel Michael, the prince of the heavenly host, appeared glorious and terrible against the sky. With one foot on the sea and one foot on the land he blew from the archangelical trumpet the brazen death of time. The three blasts of the angel filled all the universe.[22] Time is, time was but time shall be no more. At the last blast the souls of universal humanity throng towards the valley of Jehoshaphat,[23] rich and poor, gentle and simple, wise and foolish, good and wicked. The soul of every human being that has ever existed, the souls of all those who shall yet be born, all the sons and daughters of Adam, all are assembled on that supreme day. And lo the supreme judge is coming! No longer the lowly Lamb of God, no longer the meek Jesus of Nazareth, no longer the Man of Sorrows, no longer the Good Shepherd, He is seen now coming upon the clouds, in great power and majesty, attended by nine choirs of angels, angels and archangels, principalities, powers and virtues, thrones and dominations, cherubim and seraphim, God Omnipotent, God Everlasting. He speaks: and His voice is heard even at the farthest limits of space, even in the bottomless abyss. Supreme Judge, from His sentence there will be and can be no appeal. He calls the just to His side, bidding them enter into the kingdom, the eternity of bliss, prepared for them. The unjust He casts from Him, crying in His offended majesty: *Depart from me, ye cursed, into everlasting fire which was prepared for the devil and his angels.*[24] O what agony then for the miserable sinners! Friend is torn apart from friend, children are torn from their parents, husbands from their wives. The poor sinner holds out his arms to those who were dear to him in this earthly world, to those whose simple piety perhaps he made a mock of, to those who counselled him and tried to lead him on the right path, to a kind brother, to a loving sister, to the mother and father who loved him so dearly. But it is too late: the just turn away from the wretched damned souls which now appear before the eyes of all in their hideous and evil character. O you hypocrites, O you whited sepulchres, O you who present a smooth smiling face to the world while your soul within is a foul swamp of sin, how will it fare with you in that terrible day?

And this day will come, shall come, must come; the day of death and the day of judgment. It is appointed unto man to die and after death the judgment. Death is certain. The time and manner are uncertain, whether from long disease or from some unexpected accident; the Son of God cometh at an hour when you little expect Him. Be therefore ready every moment, seeing that you may die at any moment. Death is the end of us all. Death and judgment, brought into the world by the sin of our first parents, are the dark portals that close our earthly existence, the portals that open into the unknown and the unseen, portals through which every soul must pass, alone, unaided save by its good works, without friend or brother or parent or master to help it, alone and trembling. Let that thought be ever before our minds and then we cannot sin. Death, a cause of terror to the sinner, is a blessed moment for him who has walked in the right path, fulfilling the duties of his station in life, attending to his morning and evening prayers, approaching the holy sacrament frequently and performing good and merciful works. For the pious and believing catholic, for the just man, death is no cause of terror. Was it not Addison, the great English writer, who, when on his deathbed, sent for the wicked young earl of Warwick to let him see how a christian can meet his end. He it is and he alone, the pious and believing christian, who can say in his heart:

> O grave, where is thy victory?
> O death, where is thy sting?[25]

Every word of it was for him. Against his sin, foul and secret, the whole wrath of God was aimed. The preacher's knife had probed deeply into his diseased conscience and he felt now that his soul was festering in sin. Yes, the preacher was right. God's turn had come. Like a beast in its lair his soul had lain down in its own filth but the blasts of the angel's trumpet had driven him forth from the darkness of sin into the light. The words of doom cried by the angel shattered in an instant his presumptuous peace. The wind of the last day blew through his mind; his sins, the jeweleyed harlots of his imagination, fled before the hurricane, squeaking like mice in their terror and huddled under a mane of hair.

As he crossed the square, walking homeward, the light laughter of a girl reached his burning ear. The frail gay sound smote his heart more strongly than a trumpetblast, and, not daring to lift his eyes, he turned aside and gazed, as he walked, into the shadow of the tangled shrubs. Shame rose from his smitten heart and flooded his whole being. The image of Emma appeared before him and, under her eyes, the flood of shame rushed forth anew from his heart. If she knew to what his mind had subjected her or how his brutelike lust had torn and trampled upon her innocence! Was that boyish love? Was that chivalry? Was that poetry? The sordid details of his orgies stank under his very nostrils: the sootcoated packet of pictures which he had hidden in the flue of the fireplace and in the presence of whose shameless or bashful wantonness he lay for hours sinning in thought and deed; his monstrous dreams, peopled by apelike creatures and by harlots with gleaming jewel eyes; the foul long letters he had written in the joy of guilty confession and carried secretly for days and days only to throw them under cover of night among the grass in the corner of a field or beneath some hingeless door or in some niche in the hedges where a girl might come upon them as she walked by and read them secretly. Mad! Mad! Was it possible he had done these things? A cold sweat broke out upon his forehead as the foul memories condensed within his brain.

When the agony of shame had passed from him he tried to raise his soul from its abject powerlessness. God and the Blessed Virgin were too far from him: God was too great and stern and the Blessed Virgin too pure and holy. But he imagined that he stood near Emma in a wide land and, humbly and in tears, bent and kissed the elbow of her sleeve.

In the wide land under a tender lucid evening sky, a cloud drifting westward amid a pale green sea of heaven, they stood together, children that had erred. Their error had offended deeply God's majesty though it was the error of two children, but it had not offended her whose beauty *is not like earthly beauty, dangerous to look upon, but like the morning star which is its emblem, bright and musical.*[26] The eyes were not offended which she turned upon them nor reproachful. She placed their hands together, hand in hand, and said, speaking to their hearts:

—Take hands, Stephen and Emma. It is a beautiful evening now in heaven. You have erred but you are always my children. It is one heart that loves another heart. Take hands together, my dear children, and you will be happy together and your hearts will love each other.

The chapel was flooded by the dull scarlet light that filtered through the lowered blinds; and through the fissure between the last blind and the sash a shaft of wan light entered like a spear and touched the embossed brasses of the candlesticks upon the altar that gleamed like the battleworn mail armour of angels.

Rain was falling on the chapel, on the garden, on the college. It would rain for ever, noiselessly. The water would rise inch by inch, covering the grass and shrubs, covering the trees and houses, covering the monuments and the mountain tops. All life would be choked off, noiselessly: birds, men, elephants, pigs, children: noiselessly floating corpses amid the litter of the wreckage of the world. Forty days and forty nights the rain would fall till the waters covered the face of the earth.[27]

It might be. Why not?

—*Hell has enlarged its soul and opened its mouth without any limits*[28]—words taken, my dear little brothers in Christ Jesus, from the book of Isaias, fifth chapter, fourteenth verse. In the name of the Father and of the Son and of the Holy Ghost. Amen.

The preacher took a chainless watch from a pocket within his soutane and, having considered its dial for a moment in silence, placed it silently before him on the table.

He began to speak in a quiet tone.

—Adam and Eve, my dear boys, were, as you know, our first parents and you will remember that they were created by God in order that the seats in heaven left vacant by the fall of Lucifer and his rebellious angels might be filled again. Lucifer, we are told, was a son of the morning,[29] a radiant and mighty angel; yet he fell: he fell and there fell with him a third part of the host of heaven: he fell and was hurled with his rebellious angels into hell. What his sin was we cannot say. Theologians consider that it was the sin of pride, the sinful thought conceived in an instant: *non serviam: I will not serve.*[30] That instant was his ruin. He offended the majesty of God by the sinful thought of one instant and God cast him out of heaven into hell for ever.

—Adam and Eve were then created by God and placed in Eden, in the plain of Damascus, that lovely garden resplendent with sunlight and colour, teeming with luxuriant vegetation. The fruitful earth gave them her bounty: beasts and birds were their willing servants: they knew not the ills our flesh is heir to, disease and poverty and death: all that a great and generous God could do for them was done. But there was one condition imposed on them by God: obedience to His word. They were not to eat of the fruit of the forbidden tree.

—Alas, my dear little boys, they too fell. The devil, once a shining angel, a son of the morning, now a foul fiend, came in the shape of a serpent, the subtlest of all the beasts of the field.[31] He envied them. He, the fallen great one, could not bear to think that man, a being of clay, should possess the inheritance which he by his sin had forfeited for ever. He came to the woman, the weaker vessel,[32] and poured the poison of his eloquence into her ear, promising her—O, the blasphemy of that promise!—that if she and Adam ate of the forbidden fruit they would become as gods,[33] nay as God Himself. Eve yielded to the wiles of the archtempter. She ate the apple and gave it also to Adam who had not the moral courage to resist her. The poison tongue of Satan had done its work. They fell.

—And then the voice of God was heard in that garden, calling His creature man to account:[34] and Michael, prince of the heavenly host, with a sword of flame in his hand appeared before the guilty pair and drove them forth from Eden[35] into the world, the world of sickness and striving, of cruelty and disappointment, of labour and hardship, to earn their bread in the sweat of their brow.[36] But even then how merciful was God! He took pity on our poor degraded parents and promised that in the fulness of time He would send down from heaven One who would redeem them, make them once more children of God and heirs to the kingdom of heaven: and that One, that Redeemer of fallen man, was to be God's only begotten

Son, the Second Person of the Most Blessed Trinity, the Eternal Word.[37]

—He came. He was born of a virgin pure, Mary the virgin mother. He was born in a poor cowhouse in Judea and lived as a humble carpenter for thirty years until the hour of His mission had come. And then, filled with love for men, He went forth and called to men to hear the new gospel.[38]

—Did they listen? Yes, they listened but would not hear. He was seized and bound like a common criminal, mocked at as a fool, set aside to give place to a public robber, scourged with five thousands lashes crowned with a crown of thorns, hustled through the streets by the jewish rabble and the Roman soldiery, stripped of His garments and hanged upon a gibbet and His side was pierced with a lance and from the wounded body of Our Lord water and blood issued continually.[39]

—Yet even then, in that hour of supreme agony, Our Merciful Redeemer had pity for mankind. Yet even there, on the hill of Calvary, He founded the holy catholic church against which, it is promised, the gates of hell shall not prevail.[40] He founded it upon the rock of ages[41] and endowed it with His grace, with sacraments and sacrifice, and promised that if men would obey the word of His church they would still enter into eternal life but if, after all that had been done for them, they still persisted in their wickedness there remained for them an eternity of torment: hell.

The preacher's voice sank. He paused, joined his palms for an instant, parted them. Then he resumed:

—Now[42] let us try for a moment to realise, as far as we can, the nature of that abode of the damned which the justice of an offended God has called into existence for the eternal punishment of sinners. Hell is a strait and dark and foulsmelling prison, an abode of demons and lost souls, filled with fire and smoke. The straitness of this prisonhouse is expressly designed by God to punish those who refused to be bound by His laws. In earthly prisons the poor captive has at least some liberty of movement, were it only within the four walls of his cell or in the gloomy yard of his prison. Not so in hell. There, by reason of the great number of the damned, the prisoners are heaped together in their awful prison, the walls of which are said to be four thousand miles thick: and the damned are so utterly bound and helpless that, as a blessed saint, saint Anselm, writes in his book on similitudes, they are not even able to remove from the eye a worm that gnaws it.[43]

—They lie in exterior darkness. For, remember, the fire of hell gives forth no light. As, at the command of God, the fire of the Babylonian furnace lost its heat but not its light[44] so, at the command of God, the fire of hell, while retaining the intensity of its heat, burns eternally in darkness. It is a neverending storm of darkness, dark flames and dark smoke of burning brimstone, amid which the bodies are heaped one upon another without even a glimpse of air. Of all the plagues with which the land of the Pharaohs was smitten one plague alone, that of darkness, was called horrible.[45] What name, then, shall we give to the darkness of hell which is to last not for three days alone but for all eternity?

—The horror of this strait and dark prison is increased by its awful stench. All the filth of the world, all the offal and scum of the world, we are told, shall run there as to a vast reeking sewer when the terrible conflagration of the last day has purged the world. The brimstone too which burns there in such prodigious quantity fills all hell with its intolerable stench; and the bodies of the damned themselves exhale such a pestilential odour that as saint Bonaventure says, one of them alone would suffice to infect the whole world.[46] The very air of this world, that pure element, becomes foul and unbreathable when it has been long enclosed. Consider then what must be the foulness of the air of hell. Imagine some foul and putrid corpse that has lain rotting and decomposing in the grave, a jellylike mass of liquid corruption. Imagine such a corpse a prey to flames, devoured by the fire of burning brimstone and giving off dense choking fumes of nauseous loathsome decomposition. And then imagine this sickening stench, multiplied a millionfold and a millionfold again from the millions upon millions of fetid carcasses massed together in the reeking darkness, a huge and rotting human fungus. Imagine all this and you will have some idea of the horror of the stench of hell.

—But this stench is not, horrible though it is, the greatest physical torment to which the damned are subjected. The torment of fire is the greatest torment to which the tyrant has ever subjected his fellowcreatures. Place your finger for a moment in the flame of a candle and you will feel the pain of fire. But our earthly fire was created by God for the benefit of man, to maintain in him the spark of life and to help him in the useful arts whereas the fire of hell is of another quality and was created by God to torture and punish the unrepentant sinner. Our earthly fire also consumes more or less rapidly according as the object which it attacks is more or less combustible so that human ingenuity has even succeeded in inventing chemical preparations to check or frustrate its action. But the sulphurous brimstone which burns in hell is a substance which is specially designed to burn for ever and for ever with unspeakable fury. Moreover our earthly fire destroys at the same time as it burns so that the more intense it is the shorter is its duration: but the fire of hell has this property that it preserves that which it burns and though it rages with incredible intensity it rages for ever.[47]

—Our earthly fire again, no matter how fierce or widespread it may be, is always of a limited extent: but the lake of fire in hell is boundless, shoreless and bottomless. It is on record that the devil himself, when asked the question by a certain soldier, was obliged to confess that if a whole mountain were thrown into the burning ocean of hell it would be burned up in an instant like a piece of wax. And this terrible fire will not afflict the bodies of the damned only from without but each lost soul will be a hell unto itself, the boundless fire raging in its very vitals. O, how terrible is the lot of those wretched beings! The blood seethes and boils in the veins, the brains are boiling in the skull, the heart in the breast glowing and bursting, the bowels a redhot mass of burning pulp, the tender eyes flaming like molten balls.

—And yet what I have said as to the strength and quality and boundlessness of this fire is as nothing when compared to its intensity, an intensity which it has as being the instrument chosen by divine design for the punishment of soul and body alike. It is a fire which proceeds directly from the ire of God, working not of its own activity but as an instrument of divine vengeance. As the waters of baptism cleanse the soul with the body so do the fires of punishment torture the spirit with the flesh. Every sense of the flesh is tortured and every faculty of the soul therewith: the eyes with impenetrable utter darkness, the nose with noisome odours, the ears with yells and howls and execrations, the taste with foul matter, leprous corruption, nameless suffocating filth, the touch with redhot goads and spikes, with cruel tongues of flame. And through the several torments of the senses the immortal soul is tortured eternally in its very essence amid the leagues upon leagues of glowing fires kindled in the abyss by the offended majesty of the Omnipotent God and fanned into everlasting and ever increasing fury by the breath of the anger of the Godhead.

—Consider finally that the torment of this infernal prison is increased by the company of the damned themselves. Evil company on earth is so noxious that even the plants, as if by instinct, withdraw from the company of whatsoever is deadly or hurtful to them. In hell all laws are overturned: there is no thought of family or country, of ties, of relationships. The damned howl and scream at one another, their torture and rage intensified by the presence of beings tortured and raging like themselves. All sense of humanity is forgotten. The yells of the suffering sinners fill the remotest corners of the vast abyss. The mouths of the damned are full of blasphemies against God and of hatred for their fellowsufferers and of curses against those souls which were their accomplices in sin. In olden times it was the custom to punish the parricide, the man who had raised his murderous hand against his father, by casting him into the depths of the sea in a sack in which were placed a cock, a monkey and a serpent.[48] The intention of those lawgivers who framed such a law, which seems cruel in our times, was to punish the criminal by the company of hateful and hurtful beasts. But what is the fury of those dumb beasts compared with the fury of execration which bursts from the parched lips and aching throats of the damned in hell when they behold in their companions in misery those who aided and abetted them in sin, those whose words sowed the first seeds of evil thinking and evil living in their minds, those whose immodest suggestions led them on to sin, those whose eyes tempted and allured them from the path of virtue. They turn upon those accomplices and upbraid them and curse them. But they are helpless and hopeless: it is too late now for repentance.

—Last of all consider the frightful torment to those damned souls, tempters and tempted alike, of the company of the devils. These devils will afflict the damned in two ways, by their presence and by their reproaches. We can have no idea of how horrible these devils are. Saint Catherine of Siena once saw a devil and she has written that, rather than look again for one single instant on such a frightful monster, she would prefer to walk until the end of her life along a track of red coals.[49] These devils, who were once beautiful angels, have become as hideous and ugly as they once were beautiful. They mock and jeer at the lost souls whom they dragged down to ruin. It is they, the foul demons, who are made in hell the voices of conscience. Why did you sin? Why did you lend an ear to the temptings of fiends? Why did you turn aside from your pious practices and good works? Why did you not shun the occasions of sin? Why did you not leave that evil companion? Why did you not give up that lewd habit, that impure habit? Why did you not listen to the counsels of your confessor? Why did you not, even after you had fallen the first or the second or the third or the fourth or the hundredth time, repent of your evil ways and turn to God Who only waited for your repentance to absolve you of your sins? Now the time for repentance has gone by. Time is, time was, but time shall be no more! Time was to sin in secrecy, to indulge in that sloth and pride, to covet the unlawful, to yield to the promptings of your lower nature, to live like the beasts of the field, nay worse than the beasts of the field for they, at least, are but brutes and have not reason to guide them: time was but time shall be no more. God spoke to you by so many voices but you would not hear. You would not crush out that pride and anger in your heart, you would not restore those illgotten goods, you would not obey the precepts of your holy church nor attend to your religious duties, you would not abandon those wicked companions, you would not avoid those dangerous temptations. Such is the language of those fiendish tormentors, words of taunting and of reproach, of hatred and of disgust. Of disgust, yes! For even they, the very devils, when they sinned sinned by such a sin as alone was compatible with such angelical natures, a rebellion of the intellect: and they, even they, the foul devils must turn away, revolted and disgusted, from the contemplation of those unspeakable sins by which degraded man outrages and defiles the temple of the Holy Ghost, defiles and pollutes himself.

—O, my dear little brothers in Christ, may it never be our lot to hear that language! May it never be our lot, I say! In the last day of terrible reckoning I pray fervently to God that not a single soul of those who are in this chapel today may be found among those miserable beings whom the Great Judge shall command to depart for ever from His sight, that not one of us may ever hear ringing in his ears the awful sentence of rejection: *Depart from me, ye cursed, into everlasting fire which was prepared for the devil and his angels!*[50]

He came down the aisle of the chapel, his legs shaking and the scalp of his head trembling as though it had been touched by ghostly fingers. He passed up the staircase and into the corridor along the walls of which the overcoats and waterproofs hung like gibbeted malefactors, headless and dripping and shapeless. And at every step he feared that he had already died, that his soul had been wrenched forth of the sheath of his body, that he was plunging headlong through space.

He could not grip the floor with his feet and sat heavily at his desk, opening one of his books at random and poring over it. Every word for him! It was true. God was almighty. God could call him now, call him as he sat at his desk, before he had time to be conscious of the summons. God had called him. Yes? What? Yes? His flesh shrank together as it felt the approach of the ravenous tongues of flames, dried up as it felt about it the swirl of stifling air. He had died. Yes. He was judged. A wave of fire swept through his body: the first. Again a wave. His brain began to glow. Another. His brain was simmering and bubbling within the cracking tenement of the skull. Flames burst forth from his skull like a corolla, shrieking like voices:

—Hell! Hell! Hell! Hell! Hell!

Voices spoke near him:

—On hell.

—I suppose he rubbed it into you well.

—You bet he did. He put us all into a blue funk.[51]

—That's what you fellows want: and plenty of it to make you work.

He leaned back weakly in his desk. He had not died. God had spared him still. He was still in the familiar world of the school. Mr Tate and Vincent Heron stood at the window, talking, jesting, gazing out at the bleak rain, moving their heads.

—I wish it would clear up. I had arranged to go for a spin on the bike with some fellows out by Malahide. But the roads must be kneedeep.

—It might clear up, sir.

The voices that he knew so well, the common words, the quiet of the classroom when the voices paused and the silence was filled by the sound of softly browsing cattle as the other boys munched their lunches tranquilly, lulled his aching soul.

There was still time. O Mary, refuge of sinners, intercede for him! O Virgin Undefiled, save him from the gulf of death!

The English lesson began with the hearing of the history. Royal persons, favourites, intriguers, bishops, passed like mute phantoms behind their veil of names. All had died: all had been judged. What did it profit a man to gain the whole world if he lost his soul?[52] At last he had understood: and human life lay around him, a plain of peace whereon antlike men laboured in brotherhood, their dead sleeping under quiet mounds. The elbow of his companion touched him and his heart was touched: and when he spoke to answer a question of his master he heard his own voice full of the quietude of humility and contrition.

His soul sank back deeper into depths of contrite peace, no longer able to suffer the pain of dread, and sending forth, as she sank, a faint prayer. Ah yes, he would still be spared; he would

repent in his heart and be forgiven; and then those above, those
in heaven, would see what he would do to make up for the past:
a whole life, every hour of life. Only wait.

—All, God! All, all!

A messenger came to the door to say that confessions were
being heard in the chapel. Four boys left the room; and he heard
others passing down the corridor. A tremulous chill blew round
his heart, no stronger than a little wind, and yet, listening and
suffering silently, he seemed to have laid an ear against the mus-
cle of his own heart, feeling it close and quail, listening to the
flutter of its ventricles.

No escape. He had to confess, to speak out in words what
he had done and thought, sin after sin. How? How?

—Father, I . . .

The thought slid like a cold shining rapier into his tender flesh:
confession. But not there in the chapel of the college. He would
confess all, every sin of deed and thought, sincerely: but not there
among his school companions. Far away from there in some dark
place he would murmur out his own shame: and he besought
God humbly not to be offended with him if he did not dare to
confess in the college chapel: and in utter abjection of spirit he
craved forgiveness mutely of the boyish hearts about him.

Time passed.

He sat again in the front bench of the chapel. The daylight
without was already failing and, as it fell slowly through the
dull red blinds, it seemed that the sun of the last day was going
down and that all souls were being gathered for the judgment.

—*I am cast away from the sight of Thine eyes:*[53] words taken,
my dear little brothers in Christ, from the Book of Psalms, thir-
tieth chapter, twentythird verse. In the name of the Father and
of the Son and of the Holy Ghost. Amen.

The preacher began to speak in a quiet friendly tone. His face
was kind and he joined gently the fingers of each hand, forming
a frail cage by the union of their tips.

—This morning we endeavoured, in our reflection upon hell,
to make what our holy founder calls in his book of spiritual
exercises, the composition of place.[54] We endeavoured, that is,
to imagine with the senses of the mind, in our imagination, the

material character of that awful place and of the physical torments which all who are in hell endure. This evening we shall consider for a few moments the nature of the spiritual torments of hell.

—Sin, remember, is a twofold enormity. It is a base consent to the promptings of our corrupt nature, to the lower instincts, to that which is gross and beastlike; and it is also a turning away from the counsel of our higher nature, from all that is pure and holy, from the Holy God Himself. For this reason mortal sin is punished in hell by two different forms of punishment, physical and spiritual.

—Now of all these spiritual pains by far the greatest is the pain of loss, so great, in fact, that in itself it is a torment greater than all the others. Saint Thomas, the greatest doctor of the church, the angelic doctor,[55] as he is called, says that the worst damnation consists in this that the understanding of man is totally deprived of divine light and his affection obstinately turned away from the goodness of God. God, remember, is a being infinitely good and therefore the loss of such a being must be a loss infinitely painful. In this life we have not a very clear idea of what such a loss must be but the damned in hell, for their greater torment, have a full understanding of that which they have lost and understand that they have lost it through their own sins and have lost it for ever. At the very instant of death the bonds of the flesh are broken asunder and the soul at once flies towards God. The soul tends towards God as towards the centre of her existence. Remember, my dear little boys, our souls long to be with God. We come from God, we live by God, we belong to God: we are His, inalienably His. God loves with a divine love every human soul and every human soul lives in that love. How could it be otherwise? Every breath that we draw, every thought of our brain, every instant of life proceed from God's inexhaustible goodness. And if it be pain for a mother to be parted from her child, for a man to be exiled from hearth and home, for friend to be sundered from friend, O think what pain, what anguish, it must be for the poor soul to be spurned from the presence of the supremely good and loving Creator Who has called that soul into existence from nothingness and sustained it in life and loved it with an immeasurable love. This, then, to be separated for ever from its greatest good, from God, and to feel the anguish of that separation, knowing full well that it is unchangeable, this is the greatest torment which the created soul is capable of bearing, *pœna damni*, the pain of loss.

—The second pain which will afflict the souls of the damned in hell is the pain of conscience. Just as in dead bodies worms are engendered by putrefaction so in the souls of the lost there arises a perpetual remorse from the putrefaction of sin, the sting of conscience, the worm, as Pope Innocent the Third calls it, of the triple sting.[56] The first sting inflicted by this cruel worm will be the memory of past pleasures. O what a dreadful memory will that be! In the lake of alldevouring flame the proud king will remember the pomps of his court, the wise but wicked man his libraries and instruments of research, the lover of artistic pleasures his marbles and pictures and other art treasures, he who delighted in the pleasures of the table his gorgeous feasts, his dishes prepared with such delicacy, his choice wines; the miser will remember his hoard of gold, the robber his illgotten wealth, the angry and revengeful and merciless murderers their deeds of blood and violence in which they revelled, the impure and adulterous the unspeakable and filthy pleasures in which they delighted. They will remember all this and loathe themselves and their sins. For how miserable will all those pleasures seem to the soul condemned to suffer in hellfire for ages and ages. How they will rage and fume to think that they have lost the bliss of heaven for the dross of earth, for a few pieces of metal, for vain honours, for bodily comforts, for a tingling of the nerves. They will repent indeed: and this is the second sting of the worm of conscience, a late and fruitless sorrow for sins committed. Divine justice insists that the understanding of those miserable wretches be fixed continually on the sins of which they were guilty and moreover, as saint Augustine points out, God will impart to them His own knowledge of sin so that sin will appear to them in all its hideous malice as it appears to the eyes of God Himself.[57] They will behold their sins in all their foulness and repent but it will be too late and then they will bewail the good occasions which they neglected. This is the last and deepest and most cruel sting of the worm of conscience. The conscience will say: You had time and opportunity to repent and would not. You were brought up religiously by your parents. You had the sacraments and graces and indulgences[58] of the church to aid you. You had the minister of God to preach to you, to call you back when you had strayed, to forgive you your sins, no matter how many, how abominable, if only you had confessed and repented. No. You would not. You flouted the ministers of holy religion, you turned your back on the confessional, you wallowed deeper and deeper in the mire of sin. God appealed to you, threatened you, entreated you to return to Him. O what shame, what misery! The Ruler of the universe entreated you, a creature of clay, to love Him Who made you and to keep His law. No. You would not. And now, though you were to flood all hell with your tears if you could still weep, all that sea of repentance would not gain for you what a single tear of true repentance shed during your mortal life would have gained for you. You implore now a moment of earthly life wherein to repent: in vain. That time is gone: gone for ever.

—Such is the threefold sting of conscience, the viper which gnaws the very heart's core of the wretches in hell so that filled with hellish fury they curse themselves for their folly and curse the evil companions who have brought them to such ruin and curse the devils who tempted them in life and now mock them and torture them in eternity and even revile and curse the Supreme Being Whose goodness and patience they scorned and slighted but Whose justice and power they cannot evade.

—The next spiritual pain to which the damned are subjected is the pain of extension. Man, in this earthly life, though he be capable of many evils, is not capable of them all at once inasmuch as one evil corrects and counteracts another just as one poison frequently corrects another. In hell on the contrary one torment, instead of counteracting another, lends it still greater force: and moreover as the internal faculties are more perfect than the external senses, so are they more capable of suffering. Just as every sense is afflicted with a fitting torment so is every spiritual faculty; the fancy with horrible images, the sensitive faculty with alternate longing and rage, the mind and understanding with an interior darkness more terrible even than the exterior darkness which reigns in that dreadful prison. The malice, impotent though it be, which possesses these demon souls is an evil of boundless extension, of limitless duration, a frightful state of wickedness which we can scarcely realise unless we bear in mind the enormity of sin and the hatred God bears to it.

—Opposed to this pain of extension and yet coexistent with it we have the pain of intensity. Hell is the centre of evils and, as you know, things are more intense at their centres than at their remotest points. There are no contraries or admixtures of any kind to temper or soften in the least the pains of hell. Nay, things which are good in themselves become evil in hell. Company, elsewhere a source of comfort to the afflicted, will be there a continual torment: knowledge, so much longed for as the chief good of the intellect, will there be hated worse than ignorance: light, so much coveted by all creatures from the lord of creation down to the humblest plant in the forest, will be loathed intensely. In this life our sorrows are either not very long or not very great because nature either overcomes them by habits or puts an end to them by sinking under their weight. But in hell the torments cannot be overcome by habit. For while they are of terrible intensity they are at the same time of continual variety, each pain, so to speak, taking fire from another and reendowing that which has enkindled it with a still fiercer flame. Nor can nature escape from these intense and various tortures by succumbing to them for the soul is sustained and maintained in evil so that its suffering may be the greater. Boundless extension of torment, incredible intensity of suffering, unceasing variety of torture — this is what the divine majesty, so outraged by sinners, demands, this is what the holiness of heaven, slighted and set aside for the lustful and low pleasures of the corrupt flesh, requires, this is what the blood of the innocent Lamb of God, shed for the redemption of sinners, trampled upon by the vilest of the vile, insists upon.

—Last and crowning torture of all the tortures of that awful place is the eternity of hell. Eternity! O, dread and dire word. Eternity! What mind of man can understand it? And, remember, it is an eternity of pain. Even though the pains of hell were not so terrible as they are yet they would become infinite as they are destined to last for ever. But while they are everlasting they are at the same time, as you know, intolerably intense, unbearably extensive. To bear even the sting of an insect for all eternity would be a dreadful torment. What must it be, then, to bear the manifold tortures of hell for ever? For ever! For all eternity! Not for a year or for an age but for ever. Try to imagine the awful meaning of this. You have often seen the sand on the seashore. How fine are its tiny grains! And how many of those tiny little grains go to make up the small handful which a child grasps in its play. Now imagine a mountain of that sand, a million miles high, reaching from the earth to the farthest heavens, and a million miles broad, extending to remotest space, and a million miles in thickness: and imagine such an enormous mass of countless particles of sand multiplied as often as there are leaves in the forest, drops of water in the mighty ocean, feathers on birds, scales on fish, hairs on animals, atoms in the vast expanse of the air: and imagine that at the end of every million years a little bird came to that mountain and carried away in its beak a tiny grain of that sand. How many millions upon millions of centuries would pass before that bird had carried away even a square foot of that mountain, how many eons upon eons of ages before it had carried away all. Yet at the end of that immense stretch of time not even one instant of eternity could be said to have ended. At the end of all those billions and trillions of years eternity would have scarcely begun. And if that mountain rose again after it had been all carried away and if the bird came again and carried it all away again grain by grain: and if it so rose and sank as many times as there are stars in the sky, atoms in the air, drops of water in the sea, leaves on the trees, feathers upon birds, scales upon fish, hairs upon animals, at the end of all those innumerable risings and sinkings of that immeasurably vast mountain not one single instant of eternity could be said to have ended; even then, at the end of such a period, after that eon of time the mere thought of which makes our very brain reel dizzily, eternity would have scarcely begun.

—A holy saint (one of our own fathers I believe it was) was once vouchsafed a vision of hell. It seemed to him that he stood in the midst of a great hall, dark and silent save for the ticking of a great clock. The ticking went on unceasingly; and it seemed to this saint that the sound of the ticking was the ceaseless repetition of the words: ever, never; ever, never. Ever to be in hell, never to be in heaven; ever to be shut off from the presence of God, never to enjoy the beatific vision;[59] ever to be eaten with flames, gnawed by vermin, goaded with burning spikes, never to be free from those pains; ever to have the conscience upbraid one, the memory enrage, the mind filled with darkness and despair, never to escape; ever to curse and revile the foul demons who gloat fiendishly over the misery of their dupes, never to behold the shining raiment of the blessed spirits; ever to cry out of the abyss of fire to God for an instant, a single instant, of respite from such awful agony, never to receive, even for an instant, God's pardon; ever to suffer, never to enjoy; ever to be damned, never to be saved; ever, never; ever, never. O what a dreadful punishment! An eternity of endless agony, of endless bodily and spiritual torment, without one ray of hope, without one moment of cessation, of agony limitless in extent, limitless in intensity, of torment infinitely lasting, infinitely varied, of torture that sustains eternally that which it eternally devours, of anguish that everlastingly preys upon the spirit while it racks the flesh, an eternity, every instant of which is itself an eternity, and that eternity an eternity of woe. Such is the terrible punishment decreed for those who die in mortal sin by an almighty and a just God.

—Yes, a just God! Men, reasoning always as men, are astonished that God should mete out an everlasting and infinite punishment in the fires of hell for a single grievous sin. They reason thus because, blinded by the gross illusion of the flesh and the darkness of human understanding, they are unable to comprehend the hideous malice of mortal sin. They reason thus because they are unable to comprehend that even venial sin[60] is of such a foul and hideous nature that even if the omnipotent Creator could end all the evil and misery in the world, the wars, the diseases, the robberies, the crimes, the deaths, the murders, on condition that He allowed a single venial sin to pass unpunished, a single venial sin, a lie, an angry look, a moment of wilful sloth, He, the great omnipotent God, could not do so because sin, be it in thought or deed, is a transgression of His law and God would not be God if He did not punish the transgressor.

—A sin, an instant of rebellious pride of the intellect, made Lucifer and a third part of the cohorts of angels fall from their glory. A sin, an instant of folly and weakness, drove Adam and Eve out of Eden and brought death and suffering into the world. To retrieve the consequences of that sin the Only Begotten Son of God came down to earth, lived and suffered and died a most painful death, hanging for three hours on the cross.

—O, my dear little brethren in Christ Jesus, will we then offend that good Redeemer and provoke His anger? Will we trample again upon that torn and mangled corpse? Will we spit upon that face so full of sorrow and love? Will we too, like the cruel jews and the brutal soldiers, mock that gentle and compassionate Saviour Who trod alone for our sake the awful winepress of sorrow? Every word of sin is a wound in His tender side. Every sinful act is a thorn piercing His head. Every impure thought, deliberately yielded to, is a keen lance transfixing that sacred and loving heart. No, no. It is impossible for any human being to do that which offends so deeply the divine majesty, that which is punished by an eternity of agony, that which crucifies again the Son of God and makes a mockery of Him.

—I pray to God that my poor words may have availed today to confirm in holiness those who are in a state of grace, to strengthen the wavering, to lead back to the state of grace the poor soul that has strayed if any such be among you. I pray to God, and do you pray with me, that we may repent of our sins. I will ask you now, all of you, to repeat after me the act of contrition, kneeling here in this humble chapel in the presence of God. He is there in the tabernacle burning with love for mankind, ready to comfort the afflicted. Be not afraid. No matter how many or how foul the sins if only you repent of them they will be forgiven you. Let no worldly shame hold you back. God is still the merciful Lord Who wishes not the eternal death of the sinner but rather that he be converted and live.

—He calls you to Him. You are His. He made you out of nothing. He loved you as only a God can love. His arms are open to receive you even though you have sinned against Him. Come to Him, poor sinner, poor vain and erring sinner. Now is the acceptable time. Now is the hour.

The priest rose and, turning towards the altar, knelt upon the step before the tabernacle in the fallen gloom. He waited till all in the chapel had knelt and every least noise was still. Then, raising his head, he repeated the act of contrition, phrase by phrase, with fervour. The boys answered him phrase by phrase. Stephen, his tongue cleaving to his palate, bowed his head, praying with his heart.

> —*O my God!*—
> —*O my God!*—
> —*I am heartily sorry*—
> —*I am heartily sorry*—
> —*for having offended Thee*—
> —*for having offended Thee*—
> —*and I detest my sins*—
> —*and I detest my sins*—
> —*above every other evil*—
> —*above every other evil*—
> —*because they displease Thee, my God*—
> —*because they displease Thee, my God*—
> —*Who art so deserving*—
> —*Who art so deserving*—
> —*of all my love*—
> —*of all my love*—
> —*and I firmly purpose*—
> —*and I firmly purpose*—
> —*by Thy holy grace*—
> —*by Thy holy grace*—
> —*never more to offend Thee*—

—never more to offend Thee—
—and to amend my life—
—and to amend my life—[61]

He went up to his room after dinner in order to be alone with his soul: and at every step his soul seemed to sigh: at every step his soul mounted with his feet, sighing in the ascent, through a region of viscid gloom.

He halted on the landing before the door and then, grasping the porcelain knob, opened the door quickly. He waited in fear, his soul pining within him, praying silently that death might not touch his brow as he passed over the threshold, that the fiends that inhabit darkness might not be given power over him. He waited still at the threshold as at the entrance to some dark cave. Faces were there; eyes: they waited and watched.

—We knew perfectly well of course that although it was bound to come to the light he would find considerable difficulty in endeavouring to try to induce himself to try to endeavour to ascertain the spiritual plenipotentiary and so we knew of course perfectly well—

Murmuring faces waited and watched; murmurous voices filled the dark shell of the cave. He feared intensely in spirit and in flesh but, raising his head bravely, he strode into the room firmly. A doorway, a room, the same room, same window. He told himself calmly that those words had absolutely no sense which had seemed to rise murmurously from the dark. He told himself that it was simply his room with the door open.

He closed the door and, walking swiftly to the bed, knelt beside it and covered his face with his hands. His hands were cold and damp and his limbs ached with chill. Bodily unrest and chill and weariness beset him, routing his thoughts. Why was he kneeling there like a child saying his evening prayers? To be alone with his soul, to examine his conscience, to meet his sins face to face, to recall their times and manners and circumstances, to weep over them. He could not weep. He could not summon them to his memory. He felt only an ache of soul and body, his whole being, memory, will, understanding, flesh, benumbed and weary.

That was the work of devils, to scatter his thoughts and over-
cloud his conscience, assailing him at the gates of the cowardly
and sincorrupted flesh: and, praying God timidly to forgive him
his weakness, he crawled up on to the bed and, wrapping the
blankets closely about him, covered his face again with his
hands. He had sinned. He had sinned so deeply against heaven
and before God that he was not worthy to be called God's child.

Could it be that he, Stephen Dedalus, had done those things?
His conscience sighed in answer. Yes, he had done them,
secretly, filthily, time after time, and, hardened in sinful impenitence, he had dared to wear the mask of holiness before the
tabernacle itself while his soul within was a living mass of corruption. How came it that God had not struck him dead? The
leprous company of his sins closed about him, breathing upon
him, bending over him from all sides. He strove to forget them
in an act of prayer, huddling his limbs closer together and bind-
ing down his eyelids: but the senses of his soul would not be
bound and, though his eyes were shut fast, he saw the places
where he had sinned and, though his ears were tightly covered,
he heard. He desired with all his will not to hear or see. He
desired till his frame shook under the strain of his desire and
until the senses of his soul closed. They closed for an instant
and then opened. He saw.

A field of stiff weeds and thistles and tufted nettle-bunches.
Thick among the tufts of rank stiff growth lay battered canisters
and clots and coils of solid excrement. A faint marshlight struggled upwards from all the ordure through the bristling greygreen
weeds. An evil smell, faint and foul as the light, curled upwards
sluggishly out of the canisters and from the stale crusted dung.

Creatures were in the field; one, three, six: creatures were moving in the field, hither and thither. Goatish creatures with human
faces, hornybrowed, lightly bearded and grey as indiarubber. The
malice of evil glittered in their hard eyes, as they moved hither
and thither, trailing their long tails behind them. A rictus of cruel
malignity lit up greyly their old bony faces. One was clasping
about his ribs a torn flannel waistcoat, another complained
monotonously as his beard stuck in the tufted weeds. Soft language issued from their spittleless lips as they swished in slow

circles round and round the field, winding hither and thither through the weeds, dragging their long tails amid the rattling canisters. They moved in slow circles, circling closer and closer to enclose, to enclose, soft language issuing from their lips, their long swishing tails besmeared with stale shite, thrusting upwards their terrific faces . . .

Help!

He flung the blankets from him madly to free his face and neck. That was his hell. God had allowed him to see the hell reserved for his sins: stinking, bestial, malignant, a hell of lecherous goatish fiends. For him! For him!

He sprang from the bed, the reeking odour pouring down his throat, clogging and revolting his entrails. Air! The air of heaven! He stumbled towards the window, groaning and almost fainting with sickness. At the washstand a convulsion seized him within; and, clasping his cold forehead wildly, he vomited profusely in agony.

When the fit had spent itself he walked weakly to the window and, lifting the sash, sat in a corner of the embrasure and leaned his elbow upon the sill. The rain had drawn off; and amid the moving vapours from point to point of light the city was spinning about herself a soft cocoon of yellowish haze. Heaven was still and faintly luminous and the air sweet to breathe, as in a thicket drenched with showers: and amid peace and shimmering lights and quiet fragrance he made a covenant with his heart.

He prayed:

   —He once had meant to come on earth in heavenly glory but we sinned: and then He could not safely visit us but with a shrouded majesty and a bedimmed radiance for He was God. So He came Himself in weakness not in power and He sent thee, a creature in His stead, with a creature's comeliness and lustre suited to our state. And now thy very face and form, dear mother, speak to us of the Eternal; not like earthly beauty, dangerous to look upon, but like the morning star which is thy emblem, bright and musical, breathing purity, telling of heaven and infusing peace. O harbinger of day! O light of the pilgrim!

Lead us still as thou hast led. In the dark night, across the bleak
wilderness guide us on to our Lord Jesus, guide us home.[62]

His eyes were dimmed with tears and, looking humbly up to heaven, he wept for the innocence he had lost.

When evening had fallen he left the house and the first touch of the damp dark air and the noise of the door as it closed behind him made ache again his conscience, lulled by prayer and tears. Confess! Confess! It was not enough to lull the conscience with a tear and a prayer. He had to kneel before the minister of the Holy Ghost and tell over his hidden sins truly and repentantly. Before he heard again the footboard of the housedoor trail over the threshold as it opened to let him in, before he saw again the table in the kitchen set for supper he would have knelt and confessed. It was quite simple.

The ache of conscience ceased and he walked onward swiftly through the dark streets. There were so many flagstones on the footpath of that street and so many streets in that city and so many cities in the world. Yet eternity had no end. He was in mortal sin. Even once was a mortal sin. It could happen in an instant. But how so quickly? By seeing or by thinking of seeing. The eyes see the thing, without having wished first to see. Then in an instant it happens. But does that part of the body understand or what? The serpent, the most subtle beast of the field. It must understand when it desires in one instant and then prolongs its own desire instant after instant, sinfully. It feels and understands and desires. What a horrible thing! Who made it to be like that, a bestial part of the body able to understand bestially and desire bestially? Was that then he or an inhuman thing moved by a lower soul than his soul? His soul sickened at the thought of a torpid snaky life feeding itself out of the tender marrow of his life and fattening upon the slime of lust. O why was that so? O why?[63]

He cowered in the shadow of the thought, abasing himself in the awe of God Who had made all things and all men. Madness. Who could think such a thought? And, cowering in darkness and abject, he prayed mutely to his angel guardian[64] to drive away with his sword the demon that was whispering to his brain.

The whisper ceased and he knew then clearly that his own soul had sinned in thought and word and deed wilfully through his own body. Confess! He had to confess every sin. How could he utter in words to the priest what he had done? Must, must. Or how could he explain without dying of shame? Or how could he have done such things without shame? A madman, a loathsome madman! Confess! O he would indeed to be free and sinless again! Perhaps the priest would know. O dear God!

He walked on and on through illlit streets, fearing to stand still for a moment lest it might seem that he held back from what awaited him, fearing to arrive at that towards which he still turned with longing. How beautiful must be a soul in the state of grace when God looked upon it with love!

Frowsy girls sat along the curbstones before their baskets. Their dank hair hung trailed over their brows. They were not beautiful to see as they crouched in the mire. But their souls were seen by God; and if their souls were in a state of grace they were radiant to see: and God loved them, seeing them.

A wasting breath of humiliation blew bleakly over his soul to think of how he had fallen, to feel that those souls were dearer to God than his. The wind blew over him and passed on to the myriads and myriads of other souls on whom God's favour shone now more and now less, stars now brighter and now dimmer, sustained and failing. And the glimmering souls passed away, sustained and failing, merged in a moving breath. One soul was lost; a tiny soul: his. It flickered once and went out, forgotten, lost. The end: black cold void waste.

Consciousness of place came ebbing back to him slowly over a vast tract of time unlit, unfelt, unlived. The squalid scene composed itself around him; the common accents, the burning gasjets in the shops, odours of fish and spirits and wet sawdust, moving men and women. An old woman was about to cross the street, an oilcan in her hand. He bent down and asked her was there a chapel near.

—A chapel, sir? Yes, sir. Church Street chapel.[65]

—Church?

She shifted the can to her other hand and directed him: and, as she held out her reeking withered right hand under its fringe of shawl, he bent lower towards her, saddened and soothed by her voice.

—Thank you.

—You are quite welcome, sir.

The candles on the high altar had been extinguished but the fragrance of incense still floated down the dim nave. Bearded workmen with pious faces were guiding a canopy[66] out through a sidedoor, the sacristan aiding them with quiet gestures and words. A few of the faithful still lingered, praying before one of the sidealtars or kneeling in the benches near the confessionals. He approached timidly and knelt at the last bench in the body, thankful for the peace and silence and fragrant shadow of the church. The board on which he knelt was narrow and worn and those who knelt near him were humble followers of Jesus. Jesus too had been born in poverty and had worked in the shop of a carpenter, cutting boards and planing them, and had first spoken of the kingdom of God to poor fishermen, teaching all men to be meek and humble of heart.

He bowed his head upon his hands, bidding his heart be meek and humble that he might be like those who knelt beside him and his prayer as acceptable as theirs. He prayed beside them but it was hard. His soul was foul with sin and he dared not ask forgiveness with the simple trust of those whom Jesus, in the mysterious ways of God, had called first His side, the carpenters, the fishermen, poor and simple people following a lowly trade, handling and shaping the wood of trees, mending their nets with patience.

A tall figure came down the aisle and the penitents stirred: and at the last moment, glancing up swiftly, he saw a long grey beard and the brown habit of a capuchin.[67] The priest entered the box and was hidden. Two penitents rose and entered the confessional at either side. The wooden slide was drawn back and the faint murmur of a voice troubled the silence.

His blood began to murmur in his veins, murmuring like a sinful city summoned from its sleep to hear its doom. Little flakes of fire fell and powdery ashes fell softly, alighting on the houses of men. They stirred, waking from sleep, troubled by the heated air.

The slide was shot back. The penitent emerged from the side of the box. The farther slide was drawn. A woman entered quietly and deftly where the first penitent had knelt. The faint murmur began again.

He could still leave the chapel. He could stand up, put one foot before the other and walk out softly and then run, run, run swiftly through the dark streets. He could still escape from the shame. Had it been any terrible crime but that one sin! Had it been murder! Little fiery flakes fell and touched him at all points, shameful thoughts, shameful words, shameful acts. Shame covered him wholly like fine glowing ashes falling continually. To say it in words! His soul, stifling and helpless, would cease to be.

The slide was shot back. A penitent emerged from the farther side of the box. The near slide was drawn. A penitent entered where the other penitent had come out. A soft whispering noise floated in vaporous cloudlets out of the box. It was the woman; soft whispering cloudlets, soft whispering vapour, whispering and vanishing.

He beat his breast with his fist humbly, secretly under cover of the wooden armrest. He would be at one with others and with God. He would love his neighbour. He would love God Who had made and loved him. He would kneel and pray with others and be happy. God would look down on him and on them and would love them all.

It was easy to be good. God's yoke was sweet and light.[68] It was better never to have sinned, to have remained always a child, for God loved little children and suffered them to come to Him. It was a terrible and a sad thing to sin. But God was merciful to poor sinners who were truly sorry. How true that was! That was indeed goodness.

The slide was shot to suddenly. The penitent came out. He was next. He stood up in terror and walked blindly into the box.

At last it had come. He knelt in the silent gloom and raised his eyes to the white crucifix suspended above him. God could see that he was sorry. He would tell all his sins. His confession would be long, long. Everybody in the chapel would know then what a sinner he had been. Let them know. It was true. But God had promised to forgive him if he was sorry. He was sorry. He clasped his hands and raised them towards the white form, praying with his darkened eyes, praying with all his trembling body, swaying his head to and fro like a lost creature, praying with whimpering lips.

—Sorry! Sorry! O sorry!

The slide clicked back and his heart bounded in his breast. The face of an old priest was at the grating, averted from him, leaning upon a hand. He made the sign of the cross and prayed of the priest to bless him for he had sinned. Then, bowing his head, he repeated the *Confiteor* in fright. At the words *my most grievous fault* he ceased, breathless.[69]

—How long is it since your last confession, my child?

—A long time, father.

—A month, my child?

—Longer, father.

—Three months, my child?

—Longer, father.

—Six months?

—Eight months, father.

He had begun. The priest asked:

—And what do you remember since that time?

He began to confess his sins: masses missed, prayers not said, lies.

—Anything else, my child?

Sins of anger, envy of others, gluttony, vanity, disobedience.

—Anything else, my child?

—Sloth.

—Anything else, my child?

There was no help. He murmured:

—I . . . committed sins of impurity, father.

The priest did not turn his head.

—With yourself, my child?

—And . . . with others.

—With women, my child?

—Yes, father.

—Were they married women, my child?

He did not know. His sins trickled from his lips, one by one, trickled in shameful drops from his soul festering and oozing like a sore, a squalid stream of vice. The last sins oozed forth, sluggish, filthy. There was no more to tell. He bowed his head, overcome.

The priest was silent. Then he asked:

—How old are you, my child?

—Sixteen, father.

The priest passed his hand several times over his face. Then, resting his forehead against his hand, he leaned towards the grating and, with eyes still averted, spoke slowly. His voice was weary and old.

—You are very young, my child, he said, and let me implore of you to give up that sin. It is a terrible sin. It kills the body and it kills the soul. It is the cause of many crimes and misfortunes. Give it up, my child, for God's sake. It is dishonourable and unmanly. You cannot know where that wretched habit will lead you or where it will come against you. As long as you commit that sin, my poor child, you will never be worth one farthing to God. Pray to our mother Mary to help you. She will help you, my child. Pray to Our Blessed Lady when that sin comes into your mind. I am sure you will do that, will you not? You repent of all those sins. I am sure you do. And you will promise God now that by His holy grace you will never offend Him any more by that wicked sin. You will make that solemn promise to God, will you not?

—Yes, father.

The old and weary voice fell like sweet rain upon his quaking parching heart. How sweet and sad!

—Do so, my poor child. The devil has led you astray. Drive him back to hell when he tempts you to dishonour your body in that way—the foul spirit who hates Our Lord. Promise God now that you will give up that sin, that wretched wretched sin.

Blinded by his tears and by the light of God's mercifulness

he bent his head and heard the grave words of absolution spoken and saw the priest's hand raised above him in token of forgiveness.[70]

—God bless you, my child. Pray for me.

He knelt to say his penance, praying in a corner of the dark nave: and his prayers ascended to heaven from his purified heart like perfume streaming upwards from a heart of white rose.

The muddy streets were gay. He strode homeward, conscious of an invisible grace pervading and making light his limbs. In spite of all he had done it. He had confessed and God had pardoned him. His soul was made fair and holy once more, holy and happy.

It would be beautiful to die if God so willed. It was beautiful to live if God so willed, to live in grace a life of peace and virtue and forbearance with others.

He sat by the fire in the kitchen, not daring to speak for happiness. Till that moment he had not known how beautiful and peaceful life could be. The green square of paper pinned round the lamp cast down a tender shade. On the dresser was a plate of sausages and white puddings and on the shelf there were eggs. They would be for the breakfast in the morning after the communion in the college chapel. White pudding and eggs and sausages and cups of tea. How simple and beautiful was life after all! And life lay all before him.

In a dream he fell asleep. In a dream he rose and saw that it was morning. In a waking dream he went through the quiet morning towards the college.

The boys were all there, kneeling in their places. He knelt among them, happy and shy. The altar was heaped with fragrant masses of white flowers: and in the morning light the pale flames of the candles among the white flowers were clear and silent as his own soul.

He knelt before the altar with his classmates, holding the altar cloth with them over a living rail of hands. His hands were trembling, and his soul trembled as he heard the priest pass with the ciborium[71] from communicant to communicant.

—*Corpus Domini nostri.*

Could it be? He knelt there sinless and timid: and he would hold upon his tongue the host and God would enter his purified body.

—*In vitam eternam. Amen.*[72]

Another life! A life of grace and virtue and happiness! It was true. It was not a dream from which he would wake. The past was past.

—*Corpus Domini nostri.*

The ciborium had come to him.

IV

Sunday was dedicated to the mystery of the Holy Trinity, Monday to the Holy Ghost, Tuesday to the Guardian Angels, Wednesday to Saint Joseph, Thursday to the Most Blessed Sacrament of the Altar, Friday to the Suffering Jesus, Saturday to the Blessed Virgin Mary.[1]

Every morning he hallowed himself anew in the presence of some holy image or mystery. His day began with an heroic offering[2] of its every moment of thought or action for the intentions of the sovereign pontiff and with an early mass. The raw morning air whetted his resolute piety; and often as he knelt among the few worshippers at the sidealtar, following with his interleaved prayer-book[3] the murmur of the priest, he glanced up for an instant towards the vested figure standing in the gloom between the two candles which were the old and the new testaments[4] and imagined that he was kneeling at mass in the catacombs.[5]

His daily life was laid out in devotional areas. By means of ejaculations[6] and prayers he stored up ungrudgingly for the souls in purgatory centuries of days and quarantines and years;[7] yet the spiritual triumph which he felt in achieving with ease so many fabulous ages of canonical penances did not wholly reward his zeal of prayer since he could never know how much temporal punishment he had remitted by way of suffrage for the agonising souls: and, fearful lest in the midst of the purgatorial fire, which differed from the infernal only in that it was not everlasting, his penance might avail no more than a drop of moisture, he drove his soul daily through an increasing circle of works of supererogation.[8]

Every part of his day, divided by what he regarded now as the duties of his station in life, circled about its own centre of spiritual energy. His life seemed to have drawn near to eternity; every thought, word and deed, every instance of consciousness could be made to revibrate radiantly in heaven: and at times his sense of such immediate repercussion was so lively that he seemed to feel his soul in devotion pressing like fingers the keyboard of a great cash register and to see the amount of his purchase start forth immediately in heaven, not as a number but as a frail column of incense or as a slender flower.

The rosaries too which he said constantly—for he carried his beads loose in his trousers' pockets that he might tell them as he walked the streets—transformed themselves into coronals of flowers of such vague unearthly texture that they seemed to him as hueless and odourless as they were nameless. He offered up each of his three daily chaplets[9] that his soul might grow strong in each of the three theological virtues, in faith in the Father, Who had created him, in hope in the Son Who had redeemed him, and in love of the Holy Ghost Who had sanctified him, and this thrice triple prayer he offered to the Three Persons through Mary in the name of her joyful and sorrowful and glorious mysteries.[10]

On each of the seven days of the week he further prayed that one of the seven gifts of the Holy Ghost[11] might descend upon his soul and drive out of it day by day the seven deadly sins which had defiled it in the past; and he prayed for each gift on its appointed day, confident that it would descend upon him, though it seemed strange to him at times that wisdom and understanding and knowledge were so distinct in their nature that each should be prayed for apart from the others. Yet he believed that at some future stage of his spiritual progress this difficulty would be removed when his sinful soul had been raised up from its weakness and enlightened by the Third Person of the Most Blessed Trinity. He believed this all the more, and with trepidation, because of the divine gloom and silence wherein dwelt the unseen Paraclete,[12] Whose symbols were a dove and a mighty wind, to sin against Whom was a sin beyond forgiveness, the eternal, mysterious secret Being to Whom, as God, the priests offered up mass once a year, robed in the scarlet of the tongues of fire.[13]

The imagery through which the nature and kinship of the Three Persons of the Trinity were darkly shadowed forth in the books of devotion which he read—the Father contemplating from all eternity as in a mirror His Divine Perfections and thereby begetting eternally the Eternal Son and the Holy Spirit proceeding out of Father and Son from all eternity—were easier of acceptance by his mind by reason of their august incomprehensibility than was the simple fact that God had loved his soul from all eternity, for ages before he had been born into the world, for ages before the world itself had existed.

He had heard the names of the passions of love and hate pronounced solemnly on the stage and in the pulpit, had found them set forth solemnly in books, and had wondered why his soul was unable to harbour them for any time or to force his lips to utter their names with conviction. A brief anger had often invested him but he had never been able to make it an abiding passion and had always felt himself passing out of it as if his very body were being divested with ease of some outer skin or peel. He had felt a subtle, dark and murmurous presence penetrate his being and fire him with a brief iniquitous lust: it too had slipped beyond his grasp leaving his mind lucid and indifferent. This, it seemed, was the only love and that the only hate his soul would harbour.

But he could no longer disbelieve in the reality of love since God Himself had loved his individual soul with divine love from all eternity. Gradually, as his soul was enriched with spiritual knowledge, he saw the whole world forming one vast symmetrical expression of God's power and love. Life became a divine gift for every moment and sensation of which, were it even the sight of a single leaf hanging on the twig of a tree, his soul should praise and thank the Giver. The world for all its solid substance and complexity no longer existed for his soul save as a theorem of divine power and love and universality. So entire and unquestionable was this sense of the divine meaning in all nature granted to his soul that he could scarcely understand why it was in any way necessary that he should continue to live. Yet that was part of the divine purpose and he dared not question its use, he above all others who had sinned so deeply and so foully against the divine purpose. Meek and abased by this consciousness of the one eternal omnipresent perfect reality his soul took up again her burden of pieties, masses and prayers and sacraments and mortifications, and only then for the first time since he had brooded on the great mystery of love did he feel within him a warm movement like that of some newly born life or virtue of the soul itself. The attitude of rapture in sacred art, the raised and parted hands, the parted lips and eyes as of one about to swoon, became for him an image of the soul in prayer, humiliated and faint before her Creator.

But he had been forewarned of the dangers of spiritual exaltation and did not allow himself to desist from even the least or lowliest devotion, striving also by constant mortification to undo the sinful past rather than to achieve a saintliness fraught with peril. Each of his senses was brought under a rigorous discipline. In order to mortify the sense of sight he made it his rule to walk in the street with downcast eyes, glancing neither to right nor left and never behind him. His eyes shunned every encounter with the eyes of women. From time to time also he balked them by a sudden effort of the will, as by lifting them suddenly in the middle of an unfinished sentence and closing the book. To mortify his hearing he exerted no control over his voice which was then breaking, neither sang nor whistled and made no attempt to flee from noises which caused him painful nervous irritation such as the sharpening of knives on the knifeboard, the gathering of cinders on the fireshovel and the twigging[14] of the carpet. To mortify his smell was more difficult as he found in himself no instinctive repugnance to bad odours, whether they were the odours of the outdoor world such as those of dung and tar or the odours of his own person among which he had made many curious comparisons and experiments. He found in the end that the only odour against which his sense of smell revolted was a certain stale fishy stink like that of longstanding urine: and whenever it was possible he subjected himself to this unpleasant odour. To mortify the taste he practised strict habits at table, observed to the letter all the fasts of the church and sought by distraction to divert his mind from the savours of different foods. But it was to the

mortification of touch that he brought the most assiduous ingenuity of inventiveness. He never consciously changed his position in bed, sat in the most uncomfortable positions, suffered
patiently every itch and pain, kept away from the fire, remained
on his knees all through the mass except at the gospels,[15] left
parts of his neck and face undried so that air might sting them
and, whenever he was not saying his beads, carried his arms
stiffly at his sides like a runner and never in his pockets or clasped
behind him.

He had no temptations to sin mortally. It surprised him however to find that at the end of his course of intricate piety and
selfrestraint he was so easily at the mercy of childish and unworthy imperfections. His prayers and fasts availed him little for
the suppression of anger at hearing his mother sneeze or at being
disturbed in his devotions. It needed an immense effort of his
will to master the impulse which urged him to give outlet to
such irritation. Images of the outbursts of trivial anger which he
had often noted among his masters, their twitching mouths,
closeshut lips and flushed cheeks, recurred to his memory, dis-
couraging him, for all his practice of humility, by the comparison. To merge his life in the common tide of other lives was
harder for him than any fasting or prayer, and it was his constant failure to do this to his own satisfaction which caused in
his soul at last a sensation of spiritual dryness together with a
growth of doubts and scruples. His soul traversed a period of
desolation in which the sacraments themselves seemed to have
turned into dried up sources. His confession became a channel
for the escape of scrupulous and unrepented imperfections. His
actual reception of the eucharist did not bring him the same dissolving moments of virginal selfsurrender as did those spiritual
communions made by him sometimes at the close of some visit
to the Blessed Sacrament.[16] The book which he used for these
visits was an old neglected book written by saint Alphonsus
Liguori,[17] with fading characters and sere foxpapered leaves. A
faded world of fervent love and virginal responses seemed to be
evoked for his soul by the reading of its pages in which the
imagery of the canticles[18] was interwoven with the communicant's prayers. An inaudible voice seemed to caress the soul,

telling her names and glories, bidding her arise as for espousal and come away, bidding her look forth, a spouse, from Amana and from the mountains of the leopards;[19] and the soul seemed to answer with the same inaudible voice, surrendering herself: *Inter ubera mea commorabitur.*[20]

This idea of surrender had a perilous attraction for his mind now that he felt his soul beset once again by the insistent voices of the flesh which began to murmur to him again during his prayers and meditations. It gave him an intense sense of power to know that he could by a single act of consent, in a moment of thought, undo all that he had done. He seemed to feel a flood slowly advancing towards his naked feet and to be waiting for the first faint timid noiseless wavelet to touch his fevered skin. Then, almost at the instant of that touch, almost at the verge of sinful consent, he found himself standing far away from the flood upon a dry shore, saved by a sudden act of the will or a sudden ejaculation: and, seeing the silver line of the flood far away and beginning again its slow advance towards his feet, a new thrill of power and satisfaction shook his soul to know that he had not yielded nor undone all.

When he had eluded the flood of temptation many times in this way he grew troubled and wondered whether the grace which he had refused to lose was not being filched from him little by little. The clear certitude of his own immunity grew dim and to it succeeded a vague fear that his soul had really fallen unawares. It was with difficulty that he won back his old consciousness of his state of grace by telling himself that he had prayed to God at every temptation and that the grace which he had prayed for must have been given to him inasmuch as God was obliged to give it. The very frequency and violence of temptations showed him at last the truth of what he had heard about the trials of the saints. Frequent and violent temptations were a proof that the citadel of the soul had not fallen and that the devil raged to make it fall.

Often when he had confessed his doubts and scruples, some momentary inattention at prayer, a movement of trivial anger in his soul or a subtle wilfulness in speech or act, he was bidden by his confessor to name some sin of his past life before absolution was given him. He named it with humility and shame and repented of it once more. It humiliated and shamed him to think that he would never be freed from it wholly, however holily he might live or whatever virtues or perfections he might attain. A restless feeling of guilt would always be present with him: he would confess and repent and be absolved, confess and repent again and be absolved again, fruitlessly. Perhaps that first hasty confession wrung from him by the fear of hell had not been good? Perhaps, concerned only for his imminent doom, he had not had sincere sorrow for his sin? But the surest sign that his confession had been good and that he had sincere sorrow for his sin was, he knew, the amendment of his life.

—I have amended my life, have I not? he asked himself.

The director stood in the embrasure of the window, his back to the light, leaning an elbow on the brown cross-blind and, as he spoke and smiled, slowly dangling and looping the cord of the other blind. Stephen stood before him, following for a moment with his eyes the waning of the long summer daylight above the roofs or the slow deft movements of the priestly fingers. The priest's face was in total shadow but the waning daylight from behind him touched the deeply grooved temples and the curves of the skull. Stephen followed also with his ears the accents and intervals of the priest's voice as he spoke gravely and cordially of indifferent themes, the vacation which had just ended, the colleges of the order abroad, the transference of masters. The grave and cordial voice went on easily with its tale, and in the pauses Stephen felt bound to set it on again with respectful questions. He knew that the tale was a prelude and his mind waited for the sequel. Ever since the message of summons had come for him from the director his mind had struggled to find the meaning of the message; and during the long restless time he had sat in the college parlour waiting for the director to come in his eyes had wandered from one sober picture to another around the walls and his mind wandered from one guess to another until the meaning of the summons had almost become clear. Then, just as he was wishing that some unforeseen cause might prevent the director from coming, he had heard the handle of the door turning and the swish of a soutane.

The director had begun to speak of the dominican and franciscan orders and of the friendship between saint Thomas and saint Bonaventure.[21] The capuchin dress, he thought, was rather too . . .

Stephen's face gave back the priest's indulgent smile and, not being anxious to give an opinion, he made a slight dubitative movement with his lips.

—I believe, continued the director, that there is some talk now among the capuchins themselves of doing away with it and following the example of the other franciscans.[22]

—I suppose they would retain it in the cloister, said Stephen.

—O, certainly, said the director. For the cloister it is all right but for the street I really think it would be better to do away with, don't you?

—It must be troublesome, I imagine?

—Of course it is, of course. Just imagine when I was in Belgium I used to see them out cycling in all kinds of weather with this thing up about their knees! It was really ridiculous. *Les jupes*,[23] they call them in Belgium.

The vowel was so modified as to be indistinct.

—What do they call them?

—*Les jupes.*

—O.

Stephen smiled again in answer to the smile which he could not see on the priest's shadowed face, its image or spectre only passing rapidly across his mind as the low discreet accent fell upon his ear. He gazed calmly before him at the waning sky, glad of the cool of the evening and the faint yellow glow which hid the tiny flame kindling upon his cheek.

The names of articles of dress worn by women or of certain soft and delicate stuffs used in their making brought always to his mind a delicate and sinful perfume. As a boy he had imagined the reins by which horses are driven as slender silken bands and it shocked him to feel at Stradbrook[24] the greasy leather of harness. It had shocked him too when he had felt for the first time beneath his tremulous fingers the brittle texture of a woman's stocking for, retaining nothing of all he read save that which seemed to him an echo or a prophecy of his own state, it was only amid softworded phrases or within rosesoft stuffs that he dared to conceive of the soul or body of a woman moving with tender life.

But the phrase on the priest's lips was disingenuous for he knew that a priest should not speak lightly on that theme. The phrase had been spoken lightly with design and he felt that his face was being searched by the eyes in the shadow. Whatever he had heard or read of the craft of jesuits he had put aside frankly as not borne out by his own experience. His masters, even when they had not attracted him, had seemed to him always intelligent and serious priests, athletic and highspirited prefects. He thought of them as men who washed their bodies briskly with cold water and wore clean cold linen. During all the years he had lived among them in Clongowes and in Belvedere he had received only two pandies and, though these had been dealt him in the wrong, he knew that he had often escaped punishment. During all those years he had never heard from any of his masters a flippant word: it was they who had taught him christian doctrine and urged him to live a good life and, when he had fallen into grievous sin, it was they who had led him back to grace. Their presence had made him diffident of himself when he was a muff[25] in Clongowes and it had made him diffident of himself also while he had held his equivocal position[26] in Belvedere. A constant sense of this had remained with him up to the last year of his school life. He had never once disobeyed or allowed turbulent companions to seduce him from his habit of quiet obedience: and, even when he doubted some statement of a master, he had never presumed to doubt openly. Lately some of their judgments had sounded a little childish in his ears and had made him feel a regret and pity as though he were slowly passing out of an accustomed world and were hearing its language for the last time. One day when some boys had gathered round a priest under the shed near the chapel, he had heard the priest say:

—I believe that Lord Macaulay[27] was a man who probably

never committed a mortal sin in his life, that is to say, a deliberate mortal sin.

Some of the boys had then asked the priest if Victor Hugo[28] were not the greatest French writer. The priest had answered that Victor Hugo had never written half so well when he had turned against the church as he had written when he was a catholic.

—But there are many eminent French critics, said the priest, who consider that even Victor Hugo, great as he certainly was, had not so pure a French style as Louis Veuillot.[29]

The tiny flame which the priest's allusion had kindled upon Stephen's cheek had sunk down again and his eyes were still fixed calmly on the colourless sky. But an unresting doubt flew hither and thither before his mind. Masked memories passed quickly before him: he recognised scenes and persons yet he was conscious that he had failed to perceive some vital circumstance in them. He saw himself walking about the grounds watching the sports in Clongowes and eating slim jim[30] out of his cricketcap. Some jesuits were walking round the cycletrack in the company of ladies. The echoes of certain expressions used in Clongowes sounded in remote caves of his mind.

His ears were listening to these distant echoes amid the silence of the parlour when he became aware that the priest was addressing him in a different voice.

—I sent for you today, Stephen, because I wished to speak to you on a very important subject.

—Yes, sir.

—Have you ever felt that you had a vocation?

Stephen parted his lips to answer yes and then withheld the word suddenly. The priest waited for the answer and added:

—I mean have you ever felt within yourself, in your soul, a desire to join the order. Think.

—I have sometimes thought of it, said Stephen.

The priest let the blindcord fall to one side and, uniting his hands, leaned his chin gravely upon them, communing with himself.

—In a college like this, he said at length, there is one boy or perhaps two or three boys whom God calls to the religious life.

Such a boy is marked off from his companions by his piety, by the good example he shows to others. He is looked up to by them; he is chosen perhaps as prefect by his fellow sodalists. And you, Stephen, have been such a boy in this college, prefect of Our Blessed Lady's sodality. Perhaps you are the boy in this college whom God designs to call to Himself.

A strong note of pride reinforcing the gravity of the priest's voice made Stephen's heart quicken in response.

—To receive that call, Stephen, said the priest, is the greatest honour that the Almighty God can bestow upon a man. No king or emperor on this earth has the power of the priest of God. No angel or archangel in heaven, no saint, not even the Blessed Virgin herself has the power of a priest of God: the power of the keys, the power to bind and to loose from sin,[31] the power of exorcism, the power to cast out from the creatures of God the evil spirits that have power over them, the power, the authority, to make the great God of Heaven come down upon the altar and take the form of bread and wine. What an awful power, Stephen!

A flame began to flutter again on Stephen's cheek as he heard in this proud address an echo of his own proud musings. How often had he seen himself as a priest wielding calmly and humbly the awful power of which angels and saints stood in reverence! His soul had loved to muse in secret on this desire. He had seen himself, a young and silentmannered priest, entering a confessional swiftly, ascending the altarsteps, incensing, genuflecting, accomplishing the vague acts of the priesthood which pleased him by reason of their semblance of reality and of their distance from it. In that dim life which he had lived through in his musings he had assumed the voices and gestures which he had noted with various priests. He had bent his knee sideways like such a one, he had shaken the thurible[32] only slightly like such a one, his chasuble[33] had swung open like that of such another as he had turned to the altar again after having blessed the people. And above all it had pleased him to fill the second place in those dim scenes of his imagining. He shrank from the dignity of celebrant because it displeased him to imagine that all the vague pomp should end in his own person or that the ritual should assign to him so clear and final an office. He longed for the minor sacred offices, to be vested with the tunicle of subdeacon[34] at high mass, to stand aloof from the altar, forgotten by the people, his shoulders covered with a humeral veil,[35] holding the paten[36] within its folds, or, when the sacrifice had been accomplished, to stand as deacon in a dalmatic of cloth of gold[37] on the step below the celebrant, his hands joined and his face towards the people, and sing the chant *Ite, missa est.*[38] If ever he had seen himself celebrant it was as in the pictures of the mass in his child's massbook, in a church without worshippers, save for the angel of the sacrifice, at a bare altar and served by an acolyte scarcely more boyish than himself. In vague sacrificial or sacramental acts alone his will seemed drawn to go forth to encounter reality: and it was partly the absence of an appointed rite which had always constrained him to inaction whether he had allowed silence to cover his anger or pride or had suffered only an embrace he longed to give.

He listened in reverent silence now to the priest's appeal and through the words he heard even more distinctly a voice bidding him approach, offering him secret knowledge and secret power. He would know then what was the sin of Simon Magus and what the sin against the Holy Ghost for which there was no forgiveness.[39] He would know obscure things, hidden from others, from those who were conceived and born children of wrath. He would know the sins, the sinful longings and sinful thoughts and sinful acts, of others, hearing them murmured into his ears in the confessional under the shame of a darkened chapel by the lips of women and of girls: but rendered immune mysteriously at his ordination by the imposition of hands his soul would pass again uncontaminated to the white peace of the altar. No touch of sin would linger upon the hands with which he would elevate and break the host; no touch of sin would linger on his lips in prayer to make him eat and drink damnation to himself, not discerning the body of the Lord.[40] He would hold his secret knowledge and secret power, being as sinless as the innocent: and he would be a priest for ever according to the order of Melchisedec.[41]

—I will offer up my mass tomorrow morning, said the director, that Almighty God may reveal to you His holy will. And let you, Stephen, make a novena to your holy patron saint, the first martyr,[42] who is very powerful with God, that God may enlighten your mind. But you must be quite sure, Stephen, that you have a vocation because it would be terrible if you found afterwards that you had none. Once a priest always a priest, remember. Your catechism tells you that the sacrament of Holy Orders is one of those which can be received only once because it imprints on the soul an indelible spiritual mark which can never be effaced. It is before you must weigh well, not after. It is a solemn question, Stephen, because on it may depend the salvation of your eternal soul. But we will pray to God together.

He held open the heavy hall door and gave his hand as if already to a companion in the spiritual life. Stephen passed out on to the wide platform above the steps and was conscious of the caress of mild evening air. Towards Findlater's church[43] a quarter of young men were striding along with linked arms, swaying their heads and stepping to the agile melody of their leader's concertina. The music passed in an instant, as the first bars of sudden music always did, over the fantastic fabrics of his mind, dissolving them painlessly and noiselessly as a sudden wave dissolves the sandbuilt turrets of children. Smiling at the trivial air he raised his eyes to the priest's face and, seeing in it a mirthless reflection of the sunken day, detached his hand slowly which had acquiesced faintly in that companionship.

As he descended the steps the impression which effaced his troubled selfcommunion was that of a mirthless mask reflecting a sunken day from the threshold of the college. The shadow, then, of the life of the college passed gravely over his consciousness. It was a grave and ordered and passionless life that awaited him, a life without material cares. He wondered how he would pass the first night in the novitiate and with what dismay he would wake the first morning in the dormitory. The troubling odour of the long corridors of Clongowes came back to him and he heard the discreet murmur of the burning gasflames. At once from every part of his being unrest began to irradiate. A feverish quickening of his pulses followed and a din of meaningless words drove his reasoned thoughts hither and thither confusedly. His lungs dilated and sank as if he were inhaling a warm moist unsustaining air and he smelt again the warm moist air which hung in the bath in Clongowes above the sluggish turfcoloured water.

Some instinct, waking at these memories, stronger than education or piety, quickened within him at every near approach to that life, an instinct subtle and hostile, and armed him against acquiescence. The chill and order of the life repelled him. He saw himself rising in the cold of the morning and filing down with the others to early mass and trying vainly to struggle with his prayers against the fainting sickness of his stomach.[44] He saw himself sitting at dinner with the community of a college. What, then, had become of that deeprooted shyness of his which had made him loth to eat or drink under a strange roof? What had come of the pride of his spirit which had always made him conceive himself as a being apart in every order?

The Reverend Stephen Dedalus, S. J.[45]

His name in that new life leaped into characters before his eyes and to it there followed a mental sensation of an undefined face or colour of a face. The colour faded and became strong like a changing glow of pallid brick red. Was it the raw reddish glow he had so often seen on wintry mornings on the shaven gills of the priests? The face was eyeless and sourfavoured and devout, shot with pink tinges of suffocated anger. Was it not a mental spectre of the face of one of the jesuits whom some of the boys called Lantern Jaws and others Foxy Campbell?

He was passing at that moment before the jesuit house in Gardiner Street,[46] and wondered vaguely which window would be his if he ever joined the order. Then he wondered at the vagueness of his wonder, at the remoteness of his soul from what he had hitherto imagined her sanctuary, at the frail hold which so many years of order and obedience had of him when once a definite and irrevocable act of his threatened to end for ever, in time and in eternity, his freedom. The voice of the director urging upon him the proud claims of the church and the mystery and power of the priestly office repeated itself idly in his memory. His soul was not there to hear and greet it and he knew now that the exhortation he had listened to had already fallen into an idle formal tale. He would never swing the thurible before the tabernacle as priest. His destiny was to be elusive of social or religious orders. The wisdom of the priest's appeal did not touch him to the quick. He was destined to learn his own wisdom apart from others or to learn the wisdom of others himself wandering among the snares of the world.

The snares of the world were its ways of sin. He would fall. He had not yet fallen but he would fall silently, in an instant. Not to fall was too hard, too hard: and he felt the silent lapse of his soul, as it would be at some instant to come, falling, falling but not yet fallen, still unfallen but about to fall.

He crossed the bridge over the stream of the Tolka[47] and turned his eyes coldly for an instant towards the faded blue shrine of the Blessed Virgin which stood fowlwise on a pole in the middle of a hamshaped encampment of poor cottages. Then, bending to the left, he followed the lane which led up to his house. The faint sour stink of rotted cabbages came towards him from the kitchengardens on the rising ground above the river. He smiled to think that it was this disorder, the misrule and confusion of his father's house and the stagnation of vegetable life, which was to win the day in his soul. Then a short laugh broke from his lips as he thought of that solitary farm-hand in the kitchengardens behind their house whom they had nicknamed the man with the hat. A second laugh, taking rise from the first after a pause, broke from him involuntarily as he thought of how the man with the hat worked, considering in turn the four points of the sky and then regretfully plunging his spade in the earth.

He pushed open the latchless door of the porch and passed through the naked hallway into the kitchen. A group of his brothers and sisters was sitting round the table. Tea was nearly over and only the last of the second watered[48] tea remained in the bottoms of the small glass-jars and jampots which did service for teacups. Discarded crusts and lumps of sugared bread, turned brown by the tea which had been poured over them, lay scattered on the table. Little wells of tea lay here and there on the board and a knife with a broken ivory handle was stuck through the pith of a ravaged turnover.

The sad quiet greyblue glow of the dying day came through the window and the open door, covering over and allaying quietly a sudden instinct of remorse in Stephen's heart. All that had been denied them had been freely given to him, the eldest: but the quiet glow of evening showed him in their faces no sign of rancour.

He sat near them at the table and asked where his father and mother were. One answered:

—Goneboro toboro lookboro atboro aboro houseboro.

Still another removal! A boy named Fallon in Belvedere had often asked him with a silly laugh why they moved so often. A frown of scorn darkened quickly his forehead as he heard again the silly laugh of the questioner.

He asked:

—Why are we on the move again, if it's a fair question?

The same sister answered:

—Becauseboro theboro landboro lordboro willboro putboro usboro outboro.

The voice of his youngest brother from the farther side of the fireplace began to sing the air *Oft in the Stilly Night*.⁴⁹ One by one the others took up the air until a full choir of voices was singing. They would sing so for hours, melody after melody, glee after glee, till the last pale light died down on the horizon, till the first dark nightclouds came forth and night fell.

He waited for some moments, listening, before he too took up the air with them. He was listening with pain of spirit to the overtone of weariness behind their frail fresh innocent voices. Even before they set out on life's journey they seemed weary already of the way.

He heard the choir of voices in the kitchen echoed and multiplied through an endless reverberation of the choirs of endless generations of children: and heard in all the echoes an echo also of the recurring note of weariness and pain. All seemed weary of life even before entering upon it. And he remembered that Newman had heard this note also in the broken lines of Virgil *giving utterance, like the voice of Nature herself, to that pain and weariness yet hope of better things which has been the experience of her children in every time.*[50]

He could wait no longer.

From the door of Byron's publichouse to the gate of Clontarf Chapel,[51] from the gate of Clontarf Chapel to the door of Byron's publichouse and then back again to the chapel and then back again to the publichouse he had paced slowly at first, planting his steps scrupulously in the spaces of the patchwork of the footpath, then timing their fall to the fall of verses. A full hour had passed since his father had gone in with Dan Crosby, the tutor, to find out for him something about the university.[52] For a full hour he had paced up and down, waiting: but he could wait no longer.

He set off abruptly for the Bull,[53] walking rapidly lest his father's shrill whistle might call him back; and in a few moments he had rounded the curve at the police barrack and was safe.

Yes, his mother was hostile to the idea, as he had read from her listless silence. Yet her mistrust pricked him more keenly than his father's pride and he thought coldly how he had watched the faith which was fading down in his soul aging and strengthening in her eyes. A dim antagonism gathered force within him and darkened his mind as a cloud against her disloyalty: and when it passed, cloudlike, leaving his mind serene and dutiful towards her again, he was made aware dimly and without regret of a first noiseless sundering of their lives.

The university! So he had passed beyond the challenge of the sentries who had stood as guardians of his boyhood and had sought to keep him among them that he might be subject to them and serve their ends. Pride after satisfaction uplifted him like long slow waves. The end he had been born to serve yet did not see had led him to escape by an unseen path: and now it beckoned to him once more and a new adventure was about to be opened to him. It seemed to him that he heard notes of fitful music leaping upwards a tone and downwards a diminished fourth, upwards a tone and downwards a major third, like triple-branching flames leaping fitfully, flame after flame, out of a midnight wood. It was an elfin prelude, endless and formless; and, as it grew wilder and faster, the flames leaping out of time, he seemed to hear from under the boughs and grasses wild creatures racing, their feet pattering like rain upon the leaves. Their feet passed in pattering tumult over his mind, the feet of hares and rabbits, the feet of harts and hinds and antelopes, until he heard them no more and remembered only a proud cadence from Newman: *Whose feet are as the feet of harts and underneath the everlasting arms.*[54]

The pride of that dim image brought back to his mind the dignity of the office he had refused. All through his boyhood he had mused upon that which he had so often thought to be his destiny and when the moment had come for him to obey the call he had turned aside, obeying a wayward instinct. Now time lay between: the oils of ordination would never anoint his body. He had refused. Why?

He turned seaward from the road at Dollymount[55] and as he passed on to the thin wooden bridge he felt the planks shaking with the tramp of heavily shod feet. A squad of christian brothers[56] was on its way back from the Bull and had begun to pass, two by two, across the bridge. Soon the whole bridge was trembling and resounding. The uncouth faces passed him two by two, stained yellow or red or livid by the sea, and as he strove to look at them with ease and indifference, a faint stain of personal shame and commiseration rose to his own face. Angry with himself he tried to hide his face from their eyes by gazing down sideways into the shallow swirling water under the bridge but he still saw a reflection therein of their topheavy silk hats, and humble tapelike collars and loosely hanging clerical clothes.

—Brother Hickey.

Brother Quaid.

Brother MacArdle.

Brother Keogh.

Their piety would be like their names, like their faces, like their clothes, and it was idle for him to tell himself that their humble and contrite hearts, it might be, paid a far richer tribute of devotion than his had ever been, a gift tenfold more acceptable than his elaborate adoration. It was idle for him to move himself to be generous towards them, to tell himself that if he ever came to their gates, stripped of his pride, beaten and in beggar's weeds, that they would be generous towards him, loving him as themselves. Idle and embittering, finally, to argue, against his own dispassionate certitude, that the commandment of love bade us not to love our neighbour as ourselves with the same amount and intensity of love but to love him as ourselves with the same kind of love.

He drew forth a phrase from his treasure and spoke it softly to himself:

—A day of dappled seaborne clouds.[57]

The phrase and the day and the scene harmonised in a chord. Words. Was it their colours? He allowed them to glow and fade, hue after hue: sunrise gold, the russet and green of apple orchards, azure of waves, the greyfringed fleece of clouds. No, it was not their colours: it was the poise and balance of the period itself. Did he then love the rhythmic rise and fall of words better than their associations of legend and colour? Or was it that, being as weak of sight as he was shy of mind, he drew less pleasure from the reflection of the glowing sensible world through the prism of a language manycoloured and richly storied than from the contemplation of an inner world of individual emotions mirrored perfectly in a lucid supple periodic prose?

He passed from the trembling bridge on to firm land again. At that instant, as it seemed to him, the air was chilled and looking askance towards the water he saw a flying squall darkening and crisping suddenly the tide. A faint click at his heart, a faint throb in his throat told him once more of how his flesh dreaded the cold infrahuman odour of the sea: yet he did not strike across the downs on his left but held straight on along the spine of rocks that pointed against the river's mouth.

A veiled sunlight lit up faintly the grey sheet of water where the river was embayed. In the distance along the course of the slowflowing Liffey slender masts flecked the sky and, more distant still, the dim fabric of the city lay prone in haze. Like a scene on some vague arras, old as man's weariness, the image of the seventh city of christendom[58] was visible to him across the timeless air, no older nor more weary nor less patient of subjection than in the days of the thingmote.[59]

Disheartened, he raised his eyes towards the slowdrifting clouds, dappled and seaborne. They were voyaging across the deserts of the sky, a host of nomads on the march, voyaging high over Ireland, westward bound. The Europe they had come from lay out there beyond the Irish Sea, Europe of strange tongues and valleyed and woodbegirt and citadelled and of entrenched and marshalled races. He heard a confused music within him as of memories and names which he was almost conscious of but could not capture even for an instant; then the music seemed to recede, to recede, to recede: and from each receding trail of nebulous music there fell always one longdrawn calling note, piercing like a star the dusk of silence. Again! Again! Again! A voice from beyond the world was calling.

—Hello, Stephanos!

—Here comes The Dedalus!

—Ao! . . . Eh, give it over, Dwyer, I'm telling you or I'll give you a stuff in the kisser for yourself.[60] . . . Ao!

—Good man, Towser! Duck him!

—Come along, Dedalus! Bous Stephanoumenos! Bous Stephaneforos![61]

—Duck him! Guzzle him now, Towser!

—Help! Help! . . . Ao!

He recognised their speech collectively before he distinguished their faces. The mere sight of that medley of wet nakedness chilled him to the bone. Their bodies, corpsewhite or suffused with a pallid golden light or rawly tanned by the sun, gleamed with the wet of the sea. Their divingstone, poised on its rude supports and rocking under their plunges, and the roughhewn stones of the sloping breakwater over which they scrambled in their horseplay, gleamed with cold wet lustre. The towels with which they smacked their bodies were heavy with cold seawater: and drenched with cold brine was their matted hair.

He stood still in deference to their calls and parried their banter with easy words. How characterless they looked: Shuley without his deep unbuttoned collar, Ennis without his scarlet belt with the snaky clasp, and Connolly without his Norfolk coat with the flapless side-pockets! It was a pain to see them and a swordlike pain to see the signs of adolescence that made repellent their pitiable nakedness. Perhaps they had taken refuge in number and noise from the secret dread in their souls. But he, apart from them and in silence, remembered in what dread he stood of the mystery of his own body.

—Stephanos Dedalos! Bous Stephanoumenos! Bous Stephaneforos!

Their banter was not new to him and now it flattered his mild proud sovereignty. Now, as never before, his strange name seemed to him a prophecy. So timeless seemed the grey warm air, so fluid and impersonal his own mood, that all ages were as one to him. A moment before the ghost of the ancient kingdom of the Danes had looked forth through the vesture of the haze-wrapped city. Now, at the name of the fabulous artificer,[62] he seemed to hear the noise of dim waves and to see a winged form flying above the waves and slowly climbing the air. What did it mean? Was it a quaint device opening a page of some medieval book of prophecies and symbols, a hawklike man flying sunward above the sea, a prophecy of the end he had been born to serve and had been following through the mists of childhood and boyhood, a symbol of the artist forging anew in his workshop out of the sluggish matter of the earth a new soaring impalpable imperishable being?

His heart trembled; his breath came faster and a wild spirit passed over his limbs as though he were soaring sunward. His heart trembled in an ecstasy of fear and his soul was in flight. His soul was soaring in an air beyond the world and the body he knew was purified in a breath and delivered of incertitude and made radiant and commingled with the element of the spirit. An ecstasy of flight made radiant his eyes and wild his breath and tremulous and wild and radiant his windswept limbs.

—One! Two! . . . Look out!

—O, cripes, I'm drownded!

—One! Two! Three and away!

—Me next! Me next!

—One! . . . Uk!

—Stephaneforos!

His throat ached with a desire to cry aloud, the cry of a hawk or eagle on high, to cry piercingly of his deliverance to the winds. This was the call of life to his soul not the dull gross voice of the world of duties and despair, not the inhuman voice that had called him to the pale service of the altar. An instant of wild flight had delivered him and the cry of triumph which his lips withheld cleft his brain.

—Stephaneforos!

What were they now but cerements shaken from the body of death—the fear he had walked in night and day, the incertitude that had ringed him round, the shame that had abased him within and without—cerements, the linens of the grave?

His soul had arisen from the grave of boyhood, spurning her graveclothes. Yes! Yes! Yes! He would create proudly out of the freedom and power of his soul, as the great artificer whose name he bore, a living thing, new and soaring and beautiful, impalpable, imperishable.

He started up nervously from the stoneblock for he could no longer quench the flame in his blood. He felt his cheeks aflame and his throat throbbing with song. There was a lust of wandering in his feet that burned to set out for the ends of the earth. On! On! his heart seemed to cry. Evening would deepen above the sea, night fall upon the plains, dawn glimmer before the wanderer and show him strange fields and hills and faces. Where?

He looked northward towards Howth.[63] The sea had fallen below the line of seawrack on the shallow side of the breakwater and already the tide was running out fast along the foreshore. Already one long oval bank of sand lay warm and dry amid the wavelets. Here and there warm isles of sand gleamed above the shallow tide, and about the isles and around the long bank and amid the shallow currents of the beach were lightclad gayclad figures, wading and delving.

In a few moments he was barefoot, his stockings folded in his pockets and his canvas shoes dangling by their knotted laces over his shoulders: and, picking a pointed salteaten stick out of the jetsam among the rocks, he clambered down the slope of the breakwater.

There was a long rivulet in the strand: and, as he waded slowly up its course, he wondered at the endless drift of seaweed. Emerald and black and russet and olive, it moved beneath the current, swaying and turning. The water of the rivulet was dark with endless drift and mirrored the highdrifting clouds. The clouds were drifting above him silently and silently the seatangle was drifting below him; and the grey warm air was still: and a new wild life was singing in his veins.

Where was his boyhood now? Where was the soul that had hung back from her destiny, to brood alone upon the shame of her wounds and in her house of squalor and subterfuge to queen it in faded cerements and in wreaths that withered at the touch? Or where was he?

He was alone. He was unheeded, happy and near to the wild heart of life. He was alone and young and wilful and wild-hearted, alone amid a waste of wild air and brackish waters and the seaharvest of shells and tangle and veiled grey sunlight and gayclad lightclad figures, of children and girls and voices childish and girlish in the air.

A girl stood before him in midstream, alone and still, gazing out to sea. She seemed like one whom magic had changed into the likeness of a strange and beautiful seabird. Her long slender bare legs were delicate as a crane's and pure save where an emerald trail of seaweed had fashioned itself as a sign upon the flesh. Her thighs, fuller and softhued as ivory, were bared almost to the hips where the white fringes of her drawers were like featherings of soft white down. Her slateblue skirts were kilted boldly about her waist and dovetailed behind her. Her bosom was as a bird's soft and slight, slight and soft as the breast of some darkplumaged dove. But her long fair hair was girlish: and girlish, and touched with the wonder of mortal beauty, her face.

She was alone and still, gazing out to sea; and when she felt his presence and the worship of his eyes her eyes turned to him in quiet sufferance of his gaze, without shame or wantonness. Long, long she suffered his gaze and then quietly withdrew her eyes from his and bent them towards the stream, gently stirring the water with her foot hither and thither. The first faint noise of gently moving water broke the silence, low and faint and whispering, faint as the bells of sleep; hither and thither, hither and thither: and a faint flame trembled on her cheek.

—Heavenly God! cried Stephen's soul, in an outburst of profane joy.

He turned away from her suddenly and set off across the strand. His cheeks were aflame; his body was aglow; his limbs were trembling. On and on and on and on he strode, far out over the sands, singing wildly to the sea, crying to greet the advent of the life that had cried to him.

Her image had passed into his soul for ever and no word had broken the holy silence of his ecstasy. Her eyes had called him and his soul had leaped at the call. To live, to err, to fall, to triumph, to recreate life out of life! A wild angel had appeared to him, the angel of mortal youth and beauty, an envoy from the fair courts of life, to throw open before him in an instant of ecstasy the gates of all the ways of error and glory. On and on and on and on!

He halted suddenly and heard his heart in the silence. How far had he walked? What hour was it?

There was no human figure near him nor any sound borne to him over the air. But the tide was near the turn and already the day was on the wane. He turned landward and ran towards the shore and, running up the sloping beach, reckless of the sharp shingle, found a sandy nook amid a ring of tufted sandknolls and lay down there that the peace and silence of the evening might still the riot of his blood.

He felt above him the vast indifferent dome and the calm processes of the heavenly bodies; and the earth beneath him, the earth that had borne him, had taken him to her breast.

He closed his eyes in the languor of sleep. His eyelids trembled as if they felt the vast cyclic movement of the earth and her watchers, trembled as if they felt the strange light of some new world. His soul was swooning into some new world, fantastic, dim, uncertain as under sea, traversed by cloudy shapes and beings. A world, a glimmer, or a flower? Glimmering and trembling, trembling and unfolding, a breaking light, an opening flower, it spread in endless succession to itself, breaking in full

crimson and unfolding and fading to palest rose, leaf by leaf
and wave of light by wave of light, flooding all the heavens with
its soft flushes, every flush deeper than the other.

Evening had fallen when he woke and the sand and arid
grasses of his bed glowed no longer. He rose slowly and, recall-
ing the rapture of his sleep, sighed at its joy.

He climbed to the crest of the sandhill and gazed about him.
Evening had fallen. A rim of the young moon cleft the pale waste
of sky like the rim of a silver hoop embedded in grey sand; and
the tide was flowing in fast to the land with a low whisper of her
waves, islanding a few last figures in distant pools.

V

He drained his third cup of watery tea to the dregs and set to chewing the crusts of fried bread that were scattered near him, staring into the dark pool of the jar. The yellow dripping had been scooped out like a boghole and the pool under it brought back to his memory the dark turfcoloured water of the bath in Clongowes. The box of pawntickets at his elbow had just been rifled and he took up idly one after another in his greasy fingers the blue and white dockets, scrawled and sanded and creased and bearing the name of the pledger as Daly or MacEvoy.[1]

1 Pair Buskins.
1 D. Coat.
3 Articles and White.
1 Man's Pants.

Then he put them aside and gazed thoughtfully at the lid of the box, speckled with lousemarks, and asked vaguely:

—How much is the clock fast now?

His mother straightened the battered alarmclock that was lying on its side in the middle of the kitchen mantelpiece until its dial showed a quarter to twelve and then laid it once more on its side.

—An hour and twentyfive minutes, she said. The right time now is twenty past ten. The dear knows[2] you might try to be in time for your lectures.

—Fill out the place for me to wash, said Stephen.

—Katey, fill out the place for Stephen to wash.

—Boody, fill out the place for Stephen to wash.

—I can't, I'm going for blue.[3] Fill it out, you, Maggie.

When the enamelled basin had been fitted into the well of the sink and the old washingglove flung on the side of it he allowed his mother to scrub his neck and root into the folds of his ears and into the interstices at the wings of his nose.

—Well, it's a poor case, she said, when a university student is so dirty that his mother has to wash him.

—But it gives you pleasure, said Stephen calmly.

An earsplitting whistle was heard from upstairs and his mother thrust a damp overall into his hands, saying:

—Dry yourself and hurry out for the love of goodness.

A second shrill whistle, prolonged angrily, brought one of the girls to the foot of the staircase.

—Yes, father?

—Is your lazy bitch of a brother gone out yet?

—Yes, father.

—Sure?

—Yes, father.

—Hm!

The girl came back making signs to him to be quick and go out quietly by the back. Stephen laughed and said:

—He has a curious idea of genders if he thinks a bitch is masculine.

—Ah, it's a scandalous shame for you, Stephen, said his mother, and you'll live to rue the day you set your foot in that place. I know how it has changed you.

—Good morning, everybody, said Stephen, smiling and kissing the tips of his fingers in adieu.

The lane behind the terrace was waterlogged and as he went down it slowly, choosing his steps amid heaps of wet rubbish, he heard a mad nun screeching in the nuns' madhouse beyond the wall.[4]

—Jesus! O Jesus! Jesus!

He shook the sound out of his ears by an angry toss of his head and hurried on, stumbling through the mouldering offal, his heart already bitten by an ache of loathing and bitterness. His father's whistle, his mother's mutterings, the screech of an unseen maniac were to him now so many voices offending and threatening to humble the pride of his youth. He drove their echoes even out of his heart with an execration: but, as he walked down the avenue and felt the grey morning light falling about him through the dripping trees and smelt the strange wild smell of the wet leaves and bark, his soul was loosed of her miseries.

The rainladen trees of the avenue evoked in him, as always, memories of the girls and women in the plays of Gerhart Hauptmann;[5] and the memory of their pale sorrows and the fragrance falling from the wet branches mingled in a mood of quiet joy. His morning walk across the city had begun, and he foreknew that as he passed the sloblands of Fairview[6] he would think of the cloistral silverveined prose of Newman,[7] that as he walked along the North Strand Road, glancing idly at the windows of the provision shops, he would recall the dark humour of Guido Cavalcanti[8] and smile, that as he went by Baird's stonecutting works in Talbot Place the spirit of Ibsen[9] would blow through him like a keen wind, a spirit of wayward boyish beauty, and that passing a grimy marinedealer's shop beyond the Liffey he would repeat the song by Ben Jonson which begins:

I was not wearier where I lay.[10]

His mind, when wearied of its search for the essence of beauty amid the spectral words of Aristotle or Aquinas, turned often for its pleasure to the dainty songs of the Elizabethans. His mind, in the vesture of a doubting monk, stood often in shadow under the windows of that age, to hear the grave and mocking music of the lutenists or the frank laughter of waistcoateers[11] until a laugh too low, a phrase, tarnished by time, of chambering[12] and false honour, stung his monkish pride and drove him on from his lurkingplace.

The lore which he was believed to pass his days brooding upon so that it had rapt him from the companionships of youth was only a garner of slender sentences from Aristotle's poetics and psychology[13] and a *Synopsis Philosophiæ Scholasticæ ad mentem divi Thomæ.*[14] His thinking was a dusk of doubt and selfmistrust lit up at moments by the lightnings of intuition, but lightnings of so clear a splendour that in those moments the world perished about his feet as if it had been fireconsumed: and thereafter his tongue grew heavy and he met the eyes of others with unanswering eyes for he felt that the spirit of beauty had folded him round like a mantle and that in revery at least he had been acquainted with nobility. But, when this brief pride of silence upheld him no longer, he was glad to find himself still in the midst of common lives, passing on his way amid the squalor and noise and sloth of the city fearlessly and with a light heart.

Near the hoardings on the canal he met the consumptive man with the doll's face and the brimless hat coming towards him down the slope of the bridge with little steps, tightly buttoned into his chocolate overcoat, and holding his furled umbrella a span or two from him like a diviningrod. It must be eleven, he thought, and peered into a dairy to see the time. The clock in the dairy told him that it was five minutes to five but, as he turned away, he heard a clock somewhere near him, but unseen, beating eleven strokes in swift precision. He laughed as he heard it for it made him think of MacCann[15] and he saw him a squat figure in a shooting jacket and breeches and with a fair goatee, standing in the wind at Hopkins' corner,[16] and heard him say:

—Dedalus, you're an antisocial being, wrapped up in yourself. I'm not. I'm a democrat: and I'll work and act for social liberty and equality among all classes and sexes in the United States of the Europe of the future.[17]

Eleven! Then he was late for that lecture too. What day of the week was it? He stopped at a newsagent's to read the headline of a placard. Thursday. Ten to eleven, English; eleven to twelve, French; twelve to one, physics. He fancied to himself the English lecture and felt, even at that distance, reckless and helpless. He saw the heads of his classmates meekly bent as they wrote in their notebooks the points they were bidden to note, nominal definitions, essential definitions[18] and examples or dates of birth or death, chief works, a favourable and an unfavourable criticism side by side. His own head was unbent for his thoughts wandered abroad and whether he looked around the little class of students or out of the window across the desolate gardens of the green an odour assailed him of cheerless cellardamp and decay. Another head than his, right before him in the first benches, was poised squarely above its bending fellows like the head of a priest appealing without humility to the tabernacle for the humble worshippers about him. Why was it that when he thought of Cranly he could never raise before his mind the entire image of his body but only the image of the head and face? Even now against the grey curtain of the morning he saw it before him like the phantom of a dream, the face of a severed head or deathmask, crowned on the brows by its stiff black upright hair as by an iron crown. It was a priestlike face, priestlike in its pallor, in the widewinged nose, in the shadowings below the eyes and along the jaws, priestlike in the lips that were long and bloodless and faintly smiling: and Stephen, remembering swiftly how he had told Cranly of all the tumults and unrest and longings in his soul, day after day and night by night, only to be answered by his friend's listening silence, would have told himself that it was the face of a guilty priest who heard confessions of those whom he had not power to absolve but that he felt again in memory the gaze of its dark womanish eyes.

Through this image he had a glimpse of a strange dark cavern of speculation but at once turned away from it, feeling that it was not yet the hour to enter it. But the nightshade of his friend's listlessness seemed to be diffusing in the air around him a tenuous and deadly exhalation and he found himself glancing from one casual word to another on his right or left in stolid wonder that they had been so silently emptied of instantaneous sense until every mean shop legend bound his mind like the words of a spell and his soul shrivelled up, sighing with age as he walked on in a lane among heaps of dead language. His own consciousness of language was ebbing from his brain and trickling into the very words themselves which set to band and disband themselves in wayward rhythms:

> *The ivy whines upon the wall*
> *And whines and twines upon the wall*
> *The ivy whines upon the wall*
> *The yellow ivy on the wall*
> *Ivy, ivy up the wall.*

Did any one ever hear such drivel? Lord Almighty! Who ever heard of ivy whining on a wall? Yellow ivy: that was all right. Yellow ivory also. And what about ivory ivy?

The word now shone in his brain, clearer and brighter than
any ivory sawn from the mottled tusks of elephants. *Ivory,
ivoire, avorio, ebur.*[19] One of the first examples that he had
learnt in Latin had run: *India mittit ebur;*[20] and he recalled the
shrewd northern face of the rector who had taught him to con-
strue the Metamorphoses of Ovid[21] in a courtly English, made
whimsical by the mention of porkers and potsherds and chines
of bacon. He had learnt what little he knew of the laws of
Latin verse from a ragged book written by a Portuguese priest.

Contrahit orator, variant in carmine vates.[22]

The crises and victories and secessions in Roman history were
handed on to him in the trite words *in tanto discrimine*[23] and
he had tried to peer into the social life of the city of cities
through the words *implere ollam denariorum* which the rector
had rendered sonorously as the filling of a pot with denaries.[24]
The pages of his timeworn Horace[25] never felt cold to the touch
even when his own fingers were cold: they were human pages:
and fifty years before they had been turned by the human fingers of John Duncan Inverarity and by his brother, William
Malcolm Inverarity. Yes, those were noble names on the dusky
flyleaf and, even for so poor a Latinist as he, the dusky verses
were as fragrant as though they had lain all those years in myr-
tle and lavender and vervain; but yet it wounded him to think
that he would never be but a shy guest at the feast of the world's
culture and that the monkish learning, in terms of which he
was striving to forge out an esthetic philosophy, was held no
higher by the age he lived in than the subtle and curious jar-
gons of heraldry and falconry.

The grey block of Trinity on his left,[26] set heavily in the city's
ignorance like a great dull stone set in a cumbrous ring, pulled
his mind downward; and while he was striving this way and
that to free his feet from the fetters of the reformed conscience
he came upon the droll statue of the national poet of Ireland.

He looked at it without anger: for, though sloth of the body
and of the soul crept over it like unseen vermin, over the shuffling feet and up the folds of the cloak and around the servile

head, it seemed humbly conscious of its indignity. It was a Firbolg in the borrowed cloak of a Milesian:[27] and he thought of his friend Davin,[28] the peasant student. It was a jesting name between them but the young peasant bore with it lightly saying:

—Go on, Stevie, I have a hard head, you tell me. Call me what you will.

The homely version of his christian name on the lips of his friend had touched Stephen pleasantly when first heard for he was as formal in speech with others as they were with him. Often, as he sat in Davin's rooms in Grantham Street,[29] wondering at his friend's wellmade boots that flanked the wall pair by pair and repeating for his friend's simple ear the verses and cadences of others which were the veils of his own longing and dejection, the rude Firbolg mind of his listener had drawn his mind towards it and flung it back again, drawing it by a quiet inbred courtesy of attention or by a quaint turn of old English speech or by the force of its delight in rude bodily skill—for Davin had sat at the feet of Michael Cusack, the Gael[30]—repelling swiftly and suddenly by a grossness of intelligence or by a bluntness of feeling or by a dull stare of terror in the eyes, the terror of soul of a starving Irish village in which the curfew was still a nightly fear.[31]

Side by side with his memory of the deeds of prowess of his uncle Mat Davin,[32] the athlete, the young peasant worshipped the sorrowful legend of Ireland. The gossip of his fellowstudents which strove to render the flat life of the college significant at any cost loved to think of him as a young fenian.[33] His nurse had taught him Irish and shaped his rude imagination by the broken lights of Irish myth. He stood towards this myth upon which no individual mind had ever drawn out a line of beauty and to its unwieldy tales that divided themselves as they moved down the cycles[34] in the same attitude as towards the Roman catholic religion, the attitude of a dullwitted loyal serf. Whatsoever of thought or of feeling came to him from England or by way of English culture his mind stood armed against in obedience to a password: and of the world that lay beyond England he knew only the foreign legion of France in which he spoke of serving.

Coupling this ambition with the young man's humour Stephen had often called him one of the tame geese:[35] and there

was even a point of irritation in the name pointed against that
very reluctance of speech and deed in his friend which seemed
so often to stand between Stephen's mind, eager of speculation, and the hidden ways of Irish life.

One night the young peasant, his spirit stung by the violent or
luxurious language in which Stephen escaped from the cold
silence of intellectual revolt, had called up before Stephen's mind
a strange vision. The two were walking slowly towards Davin's
room through the dark narrow streets of the poorer jews.[36]

—A thing happened to myself, Stevie, last autumn, coming
on winter, and I never told it to a living soul and you are the
first person now I ever told it to. I disremember[37] if it was October or November. It was October because it was before I came
up here to join the matriculation class.

Stephen had turned his smiling eyes towards his friend's
face, flattered by his confidence and won over to sympathy by
the speaker's simple accent.

—I was away all that day from my own place over in
Buttevant[38]—I don't know if you know where that is—at a hurling match[39] between the Croke's Own Boys and the Fearless
Thurles and by God, Stevie, that was the hard fight. My first
cousin, Fonsy Davin, was stripped to his buff[40] that day minding
cool[41] for the Limericks but he was up with the forwards half the
time and shouting like mad. I never will forget that day. One of
the Crokes made a woeful wipe at him one time with his
camann[42] and I declare to God he was within an aim's ace of getting it at the side of the temple. O, honest to God, if the crook of
it caught him that time he was done for.

—I am glad he escaped, Stephen had said with a laugh, but
surely that's not the strange thing that happened you?

—Well, I suppose that doesn't interest you but leastways there
was such noise after the match that I missed the train home and
I couldn't get any kind of a yoke[43] to give me a lift for, as luck
would have it, there was a mass meeting that same day over in
Castletownroche[44] and all the cars in the country were there. So
there was nothing for it only to stay the night or to foot it out.
Well, I started to walk and on I went and it was coming on night
when I got into the Ballyhoura hills; that's better than ten miles

from Kilmallock[45] and there's a long lonely road after that. You wouldn't see the sign of a christian house along the road or hear a sound. It was pitch dark almost. Once or twice I stopped by the way under a bush to redden my pipe and only for the dew was thick I'd have stretched out there and slept. At last, after a bend of the road, I spied a little cottage with a light in the window. I went up and knocked at the door. A voice asked who was there and I answered I was over at the match in Buttevant and was walking back and that I'd be thankful for a glass of water. After a while a young woman opened the door and brought me out a big mug of milk. She was half undressed as if she was going to bed when I knocked and she had her hair hanging; and I thought by her figure and by something in the look of her eyes that she must be carrying a child. She kept me in talk a long while at the door and I thought it strange because her breast and her shoulders were bare. She asked me was I tired and would I like to stop the night there. She said that she was all alone in the house and that her husband had gone that morning to Queenstown[46] with his sister to see her off. And all the time she was talking, Stevie, she had her eyes fixed on my face and she stood so close to me I could hear her breathing. When I handed her back the mug at last she took my hand to draw me in over the threshold and said: *Come in and stay the night here. You've no call to be frightened. There's no one in it*[47] *but ourselves.* . . . . I didn't go in, Stevie. I thanked her and went on my way again, all in a fever. At the first bend of the road I looked back and she was standing at the door.

The last words of Davin's story sang in his memory and the figure of the woman in the story stood forth, reflected in other figures of the peasant women whom he had seen standing in the doorways at Clane[48] as the college cars drove by, as a type of her race and his own, a batlike soul waking to the consciousness of itself in darkness and secrecy and loneliness and, through the eyes and voice and gesture of a woman without guile, calling the stranger to her bed.

A hand was laid on his arm and a young voice cried:

—Ah, gentleman, your own girl, sir! The first handsel[49] today, gentleman. Buy that lovely bunch. Will you, gentleman?

The blue flowers which she lifted towards him and her young blue eyes seemed to him at that instant images of guilelessness; and he halted till the image had vanished and he saw only her ragged dress and damp coarse hair and hoydenish face.

—Do, gentleman! Don't forget your own girl, sir!

—I have no money, said Stephen.

—Buy them lovely ones, will you, sir? Only a penny.

—Did you hear what I said? asked Stephen, bending towards her. I told you I had no money. I tell you again now.

—Well, sure, you will some day, sir, please God, the girl answered after an instant.

—Possibly, said Stephen, but I don't think it likely.

He left her quickly, fearing that her intimacy might turn to gibing and wishing to be out of the way before she offered her ware to another, a tourist from England or a student of Trinity.[50] Grafton Street, along which he walked, prolonged that moment of discouraged poverty. In the roadway at the head of the street a slab was set to the memory of Wolfe Tone and he remembered having been present with his father at its laying.[51] He remembered with bitterness that scene of tawdry tribute. There were four French delegates[52] in a brake and one, a plump smiling young man, held, wedged on a stick, a card on which were printed the words: *Vive l'Irlande!*[53]

But the trees in Stephen's Green were fragrant of rain and the rainsodden earth gave forth its mortal odour, a faint incense rising upward through the mould from many hearts. The soul of the gallant venal city which his elders had told him of had shrunk with time to a faint mortal odour rising from the earth and he knew that in a moment when he entered the sombre college he would be conscious of a corruption other than that of Buck Egan and Burnchapel Whaley.[54]

It was too late to go upstairs to the French class. He crossed the hall and took the corridor to the left which led to the physics theatre. The corridor was dark and silent but not unwatchful. Why did he feel that it was not unwatchful? Was it because he had heard that in Buck Whaley's time there was a secret staircase there? Or was the jesuit house extraterritorial and was he walking among aliens?[55] The Ireland of Tone and of Parnell seemed to have receded in space.[56]

He opened the door of the theatre and halted in the chilly grey light that struggled through the dusty windows. A figure was crouching before the large grate and by its leanness and greyness he knew that it was the dean of studies lighting the fire. Stephen closed the door quietly and approached the fireplace.

—Good morning, sir! Can I help you?

The priest looked up quickly and said:

—One moment now, Mr Dedalus, and you will see. There is an art in lighting a fire. We have the liberal arts and we have the useful arts. This is one of the useful arts.

—I will try to learn it, said Stephen.

—Not too much coal, said the dean, working briskly at his task, that is one of the secrets.

He produced four candlebutts from the sidepockets of his soutane and placed them deftly among the coals and twisted papers. Stephen watched him in silence. Kneeling thus on the flagstone to kindle the fire and busied with the disposition of his wisps of paper and candlebutts he seemed more than ever a humble server making ready the place of sacrifice in an empty temple, a levite of the Lord. Like a levite's robe of plain linen the faded worn soutane draped the kneeling figure of one whom the canonicals or the bellbordered ephod[57] would irk and trouble. His very body had waxed old in lowly service of the Lord—in tending the fire upon the altar, in bearing tidings secretly, in waiting upon worldlings, in striking swiftly when bidden—and yet had remained ungraced by aught of saintly or of prelatic beauty. Nay, his very soul had waxed old in that service without growing towards light and beauty or spreading abroad a sweet odour of her sanctity—a mortified will no more responsive to the thrill of its obedience than was to the thrill of love or combat his aging body, spare and sinewy, greyed with a silverpointed down.

The dean rested back on his hunkers and watched the sticks catch. Stephen, to fill the silence, said:

—I am sure I could not light a fire.

—You are an artist, are you not, Mr Dedalus? said the dean, glancing up and blinking his pale eyes. The object of the artist is the creation of the beautiful. What the beautiful is is another question.

He rubbed his hands slowly and drily over the difficulty.

—Can you solve that question now? he asked.

—Aquinas, answered Stephen, says *Pulcra sunt quæ visa placent.*[58]

—This fire before us, said the dean, will be pleasing to the eye. Will it therefore be beautiful?

—In so far as it is apprehended by the sight, which I suppose means here esthetic intellection, it will be beautiful. But Aquinas also says *Bonum est in quod tendit appetitus.*[59] In so far as it satisfies the animal craving for warmth fire is a good. In hell however it is an evil.

—Quite so, said the dean, you have certainly hit the nail on the head.

He rose nimbly and went towards the door, set it ajar and said:

—A draught is said to be a help in these matters.

As he came back to the hearth, limping slightly but with a brisk step, Stephen saw the silent soul of a jesuit look out at him from the pale loveless eyes. Like Ignatius he was lame[60] but in his eyes burned no spark of Ignatius' enthusiasm. Even the legendary craft of the company, a craft subtler and more secret than its fabled books of secret subtle wisdom, had not fired his soul with the energy of apostleship. It seemed as if he used the shifts and lore and cunning of the world, as bidden to do, for the greater glory of God, without joy in their handling or hatred of that in them which was evil but turning them, with a firm gesture of obedience, back upon themselves: and for all this silent service it seemed as if he loved not at all the master and little, if at all, the ends he served. *Similiter atque senis baculus,*[61] he was, as the founder would have had him, like a staff in an old man's hand, to be left in a corner, to be leaned on in the road at nightfall or in stress of weather, to lie with a lady's nosegay on a garden seat, to be raised in menace.

The dean returned to the hearth and began to stroke his chin.

—When may we expect to have something from you on the esthetic question? he asked.

—From me! said Stephen in astonishment. I stumble on an idea once a fortnight if I am lucky.

—These questions are very profound, Mr Dedalus, said the dean. It is like looking down from the cliffs of Moher[62] into the depths. Many go down into the depths and never come up. Only the trained diver can go down into those depths and explore them and come to the surface again.

—If you mean speculation, sir, said Stephen, I also am sure that there is no such thing as free thinking inasmuch as all thinking must be bound by its own laws.

—Ha!

—For my purpose I can work on at present by the light of one or two ideas of Aristotle and Aquinas.

—I see. I quite see your point.

—I need them only for my own use and guidance until I have done something for myself by their light. If the lamp smokes or smells I shall try to trim it. If it does not give light enough I shall sell it and buy another.

—Epictetus also had a lamp, said the dean, which was sold for a fancy price after his death.[63] It was the lamp he wrote his philosophical dissertations by. You know Epictetus?

—An old gentleman, said Stephen coarsely, who said that the soul is very like a bucketful of water.[64]

—He tells us in his homely way, the dean went on, that he put an iron lamp before a statue of one of the gods and that a thief stole the lamp. What did the philosopher do? He reflected that it was in the character of a thief to steal and determined to buy an earthen lamp next day instead of the iron lamp.[65]

A smell of molten tallow came up from the dean's candlebutts and fused itself in Stephen's consciousness with the jingle of the words, bucket and lamp and lamp and bucket. The priest's voice too had a hard jingling tone. Stephen's mind halted by instinct, checked by the strange tone and the imagery and by the priest's face which seemed like an unlit lamp or a reflector hung in a false focus. What lay behind it or within it? A dull torpor of the

soul or the dullness of the thundercloud, charged with intellection and capable of the gloom of God?

—I meant a different kind of lamp, sir, said Stephen.

—Undoubtedly, said the dean.

—One difficulty, said Stephen, in esthetic discussion is to know
whether words are being used according to the literary tradition
or according to the tradition of the marketplace. I remember a
sentence of Newman's in which he says of the Blessed Virgin that
she was detained in the full company of the saints.[66] The use of the
word in the marketplace is quite different. *I hope I am not detain-
ing you.*

—Not in the least, said the dean politely.

—No, no, said Stephen, smiling, I mean . . .

—Yes, yes: I see, said the dean quickly, I quite catch the
point: *detain.*

He thrust forward his under jaw and uttered a dry short cough.

—To return to the lamp, he said, the feeding of it is also a
nice problem. You must choose the pure oil and you must be
careful when you pour it in not to overflow it, not to pour in
more than the funnel can hold.

—What funnel? asked Stephen.

—The funnel through which you pour the oil into your lamp.

—That? said Stephen. Is that called a funnel? Is it not a
tundish?[67]

—What is a tundish?

—That. The . . . the funnel.

—Is that called a tundish in Ireland? asked the dean. I never
heard the word in my life.

—It is called a tundish in Lower Drumcondra,[68] said Stephen laughing, where they speak the best English.

—A tundish, said the dean reflectively. That is a most interesting word. I must look that word up. Upon my word I must.

His courtesy of manner rang a little false, and Stephen looked
at the English convert with the same eyes as the elder brother in
the parable may have turned on the prodigal.[69] A humble fol-
lower in the wake of clamorous conversions, a poor Englishman
in Ireland, he seemed to have entered on the stage of jesuit history when that strange play of intrigue and suffering and envy

and struggle and indignity had been all but given through—a late comer, a tardy spirit.[70] From what had he set out? Perhaps he had been born and bred among serious dissenters, seeing salvation in Jesus only and abhorring the vain pomps of the establishment. Had he felt the need of an implicit faith amid the welter of sectarianism and the jargon of its turbulent schisms, six principle men, peculiar people, seed and snake baptists, supralapsarian dogmatists?[71] Had he found the true church all of a sudden in winding up to the end like a reel of cotton some finespun line of reasoning upon insufflation or the imposition of hands or the procession of the Holy Ghost?[72] Or had Lord Christ touched him and bidden him follow, like that disciple who had sat at the receipt of custom,[73] as he sat by the door of some zincroofed chapel,[74] yawning and telling over his church pence?

The dean repeated the word yet again.

—Tundish! Well now, that is interesting!

—The question you asked me a moment ago seems to me more interesting. What is that beauty which the artist struggles to express from lumps of earth, said Stephen coldly.

The little word seemed to have turned a rapier point of his sensitiveness against this courteous and vigilant foe. He felt with a smart of dejection that the man to whom he was speaking was a countryman of Ben Jonson.[75] He thought:

—The language in which we are speaking is his before it is mine. How different are the words *home, Christ, ale, master,* on his lips and on mine! I cannot speak or write these words without unrest of spirit. His language, so familiar and so foreign, will always be for me an acquired speech. I have not made or accepted its words. My voice holds them at bay. My soul frets in the shadow of his language.

—And to distinguish between the beautiful and the sublime, the dean added. To distinguish between moral beauty and material beauty. And to inquire what kind of beauty is proper to each of the various arts. These are some interesting points we might take up.

Stephen, disheartened suddenly by the dean's firm dry tone, was silent. The dean also was silent: and through the silence a distant noise of many boots and confused voices came up the staircase.

—In pursuing these speculations, said the dean conclusively, there is however the danger of perishing of inanition. First you must take your degree. Set that before you as your first aim. Then little by little, you will see your way. I mean in every sense, your way in life and in thinking. It may be uphill pedalling at first. Take Mr Moonan. He was a long time before he got to the top. But he got there.

—I may not have his talent, said Stephen quietly.

—You never know, said the dean brightly. We never can say what is in us. I most certainly should not be despondent. *Per aspera ad astra.*[76]

He left the hearth quickly and went towards the landing to oversee the arrival of the first arts' class.

Leaning against the fireplace Stephen heard him greet briskly and impartially every student of the class and could almost see the frank smiles of the coarser students. A desolating pity began to fall like a dew upon his easily embittered heart for this faithful servingman of the knightly Loyola,[77] for this halfbrother of the clergy,[78] more venal than they in speech, more steadfast of soul than they, one whom he would never call his ghostly father:[79] and he thought how this man and his companions had earned the name of worldlings at the hands not of the unworldly only but of the worldly also for having pleaded, during all their history, at the bar of God's justice for the souls of the lax and the lukewarm and the prudent.[80]

The entry of the professor was signalled by a few rounds of Kentish fire[81] from the heavy boots of those students who sat on the highest tier of the gloomy theatre under the grey cobwebbed windows. The calling of the roll began and the responses to the names were given out in all tones until the name of Peter Byrne was reached.

—Here!

A deep bass note in response came from the upper tier, followed by coughs of protest along the other benches.

The professor paused in his reading and called the next name:

—Cranly!

No answer.

—Mr Cranly!

A smile flew across Stephen's face as he thought of his friend's studies.

—Try Leopardstown![82] said a voice from the bench behind.

Stephen glanced up quickly but Moynihan's snoutish face, outlined on the grey light, was impassive. A formula was given out. Amid the rustling of the notebooks Stephen turned back again and said:

—Give me some paper for God's sake.

—Are you as bad as that?[83] asked Moynihan with a broad grin.

He tore a sheet from his scribbler and passed it down, whispering:

—In case of necessity any layman or woman can do it.[84]

The formula which he wrote obediently on the sheet of paper, the coiling and uncoiling calculations of the professor, the spectre-like symbols of force and velocity fascinated and jaded Stephen's mind. He had heard some say that the old professor was an atheist freemason. O the grey dull day! It seemed a limbo of painless patient consciousness through which souls of mathematicians might wander, projecting long slender fabrics from plane to plane of ever rarer and paler twilight, radiating swift eddies to the last verges of a universe ever vaster, farther and more impalpable.

—So we must distinguish between elliptical and ellipsoidal. Perhaps some of you gentlemen may be familiar with the works of Mr W. S. Gilbert. In one of his songs he speaks of the billiard sharp who is condemned to play:

> On a cloth untrue
> With a twisted cue
> And elliptical billiard balls.[85]

—He means a ball having the form of the ellipsoid of the principal axes of which I spoke a moment ago.

Moynihan leaned down towards Stephen's ear and murmured:

—What price ellipsoidal balls! Chase me, ladies, I'm in the cavalry!

His fellowstudent's rude humour ran like a gust through the cloister of Stephen's mind, shaking into gay life limp priestly vestments that hung upon the walls, setting them to sway and caper in a sabbath of misrule. The forms of the community emerged from the gustblown vestments, the dean of studies, the portly florid bursar with his cap of grey hair, the president, the little priest with feathery hair who wrote devout verses, the squat peasant form of the professor of economics, the tall form of the young professor of mental science discussing on the landing a case of conscience with his class like a giraffe cropping high leafage among a herd of antelopes, the grave troubled prefect of the sodality, the plump roundheaded professor of Italian with his rogue's eyes. They came ambling and stumbling, tumbling and capering, kilting their gowns for leap frog, holding one another back, shaken with deep fast laughter, smacking one another behind and laughing at their rude malice, calling to one another by familiar nicknames, protesting with sudden dignity at some rough usage, whispering two and two behind their hands.

The professor had gone to the glass cases on the sidewall from a shelf of which he took down a set of coils, blew away the dust from many points and, bearing it carefully to the table, held a finger on it while he proceeded with his lecture. He explained that the wires in modern coils were of a compound called platinoid lately discovered by F. W. Martino.[86]

He spoke clearly the initials and surname of the discoverer. Moynihan whispered from behind:

—Good old Fresh Water Martin!

—Ask him, Stephen whispered back with weary humour, if he wants a subject for electrocution. He can have me.

Moynihan, seeing the professor bend over the coils, rose in his bench and, clacking noiselessly the fingers of his right hand, began to call with the voice of a slobbering urchin:

—Please, teacher! Please, teacher! This boy is after saying a bad word, teacher.

—Platinoid, the professor said solemnly, is preferred to German silver because it has a lower coefficient of resistance variation by changes of temperature. The platinoid wire is insulated and the covering of silk that insulates it is wound on the ebonite bobbins just where my finger is. If it were wound single an extra current would be induced in the coils. The bobbins are saturated in hot paraffin wax . . .

A sharp Ulster voice said from the bench below Stephen:

—Are we likely to be asked questions on applied science?

The professor began to juggle gravely with the terms pure science and applied science. A heavybuilt student wearing gold spectacles stared with some wonder at the questioner. Moynihan murmured from behind in his natural voice:

—Isn't MacAlister a devil for his pound of flesh?

Stephen looked down coldly on the oblong skull beneath him overgrown with tangled twinecoloured hair. The voice, the accent, the mind of the questioner offended him and he allowed the offence to carry him towards wilful unkindness, bidding his mind think that the student's father would have done better had he sent his son to Belfast to study and have saved something on the train fare by so doing.[87]

The oblong skull beneath did not turn to meet this shaft of thought and yet the shaft came back to its bowstring: for he saw in a moment the student's wheypale face.

—That thought is not mine, he said to himself quickly. It came from the comic Irishman in the bench behind. Patience. Can you say with certitude by whom the soul of your race was bartered and its elect betrayed—by the questioner or by the mocker? Patience. Remember Epictetus. It is probably in his character to ask such a question at such a moment in such a tone and to pronounce the word *science* as a monosyllable.[88]

The droning voice of the professor continued to wind itself slowly round and round the coils it spoke of, doubling, trebling, quadrupling its somnolent energy as the coil multiplied its ohms of resistance.

Moynihan's voice called from behind in echo to a distant bell:

—Closing time, gents!

The entrance hall was crowded and loud with talk. On a table near the door were two photographs[89] in frames and between them a long roll of paper bearing an irregular tail of signatures. MacCann went briskly to and fro among the students, talking

rapidly, answering rebuffs and leading one after another to the
table. In the inner hall the dean of studies stood talking to a
young professor, stroking his chin gravely and nodding his head.

Stephen, checked by the crowd at the door, halted irresolutely.
From under the wide falling leaf of a soft hat Cranly's dark eyes
were watching him.

—Have you signed? Stephen asked.

Cranly closed his long thinlipped mouth, communed with
himself an instant and answered:

—*Ego habeo.*[90]

—What is it for?

—*Quod?*[91]

—What is it for?

Cranly turned his pale face to Stephen and said blandly and
bitterly:

—*Per pax universalis.*[92]

Stephen pointed to the Csar's photograph and said:

—He has the face of a besotted Christ.

The scorn and anger in his voice brought Cranly's eyes back
from a calm survey of the walls of the hall.

—Are you annoyed? he asked.

—No, answered Stephen.

—Are you in bad humour?

—No.

—*Credo ut vos sanguinarius mendax estis*, said Cranly, *quia
facies vostra monstrat ut vos in damno malo humore estis.*[93]

Moynihan, on his way to the table, said in Stephen's ear:

—MacCann is in tiptop form. Ready to shed the last drop.
Brandnew world. No stimulants and votes for the bitches.[94]

Stephen smiled at the manner of this confidence and, when
Moynihan had passed, turned again to meet Cranly's eyes.

—Perhaps you can tell me, he said, why he pours his soul so
freely into my ear.[95] Can you?

A dull scowl appeared on Cranly's forehead. He stared at
the table where Moynihan had bent to write his name on the
roll, and then said flatly:

—A sugar![96]

—*Quis est in malo humore*, said Stephen, *ego aut vos?*[97]

Cranly did not take up the taunt. He brooded sourly on his judgment and repeated with the same flat force:

—A flaming bloody sugar, that's what he is!

It was his epitaph for all dead friendships and Stephen wondered whether it would ever be spoken in the same tone over his memory. The heavy lumpish phrase sank slowly out of hearing like a stone through a quagmire. Stephen saw it sink as he had seen many another, feeling its heaviness depress his heart. Cranly's speech, unlike that of Davin, had neither rare phrases of Elizabethan English nor quaintly turned versions of Irish idioms. Its drawl was an echo of the quays of Dublin given back by a bleak decaying seaport, its energy an echo of the sacred eloquence of Dublin given back flatly by a Wicklow pulpit.[98]

The heavy scowl faded from Cranly's face as MacCann marched briskly towards them from the other side of the hall.

—Here you are! said MacCann cheerily.

—Here I am! said Stephen.

—Late as usual. Can you not combine the progressive tendency with a respect for punctuality?

—That question is out of order, said Stephen. Next business.

His smiling eyes were fixed on a silverwrapped tablet of milk chocolate which peeped out of the propagandist's breastpocket. A little ring of listeners closed round to hear the war of wits. A lean student with olive skin and lank black hair thrust his face between the two, glancing from one to the other at each phrase and seeming to try to catch each flying phrase in his open moist mouth. Cranly took a small grey handball[99] from his pocket and began to examine it closely, turning it over and over.

—Next business? said MacCann. Hom!

He gave a loud cough of laughter, smiled broadly and tugged twice at the strawcoloured goatee which hung from his blunt chin.

—The next business is to sign the testimonial.

—Will you pay me anything if I sign? asked Stephen.

—I thought you were an idealist, said MacCann.

The gipsylike student looked about him and addressed the onlookers in an indistinct bleating voice.

—By hell, that's a queer notion. I consider that notion to be a mercenary notion.

His voice faded into silence. No heed was paid to his words. He turned his olive face, equine in expression, towards Stephen, inviting him to speak again.

MacCann began to speak with fluent energy of the Csar's rescript,[100] of Stead,[101] of general disarmament, arbitration in cases of international disputes, of the signs of the times, of the new humanity and the new gospel of life which would make it the business of the community to secure as cheaply as possible the greatest possible happiness of the greatest possible number.[102]

The gipsy student responded to the close of the period by crying:

—Three cheers for universal brotherhood!

—Go on, Temple, said a stout ruddy student near him. I'll stand you a pint after.

—I'm a believer in universal brotherhood, said Temple, glancing about him out of his dark, oval eyes. Marx is only a bloody cod.[103]

Cranly gripped his arm tightly to check his tongue, smiling uneasily, and repeated:

—Easy, easy, easy!

Temple struggled to free his arm but continued, his mouth flecked by a thin foam:

—Socialism was founded by an Irishman[104] and the first man in Europe who preached the freedom of thought was Collins.[105] Two hundred years ago. He denounced priestcraft, the philosopher of Middlesex. Three cheers for John Anthony Collins!

A thin voice from the verge of the ring replied:

—Pip! pip!

Moynihan murmured beside Stephen's ear:

—And what about John Anthony's poor little sister:

Lottie Collins lost her drawers;
Won't you kindly lend her yours?[106]

Stephen laughed and Moynihan, pleased with the result, murmured again:

—We'll have five bob each way[107] on John Anthony Collins.

—I am waiting for your answer, said MacCann briefly.

—The affair doesn't interest me in the least, said Stephen wearily. You know that well. Why do you make a scene about it?

—Good! said MacCann, smacking his lips. You are a reactionary then?

—Do you think you impress me, Stephen asked, when you flourish your wooden sword?

—Metaphors! said MacCann bluntly. Come to facts.

Stephen blushed and turned aside. MacCann stood his ground and said with hostile humour:

—Minor poets, I suppose, are above such trivial questions as the question of universal peace.

Cranly raised his head and held the handball between the two students by way of a peaceoffering, saying:

—*Pax super totum sanguinarium globum.*[108]

Stephen, moving away the bystanders, jerked his shoulder angrily in the direction of the Csar's image, saying:

—Keep your icon. If we must have a Jesus, let us have a legitimate Jesus.

—By hell, that's a good one! said the gipsy student to those about him. That's a fine expression. I like that expression immensely.

He gulped down the spittle in his throat as if he were gulping down the phrase and, fumbling at the peak of his tweed cap, turned to Stephen, saying:

—Excuse me, sir, what do you mean by that expression you uttered just now?

Feeling himself jostled by the students near him, he said to them:

—I am curious to know now what he meant by that expression.

He turned again to Stephen and said in a whisper:

—Do you believe in Jesus? I believe in man. Of course, I don't know if you believe in man. I admire you, sir. I admire the mind of man independent of all religions. Is that your opinion about the mind of Jesus?

—Go on, Temple, said the stout ruddy student, returning, as was his wont, to his first idea, that pint is waiting for you.

—He thinks I'm an imbecile, Temple explained to Stephen, because I'm a believer in the power of mind.

Cranly linked his arms into those of Stephen and his admirer and said:

—*Nos ad manum ballum jocabimus.*[109]

Stephen, in the act of being led away, caught sight of Mac-Cann's flushed bluntfeatured face.

—My signature is of no account, he said politely. You are right to go your way. Leave me to go mine.

—Dedalus, said MacCann crisply, I believe you're a good fellow but you have yet to learn the dignity of altruism and the responsibility of the human individual.

A voice said:

—Intellectual crankery is better out of this movement than in it.

Stephen, recognizing the harsh tone of MacAlister's voice, did not turn in the direction of the voice. Cranly pushed solemnly through the throng of students, linking Stephen and Temple like a celebrant attended by his ministers on his way to the altar.

Temple bent eagerly across Cranly's breast and said:

—Did you hear MacAlister what he said? That youth is jealous of you. Did you see that? I bet Cranly didn't see that. By hell, I saw that at once.

As they crossed the inner hall the dean of studies was in the act of escaping from the student with whom he had been conversing. He stood at the foot of the staircase, a foot on the lowest step, his threadbare soutane gathered about him for the ascent with womanish care, nodding his head often and repeating:

—Not a doubt of it, Mr Hackett! Very fine! Not a doubt of it!

In the middle of the hall the prefect of the college sodality[110] was speaking earnestly, in a soft querulous voice, with a boarder. As he spoke he wrinkled a little his freckled brow and bit, between his phrases, at a tiny bone pencil.

—I hope the matric men will all come. The first arts men are pretty sure. Second arts too.[111] We must make sure of the newcomers.

Temple bent again across Cranly, as they were passing through the doorway, and said in a swift whisper:

—Do you know that he is a married man? He was a married man before they converted him. He has a wife and children somewhere. By hell, I think that's the queerest notion I ever heard! Eh?

His whisper trailed off into sly cackling laughter. The moment they were through the doorway Cranly seized him rudely by the neck and shook him, saying:

—You flaming floundering fool! I'll take my dying bible[112] there isn't a bigger bloody ape, do you know, than you in the whole flaming bloody world!

Temple wriggled in his grip, laughing still with sly content, while Cranly repeated flatly at every rude shake:

—A flaming flaring bloody idiot!

They crossed the weedy garden together. The president, wrapped in a heavy loose cloak, was coming towards them along one of the walks, reading his office.[113] At the end of the walk he halted before turning and raised his eyes. The students saluted, Temple fumbling as before at the peak of his cap. They walked forward in silence. As they neared the alley Stephen could hear the thuds of the players' hands and the wet smacks of the ball and Davin's voice crying out excitedly at each stroke.

The three students halted round the box on which Davin sat to follow the game. Temple, after a few moments, sidled across to Stephen and said:

—Excuse me, I wanted to ask you do you believe that Jean Jacques Rousseau[114] was a sincere man?

Stephen laughed outright. Cranly, picking up the broken stave of a cask from the grass at his foot, turned swiftly and said sternly:

—Temple, I declare to the living God if you say another word, do you know, to anybody on any subject I'll kill you *super spottum.*[115]

—He was like you, I fancy, said Stephen, an emotional man.

—Blast him, curse him! said Cranly broadly. Don't talk to him at all. Sure, you might as well be talking, do you know, to a flaming chamberpot as talking to Temple. Go home, Temple. For God's sake, go home.

—I don't care a damn about you, Cranly, answered Temple, moving out of reach of the uplifted stave and pointing at Stephen. He's the only man I see in this institution that has an individual mind.

—Institution! Individual! cried Cranly. Go home, blast you, for you're a hopeless bloody man.

—I'm an emotional man, said Temple. That's quite rightly expressed. And I'm proud that I'm an emotionalist.

He sidled out of the alley, smiling slily. Cranly watched him with a blank expressionless face.

—Look at him! he said. Did you ever see such a go-by-the-wall?[116]

His phrase was greeted by a strange laugh from a student who lounged against the wall, his peaked cap down on his eyes. The laugh, pitched in a high key and coming from a so muscular frame, seemed like the whinny of an elephant. The student's body shook all over and, to ease his mirth, he rubbed both his hands delightedly, over his groins.

—Lynch[117] is awake, said Cranly.

Lynch, for answer, straightened himself and thrust forward his chest.

—Lynch puts out his chest, said Stephen, as a criticism of life.[118]

Lynch smote himself sonorously on the chest and said:

—Who has anything to say about my girth?

Cranly took him at the word and the two began to tussle. When their faces had flushed with the struggle they drew apart, panting. Stephen bent down towards Davin who, intent on the game, had paid no heed to the talk of the others.

—And how is my little tame goose?[119] he asked. Did he sign too? Davin nodded and said:

—And you, Stevie?

Stephen shook his head.

—You're a terrible man, Stevie, said Davin, taking the short pipe from his mouth. Always alone.

—Now that you have signed the petition for universal peace,

said Stephen, I suppose you will burn that little copybook I saw in your room.

As Davin did not answer Stephen began to quote:

—Long pace, fianna! Right incline, fianna! Fianna, by numbers, salute, one, two![120]

—That's a different question, said Davin. I'm an Irish nationalist, first and foremost. But that's you all out. You're a born sneerer, Stevie.

—When you make the next rebellion with hurleysticks, said Stephen, and want the indispensable informer,[121] tell me. I can find you a few in this college.

—I can't understand you, said Davin. One time I hear you talk against English literature. Now you talk against the Irish informers. What with your name and your ideas . . . Are you Irish at all?

—Come with me now to the office of arms[122] and I will show you the tree of my family, said Stephen.

—Then be one of us, said Davin. Why don't you learn Irish? Why did you drop out of the league class[123] after the first lesson?

—You know one reason why, answered Stephen.

Davin tossed his head and laughed.

—O, come now, he said. Is it on account of that certain young lady and Father Moran? But that's all in your own mind, Stevie. They were only talking and laughing.

Stephen paused and laid a friendly hand upon Davin's shoulder.

—Do you remember, he said, when we knew each other first? The first morning we met you asked me to show you the way to the matriculation class, putting a very strong stress on the first syllable. You remember? Then you used to address the jesuits as father,[124] you remember? I ask myself about you: *Is he as innocent as his speech?*

—I'm a simple person, said Davin. You know that. When you told me that night in Harcourt Street those things about your private life, honest to God, Stevie, I was not able to eat my dinner. I was quite bad. I was awake a long time that night. Why did you tell me those things?

—Thanks, said Stephen. You mean I am a monster.

—No, said Davin, but I wish you had not told me.

A tide began to surge beneath the calm surface of Stephen's friendliness.

—This race and this country and this life produced me, he said. I shall express myself as I am.

—Try to be one of us, repeated Davin. In your heart you are an Irishman but your pride is too powerful.

—My ancestors threw off their language and took another, Stephen said. They allowed a handful of foreigners to subject them. Do you fancy I am going to pay in my own life and person debts they made? What for?

—For our freedom, said Davin.

—No honourable and sincere man, said Stephen, has given up to you his life and his youth and his affections from the days of Tone to those of Parnell but you sold him to the enemy or failed him in need or reviled him and left him for another. And you invite me to be one of you. I'd see you damned first.

—They died for their ideals, Stevie, said Davin. Our day will come yet,[125] believe me.

Stephen, following his own thought, was silent for an instant.

—The soul is born, he said vaguely, first in those moments I told you of. It has a slow and dark birth, more mysterious than the birth of the body. When the soul of a man is born in this country there are nets flung at it to hold it back from flight. You talk to me of nationality, language, religion. I shall try to fly by those nets.

Davin knocked the ashes from his pipe.

—Too deep for me, Stevie, he said. But a man's country comes first. Ireland first, Stevie. You can be a poet or mystic after.

—Do you know what Ireland is? asked Stephen with cold violence. Ireland is the old sow that eats her farrow.

Davin rose from his box and went towards the players, shaking his head sadly. But in a moment his sadness left him and he was hotly disputing with Cranly and the two players who had finished their game. A match of four was arranged, Cranly insisting, however, that his ball should be used. He let it rebound twice or thrice to his hand and struck it strongly and swiftly towards the base of the alley, exclaiming in answer to its thud:

—Your soul!

Stephen stood with Lynch till the score began to rise. Then he plucked him by the sleeve to come away. Lynch obeyed, saying:

—Let us eke[126] go, as Cranly has it.

Stephen smiled at this sidethrust. They passed back through the garden and out through the hall where the doddering porter was pinning up a notice in the frame. At the foot of the steps they halted and Stephen took a packet of cigarettes from his pocket and offered it to his companion.

—I know you are poor, he said.

—Damn your yellow insolence, answered Lynch.

This second proof of Lynch's culture made Stephen smile again.

—It was a great day for European culture, he said, when you made up your mind to swear in yellow.[127]

They lit their cigarettes and turned to the right. After a pause Stephen began:

—Aristotle has not defined pity and terror.[128] I have. I say . . .

Lynch halted and said bluntly:

—Stop! I won't listen! I am sick. I was out last night on a yellow drunk with Horan and Goggins.

Stephen went on:

—Pity is the feeling which arrests the mind in the presence of whatsoever is grave and constant in human sufferings and unites it with the human sufferer. Terror is the feeling which arrests the mind in the presence of whatsoever is grave and constant in human sufferings and unites it with the secret cause.

—Repeat, said Lynch.

Stephen repeated the definitions slowly.

—A girl got into a hansom a few days ago, he went on, in London. She was on her way to meet her mother whom she had not seen for many years. At the corner of a street the shaft of a lorry shivered the window of the hansom in the shape of a star. A long fine needle of the shivered glass pierced her heart. She died on the instant. The reporter called it a tragic death. It is not. It is remote from terror and pity according to the terms of my definitions.

—The tragic emotion, in fact, is a face looking two ways, towards terror and towards pity, both of which are phases of it.

You see I use the word *arrest*. I mean that the tragic emotion is static. Or rather the dramatic emotion is. The feelings excited by improper art are kinetic, desire or loathing. Desire urges us to possess, to go to something; loathing urges us to abandon, to go from something. These are kinetic emotions. The arts which excite them, pornographical or didactic, are therefore improper arts. The esthetic emotion (I use the general term) is therefore static. The mind is arrested and raised above desire and loathing.

—You say that art must not excite desire, said Lynch. I told you that one day I wrote my name in pencil on the backside of the Venus of Praxiteles in the Museum.[129] Was that not desire?

—I speak of normal natures, said Stephen. You also told me that when you were a boy in that charming carmelite school[130] you ate pieces of dried cowdung.

Lynch broke again into a whinny of laughter and again rubbed both his hands over his groins but without taking them from his pockets.

—O I did! I did! he cried.

Stephen turned towards his companion and looked at him for a moment boldly in the eyes. Lynch, recovering from his laughter, answered his look from his humbled eyes. The long slender flattened skull beneath the long pointed cap brought before Stephen's mind the image of a hooded reptile. The eyes, too, were reptilelike in glint and gaze. Yet at that instant, humbled and alert in their look, they were lit by one tiny human point, the window of a shrivelled soul, poignant and selfembittered.

—As for that, Stephen said in polite parenthesis, we are all animals. I also am an animal.

—You are, said Lynch.

—But we are just now in a mental world, Stephen continued. The desire and loathing excited by improper esthetic means are really unesthetic emotions not only because they are kinetic in character but also because they are not more than physical. Our flesh shrinks from what it dreads and responds to the stimulus of what it desires by a purely reflex action of the nervous system. Our eyelid closes before we are aware that the fly is about to enter our eye.

—Not always, said Lynch critically.

—In the same way, said Stephen, your flesh responded to the stimulus of a naked statue but it was, I say, simply a reflex action of the nerves. Beauty expressed by the artist cannot awaken in us an emotion which is kinetic or a sensation which is purely physical. It awakens, or ought to awaken, or induces, or ought to induce, an esthetic stasis, an ideal pity or an ideal terror, a stasis called forth, prolonged and at last dissolved by what I call the rhythm of beauty.

—What is that exactly? asked Lynch.

—Rhythm, said Stephen, is the first formal esthetic relation of part to part in any esthetic whole or of an esthetic whole to its part or parts or of any part to the esthetic whole of which it is a part.

—If that is rhythm, said Lynch, let me hear what you call beauty: and, please remember, though I did eat a cake of cowdung once, that I admire only beauty.

Stephen raised his cap as if in greeting. Then, blushing slightly, he laid his hand on Lynch's thick tweed sleeve.

—We are right, he said, and the others are wrong. To speak of these things and to try to understand their nature and, having understood it, to try slowly and humbly and constantly to express, to press out again, from the gross earth or what it brings forth, from sound and shape and colour which are the prison gates of our soul, an image of the beauty we have come to understand— that is art.

They had reached the canal bridge[131] and, turning from their course, went on by the trees. A crude grey light, mirrored in the sluggish water, and a smell of wet branches over their heads seemed to war against the course of Stephen's thought.

—But you have not answered my question, said Lynch. What is art? What is the beauty it expresses?

—That was the first definition I gave you, you sleepyheaded wretch, said Stephen, when I began to try to think out the matter for myself. Do you remember the night? Cranly lost his temper and began to talk about Wicklow bacon.

—I remember, said Lynch. He told us about them flaming fat devils of pigs.

—Art, said Stephen, is the human disposition of sensible or

intelligible matter for an esthetic end. You remember the pigs and forget that. You are a distressing pair, you and Cranly.

Lynch made a grimace at the raw grey sky and said:

—If I am to listen to your esthetic philosophy give me at least another cigarette. I don't care about it. I don't even care about women. Damn you and damn everything. I want a job of five hundred a year. You can't get me one.

Stephen handed him the packet of cigarettes. Lynch took the last one that remained, saying simply:

—Proceed!

—Aquinas, said Stephen, says that is beautiful the apprehension of which pleases.

Lynch nodded.

—I remember that, he said. *Pulcra sunt quæ visa placent.*[132]

—He uses the word *visa*, said Stephen, to cover esthetic apprehensions of all kinds, whether through sight or hearing or through any other avenue of apprehension. This word, though it is vague, is clear enough to keep away good and evil which excite desire and loathing. It means certainly a stasis and not a kinesis. How about the true? It produces also a stasis of the mind. You would not write your name in pencil across the hypothenuse of a rightangled triangle.

—No, said Lynch, give me the hypothenuse of the Venus of Praxiteles.

—Static therefore, said Stephen. Plato, I believe, said that beauty is the splendour of truth.[133] I don't think that it has a meaning but the true and the beautiful are akin. Truth is beheld by the intellect which is appeased by the most satisfying relations of the intelligible: beauty is beheld by the imagination which is appeased by the most satisfying relations of the sensible. The first step in the direction of truth is to understand the frame and scope of the intellect itself, to comprehend the act itself of intellection. Aristotle's entire system of philosophy rests upon his book of psychology[134] and that, I think, rests on his statement that the same attribute cannot at the same time and in the same connection belong to and not belong to the same subject.[135] The first step in the direction of beauty is to understand the frame and scope of the imagination, to comprehend the act itself of esthetic apprehension. Is that clear?

—But what is beauty? asked Lynch impatiently. Out with another definition. Something we see and like! Is that the best you and Aquinas can do?

—Let us take woman, said Stephen.

—Let us take her! said Lynch fervently.

—The Greek, the Turk, the Chinese, the Copt, the Hottentot, said Stephen, all admire a different type of female beauty. That seems to be a maze out of which we cannot escape. I see however two ways out. One is this hypothesis: that every physical quality admired by men in women is in direct connection with the manifold functions of women for the propagation of the species. It may be so. The world, it seems, is drearier than even you, Lynch, imagined. For my part I dislike that way out. It leads to eugenics rather than to esthetic. It leads you out of the maze into a new gaudy lectureroom where MacCann, with one hand on *The Origin of Species*[136] and the other hand on the new testament, tells you that you admired the great flanks of Venus because you felt that she would bear you burly offspring and admired her great breasts because you felt that she would give good milk to her children and yours.

—Then MacCann is a sulphuryellow liar, said Lynch energetically.

—There remains another way out, said Stephen, laughing.

—To wit? said Lynch.

—This hypothesis, Stephen began.

A long dray laden with old iron came round the corner of Sir Patrick Dun's hospital[137] covering the end of Stephen's speech with the harsh roar of jangled and rattling metal. Lynch closed his ears and gave out oath after oath till the dray had passed. Then he turned on his heel rudely. Stephen turned also and waited for a few moments till his companion's illhumour had had its vent.

—This hypothesis, Stephen repeated, is the other way out: that, though the same object may not seem beautiful to all people, all people who admire a beautiful object find in it certain

relations which satisfy and coincide with the stages themselves
of all esthetic apprehension. These relations of the sensible, visible to you through one form and to me through another, must
be therefore the necessary qualities of beauty. Now, we can
return to our old friend saint Thomas for another pennyworth
of wisdom.

Lynch laughed.

—It amuses me vastly, he said, to hear you quoting him time
after time like a jolly round friar. Are you laughing in your sleeve?

—MacAlister, answered Stephen, would call my esthetic theory applied Aquinas. So far as this side of esthetic philosophy
extends Aquinas will carry me all along the line. When we come
to the phenomena of artistic conception, artistic gestation and
artistic reproduction I require a new terminology and a new personal experience.

—Of course, said Lynch. After all Aquinas, in spite of his
intellect, was exactly a good round friar. But you will tell me
about the new personal experience and new terminology some
other day. Hurry up and finish the first part.

—Who knows? said Stephen, smiling. Perhaps Aquinas would
understand me better than you. He was a poet himself. He wrote
a hymn for Maundy Thursday. It begins with the words *Pange
lingua gloriosi.*[138] They say it is the highest glory of the hymnal. It
is an intricate and soothing hymn. I like it: but there is no hymn
that can be put beside that mournful and majestic processional
song, the *Vexilla Regis* of Venantius Fortunatus.[139]

Lynch began to sing softly and solemnly in a deep bass voice:

> *Impleta sunt quæ concinit*
> *David fideli carmine*
> *Dicendo nationibus*
> *Regnavit a ligno Deus.*[140]

—That's great! he said, well pleased. Great music!

They turned into Lower Mount Street.[141] A few steps from
the corner a fat young man, wearing a silk neck-cloth, saluted
them and stopped.

—Did you hear the results of the exams? he asked. Griffin was plucked.[142] Halpin and O'Flynn are through the home civil.[143] Moonan got fifth place in the Indian.[144] O'Shaughnessy got fourteenth. The Irish fellows in Clarke's[145] gave them a feed last night. They all ate curry.

His pallid bloated face expressed benevolent malice and, as he had advanced through his tidings of success, his small fat-encircled eyes vanished out of sight and his weak wheezing voice out of hearing.

In reply to a question of Stephen's his eyes and his voice came forth again from their lurkingplaces.

—Yes, MacCullagh and I,[146] he said. He's taking pure mathematics and I'm taking constitutional history. There are twenty subjects. I'm taking botany too. You know I'm a member of the field club.

He drew back from the other two in a stately fashion and placed a plump woollengloved hand on his breast, from which muttered wheezing laughter at once broke forth.

—Bring us a few turnips and onions the next time you go out, said Stephen drily, to make a stew.

The fat student laughed indulgently and said:

—We are all highly respectable people in the field club. Last Saturday we went out to Glenmalure,[147] seven of us.

—With women, Donovan? said Lynch.

Donovan again laid his hand on his chest and said:

—Our end is the acquisition of knowledge.

Then he said quickly:

—I hear you are writing some essay about esthetics.

Stephen made a vague gesture of denial.

—Goethe and Lessing,[148] said Donovan, have written a lot on that subject, the classical school and the romantic school and all that. The *Laocoon*[149] interested me very much when I read it. Of course it is idealistic, German, ultraprofound.

Neither of the others spoke. Donovan took leave of them urbanely.

—I must go, he said softly and benevolently. I have a strong suspicion, amounting almost to a conviction, that my sister intended to make pancakes today for the dinner of the Donovan family.

—Goodbye, Stephen said in his wake. Don't forget the turnips for me and my mate.

Lynch gazed after him, his lip curling in slow scorn till his face resembled a devil's mask:

—To think that that yellow pancakeeating excrement can get a good job, he said at length, and I have to smoke cheap cigarettes!

They turned their faces towards Merrion Square[150] and went on for a little in silence.

—To finish what I was saying about beauty, said Stephen, the most satisfying relations of the sensible must therefore correspond to the necessary phases of artistic apprehension. Find these and you find the qualities of universal beauty. Aquinas says: *ad pulcritudinem tria requiruntur, integritas, consonantia, claritas.* I translate it so: *Three things are needed for beauty, wholeness, harmony and radiance.*[151] Do these correspond to the phases of apprehension? Are you following?

—Of course, I am, said Lynch. If you think I have an excrementitious intelligence run after Donovan and ask him to listen to you.

Stephen pointed to a basket which a butcher's boy had slung inverted on his head.

—Look at that basket, he said.

—I see it, said Lynch.

—In order to see that basket, said Stephen, your mind first of all separates the basket from the rest of the visible universe which is not the basket. The first phase of apprehension is a bounding line drawn about the object to be apprehended. An esthetic image is presented to us either in space or in time. What is audible is presented in time, what is visible is presented in space.[152] But, temporal or spatial, the esthetic image is first luminously apprehended as selfbounded and selfcontained upon the immeasurable background of space or time which is not it. You apprehend it as *one* thing. You see it as one whole. You apprehend its wholeness. That is *integritas*.

—Bull's eye! said Lynch, laughing. Go on.

—Then, said Stephen, you pass from point to point, led by its formal lines; you apprehend it as balanced part against part within its limits; you feel the rhythm of its structure. In other words the synthesis of immediate perception is followed by the analysis of apprehension. Having first felt that it is *one* thing you feel now that it is a *thing*. You apprehend it as complex, multiple, divisible, separable, made up of its parts, the results of its parts and their sum, harmonious. That is *consonantia*.

—Bull's eye again! said Lynch wittily. Tell me now what is *claritas* and you win the cigar.

—The connotation of the word, Stephen said, is rather vague. Aquinas uses a term which seems to be inexact. It baffled me for a long time. It would lead you to believe that he had in mind symbolism or idealism, the supreme quality of beauty being a light from some other world, the idea of which the matter is but the shadow, the reality of which it is but the symbol. I thought he might mean that *claritas* is the artistic discovery and representation of the divine purpose in anything or a force of generalisation which would make the esthetic image a universal one, make it outshine its proper conditions. But that is literary talk. I understand it so. When you have apprehended that basket as one thing and have then analysed it according to its form and apprehended it as a thing you make the only synthesis which is logically and esthetically permissible. You see that it is that thing which it is and no other thing. The radiance of which he speaks is the scholastic *quidditas*, the *whatness* of a thing.[153] This supreme quality is felt by the artist when the esthetic image is first conceived in his imagination. The mind in that mysterious instant Shelley likened beautifully to a fading coal.[154] The instant wherein that supreme quality of beauty, the clear radiance of the esthetic image, is apprehended luminously by the mind which has been arrested by its wholeness and fascinated by its harmony is the luminous silent stasis of esthetic pleasure, a spiritual state very like to that cardiac condition which the Italian physiologist Luigi Galvani, using a phrase almost as beautiful as Shelley's, called the enchantment of the heart.[155]

Stephen paused and, though his companion did not speak, felt that his words had called up around them a thoughtenchanted silence.

—What I have said, he began again, refers to beauty in the wider sense of the word, in the sense which the word has in the literary tradition. In the marketplace it has another sense. When we speak of beauty in the second sense of the term our judgment is influenced in the first place by the art itself and by the form of that art. The image, it is clear, must be set between the mind or senses of the artist himself and the mind or senses of others. If you bear this in memory you will see that art necessarily divides itself into three forms progressing from one to the next. These forms are: the lyrical form, the form wherein the artist presents his image in immediate relation to himself; the epical form, the form wherein he presents his image in mediate relation to himself and to others; the dramatic form, the form wherein he presents his image in immediate relation to others.

—That you told me a few nights ago, said Lynch, and we began the famous discussion.

—I have a book at home, said Stephen, in which I have written down questions which are more amusing than yours were. In finding the answers to them I found the theory of esthetic which I am trying to explain. Here are some questions I set myself: *Is a chair finely made tragic or comic? Is the portrait of Mona Lisa good if I desire to see it? Is the bust of Sir Philip Crampton*[156] *lyrical, epical or dramatic? Can excrement or a child or a louse be a work of art? If not, why not?*

—Why not, indeed? said Lynch, laughing.

—*If a man hacking in fury at a block of wood*, Stephen continued, *make there an image of a cow, is that image a work of art? If not, why not?*

—That's a lovely one, said Lynch, laughing again. That has the true scholastic stink.

—Lessing, said Stephen, should not have taken a group of statues to write of.[157] The art, being inferior, does not present the forms I spoke of distinguished clearly one from another. Even in literature, the highest and most spiritual art, the forms are often confused. The lyrical form is in fact the simplest verbal vesture of an instant of emotion, a rhythmical cry such as ages ago cheered on the man who pulled at the oar or dragged stones up a slope. He who utters it is more conscious of the instant of emotion than of himself as feeling emotion. The simplest epical form is seen emerging out of lyrical literature when the artist prolongs and broods upon himself as the centre of an epical event and this form progresses till the centre of emotional gravity is equidistant from the artist himself and from others. The narrative is no longer purely personal. The personality of the artist passes into the narration itself, flowing round and round the persons and the action like a vital sea. This progress you will see easily in that old English balled *Turpin Hero* which begins in the first person and ends in the third person.[158] The dramatic form is reached when the vitality which has flowed and eddied round each person fills every person with such vital force that he or she assumes a proper and intangible esthetic life. The personality of the artist, at first a cry or a cadence or a mood and then a fluid and lambent narrative, finally refines itself out of existence, impersonalises itself, so to speak. The esthetic image in the dramatic form is life purified in and reprojected from the human imagination. The mystery of esthetic like that of material creation is accomplished. The artist, like the God of the creation, remains within or behind or beyond or above his handiwork, invisible, refined out of existence, indifferent, paring his fingernails.

—Trying to refine them also out of existence, said Lynch.

A fine rain began to fall from the high veiled sky and they turned into the duke's lawn,[159] to reach the national library before the shower came.

—What do you mean, Lynch asked surlily, by prating about beauty and the imagination in this miserable Godforsaken island? No wonder the artist retired within or behind his handiwork after having perpetrated this country.

The rain fell faster. When they passed through the passage beside the royal Irish academy[160] they found many students sheltering under the arcade of the library. Cranly, leaning against a pillar, was picking his teeth with a sharpened match, listening

to some companions. Some girls stood near the entrance door.
Lynch whispered to Stephen:

—Your beloved is here.

Stephen took his place silently on the step below the group of
students, heedless of the rain which fell fast, turning his eyes
towards her from time to time. She too stood silently among her
companions. She has no priest to flirt with, he thought with conscious bitterness, remembering how he had seen her last. Lynch
was right. His mind, emptied of theory and courage, lapsed back
into a listless peace.

He heard the students talking among themselves. They spoke
of two friends who had passed the final medical examination,
of the chances of getting places on ocean liners, of poor and rich
practices.

—That's all a bubble. An Irish country practice is better.

—Hynes was two years in Liverpool and he says the same.
A frightful hole he said it was. Nothing but midwifery cases.
Half a crown cases.[161]

—Do you mean to say it is better to have a job here in the
country than in a rich city like that? I know a fellow . . .

—Hynes has no brains. He got through by stewing, pure
stewing.[162]

—Don't mind him. There's plenty of money to be made in a
big commercial city.

—Depends on the practice.

—*Ego credo ut vita pauperum est simpliciter atrox, simpliciter sanguinarius atrox, in Liverpoolio.*[163]

Their voices reached his ears as if from a distance in interrupted pulsation. She was preparing to go away with her companions.

The quick light shower had drawn off, tarrying in clusters of
diamonds among the shrubs of the quadrangle where an exhalation was breathed forth by the blackened earth. Their trim boots
prattled as they stood on the steps of the colonnade, talking quietly and gaily, glancing at the clouds, holding their umbrellas at
cunning angles against the few last raindrops, closing them again,
holding their skirts demurely.

And if he had judged her harshly? If her life were a simple rosary of hours, her life simple and strange as a bird's life, gay in the morning, restless all day, tired at sundown? Her heart simple and wilful as a bird's heart?

Towards dawn he awoke. O what sweet music! His soul was all dewy wet. Over his limbs in sleep pale cool waves of light had passed. He lay still, as if his soul lay amid cool waters, conscious of faint sweet music. His mind was waking slowly to a tremulous morning knowledge, a morning inspiration. A spirit filled him, pure as the purest water, sweet as dew, moving as music. But how faintly it was inbreathed, how passionlessly, as if the seraphim themselves were breathing upon him! His soul was waking slowly, fearing to awake wholly. It was that windless hour of dawn when madness wakes and strange plants open to the light and the moth flies forth silently.

An enchantment of the heart! The night had been enchanted. In a dream or vision he had known the ecstasy of seraphic life. Was it an instant of enchantment only or long hours and days and years and ages?

The instant of inspiration seemed now to be reflected from all sides at once from a multitude of cloudy circumstance of what had happened or of what might have happened. The instant flashed forth like a point of light and now from cloud on cloud of vague circumstance confused form was veiling softly its afterglow. O! In the virgin womb of the imagination the word was made flesh. Gabriel the seraph had come to the virgin's chamber.[164] An afterglow deepened within his spirit, whence the white flame had passed, deepening to a rose and ardent light. That rose and ardent light was her strange wilful heart, strange that no man had known or would know, wilful from before the beginning of the world: and lured by that ardent roselike glow the choirs of the seraphim were falling from heaven.

Are you not weary of ardent ways,
Lure of the fallen seraphim?
Tell no more of enchanted days.

The verses passed from his mind to his lips and, murmuring them over, he felt the rhythmic movement of a villanelle[165] pass through them. The roselike glow sent forth its rays of rhyme; ways, days, blaze, praise, raise. Its rays burned up the world, consumed the hearts of men and angels: the rays from the rose that was her wilful heart.

> *Your eyes have set man's heart ablaze*
> *And you have had your will of him.*
> *Are you not weary of ardent ways?*

And then? The rhythm died away, ceased, began again to move and beat. And then? Smoke, incense ascending from the altar of the world.

> *Above the flame the smoke of praise*
> *Goes up from ocean rim to rim.*
> *Tell no more of enchanted days.*

Smoke went up from the whole earth, from the vapoury oceans, smoke of her praise. The earth was like a swinging smoking swaying censer, a ball of incense, an ellipsoidal ball. The rhythm died out at once; the cry of his heart was broken. His lips began to murmur the first verses over and over; then went on stumbling through half verses, stammering and baffled; then stopped. The heart's cry was broken.

The veiled windless hour had passed and behind the panes of the naked window the morning light was gathering. A bell beat faintly very far away. A bird twittered; two birds, three. The bell and the bird ceased: and the dull white light spread itself east and west, covering the world, covering the roselight in his heart.

Fearing to lose all, he raised himself suddenly on his elbow to look for paper and pencil. There was neither on the table; only the soupplate he had eaten the rice from for supper and the candlestick with its tendrils of tallow and its paper socket, singed by the last flame. He stretched his arm wearily towards the foot of the bed, groping with his hand in the pockets of the coat that hung there. His fingers found a pencil and then a cigarette packet. He lay back and, tearing open the packet, placed the last cigarette on the windowledge and began to write out the stanzas of the villanelle in small neat letters on the rough cardboard surface.

Having written them out he lay back on the lumpy pillow, murmuring them again. The lumps of knotted flock under his head reminded him of the lumps of knotted horsehair in the sofa of her parlour on which he used to sit, smiling or serious, asking himself why he had come, displeased with her and with himself, confounded by the print of the Sacred Heart[166] above the untenanted sideboard. He saw her approach him in a lull of the talk and beg him to sing one of his curious songs. Then he saw himself sitting at the old piano, striking chords softly from its speckled keys and singing, amid the talk which had risen again in the room, to her who leaned beside the mantelpiece a dainty song of the Elizabethans, a sad and sweet loth to depart,[167] the victory chant of Agincourt,[168] the happy air of Greensleeves.[169] While he sang and she listened, or feigned to listen, his heart was at rest but when the quaint old songs had ended and he heard again the voices in the room he remembered his own sarcasm: the house where young men are called by their christian names a little too soon.

At certain instants her eyes seemed about to trust him but he had waited in vain. She passed now dancing lightly across his memory as she had been that night at the carnival ball, her white dress a little lifted, a white spray nodding in her hair. She danced lightly in the round.[170] She was dancing towards him and, as she came, her eyes were a little averted and a faint glow was on her cheek. At the pause in the chain of hands her hand had lain in his an instant, a soft merchandise.

—You are a great stranger now.

—Yes. I was born to be a monk.

—I am afraid you are a heretic.

—Are you much afraid?

For answer she had danced away from him along the chain of hands, dancing lightly and discreetly, giving herself to none. The white spray nodded to her dancing and when she was in shadow the glow was deeper on her cheek.

A monk! His own image started forth a profaner of the cloister, a heretic franciscan, willing and willing not to serve, spinning like Gherardino da Borgo San Donnino,[171] a lithe web of sophistry and whispering in her ear.

No, it was not his image. It was like the image of the young priest in whose company he had seen her last, looking at him out of dove's eyes, toying with the pages of her Irish phrasebook.

—Yes, yes, the ladies are coming round to us. I can see it every day. The ladies are with us. The best helpers the language has.

—And the church, Father Moran?

—The church too. Coming round too. The work is going ahead there too. Don't fret about the church.

Bah! he had done well to leave the room in disdain. He had done well not to salute her on the steps of the library. He had done well to leave her to flirt with her priest, to toy with a church which was the scullerymaid of christendom.

Rude brutal anger routed the last lingering instant of ecstasy from his soul. It broke up violently her fair image and flung the fragments on all sides. On all sides distorted reflections of her image started from his memory: the flowergirl in the ragged dress with damp coarse hair and a hoyden's face who had called herself his own girl and begged his handsel, the kitchengirl in the next house who sang over the clatter of her plates with the drawl of a country singer the first bars of *By Killarney's Lakes and Fells*,[172] a girl who had laughed gaily to see him stumble when the iron grating in the footpath near Cork Hill[173] had caught the broken sole of his shoe, a girl he had glanced at, attracted by her small ripe mouth as she passed out of Jacob's biscuit factory,[174] who had cried to him over her shoulder:

—Do you like what you seen of me, straight hair and curly eyebrows?

And yet he felt that, however he might revile and mock her image, his anger was also a form of homage. He had left the classroom in disdain that was not wholly sincere, feeling that perhaps the secret of her race lay behind those dark eyes upon which her long lashes flung a quick shadow. He had told himself bitterly as he walked through the streets that she was a figure of the womanhood of her country, a batlike soul waking to the consciousness of itself in darkness and secrecy and loneliness, tarrying awhile, loveless and sinless, with her mild lover and leaving him to whisper of innocent transgressions in the latticed ear of a priest.[175] His anger against her found vent in coarse railing at her paramour, whose name and voice and features offended his baffled pride: a priested peasant, with a brother a policeman in Dublin and a brother a potboy in Moycullen.[176] To him she would unveil her soul's shy nakedness, to one who was but schooled in the discharging of a formal rite rather than to him, a priest of eternal imagination, transmuting the daily bread of experience into the radiant body of everliving life.[177]

The radiant image of the eucharist united again in an instant his bitter and despairing thoughts, their cries arising unbroken in a hymn of thanksgiving.

> *Our broken cries and mournful lays*
> *Rise in one eucharistic hymn.*
> *Are you not weary of ardent ways?*

> *While sacrificing hands upraise*
> *The chalice flowing to the brim,*
> *Tell no more of enchanted days.*

He spoke the verses aloud from the first lines till the music and rhythm suffused his mind, turning it to quiet indulgence: then copied them painfully to feel them the better by seeing them; then lay back on his bolster.

The full morning light had come. No sound was to be heard: but he knew that all around him life was about to awaken in common noises, hoarse voices, sleepy prayers. Shrinking from that life he turned towards the wall, making a cowl of the blanket and staring at the great overblown scarlet flowers of the tattered wallpaper. He tried to warm his perishing joy in their scarlet glow, imagining a roseway from where he lay upwards to heaven all strewn with scarlet flowers. Weary! Weary! He too was weary of ardent ways.

A gradual warmth, a languorous weariness passed over him, descending along his spine from his closely cowled head. He felt it descend and, seeing himself as he lay, smiled. Soon he would sleep.

He had written verses for her again after ten years. Ten years before she had worn her shawl cowlwise about her head, sending sprays of her warm breath into the night air, tapping her foot upon the glassy road. It was the last tram; the lank brown horses knew it and shook their bells to the clear night in admonition. The conductor talked with the driver, both nodding often in the green light of the lamp. They stood on the steps of the tram, he on the upper, she on the lower. She came up to his step many times between their phrases and went down again and once or twice remained beside him forgetting to go down and then went down. Let be! Let be!

Ten years from that wisdom of children to his folly. If he sent her the verses? They would be read out at breakfast amid the tapping of eggshells. Folly indeed! The brothers would laugh and try to wrest the page from each other with their strong hard fingers. The suave priest, her uncle, seated in his armchair, would hold the page at arm's length, read it smiling and approve of the literary form.

No, no: that was folly. Even if he sent her the verses she would not show them to others. No, no: she could not.

He began to feel that he had wronged her. A sense of her innocence moved him almost to pity her, an innocence he had never understood till he had come to the knowledge of it through sin, an innocence which she too had not understood while she was innocent or before the strange humiliation of her nature[178] had first come upon her. Then first her soul had begun to live as his soul had when he had first sinned: and a tender compassion filled his heart as he remembered her frail pallor and her eyes, humbled and saddened by the dark shame of womanhood.

While his soul had passed from ecstasy to languor where had she been? Might it be, in the mysterious ways of spiritual life, that her soul at those same moments had been conscious of his homage? It might be.

A glow of desire kindled again his soul and fired and fulfilled all his body. Conscious of his desire she was waking from odorous sleep, the temptress of his villanelle. Her eyes, dark and with a look of languor, were opening to his eyes. Her nakedness yielded to him, radiant, warm, odorous and lavishlimbed, enfolded him like a shining cloud, enfolded him like water with a liquid life: and like a cloud of vapour or like waters circumfluent in space the liquid letters of speech, symbols of the element of mystery, flowed forth over his brain.

> *Are you not weary of ardent ways,*
> *Lure of the fallen seraphim?*
> *Tell no more of enchanted days.*
>
> *Your eyes have set man's heart ablaze*
> *And you have had your will of him.*
> *Are you not weary of ardent ways?*
>
> *Above the flame the smoke of praise*
> *Goes up from ocean rim to rim.*
> *Tell no more of enchanted days.*
>
> *Our broken cries and mournful lays*
> *Rise in one eucharistic hymn.*
> *Are you not weary of ardent ways?*
>
> *While sacrificing hands upraise*
> *The chalice flowing to the brim,*
> *Tell no more of enchanted days.*
>
> *And still you hold our longing gaze*
> *With languorous look and lavish limb!*
> *Are you not weary of ardent ways?*
> *Tell no more of enchanted days.*

What birds were they? He stood on the steps of the library to look at them, leaning wearily on his ashplant. They flew round and round the jutting shoulder of a house in Molesworth Street.[179] The air of the late March evening made clear their flight, their dark darting quivering bodies flying clearly against the sky as against a limphung cloth of smoky tenuous blue.

He watched their flight; bird after bird: a dark flash, a swerve, a flash again, a dart aside, a curve, a flutter of wings. He tried to count them before all their darting quivering bodies passed: six, ten, eleven: and wondered were they odd or even in number. Twelve, thirteen: for two came wheeling down from the upper sky. They were flying high and low but ever round and round in straight and curving lines and ever flying from left to right, circling about a temple of air.[180]

He listened to the cries: like the squeak of mice behind the wainscot: a shrill twofold note. But the notes were long and shrill and whirring, unlike the cry of vermin, falling a third or a fourth and trilled as the flying beaks clove the air. Their cry was shrill and clear and fine and falling like threads of silken light unwound from whirring spools.

The inhuman clamour soothed his ears in which his mother's sobs and reproaches murmured insistently and the dark frail quivering bodies wheeling and fluttering and swerving round an airy temple of the tenuous sky soothed his eyes which still saw the image of his mother's face.

Why was he gazing upwards from the steps of the porch, hearing their shrill twofold cry, watching their flight? For an augury of good or evil? A phrase of Cornelius Agrippa[181] flew through his mind and then there flew hither and thither shapeless thoughts from Swedenborg[182] on the correspondence of birds to things of the intellect and of how the creatures of the air have their knowledge and know their times and seasons because they, unlike man, are in the order of their life and have not perverted that order by reason.

And for ages men had gazed upward as he was gazing at birds in flight. The colonnade above him made him think vaguely of an ancient temple and the ashplant on which he leaned wearily of the curved stick of an augur.[183] A sense of fear of the unknown moved in the heart of his weariness, a fear of symbols and portents, of the hawklike man whose name he bore[184] soaring out of his captivity on osierwoven wings, of Thoth, the god of writers, writing with a reed upon a tablet and bearing on his narrow ibis head the cusped moon.[185]

He smiled as he thought of the god's image for it made him think of a bottlenosed judge in a wig, putting commas into a document which he held at arm's length and he knew that he would not have remembered the god's name but that it was like an Irish oath.[186] It was folly. But was it for this folly that he was about to leave for ever the house of prayer and prudence into which he had been born and the order of life out of which he had come?

They came back with shrill cries over the jutting shoulder of the house, flying darkly against the fading air. What birds were they? He thought that they must be swallows who had come back from the south. Then he was to go away for they were birds ever going and coming, building ever an unlasting home under the eaves of men's houses and ever leaving the homes they had built to wander.

> Bend down your faces, Oona and Aleel,
> I gaze upon them as the swallow gazes
> Upon the nest under the eave before
> He wander the loud waters.[187]

A soft liquid joy like the noise of many waters flowed over his memory and he felt in his heart the soft peace of silent spaces of fading tenuous sky above the waters, of oceanic silence, of swallows flying through the seadusk over the flowing waters.

A soft liquid joy flowed through the words where the soft long vowels hurtled noiselessly and fell away, lapping and flowing back and ever shaking the white bells of their waves in mute chime and mute peal and soft low swooning cry; and he felt that the augury he had sought in the wheeling darting birds and in the pale space of sky above him had come forth from his heart like a bird from a turret quietly and swiftly.

Symbol of departure or of loneliness? The verses crooned in the ear of his memory composed slowly before his remembering eyes the scene of the hall on the night of the opening of the

national theatre.[188] He was alone at the side of the balcony, looking out of jaded eyes at the culture of Dublin in the stalls and at
the tawdry scenecloths and human dolls framed by the garish
lamps of the stage. A burly policeman sweated behind him and
seemed at every moment about to act. The catcalls and hisses
and mocking cries ran in rude gusts round the hall from his scattered fellowstudents.

—A libel on Ireland!
—Made in Germany![189]
—Blasphemy!
—We never sold our faith!
—No Irish woman ever did it!
—We want no amateur atheists.
—We want no budding buddhists.[190]

A sudden swift hiss fell from the windows above him and he
knew that the electric lamps had been switched on in the read-
ers' room. He turned into the pillared hall, now calmly lit, went
up the staircase and passed in through the clicking turnstile.

Cranly was sitting over near the dictionaries. A thick book,
opened at the frontispiece, lay before him on the wooden rest. He
leaned back in his chair, inclining his ear like that of a confessor
to the face of the medical student who was reading to him a problem from the chess page of a journal. Stephen sat down at his
right and the priest at the other side of the table closed his copy of
The Tablet[191] with an angry snap and stood up.

Cranly gazed after him blandly and vaguely. The medical
student went on in a softer voice:

—Pawn to king's fourth.

—We had better go, Dixon, said Stephen in warning. He has
gone to complain.

Dixon folded the journal and rose with dignity, saying:

—Our men retired in good order.

—With guns and cattle, added Stephen, pointing to the title-
page of Cranly's book on which was printed *Diseases of the Ox.*[192]

As they passed through a lane of the tables Stephen said:

—Cranly, I want to speak to you.

Cranly did not answer or turn. He laid his book on the
counter and passed out, his wellshod feet sounding flatly on

the floor. On the staircase he paused and gazing absently at Dixon repeated:

—Pawn to king's bloody fourth.

—Put it that way if you like, Dixon said.

He had a quiet toneless voice and urbane manners and on a finger of his plump clean hand he displayed at moments a signet ring.

As they crossed the hall a man of dwarfish stature came towards them. Under the dome of his tiny hat his unshaven face began to smile with pleasure and he was heard to murmur. The eyes were melancholy as those of a monkey.

—Good evening, captain, said Cranly, halting.

—Good evening, gentlemen, said the stubblegrown monkeyish face.

—Warm weather for March, said Cranly. They have the windows open upstairs.

Dixon smiled and turned his ring. The blackish monkey-puckered face pursed its human mouth with gentle pleasure: and its voice purred:

—Delightful weather for March. Simply delightful.

—There are two nice young ladies upstairs, captain, tired of waiting, Dixon said.

Cranly smiled and said kindly:

—The captain has only one love: sir Walter Scott. Isn't that so, captain?

—What are you reading now, captain? Dixon asked. *The Bride of Lammermoor?*[193]

—I love old Scott, the flexible lips said. I think he writes something lovely. There is no writer can touch sir Walter Scott.

He moved a thin shrunken brown hand gently in the air in time to his praise and his thin quick eyelids beat often over his sad eyes.

Sadder to Stephen's ear was his speech: a genteel accent, low and moist, marred by errors:[194] and listening to it he wondered was the story true and was the thin blood that flowed in his shrunken frame noble and come of an incestuous love?

The park trees were heavy with rain and rain fell still and ever in the lake, lying grey like a shield. A game of swans[195] flew there and the water and the shore beneath were fouled with their green-white slime. They embraced softly, impelled by the grey rainy light, the wet silent trees, the shieldlike witnessing lake, the swans. They embraced without joy or passion, his arm about his sister's neck. A grey woollen cloak was wrapped athwart her from her shoulder to her waist: and her fair head was bent in willing shame. He had loose redbrown hair and tender shapely strong freckled hands. Face. There was no face seen. The brother's face was bent upon her fair rainfragrant hair. The hand freckled and strong and shapely and caressing was Davin's hand.

He frowned angrily upon his thought and on the shrivelled mannikin who had called it forth. His father's gibes at the Bantry gang[196] leaped out of his memory. He held them at a distance and brooded uneasily on his own thought again. Why were they not Cranly's hands? Had Davin's simplicity and innocence stung him more secretly?

He walked on across the hall with Dixon, leaving Cranly to take leave elaborately of the dwarf.

Under the colonnade Temple was standing in the midst of a little group of students. One of them cried:

—Dixon, come over till you hear. Temple is in grand form.

Temple turned on him his dark gipsy eyes.

—You're a hypocrite, O'Keeffe, he said, and Dixon's a smiler. By hell, I think that's a good literary expression.

He laughed slily, looking in Stephen's face, repeating:

—By hell, I'm delighted with that name. A smiler.

A stout student who stood below them on the steps said:

—Come back to the mistress, Temple. We want to hear about that.

—He had, faith, Temple said. And he was a married man too. And all the priests used to be dining there. By hell, I think they all had a touch.[197]

—We shall call it riding a hack to spare the hunter, said Dixon.

—Tell us, Temple, O'Keeffe said, how many quarts of porter have you in you?

—All your intellectual soul is in that phrase, O'Keeffe, said Temple with open scorn.

He moved with a shambling gait round the group and spoke to Stephen.

—Did you know that the Forsters are the kings of Belgium?[198] he asked.

Cranly came out through the door of the entrance hall, his hat thrust back on the nape of his neck and picking his teeth with care.

—And here's the wiseacre, said Temple. Do you know that about the Forsters?

He paused for an answer. Cranly dislodged a figseed from his teeth on the point of his rude toothpick and gazed at it intently.

—The Forster family, Temple said, is descended from Baldwin the First, king of Flanders. He was called the Forester. Forester and Forster are the same name. A descendant of Baldwin the First, captain Francis Forster, settled in Ireland and married the daughter of the last chieftain of Clanbrassil.[199] Then there are the Blake Forsters. That's a different branch.

—From Baldhead, king of Flanders, Cranly repeated, rooting again deliberately at his gleaming uncovered teeth.

—Where did you pick up all that history? O'Keeffe asked.

—I know all the history of your family too, Temple said, turning to Stephen. Do you know what Giraldus Cambrensis[200] says about your family?

—Is he descended from Baldwin too? asked a tall consumptive student with dark eyes.

—Baldhead, Cranly repeated, sucking at a crevice in his teeth.

—*Pernobilis et pervetusta familia,*[201] Temple said to Stephen.

The stout student who stood below them on the steps farted briefly. Dixon turned towards him saying in a soft voice:

—Did an angel speak?

Cranly turned also and said vehemently but without anger:

—Goggins, you're the flamingest dirty devil I ever met, do you know.

—I had it on my mind to say that, Goggins answered firmly. It did no one any harm, did it?

—We hope, Dixon said suavely, that it was not of the kind known to science as a *paulo post futurum.*[202]

—Didn't I tell you he was a smiler? said Temple, turning right and left. Didn't I give him that name?

—You did. We're not deaf, said the tall consumptive.

Cranly still frowned at the stout student below him. Then, with a snort of disgust, he shoved him violently down the steps.

—Go away from here, he said rudely. Go away, you stink-pot. And you are a stinkpot.

Goggins skipped down on to the gravel and at once returned to his place with good humour. Temple turned back to Stephen and asked:

—Do you believe in the law of heredity?

—Are you drunk or what are you or what are you trying to say? asked Cranly, facing round on him with an expression of wonder.

—The most profound sentence ever written, Temple said with enthusiasm, is the sentence at the end of the zoology. Reproduction is the beginning of death.

He touched Stephen timidly at the elbow and said eagerly:

—Do you feel how profound that is because you are a poet?

Cranly pointed his long forefinger.

—Look at him! he said with scorn to the others. Look at Ireland's hope!

They laughed at his words and gesture. Temple turned on him bravely, saying:

—Cranly, you're always sneering at me. I can see that. But I am as good as you any day. Do you know what I think about you now as compared with myself?

—My dear man, said Cranly urbanely, you are incapable, do you know, absolutely incapable of thinking.

—But do you know, Temple went on, what I think of you and of myself compared together?

—Out with it, Temple! the stout student cried from the steps. Get it out in bits!

Temple turned right and left, making sudden feeble gestures as he spoke.

—I'm a ballocks, he said, shaking his head in despair. I am. And I know I am. And I admit it that I am.

Dixon patted him lightly on the shoulder and said mildly:

—And it does you every credit, Temple.

—But he, Temple said, pointing to Cranly. He is a ballocks too like me. Only he doesn't know it. And that's the only difference I see.

A burst of laughter covered his words. But he turned again to Stephen and said with a sudden eagerness:

—That word is a most interesting word. That's the only English dual number. Did you know?

—Is it? Stephen said vaguely.

He was watching Cranly's firmfeatured suffering face, lit up now by a smile of false patience. The gross name had passed over it like foul water poured over an old stone image, patient of injuries: and, as he watched him, he saw him raise his hat in salute and uncover the black hair that stood up stiffly from his forehead like an iron crown.

She passed out from the porch of the library and bowed across Stephen in reply to Cranly's greeting. He also? Was there not a slight flush on Cranly's cheek? Or had it come forth at Temple's words? The light had waned. He could not see.

Did that explain his friend's listless silence, his harsh comments, the sudden intrusions of rude speech with which he had shattered so often Stephen's ardent wayward confessions? Stephen had forgiven freely for he had found this rudeness also in himself towards himself. And he remembered an evening when he had dismounted from a borrowed creaking bicycle to pray to God in a wood near Malahide.[203] He had lifted up his arms and spoken in ecstasy to the sombre nave of the trees, knowing that he stood on holy ground and in a holy hour. And when two constabularymen had come into sight round a bend in the gloomy road he had broken off his prayer to whistle loudly an air from the last pantomime.

He began to beat the frayed end of his ashplant against the base of a pillar. Had Cranly not heard him? Yet he could wait. The talk about him ceased for a moment: and a soft hiss fell again from a window above. But no other sound was in the air and the swallows whose flight he had followed with idle eyes were sleeping.

She had passed through the dusk. And therefore the air was

silent save for one soft hiss that fell. And therefore the tongues about him had ceased their babble. Darkness was falling.

Darkness falls from the air.[204]

A trembling joy, lambent as a faint light, played like a fairy host around him. But why? Her passage through the darkening air or the verse with its black vowels and its opening sound, rich and lutelike?

He walked away slowly towards the deeper shadows at the end of the colonnade, beating the stone softly with his stick to hide his revery from the students whom he had left: and allowed his mind to summon back to itself the age of Dowland and Byrd and Nash.[205]

Eyes, opening from the darkness of desire, eyes that dimmed the breaking east. What was their languid grace but the softness of chambering?[206] And what was their shimmer but the shimmer of the scum that mantled the cesspool of the court of a slobbering Stuart.[207] And he tasted in the language of memory ambered wines,[208] dying fallings of sweet airs, the proud pavan:[209] and saw with the eyes of memory kind gentlewomen in Covent Garden wooing from their balconies with sucking mouths and the poxfouled wenches of the taverns and young wives that, gaily yielding to their ravishers, clipped[210] and clipped again.

The images he had summoned gave him no pleasure. They were secret and enflaming but her image was not entangled by them. That was not the way to think of her. It was not even the way in which he thought of her. Could his mind then not trust itself? Old phrases, sweet only with a disinterred sweetness like the figseeds Cranly rooted out of his gleaming teeth.

It was not thought nor vision though he knew vaguely that her figure was passing homeward through the city. Vaguely first and then more sharply he smelt her body. A conscious unrest seethed in his blood. Yes, it was her body he smelt: a wild and languid smell: the tepid limbs over which his music had flowed desirously and the secret soft linen upon which her flesh distilled odour and a dew.

A louse crawled over the nape of his neck and, putting his thumb and forefinger deftly beneath his loose collar, he caught it. He rolled its body, tender yet brittle as a grain of rice, between thumb and finger for an instant before he let it fall from him and wondered would it live or die. There came to his mind a curious phrase from Cornelius a Lapide which said that the lice born of human sweat were not created by God with the other animals on the sixth day.[211] But the tickling of the skin of his neck made his mind raw and red. The life of his body, illclad, illfed, louse-eaten, made him close his eyelids in a sudden spasm of despair: and in the darkness he saw the brittle bright bodies of lice falling from the air and turning often as they fell. Yes; and it was not darkness that fell from the air. It was brightness.

Brightness falls from the air.[212]

He had not even remembered rightly Nash's line. All the images it had awakened were false. His mind bred vermin. His thoughts were lice born of the sweat of sloth.

He came back quickly along the colonnade towards the group of students. Well then, let her go and be damned to her. She could love some clean athlete who washed himself every morning to the waist and had black hair on his chest. Let her.

Cranly had taken another dried fig from the supply in his pocket and was eating it slowly and noisily. Temple sat on the pediment of a pillar, leaning back, his cap pulled down on his sleepy eyes. A squat young man came out of the porch, a leather portfolio tucked under his armpit. He marched towards the group, striking the flags with the heels of his boots and with the ferule of his heavy umbrella. Then, raising the umbrella in salute, he said to all:

—Good evening, sirs.

He struck the flags again and tittered while his head trembled with a slight nervous movement. The tall consumptive student and Dixon and O'Keeffe were speaking in Irish and did not answer him. Then, turning to Cranly, he said:

—Good evening, particularly to you.

He moved the umbrella in indication and tittered again. Cranly, who was still chewing the fig, answered with loud movements of his jaws.

—Good? Yes. It is a good evening.

The squat student looked at him seriously and shook his umbrella gently and reprovingly.

—I can see, he said, that you are about to make obvious remarks.

—Um, Cranly answered, holding out what remained of the halfchewed fig and jerking it towards the squat student's mouth in sign that he should eat.

The squat student did not eat it but, indulging his special humour, said gravely, still tittering and prodding his phrase with his umbrella:

—Do you intend that . . .

He broke off, pointed bluntly to the munched pulp of the fig and said loudly:

—I allude to that.

—Um, Cranly said as before.

—Do you intend that now, the squat student said, as *ipso facto* or, let us say, as so to speak?

Dixon turned aside from his group, saying:

—Goggins was waiting for you, Glynn. He has gone round to the Adelphi to look for you and Moynihan. What have you there? he asked, tapping the portfolio under Glynn's arm.

—Examination papers, Glynn answered. I give them monthly examinations to see that they are profiting by my tuition.

He also tapped the portfolio and coughed gently and smiled.

—Tuition! said Cranly rudely. I suppose you mean the barefooted children that are taught by a bloody ape like you. God help them!

He bit off the rest of the fig and flung away the butt.

—I suffer little children to come unto me,[213] Glynn said amiably.

—A bloody ape, Cranly repeated with emphasis, and a blasphemous bloody ape!

Temple stood up and, pushing past Cranly, addressed Glynn:

—That phrase you said now, he said, is from the new testament about suffer the children to come to me.

—Go to sleep again, Temple, said O'Keeffe.

—Very well, then, Temple continued, still addressing Glynn, and if Jesus suffered the children to come why does the church send them all to hell if they die unbaptised?[214] Why is that?

—Were you baptised yourself, Temple? the consumptive student asked.

—But why are they sent to hell if Jesus said they were all to come? Temple said, his eyes searching in Glynn's eyes.

Glynn coughed and said gently, holding back with difficulty the nervous titter in his voice and moving his umbrella at every word:

—And, as you remark, if it is thus I ask emphatically whence comes this thusness.

—Because the church is cruel like all old sinners, Temple said.

—Are you quite orthodox on that point, Temple? Dixon said suavely.

—Saint Augustine says that about unbaptised children going to hell,[215] Temple answered, because he was a cruel old sinner too.

—I bow to you, Dixon said, but I had the impression that limbo existed for such cases.

—Don't argue with him, Dixon, Cranly said brutally. Don't talk to him or look at him. Lead him home with a sugan[216] the way you'd lead a bleating goat.

—Limbo! Temple cried. That's a fine invention too. Like hell.

—But with the unpleasantness left out, Dixon said.

He turned smiling to the others and said:

—I think I am voicing the opinions of all present in saying so much.

—You are, Glynn said in a firm tone. On that point Ireland is united.

He struck the ferule of his umbrella on the stone floor of the colonnade.

—Hell, Temple said. I can respect that invention of the grey spouse of Satan.[217] Hell is Roman, like the walls of the Romans, strong and ugly. But what is limbo?

—Put him back into the perambulator, Cranly, O'Keeffe called out.

Cranly made a swift step towards Temple, halted, stamping his foot, crying as if to a fowl:

—Hoosh!

Temple moved away nimbly.

—Do you know what limbo is? he cried. Do you know what we call a notion like that in Roscommon?[218]

—Hoosh! Blast you! Cranly cried, clapping his hands.

—Neither my arse nor my elbow! Temple cried out scornfully. And that's what I call limbo.

—Give us that stick here, Cranly said.

He snatched the ashplant roughly from Stephen's hand and sprang down the steps: but Temple, hearing him move in pursuit, fled through the dusk like a wild creature, nimble and fleetfooted. Cranly's heavy boots were heard loudly charging across the quadrangle and then returning heavily, foiled and spurning the gravel at each step.

His step was angry and with an angry abrupt gesture he thrust the stick back into Stephen's hand. Stephen felt that his anger had another cause but, feigning patience, touched his arm slightly and said quietly:

—Cranly, I told you I wanted to speak to you. Come away.

Cranly looked at him for a few moments and asked:

—Now?

—Yes, now, Stephen said. We can't speak here. Come away.

They crossed the quadrangle together without speaking. The birdcall from *Siegfried*[219] whistled softly followed them from the steps of the porch. Cranly turned: and Dixon, who had whistled, called out:

—Where are you fellows off to? What about that game, Cranly?

They parleyed in shouts across the still air about a game of billiards to be played in the Adelphi Hotel.[220] Stephen walked on alone and out into the quiet of Kildare Street. Opposite Maple's Hotel[221] he stood to wait, patient again. The name of the hotel, a colourless polished wood, and its colourless quiet front stung him like a glance of polite disdain. He stared angrily back at the softly lit drawingroom of the hotel in which he imagined the sleek lives of the patricians of Ireland housed in calm. They thought of army commissions and land agents: peasants greeted them along the roads in the country: they knew the names of certain French dishes and gave orders to jarvies[222] in highpitched provincial voices which pierced through their skintight accents.

How could he hit their conscience or how cast his shadow over the imaginations of their daughters, before their squires begat upon them, that they might breed a race less ignoble than their own? And under the deepened dusk he felt the thoughts and desires of the race to which he belonged flitting like bats, across the dark country lanes, under trees by the edges of streams and near the poolmottled bogs. A woman had waited in the doorway as Davin had passed by at night and, offering him a cup of milk, had all but wooed him to her bed; for Davin had the mild eyes of one who could be secret. But him no woman's eyes had wooed.

His arm was taken in a strong grip and Cranly's voice said:

—Let us eke go.[223]

They walked southward in silence. Then Cranly said:

—That blithering idiot Temple! I swear to Moses, do you know, that I'll be the death of that fellow one time.

But his voice was no longer angry and Stephen wondered was he thinking of her greeting to him under the porch.

They turned to the left and walked on as before. When they had gone on so for some time Stephen said:

—Cranly, I had an unpleasant quarrel this evening.

—With your people? Cranly asked.

—With my mother.

—About religion?

—Yes, Stephen answered.

After a pause Cranly asked:

—What age is your mother?

—Not old, Stephen said. She wishes me to make my easter duty.[224]

—And will you?

—I will not, Stephen said.

—Why not? Cranly said.

—I will not serve,[225] answered Stephen.

—That remark was made before, Cranly said calmly.

—It is made behind now, said Stephen hotly.

Cranly pressed Stephen's arm, saying:

—Go easy, my dear man. You're an excitable bloody man, do you know.

He laughed nervously as he spoke and, looking up into Stephen's face with moved and friendly eyes, said:

—Do you know that you are an excitable man?

—I daresay I am, said Stephen, laughing also.

Their minds, lately estranged, seemed suddenly to have been drawn closer, one to the other.

—Do you believe in the eucharist? Cranly asked.

—I do not, Stephen said.

—Do you disbelieve then?

—I neither believe in it nor disbelieve in it, Stephen answered.

—Many persons have doubts, even religious persons, yet they overcome them or put them aside, Cranly said. Are your doubts on that point too strong?

—I do not wish to overcome them, Stephen answered.

Cranly, embarrassed for a moment, took another fig from his pocket and was about to eat it when Stephen said:

—Don't, please. You cannot discuss this question with your mouth full of chewed fig.

Cranly examined the fig by the light of a lamp under which he halted. Then he smelt it with both nostrils, bit a tiny piece, spat it out and threw the fig rudely into the gutter. Addressing it as it lay, he said:

—Depart from me, ye cursed, into everlasting fire![226]

Taking Stephen's arm, he went on again and said:

—Do you not fear that those words may be spoken to you on the day of judgment?

—What is offered me on the other hand? Stephen asked. An eternity of bliss in the company of the dean of studies?

—Remember, Cranly said, that he would be glorified.

—Ay, Stephen said somewhat bitterly, bright, agile, impassible and, above all, subtle.[227]

—It is a curious thing, do you know, Cranly said dispassionately, how your mind is supersaturated with the religion in which you say you disbelieve. Did you believe in it when you were at school? I bet you did.

—I did, Stephen answered.

—And were you happier then? Cranly asked softly. Happier than you are now, for instance?

—Often happy, Stephen said, and often unhappy. I was someone else then.

—How someone else? What do you mean by that statement?

—I mean, said Stephen, that I was not myself as I am now, as I had to become.

—Not as you are now, not as you had to become, Cranly repeated. Let me ask you a question. Do you love your mother?

Stephen shook his head slowly.

—I don't know what your words mean, he said simply.

—Have you never loved anyone? Cranly asked.

—Do you mean women?

—I am not speaking of that, Cranly said in a colder tone. I ask you if you ever felt love towards anyone or anything.

Stephen walked on beside his friend, staring gloomily at the footpath.

—I tried to love God, he said at length. It seems now I failed. It is very difficult. I tried to unite my will with the will of God instant by instant. In that I did not always fail. I could perhaps do that still . . .

Cranly cut him short by asking:

—Has your mother had a happy life?

—How do I know? Stephen said.

—How many children had she?

—Nine or ten, Stephen answered. Some died.

—Was your father. . . . Cranly interrupted himself for an instant: and then said: I don't want to pry into your family affairs. But was your father what is called well-to-do? I mean when you were growing up?

—Yes, Stephen said.

—What was he? Cranly asked after a pause.

Stephen began to enumerate glibly his father's attributes.

—A medical student, an oarsman, a tenor, an amateur actor, a shouting politician, a small landlord, a small investor, a drinker, a good fellow, a storyteller, somebody's secretary, something in a distillery, a taxgatherer, a bankrupt and at present a praiser of his own past.

Cranly laughed, tightening his grip on Stephen's arm, and said:

—The distillery is damn good.

—Is there anything else you want to know? Stephen asked.

—Are you in good circumstances at present?

—Do I look it? Stephen asked bluntly.

—So then, Cranly went on musingly, you were born in the lap of luxury.

He used the phrase broadly and loudly as he often used technical expressions as if he wished his hearer to understand that they were used by him without conviction.

—Your mother must have gone through a good deal of suffering, he said then. Would you not try to save her from suffering more even it . . . or would you?

—If I could, Stephen said. That would cost me very little.

—Then do so, Cranly said. Do as she wishes you to do. What is it for you? You disbelieve in it. It is a form: nothing else. And you will set her mind at rest.

He ceased and, as Stephen did not reply, remained silent. Then, as if giving utterance to the process of his own thought, he said:

—Whatever else is unsure in this stinking dunghill of a world a mother's love is not. Your mother brings you into the world, carries you first in her body. What do we know about what she feels? But whatever she feels, it, at least, must be real. It must be. What are our ideas or ambitions? Play. Ideas! Why, that bloody bleating goat Temple has ideas. MacCann has ideas too. Every jackass going the roads thinks he has ideas.

Stephen, who had been listening to the unspoken speech behind the words, said with assumed carelessness:

—Pascal, if I remember rightly, would not suffer his mother to kiss him as he feared the contact of her sex.[228]

—Pascal was a pig, said Cranly.

—Aloysius Gonzaga,[229] I think, was of the same mind, Stephen said.

—And he was another pig then, said Cranly.

—The church calls him a saint, Stephen objected.

—I don't care a flaming damn what anyone calls him, Cranly said rudely and flatly. I call him a pig.

Stephen, preparing the words neatly in his mind, continued:

—Jesus, too, seems to have treated his mother with scant courtesy in public but Suarez, a jesuit theologian and Spanish gentleman,[230] has apologised for him.

—Did the idea ever occur to you, Cranly asked, that Jesus was not what he pretended to be?

—The first person to whom that idea occurred, Stephen answered, was Jesus himself.

—I mean, Cranly said, hardening in his speech, did the idea ever occur to you that he was himself a conscious hypocrite, what he called the jews of his time, a whited sepulchre?[231] Or, to put it more plainly, that he was a blackguard?

—That idea never occurred to me, Stephen answered. But I am curious to know are you trying to make a convert of me or a pervert[232] of yourself?

He turned towards his friend's face and saw there a raw smile which some force of will strove to make finely significant.

Cranly asked suddenly in a plain sensible tone:

—Tell me the truth. Were you at all shocked by what I said?

—Somewhat, Stephen said.

—And why were you shocked, Cranly pressed on in the same tone, if you feel sure that our religion is false and that Jesus was not the son of God?

—I am not at all sure of it, Stephen said. He is more like a son of God than a son of Mary.

—And is that why you will not communicate, Cranly asked, because you are not sure of that too, because you feel that the host too may be the body and blood of the son of God and not a wafer of bread? And because you fear that it may be?

—Yes, Stephen said quietly. I feel that and I also fear it.

—I see, Cranly said.

Stephen, struck by his tone of closure, reopened the discussion at once by saying:

—I fear many things: dogs, horses, firearms, the sea, thunderstorms, machinery, the country roads at night.

—But why do you fear a bit of bread?

—I imagine, Stephen said, that there is a malevolent reality behind those things I say I fear.

—Do you fear then, Cranly asked, that the God of the Roman catholics would strike you dead and damn you if you made a sacrilegious communion?[233]

—The God of the Roman catholics could do that now, Stephen said. I fear more than that the chemical action which would be set up in my soul by a false homage to a symbol behind which are massed twenty centuries of authority and veneration.

—Would you, Cranly asked, in extreme danger commit that particular sacrilege? For instance, if you lived in the penal days?[234]

—I cannot answer for the past, Stephen replied. Possibly not.

—Then, said Cranly, you do not intend to become a protestant?

—I said that I had lost the faith, Stephen answered, but not that I had lost selfrespect. What kind of liberation would that be to forsake an absurdity which is logical and coherent and to embrace one which is illogical and incoherent?

They had walked on towards the township of Pembroke[235] and now, as they went on slowly along the avenues, the trees and the scattered lights in the villas soothed their minds. The air of wealth and repose diffused about them seemed to comfort their neediness. Behind a hedge of laurel a light glimmered in the window of a kitchen and the voice of a servant was heard singing as she sharpened knives. She sang, in short broken bars, *Rosie O'Grady*.[236]

Cranly stopped to listen, saying:

—*Mulier cantat.*[237]

The soft beauty of the Latin words touched with an enchanting touch the dark of the evening, with a touch fainter and more persuading than the touch of music or of a woman's hand. The strife of their minds was quelled. The figure of woman as she appears in the liturgy of the church passed silently through the darkness: a whiterobed figure, small and slender as a boy and with a falling girdle. Her voice, frail and high as a boy's, was heard intoning from a distant choir the first words of a woman which pierce the gloom and clamour of the first chanting of the passion:

—*Et tu cum Jesu Galilœo eras.*[238]

And all hearts were touched and turned to her voice, shining like a young star, shining clearer as the voice intoned the prop-aroxyton[239] and more faintly as the cadence died.

The singing ceased. They went on together, Cranly repeating in strongly stressed rhythm the end of the refrain:

> *And when we are married,*
> *O, how happy we'll be*
> *For I love sweet Rosie O'Grady*
> *And Rosie O'Grady loves me.*

—There's real poetry for you, he said. There's real love.

He glanced sideways at Stephen with a strange smile and said:

—Do you consider that poetry? Or do you know what the words mean?

—I want to see Rosie first, said Stephen.

—She's easy to find, Cranly said.

His hat had come down on his forehead. He shoved it back: and in the shadow of the trees Stephen saw his pale face, framed by the dark, and his large dark eyes. Yes. His face was handsome: and his body was strong and hard. He had spoken of a mother's love. He felt then the sufferings of women, the weaknesses of their bodies and souls: and would shield them with a strong and resolute arm and bow his mind to them.

Away then: it is time to go. A voice spoke softly to Stephen's lonely heart, bidding him go and telling him that his friendship was coming to an end. Yes; he would go. He could not strive against another. He knew his part.

—Probably I shall go away, he said.

—Where? Cranly asked.

—Where I can, Stephen said.

—Yes, Cranly said. It might be difficult for you to live here now. But is it that that makes you go?

—I have to go, Stephen answered.

—Because, Cranly continued, you need not look upon yourself as driven away if you do not wish to go or as a heretic or an outlaw. There are many good believers who think as you do. Would that surprise you? The church is not the stone building nor even the clergy and their dogmas. It is the whole mass of those born into it. I don't know what you wish to do in life. Is it what you told me the night we were standing outside Harcourt Street station?²⁴⁰

—Yes, Stephen said, smiling in spite of himself at Cranly's way of remembering thoughts in connection with places. The night you spent half an hour wrangling with Doherty about the shortest way from Sallygap to Larras.²⁴¹

—Pothead! Cranly said with calm contempt. What does he know about the way from Sallygap to Larras? Or what does he know about anything for that matter? And the big slobbering washingpot head of him!

He broke out into a loud long laugh.

—Well? Stephen said. Do you remember the rest?

—What you said, is it? Cranly asked. Yes, I remember it. To discover the mode of life or of art whereby your spirit could express itself in unfettered freedom.

Stephen raised his hat in acknowledgment.

—Freedom! Cranly repeated. But you are not free enough yet to commit a sacrilege. Tell me, would you rob?

—I would beg first, Stephen said.

—And if you got nothing, would you rob?

—You wish me to say, Stephen answered, that the rights of property are provisional and that in certain circumstances it is not unlawful to rob. Everyone would act in that belief. So I will not make you that answer. Apply to the jesuit theologian Juan Mariana de Talavera who will also explain to you in what circumstances you may lawfully kill your king and whether you had better hand him his poison in a goblet or smear it for him upon his robe or his saddlebow.²⁴² Ask me rather would I suffer others to rob me or, if they did, would I call down upon them what I believe is called the chastisement of the secular arm?²⁴³

—And would you?

—I think, Stephen said, it would pain me as much to do so as to be robbed.

—I see, Cranly said.

He produced his match and began to clean the crevice between two teeth. Then he said carelessly:

—Tell me, for example, would you deflower a virgin?

—Excuse me, Stephen said politely, is that not the ambition of most young gentlemen?

—What then is your point of view? Cranly asked.

His last phrase, soursmelling as the smoke of charcoal and disheartening, excited Stephen's brain, over which its fumes seemed to brood.

—Look here, Cranly, he said. You have asked me what I would do and what I would not do. I will tell you what I will do and what I will not do. I will not serve that in which I no longer believe whether it call itself my home, my fatherland or my church: and I will try to express myself in some mode of life or art as freely as I can and as wholly as I can, using for my defence the only arms I allow myself to use—silence, exile, and cunning.

Cranly seized his arm and steered him round so as to head back towards Leeson Park.[244] He laughed almost slily and pressed Stephen's arm with an elder's affection.

—Cunning indeed! he said. Is it you? You poor poet, you!

—And you made me confess to you, Stephen said, thrilled by his touch, as I have confessed to you so many other things, have I not?

—Yes, my child, Cranly said, still gaily.

—You made me confess the fears that I have. But I will tell you also what I do not fear. I do not fear to be alone or to be spurned for another or to leave whatever I have to leave. And I am not afraid to make a mistake, even a great mistake, a lifelong mistake and perhaps as long as eternity too.

Cranly, now grave again, slowed his pace and said:

—Alone, quite alone. You have no fear of that. And you know what that word means? Not only to be separate from all others but to have not even one friend.

—I will take the risk, said Stephen.

—And not to have any one person, Cranly said, who would be more than a friend, more even than the noblest and truest friend a man ever had.

His words seemed to have struck some deep chord in his own nature. Had he spoken of himself, of himself as he was or wished to be? Stephen watched his face for some moments in silence. A cold sadness was there. He had spoken of himself, of his own loneliness which he feared.

—Of whom are you speaking? Stephen asked at length.

Cranly did not answer.

20 *March:* Long talk with Cranly on the subject of my revolt. He had his grand manner on. I supple and suave. Attacked me on the score of love for one's mother. Tried to imagine his mother: cannot. Told me once, in a moment of thoughtlessness, his father was sixtyone when he was born. Can see him. Strong farmer type. Pepper and salt suit. Square feet. Unkempt grizzled beard. Probably attends coursing matches.²⁴⁵ Pays his dues regularly but not plentifully to Father Dwyer of Larras. Sometimes talks to girls after nightfall. But his mother? Very young or very old? Hardly the first. If so, Cranly would not have spoken as he did. Old then. Probably, and neglected. Hence Cranly's despair of soul: the child of exhausted loins.

21 *March, morning:* Thought this in bed last night but was too lazy and free to add it. Free, yes. The exhausted loins are those of Elisabeth and Zachary.²⁴⁶ Then he is the precursor. Item: he eats chiefly belly bacon and dried figs. Read locusts and wild honey. Also, when thinking of him, saw always a stern severed head or deathmask as if outlined on a grey curtain or veronica.²⁴⁷ Decollation they call it in the fold. Puzzled for the moment by saint John at the Latin gate. What do I see? A decollated precursor trying to pick the lock.²⁴⁸

21 *March, night:* Free. Soulfree and fancyfree. Let the dead bury the dead. Ay. And let the dead marry the dead.²⁴⁹

22 *March:* In company with Lynch followed a sizable hospital nurse. Lynch's idea. Dislike it. Two lean hungry greyhounds walking after a heifer.

23 *March:* Have not seen her since that night. Unwell? Sits at the fire perhaps with mamma's shawl on her shoulders. But not peevish. A nice bowl of gruel? Won't you now?

24 *March:* Began with a discussion with my mother. Subject: B. V. M.[250] Handicapped by my sex and youth. To escape held up relations between Jesus and Papa against those between Mary and her son. Said religion was not a lying-in hospital.[251] Mother indulgent. Said I have a queer mind and have read too much. Not true. Have read little and understood less. Then she said I would come back to faith because I had a restless mind. This means to leave church by backdoor of sin and reenter through the skylight of repentance. Cannot repent. Told her so and asked for sixpence. Got threepence.

Then went to college. Other wrangle with little roundhead rogue'seye Ghezzi.[252] This time about Bruno the Nolan.[253] Began in Italian and ended in pidgin English. He said Bruno was a terrible heretic. I said he was terribly burned. He agreed to this with some sorrow. Then gave me recipe for what he calls *risotto alla bergamasca*.[254] When he pronounces a soft o he protrudes his full carnal lips as if he kissed the vowel. Has he? And could he repent? Yes, he could: and cry two round rogue's tears, one from each eye.

Crossing Stephen's, that is, my green,[255] remembered that his countrymen and not mine had invented what Cranly the other night called our religion. A quarter of them, soldiers of the ninetyseventh infantry regiment, sat at the foot of the cross and tossed up dice for the overcoat of the crucified.[256]

Went to library. Tried to read three reviews. Useless. She is not out yet. Am I alarmed? About what? That she will never be out again.

Blake wrote:

> *I wonder if William Bond will die*
> *For assuredly he is very ill.*[257]

Alas, poor William!

I was once at a diorama in Rotunda.[258] At the end were pictures of big nobs. Among them William Ewart Gladstone,[259] just then dead. Orchestra played O, *Willie, we have missed you.*[260]

A race of clodhoppers![261]

25 *March, morning:* A troubled night of dreams. Want to get them off my chest.

A long curving gallery. From the floor ascend pillars of dark vapours. It is peopled by the images of fabulous kings, set in stone. Their hands are folded upon their knees in token of weariness and their eyes are darkened for the errors of men go up before them for ever as dark vapours.

Strange figures advance from a cave. They are not as tall as men. One does not seem to stand quite apart from another. Their faces are phosphorescent, with darker streaks. They peer at me and their eyes seem to ask me something. They do not speak.

30 *March:* This evening Cranly was in the porch of the library, proposing a problem to Dixon and her brother. A mother let her child fall into the Nile. Still harping on the mother.[262] A crocodile seized the child. Mother asked it back. Crocodile said all right if she told him what he was going to do with the child, eat it or not eat it.[263]

This mentality, Lepidus would say, is indeed bred out of your mud by the operation of your sun.[264]

And mine? Is it not too? Then into Nilemud with it!

1 *April:* Disapprove of this last phrase.

2 *April:* Saw her drinking tea and eating cakes in Johnston, Mooney and O'Brien's.[265] Rather, lynxeyed Lynch saw her as we passed. He tells me Cranly was invited there by brother. Did he bring his crocodile? Is he the shining light now? Well, I discovered him. I protest I did. Shining quietly behind a bushel of Wicklow bran.[266]

3 *April:* Met Davin at the cigar shop opposite Findlater's church.[267] He was in a black sweater and had a hurleystick. Asked me was it true I was going away and why. Told him the shortest way to Tara was *via* Holyhead.[268] Just then my father came up. Introduction. Father, polite and observant. Asked Davin if he might offer him some refreshment. Davin could not, was going to meeting. When we came away father told me he had a good honest eye. Asked me why I did not join a rowing club. I pretended to think it over. Told me then how he broke Pennyfeather's heart.[269] Wants me to read law. Says I was cut out for that. More mud, more crocodiles.

5 *April:* Wild spring. Scudding clouds. O life! Dark stream of swirling bogwater on which appletrees have cast down their delicate flowers. Eyes of girls among the leaves. Girls demure and romping. All fair or auburn: no dark ones. They blush better. Houp-la!

6 *April:* Certainly she remembers the past. Lynch says all women do. Then she remembers the time of her childhood—and mine if I was ever a child. The past is consumed in the present and the present is living only because it brings forth the future. Statues of women, if Lynch be right, should always be fully draped, one hand of the woman feeling regretfully her own hinder parts.

6 *April, later:* Michael Robartes remembers forgotten beauty and, when his arms wrap her round, he presses in his arms the loveliness which has long faded from the world.[270] Not this. Not at all. I desire to press in my arms the loveliness which has not yet come into the world.

10 *April:* Faintly, under the heavy night, through the silence of the city which has turned from dreams to dreamless sleep as a weary lover whom no caresses move, the sound of hoofs upon the road. Not so faintly now as they come near the bridge: and in a moment as they pass the darkened windows the silence is cloven by alarm as by an arrow. They are heard now far away, hoofs that shine amid the heavy night as gems, hurrying beyond the sleeping fields to what journey's end—what heart?—bearing what tidings?

11 *April:* Read what I wrote last night. Vague words for a vague emotion. Would she like it? I think so. Then I should have to like it also.

13 *April:* That tundish has been on my mind for a long time. I looked it up and find it English and good old blunt English too. Damn the dean of studies and his funnel! What did he come here for to teach us his own language or to learn it from us? Damn him one way or the other!

14 *April:* John Alphonsus Mulrennan has just returned from the west of Ireland. (European and Asiatic papers please copy.) He told us he met an old man there in a mountain cabin. Old man had red eyes and short pipe. Old man spoke Irish.

Mulrennan spoke Irish. Then old man and Mulrennan spoke English. Mulrennan spoke to him about universe and stars. Old man sat, listened, smoked, spat. Then said:

—Ah, there must be terrible queer creatures at the latter end of the world.[271]

I fear him. I fear his redrimmed horny eyes. It is with him I must struggle all through this night till day come, till he or I lie dead, gripping him by the sinewy throat till . . . Till what? Till he yield to me? No. I mean him no harm.

15 *April:* Met her today pointblank in Grafton Street. The crowd brought us together. We both stopped. She asked me why I never came, said she had heard all sorts of stories about me. This was only to gain time. Asked me, was I writing poems? About whom? I asked her. This confused her more and I felt sorry and mean. Turned off that valve at once and opened the spiritual-heroic refrigerating apparatus, invented and patented in all countries by Dante Alighieri.[272] Talked rapidly of myself and my plans. In the midst of it unluckily I made a sudden gesture of a revolutionary nature. I must have looked like a fellow throwing a handful of peas into the air. People began to look at us. She shook hands a moment after and, in going away, said she hoped I would do what I said.

Now I call that friendly, don't you?

Yes, I liked her today. A little or much? Don't know. I liked her and it seems a new feeling to me. Then, in that case, all the rest, all that I thought I thought and all that I felt I felt, all the rest before now, in fact . . . O, give it up, old chap! Sleep it off!

16 *April:* Away! Away!

The spell of arms and voices: the white arms of roads, their promise of close embraces and the black arms of tall ships that stand against the moon, their tale of distant nations. They are held out to say: We are alone. Come. And the voices say with them: We are your kinsmen. And the air is thick with their company as they call to me, their kinsman, making ready to go, shaking the wings of their exultant and terrible youth.

26 *April:* Mother is putting my new secondhand clothes in order. She prays now, she says, that I may learn in my own life and away from home and friends what the heart is and what it

feels. Amen. So be it. Welcome, O life! I go to encounter for the millionth time the reality of experience and to forge in the smithy of my soul the uncreated conscience of my race.

27 *April:* Old father, old artificer, stand me now and ever in good stead.[273]

DUBLIN 1904
TRIESTE 1914

Notes

Anyone who attempts to annotate *Portrait* owes a great debt to Chester Anderson for his annotations to the Viking Critical Library edition (1968) and to Don Gifford for *Joyce Annotated* (2nd edition, University of California Press, Berkeley, Los Angeles, London, 1982). On those occasions when I have taken information directly from them that I could not find elsewhere, I have indicated the source with an (A) or a (G).

EPIGRAPH

Et ignotas animum dimittit in artes Ovid, *Metamorphoses*, VIII, 188: 'And he applies his mind to obscure arts.' The 'he' in question is Daedalus, father of Icarus, who fashioned wings for himself and his son to escape from the Cretan labyrinth he had created to house the Minotaur, the half-bull, half-man offspring of Queen Pasiphae and an artificial bull. The name Daedalus in Greek means 'cunning artificer'. Icarus flies too near the sun, his wings melt and disintegrate and he falls into the sea. Daedalus arrives safely in Sicily. The father and the son are often taken as prototypes of the classical and of the romantic artist respectively.

I

1. *lemon platt*: a plaited candy stick. *Tuckoo* was a nickname for the infant Joyce (*Letters*, III, 212).
2. *Michael Davitt . . . Parnell*: Michael Davitt (1846–1906) founded the Land League (1879), an organization financed by the Irish Republican Brotherhood (IRB), the Fenians in the USA, and the

Irish Parliamentary Party, under Parnell's leadership. It was devoted to the abolition of landlordism and the protection of tenants. Davitt's association with Parnell united the revolutionary, constitutional and agrarian elements in Ireland into a formidable weapon that Charles Stewart Parnell (1846–91) wielded with great skill in his campaign for Home Rule – that is, the establishment in Dublin of an Irish legislature with responsibility for domestic affairs. However, it was Parnell's irresponsible conduct of his domestic affair with Katharine O'Shea, the wife of a parliamentary colleague, that led to his being cited as co-respondent in a divorce case. As a consequence, he was abandoned by William Ewart Gladstone, the English Prime Minister and leader of the Liberal Party, by the Roman Catholic Church in Ireland and, in a famous series of meetings in Committee Room 15 of the House of Commons in December 1890, by the Irish Parliamentary Party of which he was 'the Chief'. (This is referred to in the title of Joyce's story 'Ivy Day in the Committee Room' in *Dubliners*.) Parnell died soon after, on 6 October 1891. Davitt and Parnell were in effective alliance from 1879 to 1882; thereafter the divergences in their political views became increasingly sharp. Davitt was one of the first and most vocal of those who opposed Parnell's attempt to retain the leadership after the divorce scandal.

3. *cachou*: a candy made from cashew nuts. (G)

4. *Pull out his eyes . . . Apologise*: derived from song XXIII of Isaac Watts' *Divine Songs Attempted in Easy Language for the Use of Children* (London, 1715). (G)

5. *third line*: the students were divided into three age groups: those under thirteen were in the third line; those from thirteen to fifteen were in the lower line; and from fifteen to eighteen, in the higher line.

6. *greaves in his number and a hamper in the refectory*: he has shin-guards – to protect him from football injuries – in his numbered locker, and special food, provided by his family, to replace or supplement the school meals. Kickham seems to have had solicitous parents.

7. *Stephen Dedalus*: the name conjoins the first Christian martyr, St Stephen, stoned to death outside Jerusalem in 34 AD, and the great pagan artificer–artist hero, Daedalus.

8. *magistrate*: after long exclusion, Catholics in the late nineteenth century had some avenues of advancement open to them in the judicial system. Yet even the longing for the social status conferred by a magistracy rarely outweighed the recognition that

membership of the degraded and degrading legal system in Ireland was inadvisable for Catholics, especially in troubled times. Few of the sixty-four Resident Magistrates in Ireland at that time were Catholic. During the Land War of 1879–82, in which Davitt and Parnell were among the leaders, 'Special' Resident Magistrates were appointed.

9. *peach*: inform.

10. *rector*: the rector is the ecclesiastic who has charge of the government of a college. He is superior to the prefect of studies and the prefect of discipline, both of whom are also ecclesiastics. The rector of Clongowes at this time was the Reverend John Conmee, SJ, who also appears in the *Wandering Rocks* episode of *Ulysses*.

11. *scrimmage*: in rugby football, a scrum, a set piece in which the opposing forwards lock together to form a low arch into which the ball is fed and from which it is released again by foot. The game played here is not, as has sometimes been claimed, Gaelic football. Stephen seems to be playing in the line of backs, probably on the wing, and is devoting his energies to avoiding any contact with either ball or opposing player. Rugby, like cricket, would have been considered to be a proper game for a college like Clongowes with its 'public school' ethos. Gaelic football's revival dates from 1884, but its later political victories were not won on the playing fields of Clongowes.

12. *seventyseven to seventysix*: the number of days to go to the end of first term.

13. *He wondered . . . the windows*: Archibald Hamilton Rowan (1751–1834) was a member of the radical United Irishmen organization that had sought to establish in Ireland a version of French revolutionary republican ideals. He was arrested in 1794 but escaped his troop escort and hid in Clongowes Wood Castle, as it then was. He is reputed to have thrown his hat from the library window on to the ha-ha outside, thus deceiving the British soldiers into believing that he had escaped in that direction. The legend has it that he hid in a secret room in the castle until he was smuggled in safety to France some time later. (G)

A ha-ha is a bank or dry moat designed to keep cattle off the lawns and gardens surrounding a house without obstructing the view.

Clongowes Wood Castle was sold to the Jesuit order in 1814 and became the centre of the complex of buildings forming Clongowes Wood College, SJ.

14. *Doctor Cornwell's Spelling Book . . . one of animals*: A Grammar for Beginners (1838), an introduction to *An English School Grammar* (1839), both by James Cornwell and Alexander Allen, were standard in primary and intermediate schools in Ireland at this time. The Intermediate Education Act of 1878 established a system of public examinations and payment to school managers on the basis of results obtained therein. This encouraged systematic cramming; texts such as these were designed to cater to this kind of education. Young Stephen's frequent quotations from classroom material are typical of the memorizing of set pieces practised at Clongowes and other schools.

Thomas, Cardinal Wolsey (1475?–1530), fell from grace because he could not persuade the Pope to declare Henry VIII's first marriage void. He died at the Abbey of Saint Mary Pré, near Leicester, in England.

15. *square ditch*: the square is an open water closet behind the dormitory; the ditch is the cesspool for this WC. (A)

16. *hacking chestnut*: chestnuts were suspended on a string and one was struck against the other until one of them broke.

17. *suck*: favourite, sycophant.

18. *Wicklow Hotel*: in Wicklow Street, in central Dublin.

19. *York! . . . Lancaster!*: the names of the opposing English houses in the dynastic Wars of the Roses (1445–85). Ireland supported Yorkshire, whose emblem was the white rose, against Lancaster, the red rose. This was noted by the victorious Lancastrian dynasty. The competitive spirit in learning fostered by the Jesuits was in accord with the examination system inaugurated in 1878.

20. *a wax*: a bad temper.

21. *elements*: that is, in spelling, grammar, writing, arithmetic, geography, history and Latin.

22. *green rose*: possibly the references to red, green and roses are covert allusions to Ireland, traditionally associated with the rose in its dark or sacrificially crimson shades. But it is more likely that Stephen is here considering the relation between what is possible in the world and what is possible in words.

23. *Dalkey*: a village on the coast, eight miles south-east of Dublin and one of the stops on the railway journey from the more southerly Bray, where Joyce's family lived, to Dublin.

24. *Tullabeg*: in 1886, St Stanislaus's College, Tullabeg, became the home of the Jesuit Novitiate in Ireland. It closed in 1990.

25. *kiss your mother*: probably a reference to St Aloysius Gonzaga (1568–91), a famous Jesuit who is reputed to have avoided even looking at his mother. This version of the Oedipal complex understandably worries Stephen. Kissing his mother or being kissed by her is an anxiety that recurs within a few paragraphs and again on pp. 16, 224.

26. *for a cod*: for a joke.

27. *something in the paper about it*: the fictive time of the novel is a little elusive. Parnell died on 6 October 1891. The most intense newspaper coverage of the split in the Irish Parliamentary Party and in the country at large over Parnell's leadership took place between November and December 1890. But the effects of the split reverberated for a generation.

28. *O Lord, open our lips . . . to help us!*: the opening lines of Matins in the Divine Office; the second and fourth lines are the responses. (G) The office was recited daily from the Breviary; it was an obligation for all in holy orders to recite the office at the canonical hours – Matins and Lauds, Prime, Tierce, Sext, None, Vespers and Compline.

29. *Clane . . . Sallins*: a village one and a half miles from the college and a village just over four miles from Clongowes, respectively.

30. *Visit, we beseech Thee . . . Amen*: the last prayer before the conclusion of Compline, the last of the canonical hours in the Divine Office.

31. *the white cloak of a marshal*: Maximilian Ulysses, Count von Browne, was the Austrian-born son of an Irish Jacobite whose family had owned Clongowes Wood in the eighteenth century. He became a marshal in the Austrian army and was killed at the battle of Prague in 1757. It is said that on the day of his death his blood-stained ghost appeared to the servants in his ancestral home.

32. *Bodenstown*: this townland in County Kildare contains the churchyard in which Wolfe Tone, the father of Irish republicanism, is buried. Tone's reputation was emerging from comparative eclipse as the centenary of the 1798 rebellion approached. Perhaps it is to Tone's grave that the drivers are pointing their whips.

33. *Was that right?*: see note 25, above.

34. *a marshal now*: either Stephen is confusing his father with the marshal Browne who reputedly haunted Clongowes or he has been told that his father's new position as a functionary in the corporation tax-gatherer's office merits the title. The word can be used in this way and Simon Dedalus would readily appropriate it to inflate his menial status. Worries about social status and sex are among the early gifts bestowed upon Stephen by his parents.

35. *don't spy on us, sure you won't?*: that is, don't inform against me.

36. *Father Minister*: vice-rector, a priest appointed by the rector as a housemaster whose duties are distinct from academic matters.

37. *Hayfoot! Strawfoot!*: after the practice of tying a wisp of hay to a rural recruit's left foot, a wisp of straw to his right, to teach him how to march. (G)

38. *Brother Michael*: a brother is a member of the second of the six grades of membership in the Company of Jesus – a temporal coadjutor. He would perform many household duties and services.

39. *dead mass*: a Mass for the dead, a Requiem Mass. The colours of the vestments for such a Mass would be black and gold.

40. *Dingdong! . . . carry my soul away*: anonymous nursery rhyme.

41. *Athy*: a town in County Kildare, forty-three miles southwest of Dublin.

42. *the liberator*: Daniel O'Connell (1775–1847), the leader of Catholic Ireland in the first four decades of the nineteenth century. He wrested Catholic emancipation from a reluctant British government in 1829 and thereby earned himself the soubriquet, 'the Liberator'.

43. *Parnell! Parnell! He is dead!*: Parnell's body was brought from England, where he died, to Dun Laoghaire (then Kingstown) on 11 October. It was met by a large and grieving crowd among which was Yeats, there to meet Maud Gonne. Yeats described the funeral and burial of Parnell as the event that closed the Irish nineteenth century.

44. *boss*: a kind of footstool.

45. *cramped fingers . . . Queen Victoria*: Mr Casey was a Fenian (Irish revolutionary) prisoner who had been sentenced to hard labour, picking oakum, in one of Her Majesty's (Queen Victoria's) prisons.

46. *the Head*: Bray Head, a promontory overlooking the seaside town.

47. *that champagne*: explosives.

48. *Bless us, O Lord . . . Amen*: a standard prayer recited before meals.

49. *Dunn's of D'Olier Street*: a fashionable shop in central Dublin.

50. *Ally Daly*: Dublin slang for the genuine article, the best.

51. *pandybat . . . turkey?*: a pandybat is a reinforced leather strap, used for punishment in schools. Mr Barrett calls it a turkey because it makes the hands, when struck, turn red.

52. *The bishops . . . the English people?*: in November 1890, Parnell's divorce case came up for trial. The British Prime Minister, Gladstone, published a letter on 26 November in which he informed the Irish Parliamentary Party that so long as Parnell remained leader there could be no alliance with the British Liberal Party. Parnell refused to resign his chairmanship of the Party. On 29 November he published his *Manifesto to the Irish People*, an intemperate attack on his enemies. The Catholic hierarchy intervened decisively in December, just before the Parliamentary Party met to consider Parnell's position. Forty-four members went against Parnell, twenty-seven stayed loyal to him. Parnell's subsequent by-election campaigns were attended by great bitterness, denunciations of and by the clergy, and an appeal by Parnell to the physical-force movement, the Fenians, traditional enemies of the clergy. Parnellites saw their leader as betrayed by the Gladstonian Liberals, the Irish Catholic clergy and his own Party. Others (like Michael Davitt) saw the choice as one between Home Rule and Parnell. The Fenian Mr Casey's support for Parnell would have confirmed middle-class Irish Catholic hostility to him.

53. *Woe be to the man . . . little ones*: Luke 17:1–2.

54. *Billy . . . tub of guts up in Armagh?*: respectively, William Joseph Walsh (1841–1921), Catholic archbishop of Dublin (1885–1921), and Michael Logue (1839–1924), archbishop of Armagh and Roman Catholic Primate of All-Ireland (1887–1924). Walsh's appointment to the See of Dublin was strongly opposed by the British government because of his strong nationalist sympathies. He was a strong supporter of Parnell and played a leading role in restraining the Irish clergy from involvement in the crisis. But on 3 December 1890 he sent a telegram to the Irish Parliamentary Party, then in session in Committee Room 15, calling on it to 'act manfully' – that is, to get rid of Parnell as leader. Michael Logue opposed Parnell's leadership of the Irish Parliamentary Party after the divorce. He became a cardinal in 1893.

55. *Lord Leitrim's coachman*: William Sydney Clements, Earl of Leitrim (1806–78), was a conservative politician and notoriously vicious landlord with large estates in counties Lei trim and Donegal in the north-west of Ireland. He was assassinated in 1878 by three local men who were never arrested, although a memorial to them was erected in 1960. The assassination was a prelude to the Land War, which broke out a year later. Leitrim's coachman tried to save him; the phrase indicates contempt for an Irishman who would slavishly try to protect or support his own and his people's

oppressor. The Catholic Church has often been accused of performing this role because of its regular, if strategically enthusiastic, support for the British government in Ireland.

56. *renegade catholics*: Mr Casey is referring to the practice, quite
common under the Penal Laws in Ireland, of changing one's faith
from Catholicism to Protestantism in order to retain property or
the means of survival. A proper nationalist pedigree would bear
no such stain. The boast is perfectly compatible with the anti-
clericalism that accompanies it.

57. *blackest protestant*: that is, a Protestant of the deepest anti-
Catholic dye; a common epithet in Ireland.

58. *O, come all . . . to mass*: a parody of the standard Irish ballad
that begins with 'Come all ye (or you) . . .'.

59. *chainies*: flawed or damaged chinaware. Mrs Riordan, the original for Dante, is said by Richard Ellmann to have forsaken her
ambition to become a nun when her brother left her a fortune,
made out of trading with African natives.

60. *Tower of Ivory . . . House of Gold!*: a Litany is a form of united
prayer by alternate sentences, in which the clergy lead and the
people respond. The Litany of Our Lady came into general use
about the thirteenth century, spread by pilgrims who heard it
sung in the Santa Casa of Loreto in Italy. It is usually sung or
chanted at Benediction. It is one of the four forms of Litany rec-
ognized by the Church. Devotion to Mary was often repudiated
by Protestants as an infantile form of Catholic idolatry.

61. *Priesthunter!*: not so much a reference to Parnell's belated attacks
on the clergy who had condemned him, as an insult to those
Catholics who, in supporting Parnell, were akin to the priesthunt-
ers who had in penal times collected blood-money by informing
on the proscribed clergy.

62. *The Paris Funds! Mr Fox! Kitty O'Shea!*: the Irish Parliamentary Party held funds in Paris to avoid sequestration of them by
the British government. Parnell used these to finance his last
campaign. It was rumoured that he used these moneys to finance
his affair with Katharine O'Shea. Fox was one of the pseud-
onyms he used in his communications with her. The diminutive
form 'Kitty' for 'Katharine' was sexually insulting.

63. *Tullamore*: Tullamore, fifty miles west of Dublin, produced a
famous 'plug (or chewing) tobacco'.

64. *Cabinteely road*: Mr Casey had gone by car on the inland route
towards Dublin, through the village of Cabinteely, possibly to

avoid arrest. Sergeant O'Neill may have been warning him of his imminent arrest at the railway station.

65. *It is true for them*: an expression taken from Irish; it means, 'They (the clergy) are in control, have the upper hand.'

66. *priestridden*: the reorganization of the Catholic Church in Ireland after the Famine was undertaken by Cardinal Paul Cullen (1803–78). He wanted the Irish Parliamentary Party to become, in effect, a Catholic lobby and to link itself closely to the British Liberal Party. He was deeply opposed to the Fenians.

67. *whiteboy*: the Whiteboys were an agrarian secret society that flourished initially in the 1760s. They wore white garments to help identify one another at night during their raids on stock, farmhouses and the like. Their grievances were payments of tithes, raised rents, enclosures and various taxes. Whiteboyism endured, in different forms, into the nineteenth century. The movement was condemned on several occasions by the Catholic Church.

68. *put his two feet under his mahogany*: sit at his table, receive his hospitality.

69. *Touch them not . . . apple of My eye*: Zachariah 2:8.

70. *Lanigan . . . Cornwallis*: James Lanigan (d. 1812) was Bishop of Ossory. He presented a complimentary address to Lord Cornwallis in 1799, on foot of a decision by the Catholic hierarchy to accept a proposal of Catholic emancipation in exchange for granting to the British government the right to veto the appointment of Catholic bishops. Charles Cornwallis, first marquis and second earl, who had surrendered to Washington at Yorktown in 1781, was Commander-in-Chief and Lord Lieutenant of Ireland (1798–1801). He suppressed the rebellion of 1798 and worked to secure the Union of Great Britain and Ireland. He was authorized to assure the Catholic hierarchy that emancipation would follow union. He resigned when King George III refused to honour the promise of emancipation. The Act of Union abolished the Irish parliament and made provision for Irish representation at Westminster. It remained in force from 1801 to 1922.

71. *catholic emancipation*: the act of 1829 admitted Catholics to a wide range of public offices from which they had been excluded. The measure was vigorously supported by the Catholic Church, which had helped Daniel O'Connell, the Liberator (see note 42, above), to mobilize the Catholic population in his campaign.

72. *fenian movement . . . confessionbox*: 'Fenians' was the name given to the republican organization founded on St Patrick's

Day, 1858, in New York, simultaneously with the Irish Republican Brotherhood (IRB), founded in Dublin. The name commemorated the ancient warriors of Ireland, the Fianna. The Fenians supplied men to the IRB and were subject to the Supreme Council of the IRB. The Catholic clergy denounced both the Fenians and the IRB and generally regarded both organizations as one. Absolution was sometimes withheld at confession from those who admitted membership of the movement, although the hierarchy was more hostile than the regular clergy.

73. *Terence Bellew MacManus*: MacManus (1823–60) had been a supporter of O'Connell, a Young Irelander and a Fenian. He was transported to Australia, escaped and made his way to the USA, where he died eight years later. The IRB brought his body home for burial; Cardinal Paul Cullen (1803–78) refused permission for a lying-in-state in the Catholic Pro-Cathedral in Dublin and banned participation by the Catholic clergy. The ban was broken by one priest, the funeral was one of the largest ever seen in Dublin and a propaganda success for the Fenians.

74. *Paul Cullen*: Cullen (see above) was the first Irish cardinal (1866) and a resolute organizer of the Catholic Church. (See also note 66, above.)

75. *My dead king!*: one of Parnell's soubriquets was 'the uncrowned king of Ireland'.

76. *Hill of Lyons*: a hill six miles east of Clongowes Wood College.

77. *minister*: the vice-rector.

78. *car*: a two-wheeled horse-drawn vehicle.

79. *fecked*: stolen.

80. *scut*: ran away.

81. *boatbearer*: the server who carries the vessel that holds the incense before it is transferred to the censer (or thurible, a vessel with chains attached) in the rite of Benediction. In this rite the priest takes the Host from the tabernacle, places it in the monstrance and then places the monstrance on a throne above the tabernacle. The incense is then transferred to the thurible, burnt and the thurible swung before the Host.

82. *the little altar in the wood*: there is an altar in the wood or park adjoining Clongowes at which Benediction was performed.

83. *a sprinter*: a racing cyclist.

84. *cricket was coming*: rugby football, a winter sport, was giving way to cricket, a summer game.

85. *prof*: captain of the cricket team.

86. *rounders*: a mild version of baseball.

87. *twisters and lobs*: names for different kinds of bowling in cricket.

88. *smugging*: amorous homosexual behaviour.

89. *Balbus . . . wall*: probably a translation of a paradigm sentence in a Latin primer.

90. *Julius Cæsar . . . Belly*: Julius Caesar wrote *Commentarii de Bello Gallico* (*Commentaries on the Gallic War*).

91. *six and eight*: referring to the combination of strokes on the hand in punishment: three on each hand, followed by four on each.

92. *ferulæ*: strokes. The teacher writes the number to be given on a piece of paper, which the boy then delivers to the prefect of studies who administers them.

93. *twice nine*: nine strokes on each hand.

94. *the vital spot*: the buttocks – that is, they will be flogged.

95. *a wax*: a bad temper.

96. *monstrance*: the vessel in which the Host is exposed at Benediction. It has a stem and base like a chalice, and the upper part is fashioned to represent the rays of golden light issuing from the sun (the Host) at its centre.

97. *Napoleon . . . first holy communion*: an apocryphal story, designed to indicate that the French Emperor, for all his glorious achievements, was happier when he first received the sacrament that brought him into communion with God.

98. *mare . . . plural*: the Latin word for 'sea', declined through its six cases, of which the ablative is the last.

99. *minister . . . rector . . . provincial . . . general*: the hierarchy of the Company of Jesus, in ascending order. The provincial is in charge of a province (in this case, Ireland) and the general is in overall command. He stays in Rome and is himself subject to the Pope. However, confessors are chosen from among the members of the order; no rule of seniority obtains in this respect.

100. *Tomorrow and tomorrow and tomorrow*: *Macbeth*, Act V, scene v.

101. *The senate and the Roman people*: the opening phrase of Roman senatorial decrees: 'Senatus populusque Romanus', usually abbreviated as SPQR.

102. *Lent*: the penitential period of forty days preceding Easter during which various regulations about fasting are observed. Fish would replace meat in this regimen.

103. *Magnall's Questions*: Richmal Magnall (1769–1820) published *Historical and Miscellaneous Questions for the Use of Young People* in 1800. It remained in use throughout the nineteenth century.

104. *Peter Parley's Tales*: Peter Parley was the pseudonym of Samuel Griswold Goodrich (1793–1860), author of *Peter Parley's Tales about Ancient and Modern Greece* (Boston, 1832) and *Peter Parley's Tales about Ancient and Modern Rome* (Boston, 1833). (G)
105. *saint Ignatius Loyola . . . Gloriam*: Saint Ignatius of Loyola (1491–1556), the founder of the Company of Jesus, is traditionally represented in this pose. The book signifies the constitution of the order, which he wrote, and his famous *Spiritual Exercises*. *Ad Majorem Dei Gloriam*, 'To the Greater Glory of God', is the motto of the Society.
106. *saint Francis . . . John Berchmans*: St Francis Xavier (1506–52), the most famous of Loyola's disciples, went as a missionary to India and Japan. He is often portrayed pointing to the crucifix on his chest, indicating the centrality of the cross to his mission.

    Lorenzo Ricci (1703–75) was elected general of the Company of Jesus in 1758. Hence the (red) beretta, the mark of a cardinal.

    Stanislaus Kostka (1550–68), Aloysius Gonzaga (1568–91) and John Berchmans (1599–1621) were all Jesuit saints (Berchmans was canonized in 1888) whose early deaths and heroic dedication made them models for the youth of Jesuit schools.
107. *Major Barton's*: the Barton estate at Straffan House was just over two miles from the school.
108. *gallnuts*: excrescences on trees caused by insects.
109. *long shies*: long throws practised by fielders who had to return the ball to the batting crease in cricket.

II

1. *black twist*: tobacco twisted in a cord.
2. *All serene*: equivalent of 'no problem'; Uncle Charles avoids disputes.
3. *creased*: possibly should be 'greased'.
4. *O, twine . . . of Blarney*: 'O, Twine Me a Bower' is a ballad by Thomas Crofton Croker (1798–1854), an Irish antiquarian; music by Alexander Roche. (G) 'Blue eyes and golden hair' possibly refers to the song 'Blue Eyes' by James L. Molloy (1837–1909); more likely 'I Would not Give My Irish Wife', a song by Thomas D'Arcy McGee (1825–68), a journalist and prominent member of the Young Ireland movement. The third stanza provides the Irish wife with eyes and hair of the appropriate hues. 'The Groves of

Blarney' is a famous song by J. Alfred Milliken (1767–1815), written in 1797–8.

5. *Blackrock*: a suburb south of Dublin to which the Joyce family had moved in 1892. The house they occupied in Carysfort Avenue still survives.

6. *order list had been booked*: that is, when the list of items had been ordered, either for delivery or for collection later.

7. *Uncle Charles . . . the porch*: Uncle Charles would make a desultory sign of the cross over Stephen with the holy water. It was traditional to bless oneself at the font on entering and leaving the church.

8. *Stillorgan . . . Sandyford*: all of the places named here were then villages that lay within a couple of miles of Blackrock.

9. *nearer their hearts . . . Munster*: 'nearer' is slightly odd – nearer than what? – and perhaps should be 'near'. Munster is the southern province of Ireland; its capital, Cork, is the native place of Stephen's father and uncle.

10. *The Count of Monte Cristo*: a famous adventure novel (1844) by Alexandre Dumas père (1802–70). The 'dark avenger' is the hero Edmond Dantes, who escapes from jail and, as the Count, sets forth to avenge the wrong done to him.

11. *island cave*: Dantes discovers a treasure in a cave on the island of Monte Cristo. He converts it into a hideout.

12. *Mercedes*: the beloved of Dantes who ultimately comes to live in a cottage in Marseilles.

13. *Madam, I never eat muscatel grapes*: a quotation from the novel. Dantes twice makes this declaration to Mercedes.

14. *castle*: one of several Martello towers built on Dublin Bay to defend against a possible invasion by the French during the Napoleonic wars. Joyce was later (1904) to live in one of them and make it the setting for the opening of *Ulysses*.

15. *Carrickmines . . . Stradbrook*: villages south of Blackrock.

16. *mare's hoofs . . . behind him*: the horse-drawn milk cart, containing a large milk churn, followed the tram track that linked Blackrock along the coast, via the Rock Road, to Dublin.

17. *Merrion Road*: this road continues Rock Road and can be seen from the railway line that runs parallel between it and Dublin Bay.

18. *the customhouse*: the family now lives on the northside of Dublin, near Mountjoy Square and Gardiner Street, once-fashionable areas that were then deteriorating rapidly. The Custom House,

built in 1791, stands on the river at the end of Gardiner Street; it is one of the most impressive public buildings in the city.

19. *stone of coal*: a fourteen-pound bag.

20. *Harold's Cross*: an inner suburb of Dublin.

21. *A. M. D. G.*: *Ad Majorem Dei Gloriam* ('For the Greater Glory of God').

22. *To E—— C——*: Identified in Chapter III as Emma; in *Stephen Hero* there is a young woman, similarly brooded upon, named Emma Clery.

23. *Lord Byron*: George Gordon, Lord Byron (1788–1824), the English Romantic poet.

24. *second moiety notices*: notices demanding payment of city rates for the second half (moiety) of the financial year. Stephen's father has received more than one notice, another indication of his inability or reluctance to pay his way, although Joyce's father had a job as Collector of Rates and would have had many such notices to send out.

25. *L. D. S.*: *Laus Deo Semper* ('Praise to God Always'), a Jesuit motto traditionally placed at the end of a school exercise.

26. *provincial of the order*: the reference is to Fr John Conmee, SJ, prefect of studies at Belvedere College, the Jesuit school in north Dublin. He was later to become provincial – i.e., in charge of the Irish province – of the Jesuit order.

27. *christian brothers*: the Irish Christian Brothers, founded in 1802, was a teaching order that provided elementary education to those who could not afford any. By this time they had become a powerful force in Irish education. Stephen's father is a snob. There was much more social status attached to a Jesuit education, even when provided, as in this case, for free.

28. *Maurice*: Stephen's younger brother, modelled on Joyce's younger brother Stanislaus, especially by the near-anonymity conferred upon him.

29. *twice nine*: see Chapter I, note 93.

30. *Whitsuntide*: the week beginning with Pentecost Sunday, the seventh Sunday after Easter, commemorating the descent of the Holy Spirit on the Apostles.

31. *He that will not . . . heathena and the publicana*: Matthew 18:-16–17. In a school play in 1898 Joyce did in fact ignore the script and imitate the Rector of the College.

32. *blankety blank*: substitute for a real curse.

33. *one sure five*: a certainty.

34. *the Confiteor*: Stephen admits, as in the prayer the *Confiteor* the supplicant confesses and admits to having sinned.

35. *without . . . ever reaching*: Stephen's heresy consists in the fact that he has denied that the soul could ever come closer to divine perfection. It is orthodox, of course, to say that it can never attain it.

36. *Drumcondra Road*: a main road from Dublin through the suburb of Drumcondra to the north.

37. *Clonliffe Road*: an important thoroughfare off Drumcondra Road.

38. *Captain Marryat*: Captain Frederick Marryat (1792–1848), a popular writer of adventure stories, of which *The Children of the New Forest* (1847) is the best-known.

39. *Newman*: John Henry, Cardinal Newman (1801–90), the most famous convert to Roman Catholicism in nineteenth-century England. Although he is an orthodox choice in some respects, he is an esoteric one for a schoolboy.

40. *Tennyson*: Alfred, Lord Tennyson (1809–92), poet laureate and then still resonant in reputation.

41. *As Tyson . . . Kafoozelum*: a variation on an anonymous ballad, 'The Daughter of Jerusalem', which had many versions and an alternative title, 'The Harlot of Jerusalem'.

42. *trans*: a translation or crib.

43. *Jones's Road*: leads back towards the city centre.

44. *bake*: hot and bothered.

45. *her fallen language and tradition*: among the organizations founded in these years to promote the Irish language and tradition were the Gaelic Athletic Association (1884), the Gaelic League (1893), Na Fianna Eireann (1909), a republican youth movement, and the Irish Volunteers (1913).

46. *The Lily of Killarney*: an opera (1862) composed by Sir Julius Benedict (1804–85), based on Dion Boucicault's popular melodrama *The Colleen Bawn* (1861) which was itself based on Gerald Griffin's novel *The Collegians* (1829). It is a classic example of Irish Victorian musical taste.

47. *George's Street*: a street close to Belvedere College.

48. *Lotts*: Lotts Lane, close to the river Liffey in central Dublin. Stephen has walked from the college to the corner of Marlborough Street, where the Abbey Theatre now stands.

49. *Kingsbridge*: a railway station (now Heuston Station) that serves the south and west.

50. *Maryborough*: a town fifty miles from Dublin.
51. *Mallow*: a town in County Cork. The train has travelled ninety-five miles while Stephen has been asleep – almost four hours.
52. *Victoria Hotel*: then the most fashionable hotel in Cork city.
53. *'Tis youth and folly . . . The mountain dew*: the verses are from an anonymous ballad, 'Love is Pleasin', Love is Teasin' '.
54. *come-all-yous*: popular street ballads that traditionally began with the invocation 'Come all you . . .'.
55. *drisheens*: a black or white pudding made of the intestines of sheep.
56. *Queen's College*: the three Queen's Colleges in Belfast, Cork and Galway were linked in 1850 to form the Queen's University in Ireland. The Cork and Galway colleges became part of the National University of Ireland in 1908. The Queen's College referred to here is now University College, Cork.
57. *the Mardyke*: a then-fashionable promenade leading west from the city.
58. *Groceries*: a pub that also sold groceries.
59. *marked*: when their names had been marked as present for class, they then left for the pub.
60. *Tantiles*: an area in west County Cork.
61. *street arabs*: children from slum areas.
62. *maneens*: young boys trying to behave as grown men. The diminutive form is mildly contemptuous.
63. *Queenstown*: the port city for Cork, now Cobh.
64. *first communion*: the sacrament of the eucharist, first administered at the age of seven.
65. *slim jim*: a confection of marshmallow and sugar powder.
66. *lob*: slang for a penny.
67. *jackeen*: a brazen Dubliner, usually working class.
68. *Lee*: the river on which Cork stands.
69. *Dilectus*: a phrase book of Latin quotations. (G)
70. *Tempora . . . illis*: 'Circumstances change and we change with them.' Both are correct; the question is pedantic.
71. *Yerra*: from the Irish, *a Dhi Ara*, a deprecatory exclamation.
72. *Sunday's Well*: a Cork suburb.
73. *Art thou . . . companionless*: from 'To the Moon' by Percy Bysshe Shelley (1792–1822).
74. *Foster Place*: a cul-de-sac beside the Bank of Ireland in College Green, central Dublin.
75. *old Irish parliament*: the Bank of Ireland building used to house the Irish parliament, abolished by the Act of Union (1800).

76. *Hely Hutchinson ... Flood ... Grattan ... Bushe*: John Hely-Hutchinson (1724–94), orator and economist; Henry Flood (1732–91), orator and an outstanding member of the Irish parliamentary opposition; Henry Grattan (1746–1820), the leading figure in the Irish parliamentary struggle for legislative independence, achieved in 1782. The period from 1782 to 1800 is often referred to as 'Grattan's Parliament; and Charles Kendal Bushe (1767–1843), an Irish judge, an opponent of the Union and a famous orator.

77. *as I roved out ... July*: so many Irish songs begin with this or similar phrases that it has come to betoken something or someone who is unworthy of credit and of little value.

78. *Barnardo's*: an expensive furriers.

79. *Underdone's*: a famous French restaurant, Jammet's. According to Richard Ellmann, this is probably the Joyce family nickname for it.

80. *Ingomar ... Lady of Lyons*: *Ingomar the Barbarian* (1851), a play by Maria Ann Lovell (G); *The Lady of Lyons* (1838), a romantic comedy by Edward Bulwer-Lytton.

81. *in mortal sin*: to be in a state of spiritual death because of some grave sin.

82. *Claude Melnotte*: the hero of the Bulwer-Lytton play *The Lady of Lyons*.

III

1. *Shelley's fragment ... weariness*: see Chapter II, note 73.

2. *sanctifying grace ... actual grace*: in Catholic doctrine, internal grace is divided into two kinds – sanctifying and actual. Sanctifying grace inheres in the substance of the soul; its presence is incompatible with mortal sin. It is a gift freely given, never merited. Actual grace is an impulse that excites the mind to the performance of a good act, the grace of operation; but it only becomes efficacious if the mind is willing to continue with the good works already begun – the grace of cooperation.

3. *four deep ... see nor hear*: although outside the church door, the worshippers are deemed to be morally present at the Mass. Although much decried by the clergy, this kind of lurking attendance was widely practised, chiefly by men.

4. *sodality of the Blessed Virgin Mary*: a sodality is an association of lay people that meets regularly for pious exercises in obedience to a set of rules framed to promote a specific end – in this case, to

give honour to the Blessed Virgin. Stephen's prefecture is an acknowledgement of his piety.

5. *the little office*: this collection of prayers, consisting of psalms and lessons, is said on all Saturdays in the Roman Catholic Church.

6. *emblems . . . cultus among men*: these emblems are to be found in the Psalms; the history of the growth of the cult of Mary is given in Cardinal Newman's 'The Glories of Mary for the Sake of her Son' in *Discourses to Mixed Congregations* (1849), in his *Development of Christian Doctrine* (1845) and in his *Letter to Dr Pusey* (1843).

7. *Quasi cedrus . . . odoris*: Ecclesiasticus 24:17–20.

> I was exalted like a cedar of Lebanon and as a cypress tree on Mount Sion. I was exalted like a palm tree in Gades, and as a rose plant in Jericho. As a fair olive tree in the plains, and as a plane tree by the water in the streets was I exalted. I gave a sweet smell like cinnamon and an aromatical balm! I yielded a sweet odour like the best myrrh.

8. *morning star*: one of the titles given to Mary in the Litany of the Blessed Virgin, deriving from patristic literature.

9. *bright . . . peace*: from Newman's 'The Glories of Mary' in *Discourses to Mixed Congregations*.

10. *sums and cuts*: arithmetic and geometrical theorems.

11. *game ball . . . scut the whole hour*: meaning, 'that's the class over; we can skip the whole hour.'

12. *guilty of all*: Epistle of James 2:10: 'Whoever keeps the law but offend in one part has become guilty in all.'

13. *From the evil seed . . . whole being had sunk*: Stephen has enumerated the seven deadly sins – Lust, Pride, Covetousness, Envy, Gluttony, Anger, Sloth.

14. *If a man . . . huge fortune?*: Stephen is rehearsing one of the standard puzzles about the doctrine of restitution. He is not, as has been said, inviting a simoniacal answer in which something temporal is exchanged for something spiritual.

15. *If a layman . . . valid?*: exercises in scrupulousness, the estimation of an action on grounds unworthy of serious consideration.

16. *How comes it . . . possess the land?*: the beatitudes, eight in number, were pronounced at the beginning of the Sermon on the Mount, Matthew 5:3–4 (Douay). The first two are: 'Blessed are the poor in spirit: for theirs is the kingdom of heaven. Blessed are the meek: for they shall possess the land.'

17. *Why was the sacrament . . . and as man?*: all of these questions are answered in standard doctrine and in the catechism Stephen would have studied at school.

18. *A great fisher of souls*: the phrase is adapted from the words of Jesus in Matthew 4:19, 'fishers of men'. The potted history of St Francis Xavier (1506–52), the second-in-command to the founder of the Jesuit order, St Ignatius Loyola (1491–1556), is traditional and true in its main features.

19. *Ecclesiastes . . . fortieth verse*: in fact, it is Ecclesiasticus 7:40 (Douay). The 'last things' are death, judgement, heaven and hell.

20. *What doth it profit . . . immortal soul?*: Matthew 16:26.

21. *the particular judgment*: the belief that souls are judged at the moment and in the place of death. The soul finds the place that belongs to it in heaven, purgatory or hell. At the general judgement, all humankind is judged and all sins, even of the just, are revealed.

22. *The stars . . . all the universe*: the passage is composed of phrases from the Book of Revelation, especially chapters 6 and 10.

23. *Jehoshaphat*: a valley east of Jerusalem, the valley of decision mentioned in Joel 3:2.

24. *Depart from me . . . his angels*: Matthew 25:41. Most of the preceding passage draws heavily on Matthew's description of the Last Judgement in Matthew 25:36–41.

25. *O grave . . . thy sting?*: adapted from I Corinthians 15:55 by Alexander Pope in his poem 'The Dying Christian to His Soul'. Joseph Addison (1672–1719) is said to have sent from his deathbed for his stepson, the Earl of Warwick, for whose wickedness there is no evidence, and to have said to him, 'See in what peace a Christian can die.'

26. *is not like . . . bright and musical*: from Cardinal Newman. See note 9, above.

27. *waters covered . . . the earth*: Genesis 7:4.

28. *Hell . . . limits*: Isaiah 5:14.

29. *Lucifer . . . son of the morning*: Isaiah 14:12.

30. *non serviam . . . serve*: traditionally, Lucifer's declaration. Cf. Jeremiah 2:20.

31. *a serpent . . . field*: Genesis 3:1.

32. *the weaker vessel*: I Peter 3:7.

33. *become as gods*: Genesis 3:4–5.

34. *voice of God . . . account*: Genesis 3:8–9.

35. *Michael . . . Eden*: Genesis 3:24.

36. *to earn their bread . . . brow*: Genesis 3:19.

37. *He took pity on . . . the Eternal Word*: based on various passages from the proto-evangelium (Genesis 3:15) to the testimony of John the Baptist (John 1:29).

38. *He came . . . the new gospel*: Luke 2:7, John 1:17.

39. *They listened . . . blood issued continually*: a slightly embellished account of Christ's passion as told in the Gospels.

40. *He founded . . . prevail*: Matthew 16:18–19. Joyce liked the idea that the Church was founded upon a pun – i.e., the Latin for Peter, *Petrus*, also means a rock.

41. *rock of ages*: the title of a Protestant hymn by Augustus Toplady (1740–78).

42. *Now . . .* : from this point the sermon by Fr Arnall is modelled on Giovani Pietro Pinamonti's *Hell Opened to Christians, to Caution Them from Entering into It* (1688), a Dublin translation of which appeared in 1868. Pinamonti's treatise also adheres to many of the precepts enjoined in *The Spiritual Exercises* (1548) of St Ignatius Loyola, which recommend, among other meditations, a meditation on hell in which its physical characteristics and the accompanying sensations are intensely imagined. See James R. Thrane, 'Joyce's Sermon on Hell: Its Sources and its Backgrounds', *A James Joyce Miscellany: Third Series*, ed. M. Magalaner (Carbondale, Ill.: 1962), pp. 33–78.

43. *saint Anselm . . . that gnaws it*: Pinamonti misquoting St Anselm (*c.* 1033–1109). Besides fire, the other cause of 'positive punishment' in hell is 'the worm that never dies' – the anguish of remorse, for which this is a traditional figure. The punishments of the damned are of two kinds – *poena damni* is the punishment of loss of the sovereign good; *poena sensus* are all the other torments that the damned experience.

44. *Babylonian furnace . . . light*: Daniel 3:19–27.

45. *Of all the plagues . . . horrible*: Exodus 10:21ff.

46. *Bonaventure . . . infect the whole world*: Pinamonti's adaptation of St Bonaventure (1221–74).

47. *The torment of fire . . . rages for ever*: this passage is a redaction by Pinamonti of Suarez, St Thomas Aquinas, Vazquez and others. Many commentators were concerned with the problem of how disembodied spirits suffered from material fire. The consensus was that the pain they suffered was more intense than physical pain because the fire happily combined its usual capacity to inflict torment on bodies with a preternatural capacity to do so on spiritual substances.

48. *in a sack . . . a serpent*: the Roman punishment for a parricide.

49. *Saint Catherine of Siena . . . red coals*: Pinamonti cites St Catherine of Siena (1347–80) for this detail.

50. *Depart from me . . . angels!*: Matthew 25:41.

51. *blue funk*: a state of total fear.

52. *What did it profit . . . soul?*: Matthew 16:26.

53. *I am cast away . . . eyes*: Psalm 30:23 (Douay), 31:22 (AV).

54. *our holy founder . . . composition of place*: in *The Spiritual Exercises*, St Ignatius of Loyola recommends meditating upon a physical object as an aid to contemplating a spiritual truth.

55. *Saint Thomas . . . the angelic doctor*: St Thomas Aquinas (1225–74), called the Angelic Doctor, was the greatest of the medieval theologians. His *Summa Theologica*, Part Ia, q. 64 and III, qq. 97–9, deals with this issue.

56. *Pope Innocent the Third . . . the triple sting*: Pope Innocent III (1161–1216) is cited by Pinamonti on the worm of conscience: 'The Memory will afflict, late repentance will trouble, and want of time will torment.' (G)

57. *saint Augustine . . . God Himself*: this is adapted from Pinamonti's conflation of St Augustine's remarks on the pain of the damned in *De Civitas Dei* and *Enchiridion*.

58. *sacraments . . . indulgences*: a sacrament is a visible sign of invisible grace instituted for the justification of mankind. There are seven sacraments – Baptism, Penance, Holy Communion, Confirmation, Matrimony, Holy Orders, Extreme Unction. An indulgence is the remission of the temporal punishment that derives from sin; it is only effective when the sin has been forgiven.

59. *beatific vision*: the sight of God, face to face, the essential bliss of angels and humankind.

60. *mortal sin . . . venial sin*: mortal sin destroys the soul; venial sin infects it but leaves it in a reparable condition. Venial sin is, after mortal sin, the greatest of all evils.

61. *O my God! . . . and to amend my life*: one phrase has been omitted: 'Who art so deserving' should read 'Who for thy infinite goodness art so deserving'. This is probably inadvertent but unfortunate since a perfect act of contrition involves sorrow for sin arising from a recognition of God's infinite goodness.

62. *He once had meant . . . Jesus, guide us home*: cited from Newman's 'The Glories of Mary for the Sake of her Son', discourse XVII in *Discourses to Mixed Congregations* (1849).

63. *The ache of conscience . . . O why?*: Stephen, associating sexual arousal with sin, is, according to Catholic doctrine, in error.

Concupiscence is the appetite of the fallen state. It is an incentive to sin, not a sin in itself.

64. *angel guardian*: Catholic belief assigns an angel guardian to every person as a defence against evil and a help towards salvation.

65. *Church Street chapel*: a Franciscan Capuchin friary in central Dublin.

66. *a canopy*: sometimes called a baldacchino, the canopy is carried over the priest who bears the blessed Sacrament in procession on feast days.

67. *brown habit of a capuchin*: members of the Capuchin order, a reform of the Franciscan order, were bearded and wore the long pointed *capuche*, or cowl. Otherwise they had the brown habit and white robe-belt of the Franciscans.

68. *God's yoke . . . light*: cf. Matthew 11:29–30.

69. *Confiteor . . . breathless*: the penitential prayer in which the penitent confesses to his sins and his responsibility for them. Stephen stops in mid-prayer, before the pleas for absolution and forgiveness.

70. *absolution . . . forgiveness*: the priest would say the words of absolution in Latin while making the sign of the cross over the penitent.

71. *ciborium*: the cup or chalice in which the eucharistic wafer is carried. This use of the word was confined to Ireland and England. On the Continent, ciborium meant a canopy.

72. *Corpus Domini nostri . . . In vitam eternam*: '(May) The Body of Our Lord (lead you to) Life Everlasting', the first and last three words spoken by the priest as he administers communion.

IV

1. *Sunday was dedicated . . . Virgin Mary*: adapted from *The Sodality Manual; or a Collection of Prayers and Spiritual Exercises for Members of the Sodality of the Blessed Virgin Mary* (Dublin, 1896), from the section entitled 'Devotions for Every Day of the Week'. (G)

2. *heroic offering*: 'heroic' in this instance means an act by which the agent offers to God all the satisfactory works which he performs in his lifetime for the sake of another or others – in this case for the sake of the Pope.

3. *interleaved prayerbook*: a prayerbook containing devotional and in memoriam cards; a serious sign of piety.

4. *two candles . . . old and the new testaments*: at low mass, two lit candles flanked the crucifix, the two lights of the Old and New Testaments that illuminated Christ's sacrifice.

5. *catacombs*: under Roman persecution, the early Christians celebrated Mass in the catacombs with the marble slab of a sepulchre serving as an altar.

6. *ejaculations*: short exclamatory prayers.

7. *days and quarantines and years*: a quarantine is a period of forty days. Stephen is offering up his prayers and devotions for the sake of the souls in purgatory. They gain remission of punishment; he gains in holiness and discipline.

8. *works of supererogation*: he did more than was required for fear that should not be enough.

9. *chaplets*: a rosary consists of fifteen decades of Aves, preceded by a Pater Noster and followed by a Gloria. Each decade is dedicated to a mystery of religion; the rosary itself is divided into three chaplets of five decades each. The first chaplet is given to contemplation of the five joyful mysteries, the second to the five sorrowful mysteries and the third to the five glorious mysteries. All of these mysteries are mediated through the Blessed Virgin Mary.

10. *. . . mysteries*: Stephen says three chaplets to strengthen his hold on the three theological virtues – Faith, Hope and Charity – each identified with one of the Three Persons in God and each assigned to one of the three sets of mysteries.

11. *seven gifts of the Holy Ghost*: Wisdom, Understanding, Counsel, Piety, Fortitude, Knowledge, Fear of the Lord.

12. *the unseen Paraclete*: a name given to the Holy Ghost, the Third Person of the Trinity. 'Paraclete' means advocate or pleader. The name appears in the Gospel of St John.

13. *Whose symbols . . . fire*: the New Testament emblems for the Holy Ghost were those of the dove and the wind. The descent of the Holy Ghost upon the Apostles is celebrated at Pentecost (Whit Sunday), when the vestments are red to commemorate the 'cloven tongues like as of fire' (Acts 2:3) that descended upon them. The six sins against the Holy Ghost are Presumption of God's Mercy, Despair, Resisting Christian truth, Envy at another's spiritual good, Obstinacy in Sin, Final Impenitence. For the last of these there is no forgiveness.

14. *twigging*: brushing with a stiff (twig) broom.

15. *remained on his knees ... gospels*: it was obligatory to stand up at the reading of the gospels. In the interval, Stephen remained kneeling; many others would sit rather than kneel, except at the consecration.

16. *visit to the Blessed Sacrament*: a visit to the church to pray before the tabernacle where the host resided.

17. *book ... saint Alphonsus Liguori*: St Alphonsus (1696–1787) wrote *Visits to the Most Blessed Sacrament*.

18. *canticles*: in the Douay Bible, the Canticle of Canticles, cited by St Alphonsus.

19. *from Amana ... leopards*: phrases from the Canticle of Canticles 4:8.

20. *Inter ubera mea commorabitur*: 'He shall lie between my breasts', Canticle of Canticles 1:13.

21. *saint Thomas and saint Bonaventure*: St Bonaventure (c. 1221–74), a Franciscan, and St Thomas Aquinas (1225–74), a Dominican, were friends at the University of Paris.

22. See Chapter III, note 67.

23. *Les jupes*: French for 'skirts'.

24. *Stradbrook*: a village near Blackrock where the young Stephen had travelled in a milk cart (see Chapter II, note 16).

25. *a muff*: a beginner.

26. *equivocal position*: Stephen paid no fees; he was there by special arrangement.

27. *Lord Macaulay*: Thomas Babington Macaulay (1800–1859), English historian, essayist, politician. The remark is inane.

28. *Victor Hugo*: (1802–85), dominant figure in French Romanticism.

29. *Louis Veuillot*: (1813–83), French journalist and militant defender of the Papacy.

30. *slim jim*: see Chapter II, note 65.

31. *the power of the keys ... sin*: the power to hear confession and to give (or withhold) absolution.

32. *thurible*: the vessel in which incense is burned.

33. *chasuble*: the outer sleeveless vestment worn by a priest at Mass.

34. *tunicle of subdeacon*: short outer vestment worn by the assistant to the deacon who is himself assistant to the priest.

35. *humeral veil*: an oblong veil or scarf worn on the shoulders by the subdeacon at High Mass. Sacred vessels are wrapped in it when he handles them.

36. *paten*: a plate used to hold the consecrated Host at Mass.

37. *dalmatic of cloth of gold*: the dalmatic is a vestment open on each side, with wide sleeves and marked with two stripes. Its colour should conform to that of the priest's chasuble. It is worn by deacons at High Mass.

38. *Ite, missa est*: the words that end the Mass – 'Go, the Mass is ended.'

39. *Simon Magus . . . no forgiveness*: Simon Magus offered money in exchange for spiritual power – hence the sin of simony. The sin against the Holy Ghost was Final Impenitence, involving a refusal to acknowledge even the existence of a spiritual force for good.

40. *eat and drink . . . Lord*: I Corinthians 11:27.

41. *order of Melchisedec*: Hebrews 5:6–7.

42. *novena . . . patron saint, the first martyr*: a novena is a period of nine days devoted to special prayer dedicated to a saint or the Virgin for a particular goal or purpose. Stephen was the first Christian martyr, stoned to death outside the walls of Jerusalem.

43. *Findlater's church*: a Presbyterian church in Rutland (now Parnell) Square.

44. *the fainting sickness of his stomach*: because he would, as a novice, be fasting from the night before in order to be able to receive Holy Communion.

45. *S. J.*: Society of Jesus.

46. *Jesuit house in Gardiner Street*: the house attached to the Jesuit church of St Francis Xavier in Gardiner Street Upper, off Mountjoy Square, north-east of the city centre.

47. *bridge . . . Tolka*: the Tolka is one of the Dublin rivers; the bridge is Ballybough bridge.

48. *second watered tea*: hot water had been poured for a second time on the tealeaves to make another pot – a sign of poverty.

49. *Oft in the Stilly Night*: a popular song by Thomas Moore (1779–1852), Ireland's national bard.

50. *Newman . . . every time*: the quotation is from Newman's *An Essay in Aid of a Grammar of Assent* (1881).

51. *Clontarf Chapel*: on the Clontarf Road in north Dublin.

52. *the university*: University College, Dublin. Crosby is obviously a tutor there and Simon Dedalus is looking for information about it.

53. *the Bull*: a seawall that runs from the shore at Clontarf into Dublin Bay.

54. *Whose feet . . . the everlasting arms*: a quotation from Newman's *The Idea of a University Defined and Illustrated*, Discourse I (1873). Newman had delivered this as a speech when he

was rector of the new Catholic University in Dublin in 1854–8. As University College, the Catholic University was administered by the Jesuits from 1883 to 1908.

55. *Dollymount*: Stephen is turning to cross a footbridge that links Clontarf to the Bull Wall and marks the boundary with the area known as Dollymount.

56. *christian brothers*: see Chapter II, note 27.

57. *A day . . . clouds*: an inaccurate quotation from *The Testimony of the Rocks; or, Geology in Its Bearings on the Two Theologies, Natural and Revealed* (Boston, 1857), by Hugh Miller (1805–56). Miller wrote 'breeze-borne' not 'sea-borne'. (G)

58. *seventh city of christendom*: the phrase seems to be Joyce's own.

59. *thingmote*: the place of the Scandinavian council of law, a huge mound (thingmount) in the centre of Dublin, demolished in the late seventeenth century.

60. *a stuff in the kisser*: a blow in the face.

61. *Bous Stephanoumenos! Bous Stephaneforos!*: Greek for 'Ox as garland-bearer of the sacrifice'; and for the 'ox- or bullsoul of Stephen'.

62. *artificer*: Daedalus, father of Icarus.

63. *Howth*: the north-east headland of Dublin Bay.

V

1. *Daly or MacEvoy*: assumed names for the pawnshop.

2. *The dear knows*: God knows. The Irish words for 'God' and 'deer' were the same (*Fiadh*); to avoid speaking God's name, the word for 'deer' was used instead. In its passage to English, 'deer' became 'dear'.

3. *I'm going for blue*: she is going out to get blue, a laundry powder.

4. *nuns' madhouse beyond the wall*: St Vincent's Lunatic Asylum in Fairview, run by nuns. The Dedalus family's new abode corresponds to the Joyce family address at 8 Royal Terrace in Fairview.

5. *Gerhart Hauptmann*: German author (1862–1946). Women in his plays tended to be of the pallid-pathetic school.

6. *the sloblands of Fairview*: the tidal flats where the Tolka river enters Dublin Bay. Now reclaimed land, much of the infill was provided by the debris left by the Rising of 1916.

7. *prose of Newman*: the delicacy of Newman's prose is his counteragent to the sloblands.

8. *Guido Cavalcanti*: Italian poet (1259–1300) whose famous poetic style, developed for the expression of pure feeling, would be a contrast to the cheap world of commerce and provision shops.

9. *Talbot Place . . . Ibsen*: Henrik Ibsen (1828–1906), the great Norwegian dramatist, one of Joyce's mentors. Joyce wrote an essay on Ibsen's drama in 1900 and remarked that in *When We Dead Awaken*, the sculptor Rubek's wife (awakened from her spiritual death) is 'as a breath of keen air'. This may be the association with the stonecutter's works. But part of the meaning of this programmed journey to the university, with all its attendant associations, is its privacy. Stephen is creating an imaginative world that runs parallel to the actual world he inhabits.

10. *Ben Jonson . . . I was not wearier where I lay*: Ben Jonson (1572–1637), English poet and dramatist. The line is from the Epilogue spoken by Aurora in *The Vision of Delight* (1617).

11. *waistcoateers*: prostitutes.

12. *chambering*: sexual promiscuity.

13. *Aristotle's poetics and psychology*: Stephen's acquaintance with Aristotle derives from a textbook selection of the *Poetics* and of the treatises *De Anima (Of the Soul)* and *De Sensu (Of the Senses)*.

14. *Synopsis Philosophiæ . . . Thomæ*: A Synopsis of Scholastic Philosophy for the Understanding of St Thomas. This may be a version of *Elementa Philosophiae ad mentem D. Thomae Aquinatis*, ed. G. M. Mancini (Rome, 1898). (A)

15. *MacCann*: this character is modelled on Francis Sheehy-Skeffington (1878–1916), a contemporary of Joyce at University College. Skeffington was an ardent pacifist, feminist and believer in the possibility of universal peace. He was murdered by a British army officer in 1916.

16. *Hopkins' corner*: Hopkins and Hopkins was a jeweller's and watchmaker's shop at the southern end of Lower Sackville (now O'Connell) Street.

17. *United States of Europe of the future*: a characteristic passion of Skeffington. The English journalist William Thomas Stead (1849–1912) published a book *The United States of Europe* in 1899.

18. *nominal definitions, essential definitions*: a distinction Aristotle makes in his *Posterior Analytics*, nominal referring to descriptions of effect and essential to analysis of cause.

19. *Ivoire, avorio, ebur*: French, Italian and Latin for 'ivory'.

20. *India mittit ebur*: 'India sends ivory.'

21. *Metamorphoses of Ovid*: Publius Ovidius Naso (43 BC–AD 18), the Roman poet whose *Metamorphoses* is a collection of verse narratives concerning miraculous transformations.

22. *Contrahit orator . . . vates*: 'The orator summarizes; the poet-prophets transform (elaborate) in their verses.' The citation is from a rule for scansion found in the *Prosodia* of the Portuguese Jesuit Emmanuel Alvarez (1526–82).

23. *in tanto discrimine*: 'in such a great crisis'.

24. *pot with denaries*: this translates the preceding Latin phrase.

25. *Horace*: a selection of the poems of Quintus Horatius Flaccus (65–8 BC), the great Roman poet.

26. *the grey block of Trinity on his left*: Trinity College, the only college of Dublin University, stands opposite the Bank of Ireland on College Green. Trinity, an Elizabethan foundation, was Protestant and Anglo-Irish in its orientation. Catholics, who had for long been denied entrance to it, were, from the 1870s, prohibited from entering it by the dictate of the Irish Catholic hierarchy. At the turn of the century, it was especially regarded as 'foreign' because it was hostile to the various revival movements, political and cultural, that had emerged.

27. *Firbolg in the borrowed cloak of a Milesian*: Firbolgs were held to be early and primitive inhabitants of Ireland. The Milesians were later, more cultivated, invaders. Thomas Moore, the object of Joyce's scorn, was then Ireland's most popular poet. His *Irish Melodies* (1808–34) were highly sentimental, although Joyce liked to sing some of them. Stephen, trying to free himself of the Protestant heritage of Trinity ('the fetters of the reformed conscience') finds himself confronted by the cultural heritage of contemporary Gaelic Catholicism, a kind of ancestral kitsch. Moore is an emblem of this aspect of Stephen's Ireland.

28. *Davin*: modelled on George Clancy (1879–1921), a contemporary of Joyce at University College. He became Lord Mayor of Limerick and was murdered by members of the Black and Tans, the notorious British Army regiment, in 1921. Stephen thinks of Davin at this point because Davin (or Clancy) was an ardent supporter of the Gaelic Athletic Association, and of the Gaelic League, one of the revival movements that made a great deal of Ireland's legendary Celtic past. (Clancy even persuaded Joyce briefly to attend Irish classes given by Padraic Pearse, the leader of the 1916 Rising.) Davin is unique in that he addresses Stephen by his first name. His other Dublin friends address him more formally as 'Dedalus'.

29. *Grantham Street*: a street to the west of University College in Stephen's Green.

30. *Michael Cusack, the Gael*: (1847–1907), the founder of the Gaelic Athletic Association, the model for the Citizen in the *Cyclops* episode of *Ulysses*.

31. *curfew was still a nightly fear*: curfew was one of the elements in many of the Coercion Acts passed at Westminster for the administration of Ireland. One hundred and five such acts were passed between 1800 and 1921.

32. *Mat Davin*: Maurice Davin (1864–1927), athlete and co-founder with Michael Cusack of the Gaelic Athletic Association. During the 1870s he and his brothers, Tom and Pat, held more than half the world's records for running, jumping, hurdling and weight-throwing. (D. J. Hickey and J. E. Doherty, *A Dictionary of Irish History 1800–1980* (Dublin, 1980).)

33. *a young fenian*: a member of the Irish Republican Brotherhood founded in 1858. The organization was dedicated to the use of physical force to remove the British from Ireland. They had a glamorous reputation.

34. *the cycles*: the great Irish epic tales belong to a number of groupings or cycles – the Ulster Cycle, the Fenian Cycle, the Cycle of the Kings, the Mythological Cycle.

35. *tame geese*: the 'Wild Geese' were the Irish Catholic soldiers who fled to the Continent after the Treaty of Limerick in 1691. There they served in the French, Spanish and Austrian armies. Davin has their ambition to serve in foreign armies but is intellectually domesticated.

36. *streets of the poorer jews*: the small Jewish community lived just north of Grantham Street.

37. *disremember*: to remember with a degree of uncertainty; not as blunt as to forget.

38. *Buttevant*: a town in County Cork.

39. *hurling match*: hurling, an old game revived by the Gaelic Athletic Association, is played by two teams of fifteen players each. The hurley is a bladed stick. The game is played at great speed and, at its best, with grace and power.

40. *stripped to his buff*: stripped naked to the waist.

41. *minding cool*: keeping goal, from Irish *cúl*, a goal.

42. *camann*: hurling stick. The text is confusing here. If Fonsy Davin was keeping goal for 'the Limericks' and one of the Crokes 'made a woeful wipe at him', then Fonsy must be playing for the Fearless Thurles. But Thurles is in Tipperary, not

Limerick. Joyce evidently associates Davin–Clancy with Limerick, and his knowledge of Gaelic games is unreliable. (I am indebted to Proinsias O Drisceoil for pointing this out.)

43. *any kind of a yoke*: any kind of vehicle or any person in charge of a vehicle.

44. *Castletownroche*: a town in County Cork, five miles from Buttevant. The 'mass meeting' is a political gathering.

45. *Ballyhoura hills . . . Kilmallock*: a walk north of more than fifteen miles into County Limerick.

46. *Queenstown*: the seaport town of Cork, now called Cobh.

47. *You've no call . . . no one in it*: 'You've no reason to be frightened; there's no one here' (Hiberno-English speech).

48. *Clane*: near Clongowes Wood College in County Kildare.

49. *first handsel*: the first crossing of the palm with silver, traditionally a sign of good luck associated with the New Year or with the beginning of a new phase or enterprise in someone's life.

50. *tourist . . . student of Trinity*: that is, someone who could afford to buy the flowers.

51. *slab . . . its laying*: a slab to the memory of Wolfe Tone (1763–98), the leader of the United Irishmen, was laid at the north-west corner of Stephen's Green on 15 August 1898, to commemorate the centenary of the Rebellion of 1798. A sculpture of Tone was to be set up at this spot but was never completed.

52. *French delegates*: France was represented since Tone had sought aid from France, had found inspiration in the French Revolution and claimed to be a soldier of the French army when he was arrested. The tribute to Tone was more impressive than Stephen would indicate. Yeats and his Fenian hero John O'Leary were among the speakers who addressed a huge and enthusiastic crowd.

53. *Vive l'Irlande!*: 'Long live Ireland!'

54. *Buck Egan and Burnchapel Whaley*: John Egan (*c.* 1750–1810) was a politician and duellist; Richard Whaley, a priest-hunter, nicknamed 'Burnchapel' because of his fondness for burning Catholic churches in the Rebellion of 1798, had a son, Thomas 'Buck' Whaley, who walked to Jerusalem and played handball against its walls for a bet. Popular legend claimed that Egan and one or both of the Whaleys celebrated black masses in the buildings that had been incorporated into University College.

55. *jesuit house . . . among aliens?*: this could mean that the Jesuit house was, by extension, a territory of the Pope.

56. *Ireland of Tone and Parnell . . . in space*: that is to say, the Ireland that might have achieved independence under these leaders

has receded in face of the aliens – the British imperium represented by the anti-Catholic Anglo-Irish, Egan and Whaley, and the Roman imperium, represented by the Jesuits.

57. *levite . . . canonicals . . . ephod*: a levite is a subordinate priest under Mosaic law. Canonicals are vestments prescribed for particular occasions. An ephod is an elaborate garment associated in the Old Testament with the High Priest. In Stephen's eyes, the dean of studies, in his faded soutane (long black outer garment), seems junior and servile. As in the case of Davin and others, servility stimulates Stephen's contempt.

58. *Pulchra sunt . . . placent*: Aquinas, *Summa Theologica*, Part I, q. 5, art. 4: '*Pulchra enim dicuntur quae visa placent*' ('We call that beautiful which pleases the sight').

59. *Bonum est . . . appetitus*: 'The good is that which all things desire.' Stephen is again quoting, but strategically, from the same passage in Aquinas.

60. *Like Ignatius he was lame*: Ignatius of Loyola was lamed by a wound received in battle. It was during convalescence from this wound that he turned his thoughts towards religious matters.

61. *Similiter atque senis baculus*: 'Similar to an old man's walking stick'. This is an Ignatian simile for the soldier of Christ in relation to his Jesuit superiors, from the *Constitution of the Society of Jesus with Explication* (1635).

62. *cliffs of Moher*: dramatic cliffs in County Clare.

63. *Epictetus . . . price after his death*: Epictetus, the Greek Stoic philosopher, considered freedom and contentment the highest good. His earthenware lamp is said to have been bought after his death by an admirer who thought that possession of it might make him a philosopher.

64. *An old gentleman . . . bucketful of water*: in his *Discourses*, Epictetus likens the soul to a bowl of water.

65. *a thief . . . iron lamp*: the story is told in the *Discourses*.

66. *a sentence of Newman's . . . saints*: the phrase is from Newman's translation of Ecclesiasticus in 'The Glories of Mary for the Sake of her Son', in *Discourses to Mixed Congregations*. (G)

67. *tundish*: this is in fact an English (Elizabethan) word, not an Irish word.

68. *Lower Drumcondra*: a northern suburb of Dublin to which the Dedalus family had removed.

69. *English convert . . . the prodigal*: the priest, modelled on a Father Darlington, is a convert to Catholicism and an Englishman in Ireland (just like Cardinal Newman, whom Stephen is so fond of

quoting). Stephen regards him, as the dutiful son in the parable regards the younger brother, as the prodigal who has wasted his substance and yet is welcomed by the father (Luke 15:11–32).

70. *clamorous conversions . . . a tardy spirit*: after Newman's conversion to Roman Catholicism in 1845, many other members of the Oxford Movement which he had led came over to Rome with him. But the dean of studies has converted long after those tempestuous years.

71. *six principle men . . . supralapsarian dogmatists?*: these are all Baptist sects. Six-Principle Baptists, founded in London in 1690, relied on six principles found in Hebrews 6:1–2; 'peculiar people', founded in the late eighteenth century in North Carolina, relied on God to cure all disease and refused all medicine; Seed-and-Snake Baptists, founded in nineteenth-century Tennessee, believed that some were of the seed of Eve and were saved, while others (most people) were of the seed of the snake and were damned; 'supralapsarian dogmatists' believed that salvation depended entirely on God. Man could do nothing in this regard. Therefore they refused all institutionalizing of religion as a waste of time and effort.

72. *insufflation . . . imposition of hands . . . procession of the Holy Ghost?*: insufflation is the blowing or breathing of spiritual life into a person; the imposition of hands, as at baptism, signifies the beginning of a new life and the expulsion of evil; the procession of the Holy Ghost is part of the doctrine of the Trinity that claims the Holy Ghost proceeds from the Father and the Son.

73. *sat at the receipt of custom*: the phrase is from Matthew (the disciple in question) 9:9.

74. *zincroofed chapel*: chapel of some dissenting sect.

75. *Ben Jonson*: Stephen, like Joyce, favoured the Elizabethan lyricists.

76. *Per aspera ad astra*: through hardship to the stars.

77. *knightly Loyola*: St Ignatius Loyola was of an aristocratic family.

78. *halfbrother of the clergy*: possibly a reference to the fact that the dean is a Jesuit, not one of the regular secular clergy; or to the fact that he is a convert and therefore not wholly of them.

79. *ghostly father*: Stephen would never address him in the conventional way as 'Father'. (He addresses him as 'sir' all through the conversation.) 'Ghostly' means both 'substitute' and 'involving the Holy Ghost', who is both Father and Son and yet proceeds from them.

80. *the souls of the lax . . . the prudent*: the Jesuits were often accused of being worldly and of catering to the more comfortable classes.

81. *Kentish fire*: a prolonged bout of applause with hands or feet. It is said to have originated in Kent at meetings held in opposition to Catholic Emancipation (1829), an Act that freed Irish Catholics from some of the penalties under which they had suffered.

82. *Leopardstown*: a racecourse in south Dublin.

83. *Are you as bad as that?*: Moynihan is asking Stephen has he been caught short so badly that he needs (toilet) paper.

84. *In case of necessity . . . can do it*: Moynihan is still trading on his joke, referring to the catechism's answer on emergency baptism.

85. *W. S. Gilbert . . . balls*: William S. Gilbert (1836–1911), who wrote the words for *The Mikado* (1885), music by Arthur S. Sullivan (1842–1900). The song is from the final act.

86. *F. W. Martino*: F. W. Martin, an American chemist.

87. *Belfast . . . train fare by so doing*: Stephen is allowing himself to think of MacAlister, the Ulster (Northern) student in the stereotyped way, as someone who is hardheaded, unimaginative, utilitarian and more suited, therefore, to the atmosphere of Queen's University in Belfast.

88. *science as a monosyllable*: that is, in his Ulster accent.

89. *two photographs*: of Tsar Nicholas II of Russia and the Tsarina Alexandra Feodorvina. The Tsar issued a 'Peace Rescript' in 1898. It resulted in the Hague Peace Conference of 1899. MacCann (Sheehy-Skeffington) was an ardent supporter of this plan for world peace.

90. *Ego habeo*: dog-Latin, 'I have'. This schoolboy joke Latin is continued in the subsequent conversation.

91. *Quod?*: 'What?'

92. *Per pax universalis*: 'for universal peace'.

93. *Credo ut vos . . . humore estis*: 'I believe you are a bloody liar because your face shows that you are in a damned bad humour.'

94. *No stimulants . . . bitches*: MacCann is a crusader for temperance and for votes for women.

95. *pours his soul so freely into my ear*: echoing Keats's 'Ode to a Nightingale' ('pours his soul abroad') and Shakespeare's *Hamlet*, in which Claudius killed the elder Hamlet by pouring poison in his ear.

96. *A sugar!*: a dead loss, a hopeless case.

97. *Quis est . . . vos?*: 'Who is in bad humour, me or you?'

98. *sacred eloquence of Dublin . . . Wicklow pulpit*: Stephen is referring here to the decay of the two 'traditions' of Irish eloquence –
the rural tradition, in which Gaelic and Elizabethan English is
deeply embedded; and the oratorical tradition of the eighteenth-
century parliamentarians. As always, the echo of decay is to be
heard most strongly in his contemporary and native Dublin
speech.

99. *handball*: used in the game of that name. Handball was one of
the games revived by the Gaelic Athletic Association. It is played
on a court with an end wall and side walls.

100. *Csar's rescript*: see note 89, above.

101. *Stead*: see note 17, above.

102. *the greatest . . . greatest possible number*: the slogan of the util-
itarians, popularized by Jeremy Bentham (1748–1832), adopted
by social democrats and some socialists.

103. *Marx . . . cod*: Marx is a joker, not to be taken seriously.

104. *Socialism . . . Irishman*: the most likely candidates for this claim
are William Thompson (1785–1833), a political economist, social
reformer and feminist, and James Bronterre O'Brien (1803–64),
an Irish lawyer and reformer involved in the English Chartist
movement (1836–48).

105. *Collins*: Anthony Collins (1676–1729), one of the eighteenth-
century deists and freethinkers. His most famous work was *Discourse of Free-thinking* (1713). In fact the first man to be called a
freethinker was the Irish deist John Toland (1670–1722).

106. *Lottie Collins . . . yours?*: Lottie Collins was an English music-
hall star in the 1890s. The lines are from a street-rhyme. (A)

107. *five bob each way*: five shillings to win or for a place, as in
horse-racing.

108. *Pax . . . globum*: 'Peace over the whole bloody globe.'

109. *Nos . . . jocabimus*: 'Let's go play handball.'

110. *prefect of the college sodality*: the student chosen to occupy the
position in college that Stephen had held at Belvedere.

111. *the matric men . . . first arts . . . second arts too*: matriculation
was the examination for entry to First Arts. Second-year examinations in the humanities were called Second Arts, as were the
students.

112. *my dying bible*: 'I'll take my dying oath on the bible that . . .'

113. *office*: prescribed prayers for different hours of the day, read by
priests from the Breviary.

114. *Jean Jacques Rousseau*: Swiss political philosopher (1712–78)
and seminal figure of European Romanticism.

115. *super spottum*: on the spot.
116. *go-by-the-wall*: slippery, sidling person.
117. *Lynch*: modelled on Joyce's acquaintance Vincent Cosgrave.
118. *Lynch . . . criticism of life*: an ironic reminder of Matthew Arnold's dictum that 'Poetry is a criticism of life.'
119. *tame goose*: see note 35, above.
120. *Long pace, fianna! . . . one, two!*: military instructions from the Fenian handbook. The word 'fenian' derives from Irish *'fianna'*, 'warriors'.
121. *rebellion with hurleysticks . . . informer*: an ironic reference to the abortive Fenian Rising of 1867; to the fact that the military training was conducted, not with rifles, but with hurley sticks; and to the venerable Irish institution of the informer. However, the Fenians and the Irish Republican Brotherhood managed to survive until 1916 without being betrayed by informers.
122. *office of arms*: in Dublin Castle where family genealogies, heraldic records and the like were held.
123. *the league class*: a class in Irish, run by the recently founded (1893) Gaelic League. Joyce attended a few classes with Clancy and was taught by Padraic Pearse.
124. *jesuits as father*: Davin failed to conform to the conventions of the Jesuit-educated Dubliners who addressed the Jesuits as 'sir'. This is, of course, an issue in Stephen's mind since his conversation with the dean of studies. See note 79, above.
125. *Our day will come yet*: a favourite Fenian slogan that survives to this day with the IRA.
126. *Let us eke go*: this is the first proof of Lynch's culture, as Joyce puts it in his *Letters* (III, 130). Lynch knows that Cranly mis-uses the archaic word 'eke' ('also'), instead of 'e'en' or 'even'.
127. *swear in yellow*: this is the second proof of Lynch's culture. 'The word yellow . . . is his personal substitution for the more sanguine hued adjective, bloody' (*Letters*, III, 130).
128. *Aristotle . . . pity and terror*: in his *Poetics*, Aristotle says that pity and terror are aroused so that tragedy may achieve catharsis.
129. *Venus of Praxiteles in the Museum*: a plaster cast of the Venus of Praxiteles, a Greek sculptor of the fourth century, then stood in the National Museum in Kildare Street.
130. *carmelite school*: a school run by the order of Our Lady of Mount Carmel.
131. *canal bridge*: a bridge on the Grand Canal in south Dublin. They now turn to walk along the tree-lined towpath.
132. *pulcra . . . placent*: see note 58, above.

133. *Plato . . . the splendour of truth*: Plato makes remarks of this nature in both the *Phaedrus* and the *Symposium*. Richard Ellmann claims that Joyce took the quotation from a letter of 1857 by Flaubert.

134. *Aristotle's entire system . . . psychology*: the reference is to Aristotle's *Metaphysics*.

135. *same attribute . . . same subject*: *Metaphysics*, book gamma, III, 105b, 19–20. (G)

136. *The Origin of Species*: Charles Darwin's great work *On the Origin of Species by means of Natural Selection* appeared in 1859, with troubling consequences for Christian belief.

137. *Sir Patrick Dun's hospital*: a hospital near the canal built in 1803 from the funds of the estate of Sir Patrick Dun (1642–1713), a physician.

138. *Maundy Thursday . . . Pange lingua gloriosi*: on the Thursday before Good Friday the hymn by St Thomas Aquinas 'Tell, my tongue, of the glorious body of Christ' (*'Pange, lingua, gloriosi corporis'*) is sung in praise of Christ's triumph on the cross as the presanctified Host – for there is no consecration on Good Friday – is carried to the altar. It is also sung on the feast of Corpus Christi.

139. *Vexilla Regis of Venantius Fortunatus*: Venantius Fortunatus (*c.* 530–600), bishop and poet, wrote the hymn '*Vexilla Regis Prodeunt*' ('The Banners of the King Advance'). It too celebrates the crucifixion and is sung on Maundy Thursday and on Passion Sunday. Venantius also wrote a hymn beginning *'Pange lingua'*.

140. *Impleta sunt . . . ligno Deus*: 'Fulfilled is all that David told/In true prophetic song of old/ Amidst the nations, God, saith he,/ Hath reigned and triumphed from the Tree.' This is the second stanza of the hymn.

141. *Lower Mount Street*: this street leads from the canal towards the city centre.

142. *plucked*: he failed the examination.

143. *home civil*: civil service examinations for places within the United Kingdom system.

144. *the Indian*: civil service examinations for places within the British administration in India.

145. *The Irish fellows in Clarke's*: presumably the fellows who had places in the Irish administration. The reference to Clarke's is obscure.

146. *MacCullagh and I*: it would seem Stephen has asked who gained top places in the matriculation examinations for the college.

147. *Glenmalure*: a valley in County Wicklow.

148. *Goethe and Lessing*: Johann Wolfgang von Goethe (1749–1832) and Gotthold Ephraim Lessing (1729–81). Donovan is mouthing clichés about Romantic and classical schools.

149. *Laocoon*: in this essay of 1766, Lessing developed a theory of the essential differences between poetry and the plastic arts. The work was left unfinished. More substantial reference is made to this essay in the *Proteus* episode of *Ulysses*.

150. *Merrion Square*: one of the great Georgian squares of Dublin. The two companions are now approaching the centre of the city.

151. *ad pulchritudinem . . . radiance*: a paraphrase of *Summa Theologica*, Part I, q. 39, art. 9.

152. *What is audible . . . space*: adapted from Chapter 15 of Lessing's *Laocoon*.

153. *quidditas, the whatness of a thing*: Stephen's theory is a conflation of various ideas and is not at all closely modelled on Aquinas. His emphasis on *quidditas* owes more to Duns Scotus (1270–1308) than to Aquinas and has remarkable resemblances to the adaptation of Scotus's theory of *haeccitas* ('thinghood') by Gerard Manley Hopkins, the English Jesuit poet who became professor of Greek at University College. In addition, Stephen is adding a characteristic romantic gloss to his redaction of Aquinas.

154. *Shelley . . . fading coal*: Shelley, *A Defence of Poetry* (1821).

155. *Luigi Galvani . . . enchantment of the heart*: Galvani (1737–98), an Italian physicist and physiologist, used the phrase to describe the momentary cessation of a frog's heartbeat during an experiment.

156. *Sir Philip Crampton*: Crampton (1777–1858) was a famous Dublin surgeon whose bust then adorned a drinking fountain near Trinity College. The bust was more famous for its grotesqueness than was Crampton for his medical skill.

157. *Lessing . . . statues to write of*: Lessing's essay takes its title from a celebrated group of statuary disinterred at Rome in the sixteenth century. It represented Laocoon and his sons in the coils of a serpent. It was generally considered to be an outstanding example of the 'noble simplicity and quiet grandeur' that Johann Joseph Wincklemann (1717–68) thought characteristic of Greek art. The dispute between the relative merits of sculpture, painting and literature was the stimulus to Lessing's essay.

158. *Turpin Hero . . . third person*: 'Turpin Hero' was the title of a song Joyce is known to have sung on occasion. Dick Turpin, the eighteenth-century English highwayman, was hanged in 1739. A number of ballads concerning him were published in broadsheets

and chapbooks. At least two of these show the shift from first- to third-person narrative, the inverse of the shift that takes place in this novel.

159. *the duke's lawn*: this is a lawn adjoining Leinster House, formerly town residence of the Duke of Leinster, now the home of the Irish Dail, or parliament. The National Library, Museum and Leinster House are all parts of one complex of buildings.

160. *the royal Irish academy*: this is in Dawson Street, a block away from Kildare Street. Joyce has made a rare mistake in his charting of a journey through Dublin.

161. *Half a crown cases*: Liverpool had slums that could compete with Dublin's. In this instance, the doctor concerned received a mere two shillings and sixpence for a delivery.

162. *stewing*: implacable study by someone not naturally gifted or bright.

163. *Ego credo . . . Liverpoolio*: more dog-Latin; 'I believe that the life of the poor is simply frightful, simply bloody frightful, in Liverpool.'

164. *Gabriel . . . virgin's chamber*: the archangel Gabriel announced the coming birth of Jesus to Mary (Luke 1:26–38). All through this section religious images and motifs are aestheticized by Stephen in a manner characteristic of the French and English 'decadence' of the late nineteenth century.

165. *villanelle*: a nineteen-line poem of five tercets and a closing quatrain, with only two rhymes repeating in the pattern *aba* in the tercets and *abaa* in the quatrain. Line 1 is repeated as lines 6, 12 and 18; line 3 as lines 9, 15, and 19. Ernest Dowson and Arthur Symons experimented with the form, as did Andrew Lang, Austin Dobson and other writers of light verse. The form was more notably revived by W. H. Auden, William Empson and Dylan Thomas.

166. *Sacred Heart*: devotion to the Sacred Heart began with a vision by a seventeenth-century French nun, Blessed Mary Alacoque. She was beatified in 1864. Cheap prints, showing the figure of Jesus exposing his heart as an emblem of his love, abounded thereafter. Every Irish Catholic home, it was felt, should have one.

167. *loth to depart*: this was a common term for songs of departure.

168. *victory chant of Agincourt*: a popular song of the fifteenth century celebrating the English victory over the French at the battle of Agincourt (1415). Equally, it could be Michael Drayton's (1563–1631) famous poem, 'Ballad of Agincourt' (1606).

169. *Greensleeves*: the name of an inconstant lady-love, the subject of a balled published in London in 1580.

170. *lightly in the round*: she performed a round dance, one of the elements in a quadrille.

171. *Gherardino da Borgo San Donnino*: (d. 1276) he was the leader of the 'Spirituals', a group within the Franciscan order that sought to restore it to its original purity. He was condemned as a heretic and died in prison.

172. *By Killarney's Lakes and Fells*: a ballad from the opera *Inisfallen* by Michael Balfe (1808–70).

173. *Cork Hill*: a side street that runs along the side of City Hall.

174. *Jacob's biscuit factory*: a famous landmark, not far from Stephen's Green.

175. *latticed ear of a priest*: referring to the lattice or grill in the confessional box to which the priest leant his ear to listen to the penitent.

176. *Moycullen*: a tiny village in County Galway.

177. *priest . . . life*: referring to the transubstantiation of bread and wine into the body and blood of Jesus Christ at the consecration.

178. *strange humiliation of her nature*: her menstrual period.

179. *Molesworth Street*: joins Kildare and Dawson Streets from the front entrance to Leinster House, itself flanked by the National Library and National Museum.

180. *a temple of air*: in Roman divination the sky was divided into sections, each called a templum. The flight of birds in the templum was a basis of prophecy.

181. *Cornelius Agrippa*: Heinrich Cornelius Agrippa von Nettesheim (1486–1535), a German philosopher, scientist and magician, discussed methods of divination in his *De Occulta Philosophia*.

182. *Swedenborg*: Emanuel Swedenborg (1688–1772), Swedish philosopher, scientist and mystic. His writings were influential with the French symbolists, especially his account of the essentially spiritual structure of the world.

183. *curved stick of an augur*: the *lituus* with which the sections of the templum were drawn out on the ground.

184. *hawklike man . . . bore*: Daedalus.

185. *Thoth . . . moon*: the ancient Egyptian God of learning, usually depicted with an ibis head and crowned with the horns of the moon. (G)

186. *like an Irish oath*: likely, 'Troth' ('True oath').

187. *Bend down . . . the loud waters*: the opening lines to the farewell speech of the Countess in Yeats's play *The Countess Cathleen* (1892).

188. *opening of the national theatre*: the first production of *The Countess Cathleen*, along with Edward Martyn's *The Heather Field*, on 8 May 1899 launched the Irish Literary Theatre, a forerunner of the Irish National Theatre Society, known from 1904 as the Abbey Theatre. Yeats's play provoked a storm of protest in the theatre and in the newspapers. Joyce applauded the play in the theatre, and refused to sign a letter of protest about it, drawn up by Sheehy-Skeffington, the model for MacCann.

189. *A libel on Ireland! Made in Germany!*: the play was thought to be a libel on Ireland because it presented the Irish as brutalized and famine-stricken and willing to sell their souls to the devil for food. The reference to Germany derives from Ernest Williams's book *Made in Germany*, an alarmist account of the impact of German industry on Britain that claimed German goods were shoddy and over-subsidized.

190. *budding buddhists*: a reference to Yeats's occult beliefs and the vogue for Eastern philosophy then widespread, especially among writers and artists.

191. *The Tablet*: a Catholic weekly published in England.

192. *Diseases of the Ox*: this is apparently the title of a chapter in a book.

193. *The Bride of Lammermoor*: Sir Walter Scott (1771–1832) published this novel in 1819 in the third series of *Tales of My Landlord*.

194. *marred by errors*: his accent is educated but his speech is not.

195. *a game of swans*: a flock of swans.

196. *the Bantry gang*: the brothers Timothy Daniel (1827–1914) and Alexander Martin Sullivan (1830–84) and their nephew, the Irish Parliamentary Party politician Timothy Healy (1855–1931). All were from the town of Bantry in Country Cork. They were regarded as betrayers of Parnell, Healy being by far the most venomous and wounding in his repudiation of 'the Chief'. Both Sullivans were journalists, politicians and newspaper-owners. Timothy is most remembered for his patriotic ballads, especially one titled 'God Save Ireland'.

197. *they all had a touch*: they all had sexual intercourse with the woman in question.

198. *Forsters . . . kings of Belgium*: they were not.

199. *chieftain of Clanbrassil*: this is all nonsense. Joyce is parodying the Irish taste for genealogy, stimulated by the new revival of interest in the past and by the nationalist eagerness to claim an Irish connection anywhere and everywhere.

200. *Giraldus Cambrensis*: Welsh chronicler and apologist for the Anglo-Norman invasion. He is one of the earliest sources for colonial misrepresentation of the Irish. His *Expugnatio Hibernica* (1169–85) and his *Topographia Hibernica* (1185?) are important works, but free of any reference to the Dedalus family.

201. *Pernobilis et pervetusta familia*: 'A very noble and ancient family'. The phrase is from the *Expugnatio* of Giraldus in reference to the Norman Fitz-Stephen (sons of Stephen) family.

202. *paulo post futurum*: 'in the very near future', a phrase used to describe one of the tenses of Greek verbs.

203. *Malahide*: a village resort nine miles north of Dublin.

204. *Darkness falls from the air*: misquotation from 'A Litany in Time of Plague' by the English author Thomas Nashe (1567–1601). Nashe's line is 'Brightness falls from the air'. See p. 217.

205. *Dowland and Byrd and Nash*: John Dowland (1563–1626), composer and lutenist, the greatest of all English songwriters; William Byrd (1543–1623), the father-figure of Elizabethan music, composed both sacred and secular music. For Nashe, see preceding note.

206. *chambering*: sexual enchantment, intercourse.

207. *slobbering Stuart*: James I of England (James VI of Scotland) (1566–1625), whose reign is associated with gloom and corruption in contrast to the glories of the Elizabethan age.

208. *ambered wines*: wines perfumed with ambergis.

209. *proud pavan*: a stately dance.

210. *clipped*: had sexual intercourse.

211. *Cornelius a Lapide . . . sixth day*: Lapide (1567–1637), a Flemish Jesuit, claimed that lice, flies, maggots and the like were not created directly by God but by spontaneous generation, as lice from sweat.

212. *Brightness . . . air*: see note 204, above.

213. *I suffer little children . . . unto me*: after Mark 10:14.

214. *why does the church . . . die unbaptised?*: in fact, Church teaching assigned them to limbo (now abolished), a place near hell where they experienced no torment, only the pain of loss of the beatific vision. Because they are unbaptized they are still stained with the guilt of Original Sin.

215. *Saint Augustine . . . hell*: Augustine did affirm the condemnation of unbaptized children in *De Correctione et Gratia (Admonition and Grace)*.

216. *sugan*: properly, 'sugán', Irish for a straw rope.

217. *grey spouse of Satan*: sin.

218. *Roscommon*: a county in Connaught, the western province of Ireland.
219. *birdcall from Siegfried*: a sequence of passages from Richard Wagner's (1813–83) opera *Siegfried* (1876), the third of the four operas in *The Ring of the Nibelungs*.
220. *Adelphi Hotel*: situated in South Anne Street, not far from the National Library.
221. *Maple's Hotel*: in Kildare Street, just a matter of yards from the Library.
222. *jarvies*: drivers of hackney coaches.
223. *Let us eke go*: see note 126, above.
224. *easter duty*: that is, to receive communion within the Octave of Easter. Since the Fourth Lateran Council it was Church Law that communion be received at least once a year and that once during Eastertide.
225. *I will not serve*: see Chapter III, note 30.
226. *Depart . . . fire*: see Chapter III, note 24.
227. *bright, agile, impassible . . . subtle*: the four transcendent qualities that will distinguish the bodies of the saints. They shall shine like the sun (bright), they shall have the power of unimpeded movement (agile), they shall be beyond the reach of pain or inconvenience (impassible) and their bodies will be subject wholly to the dominion of the soul (subtlety).
228. *Pascal . . . sex*: Blaise Pascal (1623–62), French philosopher and defender of the Jansenist position, a refined form of Catholic Calvinism, in a long dispute with Rome. The story concerning his mother is apocryphal but in line with the Jansenist suspicion of the attraction of pleasure and sentiment for the fallen nature of humankind.
229. *Aloysius Gonzaga*: see Chapter I, note 25.
230. *Suarez*: Francisco Suarez (1548–1617), a Spanish Jesuit theologian, claims that Jesus's words to his mother at the wedding in Cana, 'Woman, what have I to do with thee?', are courteous in Aramaic. (A)
231. *whited sepulchre*: Matthew 23:27.
232. *convert . . . pervert*: in this context, a pervert is someone who turns away from the true faith, a convert someone who turns or is turned towards it.
233. *sacrilegious communion*: the reception of communion by someone who knows that s/he is in a state of mortal sin.
234. *penal days*: the period in Irish history, dating from 1697 until 1829, during which laws were passed against Catholics prohibit-

ing them from the practice of their religion, and expelling them from all basic civil rights. One of the effects of the laws was probably to strengthen the Irish attachment to Catholicism.

235. *township of Pembroke*: in south-east Dublin, including Ballsbridge.

236. *Rosie O'Grady*: popular music-hall song; words and music by Maud Nugent.

237. *Mulier cantat*: 'A woman sings (is singing).'

238. *Et tu . . . eras*: 'Thou also wast with Jesus of Galilee' (Matthew 26:29). On Good Friday, the Passion according to St John is the Gospel reading. The reading from Matthew belongs to Palm Sunday, the Sunday before Easter. The woman's voice introduces the first of Peter's three denials of Christ.

239. *proparoxyton*: a word having the acute accent on the antepenult, in this case the third syllable of *Galilæ*.

240. *Harcourt Street station*: a railway terminus close to Stephen's Green, now closed.

241. *Sallygap to Larras*: Sallygap, in the Wicklow mountains, is linked most directly to Larras (or Larragh), eight miles south, by a military road.

242. *Talavera . . . saddlebow*: these ways of killing a king were approved, in certain circumstances, by the Spanish Jesuit Juan Mariana de Talavera (1536–1623).

243. *chastisement of the secular arm*: Canon law laid down that in cases of heresy the inquisitors can invoke 'the secular arm' – that is, hand the heretic over to the civil power for punishment.

244. *Leeson Park*: this gives on to Leeson Street Bridge over the Grand Canal; from there they would go on down Leeson Street, which ends at Stephen's Green.

245. *coursing matches*: Irish priests were regular attenders at 'coursing' – the pursuit of hares by greyhounds.

246. *Elisabeth and Zachary*: the parents of John the Baptist, both of whom were old.

247. *stern severed head . . . veronica*: John the Baptist was beheaded at Herod's orders on the request of Salome. The image of Christ's face was imprinted on the cloth with which Veronica wiped the face of Jesus in the procession to Calvary. John the Baptist lived on 'locusts and wild honey' during his years as a hermit in the desert.

248. *decollated . . . the lock*: the official word for the beheading of John the Baptist is the 'decollation' – known as such to those within the fold, within the Church. The Feast of St John the

Evangelist, celebrated on 6 May, commemorates his escape from his Roman persecutors near the Latin Gate. The escape was effected by divine intervention or – Stephen muses – by the intervention of the other John, St John the Baptist, to whom the Church is consecrated. This precursor of Christ picked the lock that released his namesake. His puzzlement was occasioned, it would seem, by the two St Johns and their different links with the Lateran Church.

249. *Let the dead bury . . . marry the dead*: see Luke 9:59–60 and Matthew 22:23.

250. *B.V.M.*: Blessed Virgin Mary.

251. *Jesus and Papa . . . lying-in hospital*: Stephen espouses the doctrine of the Trinity as more central to Catholic belief than the story of the Holy Family, a theme the Stephen of *Ulysses* develops, especially in the *Scylla and Charybdis* episode.

252. *Ghezzi*: the name of the Italian lecturer at University College was Father Charles Ghezzi, a Jesuit.

253. *Bruno the Nolan*: Giordano Bruno of Nola (1548–1600), burned at the stake as a heretic by the Inquisition.

254. *risotto alla bergamasca*: a rice dish as made in the city of Bergamo.

255. *my green*: Stephen's Green. Stephen is now moving to possess his experience and his Dublin.

256. *his countrymen . . . overcoat of the crucified*: Ghezzi's countrymen, the Italians, 'invented' Christianity in the symbolic dividing of Christ's garments at the foot of the Cross by Roman legionaries.

257. *I wonder . . . very ill*: 'William Bond', poem by William Blake (1757–1827).

258. *diorama in Rotunda*: a mode of scenic representation deriving from techniques of early photography and anticipatory of the cinema. The Rotunda, at the north end of Sackville (now O'Connell) Street is both a lying-in (maternity) hospital and a cinema.

259. *William Ewart Gladstone*: Gladstone died in 1898. It was he, in the view of Joyce and the Parnellites, who had inaugurated the betrayal of Parnell. Joyce regarded him as a pompous hypocrite.

260. *O, Willie, we have missed you*: song by the American songwriter Stephen Foster (1826–64).

261. *A race of clodhoppers*: the servility and the bad taste of the Irish disgust Stephen. They are sentimental in the cheapest way towards their oppressors.

262. *Still harping on the mother*: cf. Polonius in *Hamlet* (II. ii. 188–9): 'Still harping on my daughter'.

263. *Crocodile . . . eat it*: in this conundrum, the mother's only effective reply is 'You are going to eat it.' The crocodile cannot keep his word and eat the child.

264. *Lepidus . . . sun*: Lepidus in *Antony and Cleopatra* (II. vii. 29–31): 'Your serpent of Egypt is bred now of your mud by the operation of your sun. So is your crocodile.'

265. *Johnston, Mooney and O'Brien's*: a firm of biscuit-makers that ran a chain of teashops in Dublin.

266. *Shining quietly . . . bran*: Joyce explains (*Letters* III, 130) that he was referring to the New Testament phrase, 'Neither do men light a candle and put it under a bushel' (Matthew 5:15, Mark 4:21, Luke 11:33).

267. *Findlater's church*: at the corner of Rutland (now Parnell) Square North and Frederick Street North.

268. *Tara . . . Holyhead*: that is, the shortest way to Tara, the ancient site of the High Kings of Ireland, was via Holyhead, the port in Wales for the steam packets from Dublin. This would seem to mean either that exile is the quickest way to gain recognition (as a king) in your own country; or that leaving Ireland is the only way to get to know it truly; or that leaving Ireland is the only way left to restore to it some of the glory formerly associated with Tara.

269. *broke Pennyfeather's heart*: a stock phrase which Joyce (*Letters* III, 130) says 'suggests at once a disappointment in love, but men use it without explanation somewhat coquettishly, I think'.

270. *Michael Robartes . . . world*: the quotation is from Yeats's poem 'Michael Robartes Remembers Forgotten Beauty', later retitled 'He remembers forgotten Beauty', originally published in *The Wind Among the Reeds* (1899). It begins:

> When my arms wrap you round I press
> My heart upon the loveliness
> That has long faded from the world . . .

271. *John Alphonsus Mulrennan . . . the latter end of the world*: Joyce is here composing a mock obituary notice, of the kind then published, for the Gaelic Revival. The journalist is reporting on the quaint speech of the western peasant, itself a mockery of the dialects used by Lady Gregory and John Millington Synge in their plays, and disseminating it worldwide.

272. *spiritual-heroic . . . Dante Alighieri*: Stephen's objection is to the body-denying platonic love celebrated in Dante's love for Beatrice in *La Vita Nuova*.

273. *Old father . . . stead*: Stephen, as ever, is harping on the father –
in this case, Daedalus. He is both an Icarus asking for support (an
ominous request, given that Icarus fell from the sky) and an Icarus asking that Daedalus stand in his place – i.e., that the son will
become like the father and survive to create his own labyrinth
(*Ulysses, Finnegans Wake*).